RENNO—Inheritor of three generations of courage, proud bearer of the name of the first White Indian, this great chief has perfected the art of fighting with longbow, tomahawk, Spanish stiletto, and a razor-sharp war ax... but will these weapons defend him against a spirit enemy who attacks with the cruelest blow of all?

AN-DA—This beautiful Seneca maiden named Sweet Day will become a warrior woman dedicated to fighting beside the man she loves, destined to bear a fine young son, and targeted to endure a terrible fate at the hands of her brother.

HODANO—The perverse shaman of the dark side— voodoo has become his spirit guide, hatred has become his mission, and Renno, the White Indian, has become the target of his cruel plans of torture and death.

"MAD" ANTHONY WAYNE—The extraordinary commander in chief of the United States Army, his hope for victory at Fallen Timbers rests in the mighty hands of the White Indian—and in the awesome courage of his own heart.

GENERAL JAMES WILKINSON—An American traitor with a politician's clever lies, he secretly buys Indian warriors with Spanish silver and plots a fight against America's patriots—to make himself a king!

The White Indian Series
Ask your bookseller for the books you have missed

The White Indian Series
Book XIX

FALLEN
TIMBERS

Donald Clayton Porter

Created by the producers of
**The Holts: An American Dynasty,
The First Americans, and The Australians.**

Book Creations Inc., Canaan, NY • Lyle Kenyon Engel, Founder

BANTAM BOOKS
NEW YORK • TORONTO • LONDON • SYDNEY • AUCKLAND

FALLEN TIMBERS

*A Bantam Book / published by arrangement with
Book Creations, Inc.*

Bantam edition / June 1990

*Produced by Book Creations, Inc.
Lyle Kenyon Engel, Founder*

ISBN 0-553-28474-6

Published simultaneously in the United States and Canada

*Bantam Books are published by Bantam Books, a division of
Bantam Doubleday Dell Publishing Group, Inc. Its trademark,
consisting of the words "Bantam Books" and the portrayal of a
rooster, is Registered in U.S. Patent and Trademark Office and
in other countries. Marca Registrada. Bantam Books, 666 Fifth
Avenue, New York, New York 10103.*

PRINTED IN THE UNITED STATES OF AMERICA

OPM   0 9 8 7 6 5 4 3 2 1

As one who has had the pleasure of accompanying Renno on his journeys, I, the author, wish to dedicate this book to the memory of Lyle Kenyon Engel and to you, the individual who stands out among millions of Renno's friends. You have made the WHITE INDIAN Series a publishing phenomenon.

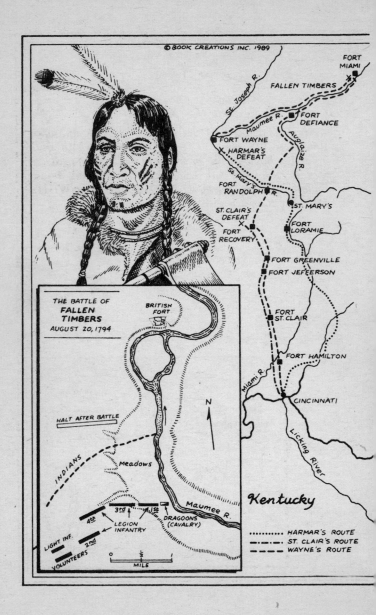

© BOOK CREATIONS INC. 1989

FORT MIAMI

FALLEN TIMBERS

St. Joseph R.

Maumee R.

FORT DEFIANCE

Auglaize R.

FORT WAYNE

HARMAR'S DEFEAT

St. Mary's R.

FORT RANDOLPH

ST. MARY'S

ST. CLAIR'S DEFEAT

FORT LORAMIE

FORT RECOVERY

FORT GREENVILLE

FORT JEFFERSON

FORT ST. CLAIR

FORT HAMILTON

Miami R.

CINCINNATI

Licking River

Kentucky

.... HARMAR'S ROUTE
—·—·— ST. CLAIR'S ROUTE
— — — WAYNE'S ROUTE

THE BATTLE OF
FALLEN TIMBERS
AUGUST 20, 1794

BRITISH FORT

N

HALT AFTER BATTLE

INDIANS

Meadows

3rd
4th
1st
DRAGOONS (CAVALRY)
LEGION INFANTRY
LIGHT INF.
2nd
VOLUNTEERS

Maumee R.

0   ½   1
MILE

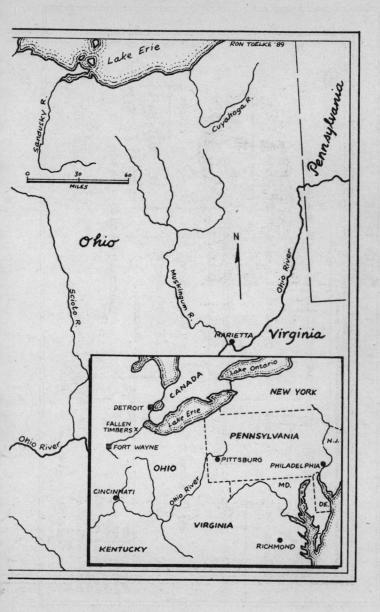

WHITE INDIAN FAMILY TREE

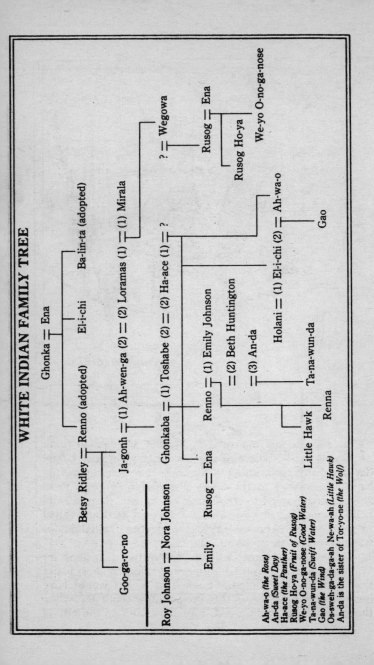

Ah-wa-o *(the Rose)*
An-da *(Sweet Day)*
Ha-ace *(the Panther)*
Rusog Ho-ya *(Fruit of Rusog)*
We-yo O-no-ga-nose *(Good Water)*
Ta-na-wun-da *(Swift Water)*
Gao *(like Wind)*
Os-sweh-ga-da-ga-ah Ne-wa-ah *(Little Hawk)*
An-da is the sister of Tor-yo-ne *(the Wolf)*

Prologue

The presidential mansion on Market Street near Sixth had drawn its share of gawkers on a pleasantly balmy day and, with the coming of darkness, presented glowing, lamp-lit windows to those few Philadelphians who were still curious enough to stroll past. Of course, there was no hope of catching a glimpse of the man whom some called "King George." The first President of the United States was not a man to go about after dark.

There were those who resented the mansion, for Washington had received numerous offers of hospitality from wealthy Philadelphians, each of whom would have been honored to house the President without fee when the government was moved from New York to the city of

1

Benjamin Franklin in 1790. But Washington had said that
the head of the nation should be no man's guest and had
rented the finest house available.

The President issued forth occasionally to visit the
gleaming new buildings that had been erected for Congress and the Supreme Court near the Pennsylvania State
House. He rode in a cream-colored, French-built coach
decorated with cupids and flowers and drawn by six pranc-
ing horses of the purest pedigree. Outriders and lackeys
accompanied the coach, and they wore the finest livery.

The President was fond of wearing black velvet suits
with many gold buckles. His hands sported yellow gloves.
Under his cocked hat topped by an ostrich plume his hair
was powdered in the style of the still-hated British gentry.
His ensemble was made complete by a fine sword in a
white leather scabbard. At public functions he shook no
man's hand, preferring to acknowledge greetings with a
stiff, small bow. He had offended a few well-wishers by
announcing that due to a proliferation of callers, he was
limiting access to his person—except for a weekly informal
reception presided over by Martha Washington—to those
who had made an appointment. His table was no longer
open to all. He invited members of Congress to dine at
the mansion on a rotation basis, served fine wines and
elaborate menus, and was criticized by some for making
the meals too coldly solemn.

In this nation made up of thirteen dissimilar states,
each more intent on its own welfare than on the general
good, the house on Market Street had come to be called
"King George's Court." Dissension, Benjamin Franklin
had once said, is both the blessing and the bane of
democracy.

Blessing or bane, there was dissension. It extended
even into the President's cabinet. It was evident in the
stilted politeness that characterized the relationship between the regal Virginian secretary of state, Thomas Jefferson,
and the sometimes brash but usually practical-minded
New Yorker, Secretary of the Treasury Alexander Hamilton.
Arriving together at the door to Washington's private

office, Hamilton, the younger, bowed Jefferson into the
room first.

"Ah, gentlemen," Washington said. "I do pray that
you will forgive me once again for tearing you away from
your hearth." He had risen and now indicated chairs for
the two men upon whom he leaned most heavily for
support and advice. A liveried black man entered on silent
feet and poured a fine port into three crystal glasses. Both
Hamilton and Jefferson waited for the President to speak.
Washington's first words were a long time in coming, and
the frank appraisal of his hard eyes made Hamilton stir
uneasily in his chair. Jefferson, however, returned the
President's stare with a slight smile.

Washington was thinking, *Thank you, Lord, for these
two excellent men*. And he was remembering how Hamilton
and the company he had raised had prevented Cornwallis
from crossing the Raritan to attack the main army. In the
years that followed, Hamilton had become one of his most
trusted aides-de-camp and envoys. Yes, Hamilton was a
rock, the rock upon which Washington was fashioning the
fiscal policy of the new nation. But Jefferson was a man to
be valued, too, even if his dependability had been proven
in a different arena, far from the battlefields of the War for
Independence. *Ah, what a waste to have these two at
polar extremes*.

"Mr. Hamilton," Washington said, having finished the
port. "At long last I have managed to digest your quite
literate and, I might add, highly technical report on the
public credit. I have taken the liberty of giving Mr.
Jefferson a copy as well."

Hamilton waited, offering only a sidelong glance in
Jefferson's direction.

It was Jefferson who spoke. "An excellent piece of
work, Mr. Hamilton, I must say. However—" The elegant
Virginian looked at Washington. The President nodded at
Jefferson to continue. Washington could handle differences
between men. "I fear, Mr. Hamilton, that you're going to
have difficulty getting your proposals through Congress."

"I anticipate no great problems," Hamilton replied
stiffly. Washington's self-consciousness about his bad teeth

did not prevent him from smiling into the hand that he raised to his mouth. *Odd*, he was thinking, *how great men can be petty and so obviously contradictory*. It had come to his ears that Jefferson had disparaged the secretary of the treasury as a "foreign-born adventurer whose financial policies are based on attitudes engendered by childhood poverty." Truly, Hamilton had known poverty when his mother and he were deserted by his father. Truly, he was foreign-born, a son of the island of Nevis in the British West Indies; and he was, perhaps, overly sensitive to slurs on his origin, for his mother, a French Huguenot, had lived with his father, James Hamilton, before her divorce from her first husband was official. But in the past Hamilton had been quick to point out that his lineage was good. He had once said, "My blood is as good as that of those who plume themselves upon their ancestry." After all, his father had been of the Scottish nobility, the fourth son of the Laird of Cambuskeith.

The President recognized that the political rivalry between Hamilton and Jefferson had deep roots and was fueled by personal considerations, for Jefferson was of the Virginia aristocracy and had married into one of the most influential colonial families, the Randolphs. Even though the Jefferson plantation was not in the aristocratic Tidewater area of Virginia, and even though the young Jefferson had, as a result, been exposed to influences more democratic than those of the Tidewater, he was, from Hamilton's viewpoint, only a shade removed from British gentry and suspect for it.

"There are those who say," Jefferson continued, "that your motives are political more than economic, that you plan to tax the poor to pay off debts to the rich merely to bind men of wealth and influence to the national government."

Now the President rolled his eyes heavenward. Hamilton had stated publicly that England had the best government in the world and thought that the government of the United States should be modeled after the England of George III. Yet Hamilton was suspicious of Jefferson without realizing that Jefferson was the true republican, not Hamilton himself. Washington was certain that one or perhaps both of these men would, in all likelihood, follow him into the office of the presidency. And each of them thought of himself as the true man of the people. Who was right? Washington thanked God that he would not have to be the one to decide that question.

"Are you saying, Mr. Jefferson, that you will be unable to support my proposals?" Hamilton asked.

"In their present form it would be difficult for me." Jefferson looked into Washington's eyes. "For this, sir, I am sorry."

A grim smile twitched Washington's lips. "A man must support his convictions, Thomas." He made a motion with his hand, and the liveried black man poured more port into his glass. "However, gentlemen, perhaps there is a solution to our dilemma." He knew that a serious clash was inevitable between his two advisers. Already the sides were forming: Jefferson and James Madison were working together to form a political party based on democratic republicanism; Hamilton, with his followers, believed in a strong federal government managed by men of means and property.

The two cabinet officers waited again as Washington sipped from his crystal glass.

"I have seen a preliminary draft of an interesting act that is being presented in Congress," Washington began.

Jefferson straightened his shoulders, obviously suspecting what was coming.

"This act," Washington said, "would establish the temporary and permanent seat of the government of the United States. I think you know of this act, Mr. Jefferson?"

"I do," Jefferson answered.

"I am considering sending a message to Congress stating that I have selected a site," Washington said.

Long moments of tense silence followed. Whatever Washington wanted, Washington got; it had been that way since Valley Forge. When the electors gathered to choose the first President of the new nation, only one name was considered—no other man was even mentioned—and that name had been George Washington's.

The President continued. "Mr. Hamilton and I are, of course, aware of your predilection for having the new capital of the United States situated on the banks of the Potomac."

Jefferson took a deep breath and held it.

"This presents—as does your disagreement with Mr. Hamilton's, and my, financial policies—some difficulty to me, Mr. Jefferson. If I support a site on the Potomac, I can be accused of being partial, for I am, after all, a Virginian."

Jefferson nodded. This was a valid concern.

Washington leaned forward. "Thomas, I believe in Mr. Hamilton's policy. We need your support."

Jefferson nodded. "I think, Mr. President, that the banks of the Potomac would make an excellent location for the seat of government. The site would be centrally located and accessible to sea transport."

"Philadelphia has the same attributes," Hamilton pointed out, "although it is less accessible from the south. And my own state, New York, has a rightful claim as well."

"Each faction can cite its own merits," Jefferson allowed.

"With my financial policy we would have a way to raise money to build a new capital," Hamilton said.

"I have talked at length with Major L'Enfant," Washington said. "He is enthusiastic about choosing an unencumbered site, and he promises to build a city that will testify to the future greatness of this nation." He shrugged, a gesture seldom seen. "However—"

Jefferson looked at Hamilton, and his face relaxed into a smile. "I think, sir, that I am being stretched a bit, as if in the rack."

"It will only be painful for a moment," Hamilton said, answering Jefferson's smile.

"Actually," Jefferson said, "I feel much better already. I am no dewy-eyed idealist when it comes to politics and compromise. What, exactly, would you like me to do in support of your economic plans?"

"That can be discussed at a later date," Washington said. "So. I have prepared a message to Congress, asking for authorization to have a plot of land surveyed on either side of the Potomac. I will leave it to the Congress to determine the exact size of this territory." He added, with true modesty, "I trust that Congress will give serious consideration to my proposal."

Hamilton laughed. "Congress will approve anything you propose, and public opinion will follow immediately."

"So that's settled, then," Washington said. "More port, gentlemen?" Both men accepted a refill of their glasses. "There is another matter that is giving me pause. I welcome your contributions and efforts." He looked at the ceiling. "I fought with and led good men to their deaths, not for love of war but for love of peace, and it seemed that peace came at Yorktown in September of 1781." He sighed. "But where is that peace now? Today the British are enforted at Niagara, Detroit, and Mackinac, on lands officially ceded to the United States by the treaty that you, Thomas, helped to draft in Paris. The governor-general of British Canada has promised arms and aid to the Indians of the northwest—we have this in writing from reputable authority. There are Spanish garrisons at St. Louis, Ste. Genevieve, Natchez, New Orleans, Mobile, and Pensacola. These two European powers—with the aid of those French who still exist in some numbers—control our western waterways. The Spanish are arming the Indians of the south, the Creek among them. And as you may know, the northwestern tribes, led by the Shawnee and the Miami, have declared that the Ohio is their last frontier, that they will fight to the death before retreating farther."

Washington paused and searched the two faces before him for reaction. "We promised our veterans land, gentlemen, and there was no land to give them. We told them to take their lands in the northwest, and many of them did just that. Now they are dying. We have sent them, our people, into a dispute that is claiming more lives than many battles of the great war. Our thirteen states are only now beginning to recover from the exhaustion of the war, and their main aim seems to be to cling not only to independence from England but independence from each other. We have no army. You, Mr. Hamilton, advocate a strong central government, but what does this government do to protect the people on the frontiers?"

Hamilton shifted in his seat.

"The frontier is ablaze, gentlemen. War parties roam from the far south to the Great Lakes, and those settlers who have survived the Indian raids have to contend with attempts by land merchants and lawyers to grab their property. These western settlers, you must remember, are, in many cases, Englishmen, Scotch-Irish, German, and Dutch. Before the war they were loyal to the Crown and had the Crown's protection. They have seen little from us, from this government, to gain their loyalties. One could hardly blame them—as their women and children are tortured or kidnapped, as their hard-won settlements are burned—if they turned to Spain, France, or England for protection—"

"Which is exactly what the foreign agitators want," Hamilton grumbled.

"I have been among them," Washington said, "and although I have had only scanty reports from the northwest of late, I think I know the settlers' state of mind. I tell you this, gentlemen: The shape and the future of this nation will be decided in the northwest. The northern tribes, united, will be a most formidable enemy. A coalition of Shawnee, Wyandot, Delaware, Mingo, Ottawa, Potawatami, Chippewa, and Miami have declared war, and they have the support of the British and the Spanish. I am thankful that the Spanish are too far away, in the Floridas, to help much—except with arming the southern Indians to spread our defenses thin."

"I have forwarded protests from the State Department to the government in London," Jefferson said.

"This matter will not be settled in London but in the forests north of the Ohio," Washington told him. "War is going on now, and it will grow more intense. These Indians have known nothing but war for hundreds of years, and in recent decades they have had excellent instructors in the art of war. They come closer to being professional soldiers than any body of troops we could muster. They have learned military skills and strategy from their fathers and their grandfathers who fought under Frontenac, Vaudreuil, Montcalm, Abercrombie, Forbes, Amherst, Pontiac, and Bradstreet. And they have studied the lessons taught by that most successful coalition of Indian tribes in the history of this land, the League of the Iroquois. In fact, Iroquois war chiefs and warriors are already among them, bringing with them the great martial tradition of the Iroquois League."

It was Jefferson who broke the silence.

"Should the Indians, with the aid of the British and Spanish, be able to hold our line of expansion at the Ohio, that means that our western boundary will forever be the Appalachian Mountains."

"Indeed," Washington agreed.

"And those vast and fertile territories between the mountains and the Mississippi will become a patchwork of foreign enclaves, Indian strongholds, and perhaps a small, independent state or two if men like George Rogers Clark prevail," Jefferson said.

Washington nodded. Thomas had a keen mind. He waited, but neither Jefferson nor Hamilton spoke.

"It would not take very much to turn the western settlers away from us," the President continued. "This we must not allow. Mr. Hamilton, I would like an estimate on the cost of raising an army, equipping it, and sending it into the Northwestern Territories."

"Yes, sir," Hamilton said.

"To do so, as you know, sir, risks war with England," Jefferson put in.

"But that's the choice, isn't it, Thomas?" Washington asked unhappily. "To give up territory that is legally ours or to risk war?"

Jefferson nodded grimly. He rose. "Shall I tell the British ambassador of your resolve, sir?"

"No, not just yet," Washington answered. "Thank you, gentlemen, for coming." He rose and nodded, satisfied. "I think this has been a most productive session, do you agree?"

"Indeed," Hamilton said, and Jefferson nodded ruefully.

*　　*　　*

Alone, Washington finished his wine. The servant entered and stated quietly that Mrs. Washington had requested that the general dress for dinner. Washington waved the man away, reached into a drawer for paper, and dipped a quill pen in ink.

My dear friend Renno,

Sometime in the past I penned a request to you, a request that I had no right to make, other than that the content was of importance not only to this new nation but to your people as well. Perhaps, in the confusion, the letter was lost, and so I address you again. It is of vital importance that I have intelligence of conditions in the territory north of the Ohio River. I know of no man more qualified to make such a survey for me.

He wrote more, signed with a flourish, closed the letter in an envelope, and applied his individual wax seal.

Chapter I

The last surge of spring growth had provided a shady canopy of green for the soft floor of the northwestern forests. To the eyes of the lone white man, the wilderness seemed to be the last place for death and war. Roy Johnson had traveled for weeks without coming face-to-face with another man, although he had occasionally gone out of his way to avoid a hunting party or a secluded village. He had traveled northeast from Knoxville, then northwesterly to see the thriving little town of Boonesborough, in Kentucky, and to hear the concerns of the rugged individualists who had braved the land west of the mountains.

A musket, a knife, and a bag of corn gave him all he needed to live well. Game was plentiful and could be taken easily, most often by snare or stealth without wasting shot and powder. His camp, in a thicket of brush, was the ultimate of simplicity: a fire made as smokeless as possible by the use of dry twigs, a bed of leaves on which to spread his one blanket, a hare roasting on a spit. While he waited for the meat to cook, he chewed moistened corn and let his memories flow. Here, in solitude, in the peaceful forest, he was beginning to see things clearly, and the sorrow of losing a beloved wife was no longer a pain in his chest equal to that of a severe wound. Nora was dead, God bless her, gone with the angels to join a beloved daughter, their Emily, and he was alone in the world save for his grandchildren, Emily's son and daughter. They— the grandchildren—were the basis of his only regret at being so far from home.

Around him the night sounds began: the hoot of an owl, the scurry of small rodents in the leaves, a sigh of wind in the high treetops. It was thus, he was thinking, with the long hunters, those men who first penetrated beyond the mountains. Their stated purpose had been to collect hides and furs, but, he suspected, it was the forest itself that attracted them, drew them to a freedom unlike any other, based on one's own ability to cope and stay alive in a land that could be hostile.

He himself had journeyed to the north with a purpose— supposedly to see for himself the conditions in the Ohio lands. But the real motives behind his long trek were to learn to live with his grief and his new loneliness; to see ground that he had never seen before and to place, perhaps, the first white foot on some of that land; to live with a fullness made sweet by the certain knowledge that at any given moment he might lose his scalp. He had become one of the restless ones.

He had seen and listened to men much like himself in Kentucky. Ever restless, they were their own law, men who scorned any vestige of authority except that of their own sinews and weapons. Those men who settled Kentucky had come first to hunt and then—in order to enjoy that one ingredient of life without which a man is not whole, a wife and family—to build their poor huts, to clear their three or four acres, and then to guard them against Indian raids and the rapacious land companies and lawyers who seemed to appear on the frontier as a natural consequence of settlement. Roy had heard settlers' complaints: They had no kind words for the federal government or for those bewigged and powdered men back in New York and Philadelphia who spoke of a great new nation and talked of taxes while the frontier flamed and westerners died under the blade of Indian tomahawks.

Roy Johnson would have a few words to report to George Washington. He would tell the President that the narrow belt of so-called civilization east of the mountains was but a tiny part of this vast continent . . . that the true riches of the land lay beyond the first natural frontier . . . and that those who had pushed westward were Americans, too. But they might not remain so unless that much-vaunted federal government either provided some protection in the new lands or forced the states to live up to their responsibilities.

Roy's task was just beginning, but already he could see the complexity of the problem. There were men in Kentucky such as George Rogers Clark, who realized that the true potential for the nation lay in the west. He had met and talked with Clark in Boonesborough and he had pieced together a picture of disillusionment. Clark dropped real hints that he just might cast his lot—and the lot of Kentucky—with any power that would come to the westerners' aid.

Clark had told Roy of an offer from the British governor of Canada to provide an army of thousands of British regulars and arms for the settlers to mount an attack on New Orleans.

The Mississippi River was Kentucky's lifeline and its principal trade route, but the Spanish sat astride the mouth of the river at New Orleans, blockading the river and confiscating any shipments of goods sent downriver by the Kentuckians.

Roy had met another man, a former military officer named James Wilkinson, during his visit in Boonesborough. Wilkinson was openly in favor of severing ties with the

United States. It was well-known that the man had made several trips to New Orleans and had gained the confidence of the Spanish governor so Wilkinson's trade goods were not confiscated upon reaching New Orleans. It was common knowledge in Kentucky that Wilkinson wanted the west to be under the protection of Spain or England— the choice to be determined by the amount of gold that either country would put into the pockets of Wilkinson himself.

Roy had also heard in Boonesborough something that had disturbed him greatly: Both Clark and Wilkinson, viewing Roy Johnson as a potential ally, had confided that they were in contact with John Sevier, who favored uniting the territory that had been the short-lived and never official state of Franklin with Kentucky and Spain. This Roy could scarcely credit, although he knew that Sevier was a disillusioned man. They had ridden into battle together, he and John Sevier, and there had been a time when the mere threat of an expedition under Sevier could bring quiet to warlike Indians.

But, Lord, if a man like Sevier felt that the west was getting short shrift from the United States, where would it all end?

Roy was eager to complete his scouting task. He was north of the Ohio, having crossed that mighty river by swimming, pushing his musket and supplies ahead of him on a makeshift raft. He was aiming his steps northeast, toward the settlement of Marietta, a distance that would take weeks to cover. He was under way with the sun after finishing the last of the rabbit for breakfast. Staying well away from the thick growth along the river's bank, he walked lightly, easily. He felt young again—vibrant and strong enough to take on the challenge of the whole vast continent. He thought of the incredible distances to the west and longed for the freedom and the time to set out in pursuit of the setting sun to see what was over that hill, and then the next.

He had roasted squirrel on a spit for a midafternoon meal, then set out to cover more miles before darkness.

He would not eat again that day, for the Indians tended to build their villages and encamp along the river. He had seen many signs of Indians during the day, and once he had hidden in deep brush to let a hunting party of three Shawnee braves pass by.

With the setting sun he approached the river once more, seeking water, and heard voices and the barking of dogs. With dusk he approached a village sitting on a small bluff over the river. Cook fires were burning, and the aroma of roasting meat wafted to him. He sought out a vantage point on a little rise looking directly down into the encampment and chewed on dry corn to dispel the hunger pangs engendered by the delicious smells coming toward him.

He stopped chewing for a few moments when, by the light of the fires, he saw two braves drag a white man from a hut and secure his bound hands to a long rope fastened to the top of a pole about ten feet high. The white man was tall, wiry, a frontiersman. His long hair was going gray and was tied behind his head with a leather thong. His buckskins were tattered and showed traces of blood here and there.

The village was a new one, raw, temporary in looks. The brush that had been cleared from the site had been burned in piles, leaving ash heaps. Roy recognized the paint and clothing styles of at least three tribes. He was not surprised to see Miami and Shawnee, but the presence of two stalwart warriors who were obviously Seneca gave him reason for thought. If the Seneca were represented in significant numbers among the tribes swearing war to the death on their Ohio River boundary, then there would certainly be other representatives from the League of the Iroquois. The league was no longer the great power that once had subjugated lesser tribes over a vast area, but he had good reason to know and respect the fighting ability of the Iroquois—especially the Seneca.

He counted thirty warriors without bothering to tally women and children. Then his attention was drawn to the captive white man as women and children fed hickory poles to a bonfire blazing near the pole to which the captive was secured. The man was seated, leaning wearily against the post, his arms overhead. Now women and children began to gather around him, taunting and jeering. Small boys and tawny young girls threw sticks and small stones at the captive. He did not try to dodge. He merely turned his head against his forearm to protect his eyes while the barrage bounced off him.

Now the warriors had completed their meals, and they began to gather around the man. Roy was not close enough to hear their orders, but suddenly several women converged on the captive, jerked him to his feet, and began to cut away his clothing, leaving him naked. He lowered his hands and tried to cover his genitals, but his face remained calm. The warriors closed in, and one lifted his musket. The sound of its firing was like a small clap of thunder. The white man winced. This was not typical Indian behavior, Roy was thinking, to make death so easy. When another musket fired, he realized that the warriors were firing charges of powder without balls into the man's naked body.

Roy considered trying to time his own fire so that a shot from his musket, with a ball, would put the captive out of his agony while the sound of his shot would be covered by the firing of an Indian's musket; but he decided quickly that it would be too risky. As for trying to rescue the captive, it was hopeless. He shook his head, thinking that his son-by-marriage, Renno, might try it, but then Roy was not the white Indian. His heart was breaking as he watched over sixty loads of powder being fired one by one into the hapless frontiersman.

To kill another man gave the victor the dead man's strength, his courage, his orenda. The scene before Roy's eyes was not unusual; the longer a victim lived under torture and abuse, the greater the strength gained by those who ultimately killed him.

"You are a rock," Roy whispered in tribute to the man who would die, ever so slowly, before his eyes. "May God take you quickly."

Powder burns had blackened the man's flesh when a tall warrior leaped forward, his knife flashing. The warrior held up first one and then both of the captive's ears to the accompaniment of shouts of approval from the other warriors and the women and children.

The hickory poles in the bonfire had burned into two pieces, leaving the middle ends glowing or flaming. A lithe young woman dashed forward with a burning hickory brand and applied the fiery end to the white man's belly. He cringed back, but the rope tied to his bound hands allowed him no escape. Other women joined in, thrusting the glowing, burning hickory poles against the man's tortured body. Younger women were picking up hot coals from the bonfire and throwing them at the man, littering the barren earth in a circle around the pole.

Through it all, not a sound escaped the captive's lips. Agony caused his ravaged skin to quiver and ripple like the skin of a horse trying to displace a fly. His lips drew back to expose strong, white teeth, and he took deep, gasping breaths, but he would not scream.

"You're playing into their hands," Roy whispered. "Scream, you damned fool! Don't be so brave. If you're brave, they'll draw it out as long as possible."

The captive rolled into a bed of hot coals. Women closed in, flinging more glowing coals atop his body. He struggled to his feet and walked, staggering, weaving, his feet being charred by the coals. Once more he fell, and it seemed to Roy that it was the end, for the man could only squirm and writhe in his efforts to stand.

Roy rose sadly, but before he walked away, he saw the captive struggle to his feet once more. A warrior moved swiftly, supporting the man's ravaged body with one arm while he deftly lifted the man's scalp to leave bone and raw flesh.

The frontiersman lifted his knee with sudden forcefulness, driving it into the warrior's crotch. The warrior screamed in pain and dropped to his knees, clutching himself, and a chorus of approval rose from the onlookers. This last defiant act pleased the man's tormentors by proving that the captive had been a worthy man, of such courage that his strength would be enough to be shared by all.

The warrior who had been kneed in the testicles climbed to his feet and hurled the bloody scalp into the white man's face. The white man fell onto his belly atop the coals and did not move. Small boys belabored the body until, from the deep shadows underneath a brush shelter, a tall, dark figure emerged. Silence fell over the village. The small boys around the fallen captive scattered.

The man moved smoothly, liquidly. His face was concealed by a cowl of wolverine fur. He knelt beside the body, seemingly immune to the fire of the glowing coals, and lifted his arms. The voice that came from under the cowl caused the hair to stand up on Roy's neck. The sound was a low, guttural chant that grew in volume, becoming more shrill until it was a shriek as irritating as fingernails scratching a slate.

The eerie shaman bent low to lift the white man. The captive spat into the face under the cowl. The man was still alive—how, Roy could not guess. There came a chilling laugh, a hissing of sound. There was enough light for Roy to see that the shaman's tongue was split, like a serpent's. A knife appeared in the cowled man's hand. It flashed repeatedly, and blood gushed from the dying man's wrists, throat, and chest. Roy, frozen in awed horror, would have sworn that at that moment he saw something white and nebulous pass from the dying man's mouth into the open, slit-tongued mouth of the Indian shaman.

The shaman rose, lifted his arms, and chanted. His voice was a hiss, like a snake's. His wolverine hood fell back, and in the light of the fires Roy saw the skeletal face, painted white and horribly scarred. One ruined eye glared with a deadly whiteness, and the one good eye reflected the fires in a red glow. Roy shuddered and turned away.

Roy came into the area of white settlement some days later, where he saw and heard of the results of the savage war in the northwest. He came upon a small cleared farm, where the entire family was dead and mutilated. He heard the whispered confession of a settler who, fleeing a war party, was faced with the choice of saving either his infant son or his mother. The man, mouth twisted, looked up at Roy with tears in his eyes.

"My boy was too young to know. He was too young to know."

It was the man's mother who was saved.

"They don't care back east," another man grated. "My sister and me—we was raided two months ago. We was hidin' in the brush. Twenty or more bucks—Miami, Shawnee, Lord knows who else. She strangled her baby at her breast when it started cryin' lest it give away our hidin' place and bring death to us all."

Roy met Inga Block, a sturdy Dutchwoman, who had killed three attacking Indians with an ax, thus saving her house and her children. Mrs. Block's husband was dead, his scalp decorating some Shawnee lodgepole. She spoke in a thick Germanic accent. "Vy ve stay? Ve hungered for dis rich land. For da first time ve are free from hunger and vant. Dat is vy."

Marietta, the first white settlement north of the Ohio, sat below rolling, wooded hills at the junction of the Ohio and the Muskingum. Roy found the people of Marietta to be different from the usual western settler: They were New Englanders, and unlike many on the frontier in Tennessee and Kentucky, they were more interested in staying than in moving on. On the opposite bank of the Ohio sat a small, wooden-palisaded fort, Fort Harmar.

"That's our army," a man of Marietta said wryly. "Safely back across the river in the United States, mind you."

It was in Marietta that Roy heard about General Josiah Harmar's expedition into the heart of the Ohio Indian country. He had marched out of Fort Washington, near the meeting of the Ohio and the Miami rivers, with 1,100 militiamen and 320 regulars. The Indians, fighting in their own territory, fell back, allowing Harmar to burn a few villages and capture stores of corn. But then Colonel John Hardin, a militia officer, had confronted the Miami war chief Little Turtle, who used the unconventional tactics of the Indian warrior, giving way one moment, advancing as if by magic at the next. The militiamen panicked before this flexible-line assault, leaving the few regulars to stand and die. After a series of routs, Harmar had withdrawn, leaving behind 183 dead, most of them hard-to-replace regulars.

At Fort Harmar, Roy talked with the young officer in charge of the small garrison. "General Harmar maintains that he was successful," the young man said, after assessing Roy Johnson as a man who would not repeat tales. "And he was. He was successful in showing Little Turtle and the rest of them just how easily we can be killed when we invade the Indians' own territory. There'll be hell to pay; you watch."

Hell came in the form of burning cabins and dying children as half a score of Indian tribes, large and small, emboldened by Harmar's defeats, sounded the war cry throughout the northwest.

A Seneca shaman with a forked tongue spoke to a gathering of chiefs. "The time is now," Hodano exhorted. "Never will this time come again. The time is now to restore the boundary, to throw the whites back across the Ohio, and to hold that line as long as rain falls from the sky and as long as winter is followed by spring."

Chapter II

Renno, white Indian and Seneca sachem, was sprawled on his back beside a clear stream. He wore only a breechclout, and the sun felt good on his bronzed skin. His tomahawk and Spanish stiletto had been removed for comfort and lay within easy reach.

In this stream down a slight slope from the Seneca and Cherokee villages, a dozen or more shiny-skinned young boys and girls romped, splashed, hooted, laughed, and in general, disturbed the peace. Renno's eyes were closed, his mind idling. Bird song came to his ears over the din of the children. He could pick out the voice of his son, Little Hawk, and the tinkling sound of his daughter's giggles. He opened one eye and lifted his head. Renna

21

was playing in the shallows, leaning down to splash water at her brother, who danced before her and contorted his features into an animate false face. Renno's heart lifted. His Renna was a living, miniaturized image of her mother, Emily of the pale hair . . . wife of his youth and love of his heart forever. Renna would, everyone agreed, become even more like Emily as she grew. Now she was only a solidly built little girl with a sunny personality, always ready with a smile, knowing that one tug from her soft tiny hand could work wonders of indulgence with her father.

Little Hawk was large for his age. He would grow to be a man as tall as his father, perhaps even taller, for the men of his mother's family, the Johnsons, had been tall. He, too, had taken his hair color from his mother, but the paleness was burnished by the sun and enriched by his Indian ancestry so that his well-shaped head was topped by a mane of tawny gold. He moved with surprising coordination, reminding Renno of a young lion, such as he had seen on the vast plains of Africa not too many months before.

These, then, his son and his daughter, were the reasons for his existence. They were the future. It had been foretold by the manitous that one day Little Hawk, Os-sweh-ga-da-ga-ah Ne-wa-ah would be a great sachem, and that was just, for the boy had the blood of sachems: of Ghonkaba, of Ja-gonh, and of the first white Indian, the great Renno. One day the fate of the tribe would rest on his shoulders. Renno offered a brief prayer to the manitous, for that responsibility was a heavy burden, even though there was peace here in the eastern heart of the Cherokee nation, two days' journey westward of Knoxville.

As free as you are now, my son, Renno was thinking, *enjoy. For one day your time will not be your own as it now is. One day you will be at the call of the tribe, and their needs will come before yours.*

So thinking, he felt a pang of loss that had been with him since he had said good-bye, in England, to the second woman he had loved, the flame-haired Beth Huntington; and for a moment he dreamed of leaving these fields and forests, this freedom, to take his children and win Beth

back. He would live as a white man in England, or
perhaps in Wilmington or the West Indies, and, with
Beth, rear Renna and Little Hawk as white children,
sending them to the finest white man's schools. But then a
hawk lazed over, riding a wind, sending one shrill, harsh
call downward.

"Brother," Renno whispered, any thoughts of leaving
his land gliding away on the hawk's soaring sweep. He,
like the hawk, was free, a creature of the wilderness. He
was not discontent. The time of the new beginning had
come with its sweetness, greening the world and enriching
the diet with fresh goodness; and there was peace. Beth?
She had come into his life as foretold by the manitous, and
she had gone, her purpose completed. Because of her,
because of the gold he had helped her to retrieve from the
far west, a measure of prosperity had come to the community, and not a longhouse or log cabin in the two villages
was without utensils made of the white man's metals.

He closed his eyes, then opened them a crack upon
hearing the stealthy approach of two naked, dripping,
small Seneca. He tensed the hard muscles in his belly as
both Little Hawk and Renna launched themselves upon
him. The three of them rolled in a tangle of arms and legs.
Renna shrilled bell-like laughter as he tickled her. Little
Hawk grunted with effort, pitting his boy's strength against
the steel muscles of his father's arms.

"Do it again," Renna begged, wanting to be tickled.

"Come into the water," Little Hawk invited. "It is
cool and wonderful." His face was serious. His manner was
often overly solemn for a boy of his age. He took his
father's hand, and Renno allowed himself to be drawn to
his feet. Renna clung to his other hand as they ran to the
stream and splashed among the clamoring urchins. Renno
held Renna high as he waded to the deep part of the
swimming hole, where the water came to his chest. Little
Hawk swam strongly, toward his father, and then clung to
Renno's back.

"It's nicer up there," Renna said, pointing upstream.
From that direction came feminine voices, older voices,
for beyond a bend, protected from prying eyes by dense

growth, was the area reserved for the young maidens of the two tribes. "An-da and Ah-wa-o are there."

"Soon you will join them," Renno said. "Soon you will become modest and will hide your body from the eyes of your brother and the others."

Renna giggled.

"She'll have to learn how to swim first," Little Hawk said solemnly.

"I can swim," Renna protested.

"Show me," Renno said, lowering her facedown into the water with his hand under her stomach. She kicked and splashed, holding her head high in a vain effort to keep water from her face.

"See?" she demanded, looking at Little Hawk with challenge in her blue eyes.

"Well," Little Hawk said, giving his father a small smile, "you're learning."

"Is it time to eat?" Renna asked.

"If you think so, it is," Renno answered.

"Well, then," Renna said.

The two children put on their clothing over their wet bodies, Little Hawk in buckskin trousers and moccasins, Renna in a short buckskin shift. Her moccasins were ornate, crafted lovingly with many decorations by her grandmother Toshabe.

El-i-chi, the Seneca's shaman, brother of Renno, tall, bronzed, and well formed, stood at the edge of the cleared gardens. Renna ran to him and threw herself into his arms, saying, "Carry me."

"Brother," Renno said in greeting.

"Tonight, at the council, you will speak...." El-i-chi said, his words half question.

"So I have said," Renno answered.

From the trees and brush along the stream came two maidens. Renno smiled as he saw his brother's face, for El-i-chi's eyes were on the taller, the girl he loved, Ah-wa-o, the Rose, daughter of the senior warrior Ha-ace, and—and this was the problem—his sister-by-marriage, for Ha-ace was the husband of their mother, Toshabe.

"I think, Renna, that El-i-chi will not carry you,"

Little Hawk said, breaking into a rare smile as he looked up at his uncle's face. "El-i-chi has other things on his mind."

"Come," Renno said, reaching for Renna.

The maiden with Ah-wa-o, An-da, Sweet Day, lowered her eyes upon seeing the sachem and his brother and walked demurely at Ah-wa-o's side. Although she was not quite as tall as Ah-wa-o, she lost nothing in comparison, for she was in the full bloom of nubility, with high, firm breasts that filled her buckskin tunic beautifully; long, shapely legs; a waist tiny enough to be spanned by the two hands of a warrior. Damp spots showed through the buckskins of both maidens, and their dark, thick hair gleamed wetly.

"An-da will carry me," Renna said.

"No one will carry you," Renno said. "You must learn to run like the wild deer."

"Yes," Renna said, eyes sparkling at the thought of a new game.

An-da lifted her eyes to look into Renno's face, and what Renno saw there caused him embarrassment, for it was obvious adoration. When he had returned to the village after a long absence, he had at first noticed An-da only as another splendid example of Seneca maidenhood—a young girl, quite decorative, coming into the age of marriageability, and beautiful to behold. As the time had passed, he had realized that she was too innocent to realize that she emanated overt evidence of her attraction to him.

"An-da will run like a deer with us," Renna piped.

An-da lowered her eyes and nodded. El-i-chi and Ah-wa-o, having serious matters to discuss, had walked off at an angle, not making directly for the village.

"Ready," Renno said. He set out at a slow trot. Little Hawk dashed ahead and yelled back over his shoulder, moving with a grace unusual in one so young. Renna had to run hard to keep up, her short legs pumping. Renno cast a glance at An-da. She ran like a warrior, with no wasted motion of her arms, her long legs moving effortlessly, the short skirt lifting with her movement to show a length of well-developed thigh.

It was a distance of perhaps two hundred yards to the first longhouse on the outskirts of the Seneca village, a long distance for a small child, but Renna ran gamely. When she began to pant, Renno slowed his pace and An-da matched him, running at his side with her head high, breathing easily through her nose. She would, Renno thought, make some young warrior a fine wife.

"I will beat you," Renna gasped, doubling her efforts to pull ahead.

"You will have to run hard, little one," Renno said.

Renna gave it her all, and Renno allowed her to pull ahead. She halted as she passed the longhouse and turned, her face flushed and eyes glowing. "See? I did beat you."

"So you did," Renno said, then told An-da, "You run well."

An-da flushed and lowered her head. "There are times, when no one is watching, that I run alone, to feel the wind in my hair and to feel the goodness of life."

Renno looked at her with new interest. He, too, relished the feeling of moving against the wind and of covering ground in long, strong strides.

"An-da will eat with us," Renna said, taking An-da's hand.

"No," An-da said, "I have imposed upon Toshabe too often."

True, since Renno's return, it seemed that An-da was quite often in Toshabe's longhouse; but she helped Ah-wa-o look after Renna and assisted Toshabe in meal preparation and cleanup.

"Toshabe will not mind," Renno said.

"Well, then," An-da said, smiling. Her teeth were white and even, and her smile was a blaze of beauty.

Some warrior, Renno thought, *will indeed be a lucky man.*

An-da and Renna went into Toshabe's longhouse. Little Hawk, who had run ahead, was in Renno's own longhouse when the sachem entered. Although many in the Cherokee village, and a few in the Seneca village, had built log cabins after the white man's fashion, Renno preferred the openness and comfort of the traditional Seneca longhouse.

Little Hawk was holding the white Indian's English longbow, trying to bend it to loop the bowstring over an end.

"You're still a bit short in the breeches for that," Renno said in English.

Little Hawk strained, and the bow bent slightly, but not nearly enough.

"Perhaps you should go see if your grandmother needs wood for the cook fire," Renno suggested.

"That is woman's work," Little Hawk protested.

"That is work for Little Hawk if Renno says."

"So," Little Hawk said. He put the longbow back in its place and left the longhouse.

The run and the warmth of the day had dried Renno's breechclout. He donned a buckskin tunic, then put his tomahawk into its place on the wall, leaving the stiletto in its sheath at his belt.

Now it was quiet. The village was settling into evening, and the smell of food and cook fires was in the air. He stood near his own fire and stared toward the patch of blue evening sky that showed through the smoke hole. His thoughts moved to the coming council, which he had called to present the case for his brother. Even though there was no blood relationship between El-i-chi and Ah-wa-o, in order for them to marry, tribal dispensation against ancient custom was needed.

But there were those who felt that too much custom had already been forgotten. The Seneca who had fought with Renno's ancestors on the side of the Americans in the White Man's War had left much behind them when they followed Ja-gonh away from the northern lands of the League of the Iroquois. By necessity, many of the old ways had been abandoned. To dispense with still another Seneca tradition would be, to many, a sadness.

The council, Renno knew, would talk and talk. No one loved an oration, either to deliver it or listen to it, more than a Seneca. Ultimately the council would decide that the changing times called for change, and El-i-chi and Ah-wa-o would be permitted to become one.

Renno hoped that he could use his prestige and influence as sachem to limit the orations regarding custom so that the council could take up other matters. He had been thinking about his own oration for some time now, for he felt that the tribe was curiously discontent. Never had he seen so many unhappy while having so much in the way of material goods. A working peace existed between the Indian villages and the white settlements around Knoxville. Aside from the usual coup raids by young warriors eager to attain manhood, peace existed to the south and the west with the Choctaw and the Chickasaw. There was no hunger; game was plentiful, and the fields were rich. And yet Renno had come home from Africa to a tribe torn by dissension. He had quickly removed one source of conflict by simply taking charge, as sachem, for the brash, fiery young Seneca war chief Tor-yo-ne had been agitating during the months of Renno's absence for the tribe to choose a new leader.

This area of thought caused Renno to frown. Admittedly he had been away too long. His duty was to his tribe. Old Ghonka had known—as had the first Renno, Ghonkaba, and Ja-gonh—that men need a leader; without strong leadership, factions form, and the purpose of the tribe is diluted. This was cause for concern, because in the wooden box where Renno kept things of value, there sat a letter from a man he respected very much, General George Washington, requesting that Renno leave his tribe once again to do service to the United States.

For long moments he hesitated, thinking to gather his weapons and run, leaving the village behind, seeking the solitude of the wilderness, and consulting his manitous. But, no, he would not—*could* not—consider leaving the tribe again so soon on a mission that would take months. A man had to know his priorities, and his first duty was to his tribe. Little Hawk and Renna, motherless, did not deserve to be temporarily fatherless as well. If Washington were to get information about conditions in the northwest and learn the feelings of the tribes making war there, the information would have to come from someone else.

El-i-chi? No, he was a helpless victim of love. He would go if he were so ordered by his sachem, but his heart would remain here, with Ah-wa-o. Who, then?

He reviewed a list of young warriors and, somewhat to his own surprise, included in that mental list the name of the Wolf, Tor-yo-ne. Tor-yo-ne had fairly recently made the trip south, passing through Kentucky on his way to bring a small group of northern Seneca to join Renno's contingent. Tor-yo-ne's contacts in the north, in the homelands of the Iroquois, would be more recent than Renno's, for, although the sachem had traveled through the ancestral lands, it had not been for quite some time. But could Tor-yo-ne be trusted? Perhaps. He was, after all, Seneca, with the blood of sachems.

Such a decision, however, could wait. Things moved slowly on the frontier and in the wilderness. First it was necessary to settle the question that had El-i-chi and Ah-wa-o dazed with love and desire. Renno put his mind back to the words he would say at the council, once the matter of young love had been resolved. Perhaps the rumors of war and change were causing the restlessness in the tribe. Or perhaps it was merely the yearning of warriors to be involved in the action, to participate in those wars raging along the entire frontier.

But Renno had no intention of mobilizing the tribe or taking his warriors into battle. In his opinion, the Seneca had already done their share. They had broken tradition and by that action had contributed to the weakening of the wonderful League of the Ho-de-no-sau-nee. They had fought for the United States in the White Man's War, and they had fought against mounted Spaniards and the Chickasaw to protect the white man's lands as well as their own. Now, if the United States once again faced war, it would be the white man's responsibility, not the Seneca's.

And yet . . . He paced. He closed his eyes and thought. The future of his tribe and, he believed, of all Indians, lay with the United States, not with Spain, France, or England. All of the old European powers had already demonstrated that they considered the Indians to be nothing more than cat's-paws, nothing more than live bodies to be thrown into battle—and not for the ultimate benefit of the Indians. The prize was a continent, and it had not mattered to the French, Spanish, or English how many Indian warriors died. The tribes that had fought against the emerging new nation had been and were continuing to be punished by seizure of their lands.

If all Indians could be united—or if they had been united when the first white men came to the shores of the continent—the situation would be different. But, except in the Iroquois League, tribal war had been a way of life, with no union possible between Indian nations. It was no use dwelling on what might have been.

In the northwest, if the reports that the northwestern tribes were uniting against the settlers north of the Ohio were true—and Renno had reason to believe they were, because he himself had traveled the frontier and had talked with Indian leaders—it would be a very bloody war. There were excellent warriors among those tribes. In Renno's own village, some warriors talked of joining that grand new coalition and retaking the northern lands seized by the United States, the original lands of the Seneca. That was folly. Therein lay death and extinction. Of that Renno was certain, for he knew, too, the might and the power of the white men. No, whatever might come, he would not fight against the United States. One day, perhaps, his Seneca would be an integral part of the United States, for that seemed to be the only solution.

Renno was in his midtwenties, a man in his prime. He was young to be a sachem, but his views had been matured in a caldron of war, intrigue, and travel. He had seen more of the North American continent than perhaps any man living, and he had set his feet on the soil of far countries. He had seen bravery and cowardice, treachery and high honor. For one moment in the solitude of his longhouse he felt that he could see the future: a tribe led by his son, Little Hawk, still a unified entity but working and living among white men, the young ones going to the white man's schools, speaking English, and wearing the

white man's clothes. A dull sadness overcame him. He
kicked the ashes of his fire with a moccasined toe and,
taking a deep breath, walked out into the evening. Little
Hawk was just coming across the clearing to summon him
to the evening meal in the longhouse of his mother and
stepfather.

El-i-chi was not present. An-da divided her time
between Renno and the two children, helping Renna cut
up the soft chunks of venison in the stew, giving Little
Hawk second helpings, and inquiring, in polite Seneca,
about Renno's needs until, self-conscious over the attention, he said, "Little one, I appreciate your concern. But I
am the best judge, after all, as to when I need more food
or when my water cup is to be refilled."

Toshabe put her hand on An-da's arm in consolation
when the girl lowered her head, ashamed. A soft smile
lifted Toshabe's lips, and she sneaked a look at Renno to
see that he, too, was aware that he had spoken sharply to
the girl. His eyes came back, again and again, to An-da's
lovely, young face.

So, Toshabe thought. *At last my son has noticed her.*
A young buck of a boy like Little Hawk needed the
calming influence of a woman, and Renna needed a mother. Renno was still a young man, and he needed the
warmth, the companionship, and the body of a woman in
his longhouse. An-da would truly be acceptable as a
daughter-by-marriage.

Twice now her son had chosen white women, so
perhaps he had learned his lesson. She knew that Renno
was appreciative of feminine beauty. He had, after all,
chosen two of the most beautiful women Toshabe had ever
seen. Had Emily lived, Toshabe would have been content,
for Emily had made every effort—until she had chosen to
go into Knoxville to give birth to Renna—to be a true
Seneca wife. Toshabe had never harbored much hope for a
successful union between Renno and Beth Huntington.
True, Beth had become a good traveler, and she had killed
in defense of herself and the group during the long

journey to the west; but Toshabe had never been able to envision Beth as a Seneca wife.

"Pay no attention," Toshabe told the girl. "This one can sometimes be tiresome." She smiled at Renno. "You should be appreciative of the politeness of this girl, for she, at least, knows and respects the customs of our people." Toshabe's voice clearly held a tone of warning, which revealed her feelings about the proposed marriage of El-i-chi and Ah-wa-o.

Renno finished his meal in silence as Ha-ace, the Panther, spoke of rumors from the west, which had been carried back to the village by young warriors after a long hunt. The warriors had reported that a segment of the Cherokee tribe had taken up arms against the white settlers.

"If that is true," Renno said, "then may the manitous give us guidance."

After the meal Renno thanked his mother, then thanked Ha-ace in formal Senecan phrases spoken gravely. When he rose and went out the door, Toshabe followed.

"I will speak in council tonight," she said.

Renno was not surprised. It was fitting that Toshabe, the senior matron of the tribe, take an active part in a decision dealing with family and tradition.

"So," Renno said. "And what will you say regarding the matter before the council?"

"What must be said will be said," she stated flatly.

The council longhouse was crowded. Seated next to his mother was his older sister, Ena. Her husband, Rusog, chief of the Cherokee, sat by her side as an honored guest, a friend. Unless asked, he would not speak. Neither El-i-chi nor Ah-wa-o was present.

It was Renno who opened the council. His opening oration was brief, merely stating the fact that El-i-chi, shaman of the tribe, son of Ghonkaba, had requested the tribal matrons' agreement to his marriage to the daughter of Ha-ace, Ah-wa-o, his sister-by-marriage.

Then it began. An outsider would not have known that the subject under consideration for well over two hours was a break from tribal marriage taboos. Yet all the oration applied to this subject—a rehashing of history, a calling up of the past greatness of the league and the Seneca.

One of the matrons, the wife of a senior warrior, spoke of time gone by, the greatness of the Seneca, and the traditions of the Iroquois. One by one the matrons spoke, some eloquently, some adequately. It seemed to Renno that the speakers were unaware that this council and these orations were, in effect, a part of the struggle to retain an identity for the tribe.

Now Toshabe spoke. "It is my son we speak of, a son who has the true love of his mother, for any mother wants peace and contentment for her sons, and wives for her sons worthy of them. Ah-wa-o is, of course, worthy. If any here has heard one word of dishonor against her, it is a lie, for never has there been a more chaste, a more true maiden than my stepdaughter. My husband, Ha-ace, and I never suspected that one day my son would love the Panther's daughter. Otherwise I would never have consented to have Ha-ace as my husband, for to a mother, a son's happiness is more important than her own. But we could not guess, and Ha-ace is my husband."

The gathered matrons nodded.

"It has been stated in this council that circumstances have forced us to abandon too many of the time-honored customs, too much of the wisdom of those who have gone before us," Toshabe continued. "I find myself saying yes, this is true."

Renno's face was expressionless, but he felt something sink inside him.

When Toshabe sat down, another matron began to speak. "Toshabe seems to have forgotten that she herself is half-French and half-Erie. And of all the families in this Seneca community, that of the great Renno has intermarried most often. I support the union of Ah-wa-o and our shaman. At least they are both Seneca."

Toshabe rose to respond. "We must go back to the very old ways. We must be committed to keeping the tribe strong and pure. True, we have relaxed our marriage

customs—especially in this place, with our small numbers—
for it has not always been possible to observe the old laws
concerning the proper matching of clans in a marriage."
She paused, glanced around, and then looked into Renno's
eyes. "But we must not, ever, adapt the customs of the
white man, which allow the mingling of blood in marriage
between cousin and cousin, for the laws are clear, and in
that way lies destruction. Now it is true that there is no
blood between my son and Ah-wa-o, and yet by tribal law
they are brother and sister."

A grunt of agreement came from several of the older
women.

Tears formed in Toshabe's eyes. "It is my honor, as
senior matron of the clan, to have a voice in decisions
regarding custom and tradition, and I, as keeper of the
custom, cannot agree to allow even a symbolic break with
this core of the marriage laws. As senior matron, I advise
that my son's marriage to his sister cannot and will not be
blessed."

"So," an old woman began, leaning back as if in
preparation to add to Toshabe's statements. But Renno
spoke first, standing. He was sachem. They would hear his
words, but he could not enforce his will in council or go
against the united wisdom of the tribe's matrons.

"You have heard my mother," he said, "and she is
wise. I cannot fault her, nor can I disagree with her words.
And yet there is this to consider: Our tribe is small. Many
of our young warriors have taken wives from our brother
tribe, the Cherokee. I find no fault in this. But we have
spoken here of the survival of our customs. Customs die
when a people die, or when, due to circumstances beyond
their control, their blood is diluted with the blood of other
nations. You know, and I could name, many tribes that
have so disappeared. For whatever reason, we—the Seneca
and other tribes as well—do not breed as prolifically as do
the white men. Remember: When last you saw a settler's
cabin, how many children played around the door?"

"It is true that the whites produce children like
rabbits," Ena said.

"A Seneca family, on the other hand, consists of one,

two, seldom more than three children," Renno said. "When the white man came, he was few. And now he swarms over the east and pushes relentlessly toward the west. We lose our warriors in battle, and tribes grow smaller." He paused to cast a benevolent smile on the gathering. "I do not say that the union of El-i-chi, my brother, and his Ah-wa-o, will increase the tribe to match the numbers of our neighbors, the white men. I do say that the blood of Renno, Ja-gonh, and Ghonkaba should be reproduced by a Seneca maiden. Once before my brother loved, and she was a Chickasaw. I speak no ill of her, but how much better that El-i-chi's sons be Seneca."

He walked to the center of the circle, held out his arms, and lifted his hands to the manitous and the sky beyond the council-house roof. "It is my belief that the manitous of the Seneca would see no harm in this union. It is my desire to see my brother have his Ah-wa-o, but I am only one voice in this council. Perhaps it is time to break with certain traditions. As surely as the seasons come and go and as the whites push farther westward, we will have to adapt and change our customs. I ask you this: Let the change start here, for in war and peace my brother has proven his worth and his loyalty to us."

The oratory continued for much longer, past the usual time when the entire village was sleeping, toward the midnight hour. Renno knew that the cause was lost, and he called for a decision. One by one the matrons cast their votes. It was the opinion of the council that to allow El-i-chi and Ah-wa-o to have the blessings of the council in a union of brother and sister would be a step toward chaos and the weakening of the tribe.

Renno found El-i-chi and Ah-wa-o in Ha-ace's long-house. They sat across the fire from each other. Little Hawk and Renna were sleeping in the small beds that Ha-ace had built for them against one wall. When Renno entered, El-i-chi sprang to his feet. He looked into Renno's face and saw the decision. His own face set in grim lines, and the blood of anger rushed upward to redden it.

"My heart aches for you," Renno said.

"Who spoke against me?" El-i-chi demanded. "There are traditions to cover that as well." His hand closed on the haft of his tomahawk.

"My brother, only two spoke *for* you," Renno said. "It is the will of the tribe."

"Only two?" El-i-chi grated. "My mother and who else?"

Renno's neck stiffened slightly. "You ask, when you had my word?" He paused. "And our mother was not the other."

El-i-chi's anger was great. "My mother spoke against us?"

Renno remained silent. Ah-wa-o was weeping softly, hiding her tears behind uplifted hands.

"My mother . . . " El-i-chi repeated with total disbelief.

"She believes she is right," Renno said.

"My mother!"

"Give it time," Renno said soothingly. "The matter can be considered again. I will talk with the matrons, one by one. Time, Brother, time."

"There has been more than enough time," El-i-chi said. "We could have been married in Wilmington, and then we could have presented them with an accomplished deed. But, no, we waited, trusting to the wisdom of the council."

El-i-chi moved swiftly, trying to push past Renno, but Renno seized his arm and held him.

"Patience," the sachem advised.

"I go," El-i-chi said coldly. He cast a look at Ah-wa-o, and the tears in her eyes touched him, causing his own eyes to sting. He spoke softly, to her and to no one else. "I go. I must think."

Renno walked to stand beside the seated Ah-wa-o. He placed his hand on her hair. "You will have patience, little Rose?"

Ah-wa-o could not speak. Her chest heaved with her sobs, but she was silent.

"There is time for you," Renno said. Helpless, he walked over to where his daughter lay sleeping and bent to cover her feet with a soft deerskin. Then he left the longhouse and stood for a long time looking up at the stars. He longed to do as El-i-chi had done—leave the village and run into the forest. But there were more important things than the love of one man for one woman. He returned to his longhouse, where hours passed before he slept.

He was not concerned when El-i-chi did not return the next day or the day after. He could imagine himself in El-i-chi's moccasins. And if it were he out there in the forest with his heart heavy, he would run; when he had purged his blood, he would rest and fast and seek his answers from the manitous. El-i-chi would return.

Indeed, he did return on the fourth day, to find Tor-yo-ne sitting on the floor of Toshabe's longhouse, silent, handsome, his eyes on Ah-wa-o, who sat across the room from him.

Ah-wa-o gave a glad little cry and made an aborted move to get to her feet when El-i-chi entered.

"You have returned," Toshabe said.

"I have," El-i-chi said.

"I thank thee that thou art well," Tor-yo-ne said in formal Seneca.

"*Do-ges,*" El-i-chi said. *Truly.* He looked at Ah-wa-o, then at Tor-yo-ne, and then at Toshabe.

"Tor-yo-ne, war chief of the Seneca, has made an offer for Ah-wa-o's hand in marriage," Toshabe said after she had moved to stand between El-i-chi and Tor-yo-ne. She knew her younger son well. El-i-chi reacted violently, his tomahawk springing into his hand, his lips curling in a snarl.

"As is his right," Toshabe said. "He spoke not as long as you had a claim to her."

El-i-chi's eyes were steely. Tor-yo-ne sat calmly, although the muscles of his arms had tensed. "We are brothers. A brother does not show his blade in a house of peace."

"I need no instructions from you," El-i-chi said, but his voice was calm. "Go, Tor-yo-ne. Go in peace." He would not dishonor his mother's house, not even under such dire provocation.

"Both of you acknowledge that this is my house," Toshabe said with acid sarcasm. "I am pleased that you have so much wisdom, and I am angered to have harsh words pass here. Therefore, both of you leave."

El-i-chi exited first. He stood in the square, tomahawk back in his belt, when Tor-yo-ne came out. For long moments they stood facing each other, eyes locked.

"I mean you no dishonor," Tor-yo-ne said at last.

"Try me not, Tor-yo-ne," El-i-chi grated. There was still a residue of anger in him, which would grow as he came to realize the consequences of the council's decision and the one he had made in his days of solitude.

Then he turned and walked back into the forest.

Chapter III

There were those who called the Cherokee Se-quo-i lazy. No one said as much to his face, for he had learned the art of war from his own chief, Rusog, and his friend Renno. Moreover, those who knew him well realized that he was not lacking in energy but was merely a bird that fashioned his own feathers. His efforts were not always directed along the customary lines of endeavor, nor had he chosen a woman.

Because he did not spend hours honing and polishing his weapons, critics pointed to his tomahawk, hanging in its place on the wall, and smiled covertly at the rust on the blade. Often, when his attentions were on his books, on his squiggles of letters on paper, or on his experiments in metalworking, he was content to allow one of his many blood relatives to provide food for his mother, some younger family members, and Se-quo-i himself.

The young man had spent a season constructing the finest log cabin in the Cherokee village, and this in itself caused some to say that he put on airs and fancied himself to be above his station in the tribe. To all this envy, Se-quo-i was oblivious. Often, when he submerged himself in his ongoing, most beloved project—reducing the complicated and numerous sounds of the Cherokee language into a coherent alphabet—he would seclude himself for days, often refusing to leave his work to eat. To date, he had isolated over sixty distinct sounds, but he was having trouble completing the catalog of sounds that made up the language, for some were not totally distinct from others.

One day, when he realized that his alphabet would probably be extended to as many as eighty-six letters, he gave up in disgust and walked outside to find that the new beginning had changed the earth once more and that life in the sun was, at least temporarily, preferable to life inside his cabin. He surprised some warriors by joining a hunt. He was the first to shoot a deer, but when the hunt was over, he sat behind his home and mused over an odd implement that he had had brought from Knoxville. It was a plow with a steel share and oak handles with which to guide it as it was pulled by a horse or a mule. This was also a departure; the horse had never been an integral part of Cherokee life. Horses were handy, but in the forest a man could make better time on foot.

All around him in the fields Cherokee women were working that season's crops in the traditional manner, a few using hand-fashioned digging sticks, others with steel-bladed hoes obtained in trade from the white man. The fields gave promise of a rich harvest: corn, beans, peas, squash, pumpkins, melons, sunflowers, and sweet potatoes. Each hill, each row, had to be tilled to prevent the weeds and grass from taking over. The white man lessened the labor of farming with this odd thing, the plow. With that one instrument, one man and a horse could do the work of many women.

Se-quo-i had made sketches of the harness used by the white farmers, and over a period of time he had almost completed a set of harnesses for one horse. On that warm, pleasant day, he decided to complete the job and try out the plow. There were a few horses in the village, and Se-quo-i set out to obtain one, trading several pieces of silver jewelry that he had fashioned himself for an old plug of an animal. Used to having only a blanket on its back topped by a warrior, the horse took an instant dislike to Se-quo-i's harness, and for an entire morning the battle between man and beast raged up and down behind Se-quo-i's cabin until a plot of ground that had been smooth and level was chewed by the prancings of horse's hooves and occasional stabs of the plowshare.

Se-quo-i's efforts attracted an audience. The onlookers were more than willing to offer suggestions, including a musket ball to the stubborn brain of the horse or, alternately, to the brain of a warrior who was fighting so hard for the dubious honor of doing women's work. Se-quo-i was beginning to think that the suggestion regarding a musket and the horse was worthy when, looking up, he saw Renno standing, arms crossed over his bare chest, a musing smile on his face. Here, at last, was a man who would understand. Se-quo-i tied the horse to a tree and, wiping sweat from his forehead, came to stand beside his friend.

"One man with a plow can do the work of many women," Se-quo-i said.

"And, idle, what will the women do?" Renno asked, smiling.

Answering in kind, Se-quo-i said, "They will have more time to wear out their teeth softening deerskin garments so that we will be better dressed."

Renno had heard about Se-quo-i's experiment with the plow and, perhaps to take his mind off the fact that El-i-chi was not yet back from his second disappearance into the wilderness, had decided to see for himself. "It will come, my friend," the sachem said. "We will learn to accept such things, for the white man can produce a surplus of food and can use that surplus for trade to obtain items he can't make himself."

"So," Se-quo-i responded, pleased that Renno understood. "Tell them." He indicated the bemused audience that had formed to watch his battle with the horse.

With a sigh of resignation, Se-quo-i went back to his work. Renno found a grassy spot, sat down, and leaned back against a small tree. The horse, rested, seemed to be determined to pull in every direction except the one indicated by Se-quo-i, but the plowshare had penetrated deep, and a crooked furrow of rich-smelling new earth was forming behind the plow, turning under the weeds and grass that had been growing in the plot. When Se-quo-i managed to turn the plow and direct it back alongside the fresh furrow, the onlookers shouted in approval, and Se-quo-i lifted one hand to wave his acknowledgment.

When he removed his hand from the oak handle, the plow twisted, the share leaped up from the earth, and, sensing the sudden ease of tension, the horse turned and tried to walk back over the fallen plow, tangling the harness.

With a few Cherokee oaths, Se-quo-i leaped forward to try to untangle the animal before his hard-worked harness was broken. The animal chose that time to rear and kick, and man and horse came tumbling down together atop the plow, Se-quo-i under the horse's weight.

Renno sprinted across the short distance. The horse was screaming in pain and fright, and there was a great deal of blood. Three Cherokee warriors came running to Renno's side. The horse was still thrashing and struggling as blood gushed from its belly, which had been penetrated by the upturned plowshare. Renno lifted his tomahawk high and put the animal out of its misery with a mighty blow between the eyes, and after a few kicks the horse was still.

Se-quo-i's face was ashen, strained. He lay under the horse and with one leg across the stock of the plow. Renno directed the warriors' efforts, and the deadweight of the horse was lifted so that Renno could pull Se-quo-i free. All the blood was not from the horse; Se-quo-i's leg had a compound fracture, with white bone showing through the flow of blood. Renno's first thought was of El-i-chi, for his brother had learned the art of healing from old Casno, but El-i-chi was in the forest, nursing his wounded heart.

"Get Melino, quickly," Renno ordered. "And my mother."

Some of Se-quo-i's young relatives left on the run, and soon the elderly Cherokee shaman, Melino, was kneeling beside Se-quo-i. And then Toshabe, running with a quickness belying her age, arrived. Because Melino was chanting a hymn of healing, Toshabe pushed the shaman aside in disgust, ripped Se-quo-i's sash from his waist, and used it to encircle the leg and, with pressure, stop the flow of blood.

"We must sing the hymns of healing," Melino protested.

"While this one dies of loss of blood?" Toshabe asked sharply. "Sing your hymns later, Shaman, when we have set the break."

Melino rose stiffly and stood with obvious insult showing on his wrinkled face.

"We will need splints," Toshabe told Renno. "Thin slats, this long." She indicated a length. "And a litter to move him into the house."

Soon the materials demanded by Toshabe were ready. She had managed to stanch the flow of blood and had loosened the sash around Se-quo-i's leg. Meanwhile, word of the accident had spread, and the older woman who was the chief healer of the Cherokee village was at Toshabe's side. The two of them worked well together. When Toshabe was ready, she spoke to the Cherokee healer, who held Se-quo-i's upper leg firmly while Renno grasped the young man under the arms.

"Now!" Toshabe said, tugging hard on the leg made crooked by the break. Se-quo-i gasped, but no other sound of pain escaped his lips. With a sharp crack, the crooked leg was extended. Blood gushed anew, and the two women busied themselves in stanching it. At last it was possible to bind the splints into place and to move Se-quo-i to his bed.

"I should have listened to those who advised putting a musket ball into that horse's head," Se-quo-i joked weakly.

"The end result was the same, using my tomahawk," Renno said.

"Rest now," Toshabe urged. "You are young. The break will heal quickly."

The next day, Se-quo-i demanded his books. If he had to be confined to his bed while his leg healed, he would put the time to good use.

At last El-i-chi returned to the village. His face was dark, brooding. Renno tried to talk to him once on the afternoon of his return, but the shaman was in no mood for conversation. Renno had heard of El-i-chi's encounter with Tor-yo-ne, but the shaman made no mention of it, so Renno decided to leave his brother alone, to let El-i-chi work out his problem by himself.

The next morning Renno was awakened by his mother shortly after sunrise.

"I feared it," Toshabe said as she stood in Renno's longhouse.

"What did you fear?" Renno asked.

"They are gone. They left the village in the dark of the night."

He didn't have to ask to know that it was El-i-chi and Ah-wa-o who had gone. Renno pulled on his clothing, and Toshabe returned to her husband. The sachem did not take the time for breakfast. He left the village, making a swing to the west, then gradually circling to the north. He had little hope of picking up the lovers' trail, for many paths came and went from the village, but he was not surprised when, past the swimming stream and a mile into the forest, he saw the message that had been left him by his brother: A hawk's feather was stuck into a small crack in a large tree and, below it, cut into the bark with a knife, a crude compass with the arrow pointing north. El-i-chi was heading toward the Seneca homelands, where the waters smoked in the autumn and the snows of winter were deep.

A feeling of total loss caused Renno to fall to his

knees. His arms reached for the sky in a futile gesture, and his heart was heavy in his chest.

"Brother, oh, my brother," he whispered.

And then he experienced a surge of anger. It was so like El-i-chi to put his own happiness first, to abandon his responsibilities as shaman, and to leave his brother to face the burden of leadership and the problems of the future alone. He leaped to his feet, but the anger was short-lived. It was replaced by a dull pain in his breast and questions in his mind. What things in life had the most value, after all? Was not the sweetest thing in life a man and woman together, a man and a woman made one?

He lifted his arms to the manitous once more, and then, with his grief an almost insupportable weight, he lowered his hands to his sides and slowly began to pound his feet into the detritus of the forest's floor in a dance of mourning. He offered a song for the dead, and the sound soared upward into the thick foliage.

Arthur St. Clair, appointed by Congress to be governor of the Northwest Territory, had been given fourteen thousand dollars by Congress to be used in conciliating the Indians. St. Clair was a man of honor, serious in his efforts to learn the true state of mind of the Indians. The Indians, however, could not understand St. Clair's confusion about their thinking, for white settlers continued to pour over their boundaries in spite of the series of killings that had proliferated after Harmar's humiliating defeat. The governor had called a peace conference to which the chiefs came, but St. Clair suspected that they had attended only to claim their monetary gifts before going back to their various lands to listen to the promises of the English agents who were constantly at work among them.

St. Clair was primarily a politician and a diplomat. His main interest was the formation of suitable local governments for such settlements as Marietta and the newly established Cincinnati. But now he had been ordered by Congress to assume military responsibility as commander of a new army, which would be allocated the sum of over three hundred thousand dollars. That force would, without question, be powerful enough to tame the northwest. It seemed ironic to him—although he did not point it out to others—that so much more money had been appropriated for war efforts than for peace.

The governor would have preferred to leave the actual fighting to others; in fact, he had actively encouraged the settlers in Kentucky to take part in the growing war and had been pleased when James Wilkinson had led a force of Kentucky volunteers north of the Ohio to burn Indian villages. But now the responsibility rested with him. Men and equipment were pouring in. An entire new infantry regiment of regular soldiers would soon be joined to his forces of militia. St. Clair was being buried by a mountain of details, so when he was informed that a Colonel Roy Johnson requested a conference with him, he seized upon that opportunity to leave his paperwork. His eyes narrowed when Roy entered the room, for Roy was the type of man that St. Clair secretly admired—the frontiersman, independent, resourceful, and unafraid of the devil himself.

"Ah, Colonel Johnson," St. Clair said, standing to extend his hand. "Your reputation precedes you."

"My bad luck, sir." Johnson smiled wryly.

"Not at all, not at all. I have heard good words about your campaigns with John Sevier. If you've come to join our war, you're more than welcome."

Johnson and St. Clair sat down. "I might be of some use, sir," Roy offered.

"Good officers experienced in fighting the Indian are in short supply," St. Clair said. "If it were within my power, I'd give you a command, but this is to be a regular army affair, I'm afraid."

"I'm not here for command, Governor. Give me a few frontiersmen, and I'll go out ahead of the army and keep you posted about what's going on."

"Excellent," St. Clair said. "Whatever you need, sir, just let me know."

"Well, sir, if I don't sound too impudent, I'd like to know just how much you, and the secretary of war, know about what you're up against."

"I can only assure you that we're not taking the situation lightly," St. Clair replied.

"Not after what happened to Harmar," Roy said.

"Indeed," St. Clair agreed. "We cannot afford another defeat for an American army." He leaned back. "Perhaps, Colonel, my task of briefing you on our knowledge would be made easier if you'd tell me first what you know about our situation."

Roy scratched his head. "Well, you're up against the most unified Indian force since the League of the Iroquois. And it's not restricted to the northwest, as you must know. You've got Indian nations—not just scattered tribes—more or less united in an effort to hold the settlers behind a line that extends roughly from the mountain headwaters of the Allegheny down the Ohio and up the Tennessee to its headwaters."

"Exactly," St. Clair agreed.

"Here in the north the main forces are made up of Delaware, Miami, Shawnee, and Wyandot, with scatterings of other tribes, including warriors from the Iroquois nations. If the war shows promise for the Indians, you'll have an old enemy involved, Joseph Brant and his Mohawk who fled to Canada after the War for Independence. Another Indian victory will bring more southern tribes against you. Right now the weakest spot in the Indian line is in the Chickasaw nation; but if American troops lose another battle, the Chickasaw might forget the treaties they've signed and join the fight."

"How about the Cherokee?" St. Clair asked.

"They're solid allies for Americans, mostly," Roy said. "Damned fine people. But there's always old Dragging Canoe."

"The name is new to me," St. Clair confessed.

"He's the prime force behind a small war party in the western part of the Cherokee nation. He's been fighting whites off and on since the war, and he's at it again."

"My God," St. Clair said. "Cherokee?"

"A small part of the tribe," Roy emphasized. "The tribe to worry about in the south is the Creek. There are more of them. In the event of an all-out Indian war, the

Creek could raise holy hell if they had Spanish arms and powder."

"Our information out of the Floridas," St. Clair said, "is that the Spanish governor is being cautious about supporting Indian wars."

"For how long?" Roy challenged. "He may be careful about raising the ire of the southern states—and the United States as a whole—by openly supporting a Creek war against us, but he's still blocking the Mississippi. And if what I heard in Boonesborough is correct, he's actively trying to influence Indian hostility here in the northwest and up and down the length of the Mississippi." He paused. "What do you know about James Wilkinson?"

"A fine man," St. Clair said. "His recent military venture has increased his stature considerably. A good man to have on one's side."

"From what I hear, the Spanish governor feels the same way."

St. Clair's face showed astonishment. "You can't be serious."

"Maybe not," Roy said, shrugging.

"You failed to mention one substantial tribe of the south," St. Clair said. "The Choctaw."

"Well, for the moment they're not a threat. Not organized for military activity like the Creek. The Creek have secure supply lines into Spanish Florida. They're in a good position, and they have the strength and determination to keep constant pressure on the frontier of Georgia and to send their war parties through Cherokee country to raid the Watauga, Tennessee, and Kentucky frontiers."

"You paint a grim picture, Colonel," St. Clair said. "I can't believe things are as out of hand as you say. Just where do you get your information?"

Roy shrugged. "Last few months I've seen a heap of country, sir. I've talked to and listened to a lot of folks. I'm from Cherokee country myself, and my son-in-law is sachem of the branch of the Seneca that went south to live with the Cherokee."

"You're saying that part of your intelligence comes from an Indian?" St. Clair asked scornfully.

"Not just any Indian," Roy said.

St. Clair mused for a moment. "Well, we will be assured of success by our overwhelming superiority of arms—"

"You haven't seen any of those new British muskets that are being used by the Shawnee and the Miami?"

St. Clair brushed the warning away with the wave of a hand. "A few. Most of them have only ancient pieces left over from the war or a bow and arrow."

"General," Roy said, "I don't know where you're getting your information, but I'd suggest that you think again if you believe you'll be marching on men armed with bows and arrows."

St. Clair smiled. "Since I respect your experience, Colonel Johnson, feel free to come to me at any time."

Roy nodded. He almost had second thoughts about joining the impending punitive expedition into the heart of the Ohio country. It seemed apparent that he knew more than St. Clair about the Indians and the overall situation. But he would be out front, with a few picked men. If the need arose, he could run like hell.

James Wilkinson, who liked to be called "colonel" after having led the Kentucky volunteers across the Ohio against undefended villages on the edge of Indian country, was at that time encamped on the banks of the mighty Ohio. He had been in the far west for three days with four hirelings and a Shawnee scout.

His patience was growing thin. He realized the difficulty of travel and was aware of the vast, watery distances down the river to New Orleans, but the extreme lateness of the man he was to meet was inexcusable. He was on the verge of giving the order to break camp when his Shawnee scout came silently into the clearing and stood before Wilkinson, who was seated on a campstool.

"They come," the Shawnee reported.

Wilkinson leaped to his feet and followed the scout to the small bluff overlooking the river. The floods of spring were past, and the muddy river flowed mightily inside its banks. Far away downriver he saw the craft—the spread of its sails and the movement of the oars. It was over two hours before the boat began to edge in toward the bank where a signal fire had been lit, and it was early evening when a dandified Spaniard made his way gingerly up the muddy bank and stood gazing imperially at Wilkinson.

"Mr. Wilkinson?" the Spaniard asked in only slightly accented English.

"I am Colonel Wilkinson."

"I greet you in the name of His Excellency, Esteban Miró, governor of the Spanish Crown territories in the Floridas and Louisiana."

"I am honored," Wilkinson said. "Come, sir, and have refreshment. We will sit while we talk."

"It is my desire to leave this wretched place as quickly as possible," the Spanish envoy said as the two men walked toward Wilkinson's camp, "so I will come directly to the point. First, I must congratulate you on your good sense, Colonel. The man who casts his lot with Spain is assuring his future."

"I will need more than words for assurance," Wilkinson said, offering the elegant Spaniard his campstool while seating himself on a fallen log.

"Many, the English among them," the envoy continued, "have thought that Spain's role in this land has faded. I will not go too deeply into that matter, except to say that any man who discounts the power of a nation that has extended its empire from the Philippines to the West Indies, from the Rocky Mountains of this continent to the southern tip of South America at Cape Horn, is a fool."

"Not exactly small potatoes," Wilkinson agreed.

"I beg your pardon?"

"I am fully aware of the achievements of Spain," Wilkinson said. "I have been a friend of Señor Miró's for a number of years, since shortly after I came to Kentucky."

"He considers you to be a true friend, and you can be assured of his support. I have been instructed to inform you that you will have the governor's aid in your efforts to form an independent Kentucky republic in alliance with Spain."

Wilkinson nodded.

"In return," the envoy continued, "the governor expects certain actions on your part."

"I anticipated nothing less," Wilkinson said.

"The governor is an ambitious man, a man of vision. He intends to add to the glory of Spain by making the entire Ohio Valley a part of Spain's possessions on this continent."

"Of course," Wilkinson said. But he was thinking that Miró might be biting off more than he could chew.

"In this respect we wholeheartedly support the Indians' efforts to throw the Americans back across the Ohio," the envoy said. "And we are prepared to back our determination with whatever monies and supplies are needed by our allies the northwestern Indians."

"Which puts you into direct competition with England," Wilkinson pointed out.

"Where England failed, we shall succeed," the envoy said confidently. "You, Colonel Wilkinson, will be our voice here, our liaison for arms and money for our allies. We have promised the coalition of tribes, through the Miami Little Turtle, a quantity of silver coin to be used to purchase guns, shot, powder, and other military necessities. You will be the man who delivers this silver."

"I'm sure that my friend the governor has made provisions to ensure that I may be compensated during this operation," Wilkinson said.

The envoy made a face of distaste at the American's obvious avarice. "Of course. The governor has authorized you to take twenty percent of the shipment for expenses and recompense for your efforts."

"So small an amount for the man who single-handedly prevented the scoundrel George Rogers Clark from sending a military expedition against New Orleans in order to open the river for trade?"

"Twenty percent of a huge amount is much."

"I remind you, my friend, that I have only to change my stance in my Kentucky and side with Clark to have a force of overwhelming strength move down the Mississippi."

"It would take more than a handful of frontiersmen to challenge Spain."

Wilkinson smiled. "But, my friend, we would not be invading *Spain*, with her might, her navy, her army. We would be attacking an isolated river town guarded by a mere handful of Spanish soldiers. On the way we would, of necessity, destroy the small garrisons at St. Louis and Ste. Genevieve. With New Orleans in the hands of the men of Kentucky, the United States would be forced to come to our aid in the event of any Spanish attempt to retake the city."

"You threaten me and Spain?" the envoy demanded angrily.

"I state the facts realistically," Wilkinson said. "My friend, I am risking a great deal to form an agreement with Spain, to aid in the turnover of vast territories to her. In return, I want to be adequately compensated. Kentucky is mine. And the money to enjoy my life is a prerequisite. If Señor Miró thinks that I am too expensive—"

"I have been authorized to offer thirty percent of the total sum of the silver shipment," the envoy said, resigned.

"Forty," Wilkinson said. "No less. After all, the Indians have received and are still receiving arms from the British. At this point, their needs for more funds with which to purchase arms are minimal."

"You remind me, sir, of a bandit from the hills in my own country," the envoy growled, his lip curling.

"Whatever," Wilkinson said, still smiling. "Forty percent. Where and when?"

"The vessel carrying the silver has already left New Orleans and is no more than a month behind me."

"Good, good," Wilkinson said. "The less attention drawn to the vessel, the better. Therefore I will not send a force downstream to meet it but will await it here on the Ohio."

"In this matter," the envoy said, "we will trust to your judgment." He rose. "I will not, sir, burden you with my presence any longer."

Wilkinson waited until the envoy was aboard his boat and the craft had been pushed out into the current before he did his little dance of triumph. The Shawnee scout, sitting with his back against a tree, watched expressionlessly.

Wilkinson knew that his fortunes were improving. First there would be the tidy profit for handling the money being sent to Little Turtle and the other war chiefs. Later there would be exclusive trade agreements with Miró in New Orleans. Vessels owned by Wilkinson would soon be floating down the Mississippi with Miró's assurance that Wilkinson's goods and his goods alone would be safe from confiscation. Little by little he would offer the inducement of free trade on the river to other merchants in Kentucky, thus building a hard core of Spanish supporters. In his dreams he could see himself with a landholding to make the medieval dukedoms of the old countries seem small in comparison. And then, with Spanish control of the west, he would be president, *king*, of the independent state of Kentucky.

He had time before the shipment of silver arrived; meanwhile, he had other business to transact. He set his course for Boonesborough, where, thanks to his eloquent pen and his voice, he had his archrival, George Rogers Clark, on the run. His letters to influential men in the government back east had succeeded in making almost everyone think that Clark, the thirty-four-year-old man who had fought so long for Kentucky statehood, was a senile drunkard.

For days, then weeks, nothing seemed to have meaning for Renno. Toshabe's best culinary efforts, even the sachem's favorite, a hominy soup the makings of which came from the Cherokee—a rich mixture of salt meat, onions, hominy, and poke greens flavored with hickory-nut milk—failed to lift his spirits. He spent many hours in Se-quo-i's cabin, sometimes listening as the young Cherokee read aloud from his collection of the white man's books, sometimes venturing a halfhearted comment on some subject pertaining to the future of the Indian.

True to Toshabe's prediction, Se-quo-i's broken leg had healed rapidly. Application of poultices made of herbs and roots had healed the lacerated skin and flesh, and the swelling had disappeared from the leg.

Renno spent the rest of his time with his children,

instructing Little Hawk in the art of arms and spoiling Renna shamelessly. Thoughts of his brother flooded his waking hours and disturbed his sleep. Perhaps he could have followed El-i-chi and found him, but it would have been difficult. If El-i-chi wanted to be lost, the chances were good that he could lose himself and Ah-wa-o in the vast forest that extended northward. And if, by some miracle of tracking or by luck Renno had caught up with the eloping couple, what could he have done? Could he have physically forced El-i-chi to return? If he could have convinced El-i-chi and Ah-wa-o that what they had done was wrong, the fact would have still remained that their union had been consummated, and they would have been held in disgrace by the entire tribe.

Ah, El-i-chi. The brothers had seen so much together and had fought side by side, often against daunting odds, in many places and in odd corners of the world. And now El-i-chi had vanished as if with the spirits, and only the manitous knew if brother would ever embrace brother again.

It seemed that An-da was always near, especially when Renno went to take his meals in his mother's house. Ena was often in Toshabe's house, too, bringing her twins, Rusog Ho-ya, Fruit of Rusog, and We-yo O-no-ga-nose, Good Water, called We-yo. The boy and the girl had passed their first birthday and were alternating crawling strongly with exploratory walking. They were curious about everything except the cook fire. Three times Ena had taught the danger and pain of fire to her twins by holding their hands painfully close to the blaze until, with shrieks of fear and an ache just short of blistering, the lesson was learned. But nothing else was safe from the marauding toddlers, who, Toshabe swore laughingly, must have taken their blood from the Cherokee thunder god, the Red Man, Asgaya Gigagei, for they could strike like lightning when one's attention was averted, bringing down an entire bed on their heads or sending the cook pots scattering with a horrible clatter.

"Had they both been born boys," Ha-ace said, "nothing would be safe."

But there was love in the longhouse, and Toshabe adored her grandchildren. Children, gifts of the manitous, were treasured above all else and allowed to go their own way as long as that way did not endanger them. In this nest of domestic noise, Renno gradually became Renno again, and once again his mind was busy, George Washington's letter foremost in his thoughts.

On the day that the splints were removed from Se-quo-i's leg a crowd gathered in his cabin, including Rusog, Ena, Toshabe, Ha-ace, and Renno. Little Hawk watched wide-eyed, and An-da held Renna, who was a bit frightened as Toshabe began to take off the wrappings. "You will not be able to put your full weight on it for some time," she cautioned as Se-quo-i eagerly raised his leg to examine the impressive scars where jagged edges of bone had once protruded.

"I have made this for you," Rusog said, producing a well-fashioned walking stick with a haft made to fit a man's hand.

"I am grateful." Se-quo-i swung his legs over the side of the bed and put his feet on the floor, using the walking stick to support part of his weight. "I'm crooked," he said quietly. Crooked he was, the broken leg twisted still and shortened. He frowned as he put a bit of weight on the leg, his shoulders falling out of line. "This cannot be."

"It is often thus with so bad a break." Toshabe spoke crisply. "Thank the manitous that you will be able to walk at all."

"I will not walk bouncing up and down crookedly for the rest of my life!" Se-quo-i thundered.

"It will improve with time," Renno said, although he did not really believe it. He felt devastated by a new source of sadness. El-i-chi was lost to him, and now another warrior who had stood at his side, who had fought with him, was crippled. He turned his face away, grieving for his friend, who would never again be whole.

A small riverboat named the *Santa Maria*, in honor of that same ship in the fleet of the great admiral Columbus, was beating its way up the Mississippi from New Orleans. Using sail when she had a favorable wind, which was rarely, and oars when she had no wind, her progress was slow. The crew was a motley gang of New Orleans waterfront riffraff mixed with only a few truly dependable men from the Spanish navy.

In command was Lieutenant Juan Revis, assigned to the mission at the request of Governor Miró from a Spanish ship of the line. Revis fervently desired to deliver the silver successfully, make his way back down the river as swiftly as possible, and rejoin his ship. And he was still long weeks away from the garrison at New Madrid, the first point of Spanish civilization upriver from New Orleans, in the land of those halfhearted friends of the Spanish, the Chickasaw.

When the river was broad and the winds favorable, the *Santa Maria* traveled into the night in spite of the grumblings of the crew. The miles passed slowly, laboriously, and still the broad, muddy river stretched before the boat, the banks a wilderness inhabited, Revis felt, by irredeemable savages.

One by one distant events were affecting the future of Renno, all without his knowledge. He could never be fully resigned to the loss of his brother from his life, but he had managed to achieve a degree of acceptance. He had not yet given in to his growing urge to seclude himself in the wilderness for fasting and communication with his manitous; although he would not have admitted it even to himself, he was fearful of what that counsel would be. He had not surrendered to the powerful desire to put miles beneath his running feet or to the pressing need to acknowledge the letter from his friend George Washington.

He seemed content. At mealtime in Toshabe's longhouse he joked and laughed with members of his family. He had grown fond of the beautiful young An-da and treated her as if she were a younger sister, teasing her and asking her what young warrior had cast his eyes at her that day. He hunted only when necessary, and he limited the distance of his hunts with iron will, fighting the desire to look past the next hill. He instructed Little Hawk and other young boys in the use of weapons and in forest lore. But to show that his contentment was, after all, a surface thing, his heart soared with excitement when he was summoned to the Cherokee council house by his brother-by-marriage, Rusog, and heard the words of a traveler from the west.

The talk was long, but the information brought was basic and simple: Representatives of the northern tribes had been in council with the Cherokee in the west, Chief Dragging Canoe the most important among them, urging that the Cherokee join in the war that was threatening to explode from the Floridas to the Great Lakes.

Afterward, Renno sat with Ena and Rusog in their lodge, brooding into the fire in silence. Rusog, as if sharing Renno's thoughts, was also silent while Ena was putting the rambunctious twins to bed.

It was Rusog who finally broke the silence. "The Cherokee will not fight in this war."

Renno looked into the eyes of his brother-by-marriage but said nothing.

"Those who travel the warpath with Dragging Canoe are few," Rusog continued. "But war attracts young men. This war must be stopped."

Renno nodded.

"I will go," Rusog said as Ena came into the room.

She nodded, not surprised.

"We will be two," Renno offered.

"This is a Cherokee affair," Rusog said, "although my brother's company would be welcome and his strong arm more so in the event of trouble."

"As you are silent as a guest in the Seneca council house, I will be silent in yours," Renno said. "But I will be there."

"So," Rusog agreed.

Chapter IV

R enno had never undertaken a major mission without a
period of fasting and praying to seek guidance from
his manitous, the spirits of those Seneca who had gone to
the Place across the River before him. Now, while Rusog
fretted impatiently back in the village, Renno was once
again alone with the spirits in the wilderness. The summer
night was alive with the sounds of insects, the call of night
birds, and the rustle of small animals. His fire burned in a
secluded glen, beneath a high, rocky cliff. The accumulation of ash and cinder showed that the fire had been fed
for some time. Renno had no food in the one-man camp.
Nearby, a little stream fed by a clear spring at the base of

58

the bluff gurgled its way westward to join a larger stream and, eventually, the Tennessee River.

For two days and into the second night he had fasted and chanted his appeal to the spirits, and now he felt purified. The hunger pangs that had attacked him during the second day were gone, leaving only a sense of peace and rightness.

A whippoorwill sang of its sadness to the narrow crescent moon in the west. The night was far gone, and still Renno was sleepless, for there seemed to be a sense of change, a charge, in the cool night air. Although he no longer felt alone, there was as yet no spirit manifestation to give him guidance. He tried to clear his mind and create a well of darkness more receptive to the feeling that others were present although unseen.

When he realized that his vision was fading, that the moon and the stars were dim, a soothing reassurance came over him. It was as if he were lost for long moments in a dark mist not of the earth. He felt a presence, but it defied identification. He knew only that he was being held in favorable regard.

He waited. Figures began to materialize, at first at a distance, and then it was as if he himself were moving through the air on the wings of a hawk, bringing him nearer so he could make out individual forms and faces. A gathering of warriors, Mohawk by their dress and paint, sat in council. Facing them were white men.

One of the white men spoke: "This is a family quarrel between us and England. The Indian, the League of the Ho-de-no-sau-nee, is not involved in this dispute. Our leaders ask that you not take up the tomahawk against King George or against us. They ask that you do not join either side but keep to your lands in peace."

It was as if Renno himself were sitting in on the council. He did not recognize the white men, but he knew the identity of the aged Mohawk chief who rose to answer, although he had never actually seen the man. It was Steyawa, and Renno felt the same astonishment as the others in the council house when Steyawa spoke.

"You who have ears, let them hear," the old chief said in the high style of an Iroquois orator. "The League of the

Ho-de-no-sau-nee will take no part in this family fight
between the white men of King George's colonies and
their father. We, the Ho-de-no-sau-nee, will sit in our
homes and let the white men fight their own battles."

Renno felt himself straining forward, trying to protest, for the Mohawk chief had no right to speak for the
entire league, for all six nations. But he could not find his
voice, and then the scene faded . . . to be replaced with a
pageant that made Renno's heart soar with pride, for he
recognized the Tree of Great Peace, the symbol of the
Great Peace that had tied the League of the Iroquois as
one for hundreds of years. He saw the symbolic fire that,
by legend, had been lit by Hiawatha, messenger of the
great prophet who first had envisioned an end to the
intertribal wars among Iroquois brothers; and Renno saw
gathered there in the council of the harvest moon the
senior warriors and elders of the Six Nations: Mohawk,
Seneca, Cayuga, Oneida, Onondaga, Tuscarora. Renno,
too, sat in that council and realized that he was being
given a great honor by the manitous, who were enabling
him to witness events that were long past.

The sachems rose one by one to speak, and one by
one they castigated the Mohawk chief Steyawa for presum-
ing to speak for the league as a whole. Steyawa sat,
stunned, and the words fell on him as if they were blows
until, his pride stung beyond endurance, he rose, straightening his old bones to stand tall and dignified. He did not
look at the others. He stalked forward, stood close to the
Fire of Great Peace, and stared downward into the flames
and coals. For two hundred and fifty years the great fire
had burned. The red glare of it etched the wrinkles in
Steyawa's face. Slowly, dramatically, he lifted his arms
until they pointed to the heavens, and then, in a low, deep
voice that carried well, he said calmly, "There is no more
League of the Ho-de-no-sau-nee."

A shiver of dread caused Renno to feel cold.

The vision darkened and became stark as Steyawa suddenly kicked the Fire of Great Peace apart. The stench of
burning leather and of scorched flesh came to Renno, but in
spite of burns on Steyawa's feet and legs, the old Mohawk

continued to kick at the fire until the embers were scattered and the living flames were no more. An eerie silence descended, and then a sudden downpour, an earsplitting roar of waters, extinguished the still-glowing coals.

The vision vanished. The crescent moon had passed behind a cloud, leaving Renno to sit in darkness as he tried to understand why he had been shown an event that had happened long ago, at the beginning of the War for Independence. Obviously it had been a dire omen for all the Six Nations; but what meaning did it have in Renno's world?

"Instruct me," he whispered, still feeling the warm, reassuring presence of the manitous. "You, my ancestors, have stood beside me in battle and have guided me well. Leave me not in ignorance of what I should do."

His heart soared, and a feeling of total peace and confidence enveloped him as a vision of a council inside a Seneca longhouse appeared to him. Again it was as if he himself sat in the council, and around him were all those who had gone before: Grim old Ghonka sat at the head, flanked by the young, strong, original Renno and Renno's son, Ja-gonh. Ghonkaba was there, and old Casno. And Ah-wen-ga, Renno's beloved grandmother, sat in shadows behind the warriors, alongside a pale-haired figure who thrilled Renno's heart—Emily. Here were all the generations of the white Indian: Ghonka, who had adopted the white child who became the first Renno; Ja-gonh, son of Renno and white Betsy, and husband of Ah-wen-ga; Ghonkaba, Renno's father. They looked at him and smiled.

"Is it my time to join you?" Renno whispered, although no sound issued from his lips. His ancestors were looking at him with love and respect and what might have been interpreted as welcome.

Renno, accepting his fate, extended his arms, reaching, trying to detain the spirits as they began to fade, and the night sounds of the forest replaced the soft crackle of the council fire in the spirit longhouse.

Then, stunned, he heard his own voice raised in a wail of protest. "Don't go yet! You have told me nothing . . . nothing."

The original white Indian faced his namesake across

the small, flickering fire. The spirit's face was set in an expression of pride and fondness.

"Old Father," Renno whispered, bowing his head.

"We take great joy in you," the spirit said, and the words filled Renno's heart. Then the spirit's face became grim. "The winds of change that extinguished the Fire of Great Peace now blow upon you. It is not for you to resist or to seek your contentment and comfort. You must go as the winds blow." The spirit began to fade.

"Leave me not, Old Father," Renno begged.

"In the book of the white man," the spirit voice said, sounding hollow, echoing in Renno's mind. "In the book called Job, which my Betsy read to me and your Emily read to you: 'He mocketh at fear, and is not affrighted; neither turneth he back from the sword. . . . He saith among the trumpets, Ha, Ha! And he smelleth the battle afar off, the thunder of the captains, and the shouting.'"

"I hear," Renno said.

"Renno," a soft, familiar voice whispered, and Emily appeared, dressed as a woman of the Seneca, her pale hair braided. "Renno . . ."

"Beloved," Renno said, longing to reach across the low flames to her but knowing that it was not to be.

"Do you remember Ezekiel, who walked the Valley of Bones?"

"I do," Renno answered.

"When they come against you, you will not be alone," the manitou said, then was gone, leaving Renno to chant his song of thanks.

Morning was not far away. In spite of his fast, he felt strong. Lying on his belly, he drank deeply from the stream, feeling the dampness of morning dew on the moss under him. He was no longer regretful that he would once again leave his family and his people. He had been assured of the rightness of his leaving.

At last he ran homeward, startling a brace of young deer into panicked flight. They leaped before him, white tails flagging their retreat, and he shouted out in happiness and for a while kept pace with them until, with a flick of tail, they left the trail and crashed off through the undergrowth.

*   *   *

Back in the village, he ate frugally. Toshabe, serving him, could see the new relaxation in his facial muscles.

"Now you are Renno," she approved. But she did not request an explanation. She knew his purpose for the stay in the forest, and his new assurance told her that he had found his answer. He was sachem. He was the man, head of the tribe, the clan, and the family. Whatever his actions now, they were directed by the spirits of the ancestors and, therefore, unquestionably right.

He found Emily's Bible, the pages curled from much use, and sought further knowledge in the book of Ezekiel: "And there was a noise, and behold a shaking, and the bones came together, bone to bone—and lo, the sinews and the flesh came upon them, and the skin covered them above: but there was no breath in them."

He felt his skin crawl, and he wondered what the quote meant for him. But he knew no fear, for his Emily had said, "You will not be alone."

"By the manitous," Renno said, breathing hard as he stood beside a quiet stream after a day of travel. "It is good, is it not, my brother?"

"It is good," Rusog agreed.

The village was far behind them now. They had traveled to the west, alternating walking with the warrior's jog, toward the farthest extension of Cherokee hunting grounds. They had skirted Cherokee villages, for the urgency of their mission precluded visiting, with Rusog's accepting the honor that was his as the preeminent Cherokee chief; had Rusog's presence been known, every village chief would have wanted to feed him lavishly and to honor him with orations.

The brothers-by-marriage had sometimes left the well-traveled trails to find new paths through the virgin wilderness. With the morning sun they ran easily, lightly, until midmorning, then they eased the pace through the heat of the day to run again in the late afternoon and into darkness, pausing only to take what game made itself readily available and to eat two meals a day, at night and at dawn. They traveled light, with only weapons and, in the event that no game presented itself, a small pack each of dried meat and that delicious and long-lasting food of the Cherokee, a hard ball of ground nuts and honey.

Once again Renno's feet knew new ground, and the beauty of the land was not lost on him. The two warriors put miles behind them until the impressive bulk of rock called Lookout Mountain by the white men rose ahead. This was where Dragging Canoe had established the Five Lower Towns of the Cherokee nation after having been driven away from the area around Chickamauga Creek by an expedition led by Colonel Evan Shelby in 1779.

Renno and Rusog paused, rested, washed themselves and their clothing in a clear creek, and then walked proudly, as befitted two sachems, toward the mountain. Renno knew that they were being watched, for he had seen the glint of the sun on metal from the rocks on both sides of the trail, but he kept his eyes forward. His hand, however, was poised to take the English longbow from his shoulder.

The village of Dragging Canoe was located well for defense, and near it was the opening to Nickajack Cave, which served as a stronghold and a storehouse. As Renno and Rusog approached, it was evident that they were expected, for the townswomen and children had turned out to line the approach to the central area of the village, and stalwart Cherokee warriors, weapons much in evidence, lined the compound. Renno noted the presence of a few bearded, ragged, dirty white men, most probably outlaws who had sought the safety of Dragging Canoe's settlement.

The hostile old Cherokee chief himself stood before his lodge, arms crossed on his chest, wearing the ceremonial feathers of his rank. Rusog and Renno stopped a few paces away.

"I greet my brother Dragging Canoe," Rusog said.

"And I greet my brother Rusog," Dragging Canoe replied, stepping forward.

"I thank you for the escort and the protection that you have afforded us these last few miles," Rusog approved.

"Dragging Canoe is not without enemies," the old chief said. "My people guard me well."

"That is good," Rusog said.

"You will eat and drink," Dragging Canoe invited. He raised a hand, and women appeared from his lodge with bowls of food and pottery jugs of water. The three chiefs sat on blankets spread in front of Dragging Canoe's lodge. The village had no large council house, but it was pleasant in the shade and open air, with the sun behind the lodge.

In accordance with custom, the three ate in silence. Dragging Canoe's warriors stood motionless, arms crossed, watching the chewing of three sets of jaws. After the meal was cleared away by the women, a pipe was passed. Renno took two puffs but expelled the smoke quickly, not liking the bite of the tobacco.

"And now, my brother Rusog," Dragging Canoe began, "I will save much time and much breath by stating what I assume to be the two possible reasons for your honoring me with your presence."

Rusog nodded.

The old chief's lips curled in a sly smile. "I pray to the spirits that the great chief of the Cherokee has at last come to his senses and realized that the white man has always been our enemy and will always be so. On the other hand, the second possibility is that you have come in a futile attempt to tell Dragging Canoe that he must give up his fight against the white man." He spread his hands. "Now I ask, which reason has brought you here?"

Rusog smiled. "I think Dragging Canoe has learned directness from the white man even while he has fought him for these many years."

"Perhaps," Dragging Canoe allowed. "But what one learns is not always better than the old ways. I am direct, my brother, because you come at a time when I am preparing for a journey."

"Then we will not keep you, my brother," Rusog said. "It is true that I have come for one of the reasons you stated, but also out of concern for you and for the Chickamauga Cherokee you lead. Many have died, Dragging Canoe, white and red alike, and many more will die. Most who die will be those we can least afford to lose—our warriors, our young men. Although Dragging Canoe may have good reason to hate the white men, to continue to

war against them is futile. The friendship that we Cherokee have formed with the Cumberland whites is worth
preserving; white and Indian must unite against those who
will threaten us in the future—the Spanish and the English. Would Dragging Canoe prefer to return to the times
when the nations of Europe gave our young men strong drink
and weapons and a pittance of gold or silver to fight wars?"

Dragging Canoe was silent for a long time. When he
spoke, it was in the tone of oratory. "All my life, from moon
to moon and from year to year, I have carried the battle to
those who come unasked into our lands. For the rest of my
life, be it long or short, I will continue this battle, for I
have been driven from the home of my ancestors. I have
been hounded, and my young men have died at the hands
of the invaders." Dragging Canoe's face was grim. "To ask
me to cease the struggle to keep that which is mine is to
ask me to cut off my arms, my legs, and my heart from my
body. Once your grandfather Loramas felt as I feel, young
Rusog, and who is to say that a man of such wisdom was
wrong? All of the Cherokee once felt as I feel and had the
courage to fight."

Rusog's shoulders straightened at this slight slur, but
he remained silent.

"I will never become the white man's lapdog," Dragging Canoe vowed. "I will live out my life in the way of
my ancestors, not owning the land on which I hunt, for no
man can own the earth. He can only use it as a gift from
the spirits and respect it. To see it shorn of its trees, to see
the good earth torn by the white man's plow, this I will
never abide."

"I hear," Rusog said quietly. "And yet, my brother,
that way lies the end of all."

"You would have us give ground slowly, allow the
plows into our forests, and see our deer slaughtered by the
whites who breed five new children to replace each one
we kill," Dragging Canoe said. "You are alone, my brother, for I have spoken with many—with Little Turtle, with
Red Jacket, with Joseph Brant himself, and with the chiefs
of the Creek—and we are the true spirit of the Indian, not
you! Not those Cherokee who build log huts like the white

man and trade for his pitiful things made of metals! I bear you no ill will, Rusog, for you are a blood brother, but I say, without malice, that you and those who think like you will be swept away. You will be dust, perhaps killed by a white man's disease or rotted into something weak and helpless by eating his tasteless food. Hear me. You came to talk peace to me. I talk war and honor to you."

"Then we are wolf and bear," Rusog said, "never to lie down together in rest."

"And you, Sachem, Renno of the Seneca, what say you?" Dragging Canoe asked.

"My brother's voice is my own," Renno said. "But I would add this." He thought he knew now the reason for his having been shown the vision of the first omen of disaster for the League of the Ho-de-no-sau-nee. "In a vision from the manitous only a moon past I saw how greatness ended. Once my people, the Six Nations of the Iroquois, faced the same decision that now faces the Cherokee, and they chose to side with England against the Americans. Now they are no more the power that once controlled the vast and rich lands from the far north even into this valley. It is said, Dragging Canoe, that Cherokee and Iroquois are blood, from common ancestors, and, indeed, we have been brothers. The Cherokee nation is great and at peace. No man can say that Renno scorns a just war—"

"I know you, Sachem," Dragging Canoe cut in. "Your honor is beyond doubt."

Renno bowed his head to acknowledge the compliment. "When the time is come to lift the tomahawk, Renno will be there. The question is against whom shall Renno's ax be raised?"

"Your father fought with the Americans, as did you," Dragging Canoe said. "I do not know the reasons for your father's decisions, but he was great, as are you. But greatness comes only with wisdom, young Sachem, which you have demonstrated and which, I trust, you will demonstrate once more when I explain." He shifted himself for comfort, and a grimace of pain fleeted across his face. They had been sitting for a long time, and he was not a young man. "We have had the Americans' promise, and

we have seen those promises broken. With each passing
moon we see more whites crossing the mountains that
were once ours alone. Where will they find land, unless it
is Cherokee land? The white man has been generous—"
he snorted to show his disgust "—in *giving* us, by solemn
treaty, land where we have lived as long as grass has grown
and the trees have leafed with the springtime. He has
given us a small portion of the land that was once ours,
with his solemn promise that it will be ours forever.
Forever, to a white man, is the length of time it takes for
him to breed more male children to carry guns to kill us.
Join me, Seneca. Join this greatest coalition of tribes in
history. Fight at my side and at the side of men such as
Little Turtle, Joseph Brant, Red Jacket, and the Creek
who is called by the white men McGillivray."

"I cannot," Renno said. "For it is in my mind, and it
is foretold to me by my manitous, that the future of my
people and of all Indians lies with the United States, not
against them."

"I am sad," Dragging Canoe said, "but I make one
more effort. We have powerful allies, Seneca."

"You speak of promises broken by the Americans,"
Renno said. "Ask those who fought with the British about
broken British promises. The Spanish? Yes, I know that
they, too, seek Indian warriors to die for them. I have
been among the Spanish, and I have seen the results of
their greed. I have seen the skeletons of Indians who were
worked to their death in the depths of the earth seeking
gold for the Spanish. Dragging Canoe is wise and a man of
honor, but perhaps he does not know the treachery of the
Spanish and the self-interest of the English. They want
this land for themselves, my friend. They will promise
anything to get warriors, bodies to march into the guns of
the Americans. But in the end, should you and they
prevail, the land will be theirs, and the same guns that are
given to you to fight the Americans will be turned on you
and your children and your children's children until they
die or become slaves."

Dragging Canoe spoke in an almost inaudible voice.
"You say, Rusog, that we are bear and wolf and will never

lie down together. This one, then, is a mountain panther."
He lowered his head sadly. "You have said, Rusog, and I
have said."

"I am sad," Rusog said, "to know that should war
come to this country of the Cherokee, and should my
brothers the Chickamauga march toward the Cumberland or
toward Knoxville, that I and mine will stand against them."

"And the Seneca," Renno added.

"I march not to the east," Dragging Canoe promised.
"My hunting grounds will be here."

"Then we will continue to be brothers," Rusog replied.

"It is good," Dragging Canoe said. "Now it is time for
me to rest. A house will be prepared for you, and women
will be available to tend your needs."

Food and drink were brought to a lodge assigned to
Rusog and Renno by two giggling, pretty young Cherokee
maidens, one of whom asked permission to speak. Rusog
smiled and nodded.

"Great Chief," the girl said, "my brother, the warrior
Little Moon, followed your father, Wegowa. Do you know
of him?"

"I know him well," Rusog said warmly. "A man of
great power, and a warrior in whom to take pride."

"Is he well?" she asked.

"He is well. He has a son of some ten years," Rusog
answered.

"Tell him that Golden Moon, his sister, gives him
greetings and that his father has passed to the land of the
old ones and that his mother is old but well."

"I will," Rusog agreed.

"Great Chief," the girl ventured shyly.

Rusog raised his eyebrows up.

"I like not this war."

"You are wise beyond your years," Rusog said.

"I am young, but I am a widow because of this war.
And soon there will be many like me."

"Perhaps Dragging Canoe will see reason," Rusog
suggested, intrigued by the girl's statement but not daring
to question her openly.

"Even now he prepares," the girl said.

Rusog nodded. Dragging Canoe had told them that he was in preparation for a journey. "I know."

"I would that you could make him relent," the girl went on. "But when he meets the Spanish and has gold and the weapons of war—"

"It is in the hands of the spirits," Rusog told her.

When the young women were gone, Rusog dislodged a piece of venison from a gap in his teeth with the point of his knife, then said, "So Dragging Canoe goes to meet the Spanish for gold and weapons of war."

"I, too, found the woman's words interesting," Renno replied with a wolfish grin.

"Like you, I have no love for the Spanish." Rusog grinned broadly. "I have a healthy regard for gold, however, and for what gold can do for our people."

"I think, Brother, that our return to our homes will be slightly delayed."

"You are wise, as always," Rusog said.

The sun was just beginning to wash a dim, red glow across the sky to the east. The forest was still; the night creatures were seeking their refuge against the day, and the animals and birds of morning were not yet about. For nearly a week Renno and Rusog had tracked Dragging Canoe and a group of at least thirty warriors westward, toward the Mississippi. Accompanying the Cherokee were three of the white outlaws who walked the path of war with the old Cherokee chief.

Renno and Rusog stayed well back from their quarry. The Seneca sachem led, treading the path silently, with Rusog moving as soundlessly behind him. Before the end of the previous day, Renno had noted that a small group of warriors had left the main body, the evidence of their divergence almost hidden—only a broken leaf testifying to the departure of someone from the trail. Perhaps they had merely gone into the forest to hunt, but when that had been the case before, no effort had been made to hide the signs. Renno had cast around in the forest to see the faint marks of five men moving parallel to the trail. Then the signs had been lost. Warriors always left some evidence of their passing, if only a bent twig, a disturbed patch of fallen leaves . . . unless there was a conscious effort to remain signless.

Now the two warriors moved silently, cautiously, using the first faint light of day to guide them. Their senses were alert, their weapons at the ready. Renno was counting on the early hour as an ally; if anyone from Dragging Canoe's party had been spying on them, they would have seen that Renno and Rusog slept until sunrise, then enjoyed a relatively leisurely breakfast before starting to move.

Their moccasins left tracks in the dew-dampened pine straw. Renno heard a faint, distant sound and halted. Rusog froze behind him. They heard nothing. Renno crept forward. The sound came again after he had moved fifty feet. Ahead the trail broadened into a natural glade, closed in by dense underbrush. Rusog cocked his head as the sound came again. An animal?

Renno opened his mouth, closed his eyes, and emitted an almost inaudible rattle; the sound was a snore. Rusog nodded. He motioned that he would creep around the clearing to the right. He melted into the undergrowth. Renno disappeared to the left, making his way with ultimate care, moving wraithlike in the dim predawn light. The snore was coming from just ahead.

Renno was within a dozen feet of the sleeping man before he saw him, seated, legs sprawled, head against the trunk of a huge sycamore. Renno, motionless, waited. Minutes later one chirp, the sound of a cricket, told him that Rusog had circled the clearing and was now on the same side, ahead of him. He moved forward, passing within a few feet of the sleeping man—one of the white outlaws from Dragging Canoe's village. His rank odor assaulted Renno's nostrils.

Four Cherokee warriors were wrapped in their blankets, feet pointed, by habit, toward the dead fire, as if it were the center of a wheel and the sleeping Cherokee, the spokes. A man stayed warmer in cold weather with his feet pointed toward the fire. Renno saw a slow movement of brush, and Rusog emerged. He nodded as if to say, "You were right, my brother. We were going to be ambushed."

But instead the would-be attackers were betrayed by their sentinel, who snored peacefully against a sycamore tree. For a moment Renno hesitated because the warriors were, after all, Cherokee. But when Rusog raised his hand, made a throat-cutting motion, and pointed at the three Cherokee nearest him, Renno nodded and pointed at the remaining Cherokee and the sleeping white man. Rusog nodded again and crept forward, knife in one hand, tomahawk in the other.

"My brother," Renno remarked aloud in a normal voice as he drew his stiletto, "shall we kill them as they sleep?"

Rusog rolled his eyes skyward as chaos erupted in the camp. With a shout of alarm a warrior was on his feet, tomahawk lifting, when Rusog met him and chopped him down like a tree. The blade at his throat sent a plume of red spewing in the growing light. Renno whirled and sent his stiletto singing a deadly song into the neck of the white sentinel, who never recovered from his confusion. The outlaw died as the blood pumped from his jugular vein. And then the melee involved three against two with Rusog performing a graceful dance of death opposite two fully awake Cherokee.

The warrior facing Renno was a large older man, no doubt a senior warrior. "Must you die, my brother?" Renno asked as the warrior edged forward, tomahawk poised. "You may go in peace upon your word that you will not raise the hatchet again against the Americans."

The Cherokee's mouth curled in contempt. He launched a blow that, had it connected, would have smashed Renno's skull. Renno sidestepped and sent his own tomahawk into soft flesh at his adversary's belly.

"Don't try to talk reason to these!" Rusog cried out as Renno's blade sank deep and sliced fatally.

Rusog was sore beset, facing two strong young warriors who were using good teamwork to render his attack ineffective. Rusog narrowly avoided being taken full in the face by a mighty slash of a blade; then he parried a stroke to his side and leaped back.

Renno asked, "Did I hear you calling me, Brother?"

"If you can find the time," Rusog grunted, avoiding still another deadly blow and evening the odds a bit by severing the biceps muscle on the fighting arm of one of the Cherokee. The warrior cried out and fell back, never to feel anything again as Renno's tomahawk cracked his skull.

"Thank you very much," Rusog said, now moving confidently toward the final enemy. "But you could have taken the whole one, I think."

"My brother has been long inactive. He needs to hone his skills," Renno joked.

He leaned against a tree and watched with interest as Rusog's foe, a strong one, seeing that retreat was impossible, attacked with a fury that drove Rusog back. But it ended with a swift plunge from the knife in Rusog's left hand, the blade finding an opening between ribs to stop the beating of the Cherokee warrior's heart. Rusog stood over the fallen man, panting. He leaned to wipe his blades on the buckskin trousers of the corpse.

"You are right," he said, straightening. "I have been too long inactive." He crouched down, clutched the dead man's dark hair, and then straightened with a grunt. "There is no honor in lifting the scalp of a brother," he decided.

"Agreed," Renno said.

"Folly," Rusog grated, spitting out his disgust.

"There will be more folly, Brother."

"And I was about to kill them as they slept," Rusog said, a revolted look on his face. "Suddenly my own people are the enemy."

"I grieve with you," Renno told him. "I have little stomach for this."

"And yet there will be more killing because of the Spanish gold. Good weapons, the strong drink of the Spanish, money to buy more of the drink and perhaps a horse—those things will attract many to Dragging Canoe's war party."

"Then we go on?" Renno asked.

"Have we a choice?"

Renno, remembering the words of his ancestor, said, "'To follow the winds as they blow will see more blood.'"

Rusog nodded darkly. "We have no choice, after all."

The journey was long. In the flat country another ambush was sprung, this one with only a few moments' warning, just enough time to allow Renno to use his longbow with deadly effect on two warriors before the Cherokee—six strong even after losing the two—burst from a thicket shouting death and war. The battle was heated, leaving both Rusog and Renno gasping from the ferocity of the struggle when six more Cherokee warriors finally lay dead.

After that they were more careful. In the distance they could see the taller trees that marked the Mississippi riverbank. They approached the Father of Waters at night, across from the lights of the Spanish fort at New Madrid. On the near shore Dragging Canoe's band was encamped, and the sentinels were posted well, making any approach so chancy that Renno and Rusog moved upstream, found a place where they could spy on the band's activities, and waited throughout the night, taking turns at sleep.

In the early morning a small riverboat flying the flag of Spain crossed the Mississippi from New Madrid, and a young, ornately uniformed Spaniard conferred for some time with Dragging Canoe in the shade of a cottonwood tree. Then the Cherokee and the boat's crew off-loaded two wooden cases that, when broken open, revealed muskets as well as a small strongbox that Dragging Canoe opened with eagerness.

"Pay from his master, the Spanish governor," Rusog grated contemptuously.

"But the hunt is not yet concluded," Renno foretold.

From their hidden position they watched the uniformed Spaniard board his vessel. The boat was pushed out into the current, but instead of crossing the river to return to New Madrid, it went upstream. There was little wind, and it blew in the wrong direction, so oars flashed and roiled the water as the boat made slow headway.

Dragging Canoe and his men, meanwhile, were brandishing their new, powerful muskets and whooping with joy. The boat passed near the point where Rusog and Renno were hidden—near enough for them to count ten men, including the Spanish officer.

"There," Renno said, indicating the boat's stern. "Dragging Canoe did not get all the muskets."

"Nor all of the gold?" Rusog suggested.

"These ten Spaniards do not have the look of warriors," Renno said.

"I fancy they will rest at night," Rusog said.

"Unless something happens to disturb that rest..." Renno told him.

It was almost no effort to keep pace with the slow-moving boat as it struggled against the river's current. They had time to roast a rabbit, eat well, and still be near the boat when, at darkness, it pulled to their side of the river and tied up to a strong snag near the shore. A stretch of water approximately twenty yards across separated the boat from the bank.

A lantern was kept burning, and a sentinel posted on the bow was illuminated by its light.

"I will take him," Rusog said.

"Would it not be best to put more distance between us and Dragging Canoe's warriors?" Renno suggested.

"But then we will have farther to carry the rifles and the gold," Rusog pointed out.

"I do not intend to break my back carrying rifles," Renno said.

"We will give them another day of life, then," Rusog assented, looking around for a likely place to make his bed.

Chapter V

Knowing that Renno might follow and try to negate the decision to have Ah-wa-o, El-i-chi had traveled far and fast for days, using care not to leave a trail. It took them many days to put the land of the Cherokee behind them. During that time they talked of many things. They laughed and occasionally acted like overgrown children at play, splashing each other in a clear, cool stream and wrestling in mock tests of strength, which El-i-chi often lost deliberately in order to have Ah-wa-o's sweet weight atop him.

At night they slept under the same blanket, but although the kisses were deep and the caresses increasingly intimate, turning El-i-chi's blood into fire—and although Ah-wa-o never said no or pulled away—he honored her. Theirs was not a temporary, animal lust. Their union was to be in the tradition of the Seneca, and to them it would be as binding and as honorable as if it had been performed in the presence of family and tribe.

It was not until they had crossed the Cumberland River into Kentucky that El-i-chi sought out a hidden place to rest. In a glen among rocks and dense forest he built a temporary shelter, killed a deer for food—until that time they had been eating lightly on small game and the dried provisions that Ah-wa-o had taken from the longhouse of Ha-ace and Toshabe—and prepared Ah-wa-o for their wedding ceremony. He laid out a small fire in a ceremonial manner, the wood for the fire chosen carefully for straightness and arranged just so in a pattern to please the manitous and the spirits of good.

They cleansed their bodies by rubbing themselves vigorously with clean, white sand in a gurgling stream, and Ah-wa-o washed and dried their buckskins. The wedding feast, venison and dried corn, was ready, the meat sending delicious aromas throughout the little glen. If they had been back in the village, everyone would have partaken of the feast, which would begin at sundown, and there would have been glad singing and dancing. In the wilderness, it was a dance for two. But El-i-chi felt no sorrow or regret, for he had never seen a more graceful dancer than his Ah-wa-o. They ate the wedding feast facing each other across the glowing fire, and to observe tradition, they slept separately.

El-i-chi was awake with the first rays of the sun. Ah-wa-o awoke to find the campsite festooned with flowers, and venison roasting over the fire. When the sun was three hours high, they stood facing it, hand in hand, as El-i-chi chanted to the manitous. He was the tribe's shaman. He had presided over the wedding ceremonies of others, and now he was performing his own, his heart full of the beauty of his bride.

Departing from the traditional ceremony, he looked down into Ah-wa-o's eyes and said, "With this we make our exile permanent. With this we cut all ties, for once it is done there is no turning back. Think well, Ah-wa-o."

"My thinking is done," she said in a strong, confident voice.

He felt as if he could swim in her dark eyes and could see through to her spirit. He chanted the old words, and then, arm in arm, they danced the stately dance of union. Now they were one. They ate and, in keeping with custom, sat side by side to receive the well-wishes of friends and relatives, except, of course, they were alone.

"I have not told you, Husband," Ah-wa-o said, "but when I was creeping out of the longhouse, my father lifted his head and looked at me. He said nothing, but he smiled, for he must have known what I was about. And so, even though he is not here, I can feel his blessing."

A surge of warmth for the Panther, Ha-ace, came to El-i-chi. He wondered if Toshabe, too, had known. He thought not, for his mother was, after all, keeper of traditions.

"One day I will clasp the arm of Ha-ace in gratitude for that."

"Will we ever see them again?" she asked.

He held her close but was silent, and his silence brought tears to her eyes. He kissed them away.

"Forgive me," she whispered. "It was only a moment. Only a moment when I wished—"

"I know," he sympathized, thinking of Renno, Ena, his mother . . . they should be with him now, smiling and wishing joy and many children for his union.

"I would face more than disgrace," she said, pushing her youthful, ripe body against his.

The day seemed endless to both. With the setting sun they walked hand in hand to the stream, and for the first time bathed together nude. El-i-chi's eyes feasted, and his evident manhood made Ah-wa-o giggle and turn her eyes away shyly, only to come back once again to feast in their turn on his body. The union was consummated with great care on El-i-chi's part. He knew the fears and sensitivity that made Ah-wa-o nervous.

They had little sleep that night, and in the early-

morning hours, when their passion surged high once
more, it was truly complete as Ah-wa-o gave a little cry
that was surprise as much as pleasure.

The traverse of Kentucky was accomplished with great
caution. The white settlers here—on the frontier of several hostile tribes, with the coalition of tribes just across the
Ohio—tended to shoot first at an Indian and then wonder
whether he was friendly or hostile. But El-i-chi, master of
woodcraft, seemed able to sense the locations of the
scattered white settlements and avoided them.

They crossed the Ohio near its junction with the Big
Sandy River and entered a wilderness of beauty and
boundless plenty. Once they had journeyed a few days
away from the river, game was so plentiful that beaten
trails had been cut through the forests, sometimes leading
to saline springs with salt licks.

It was Ah-wa-o who discovered what was to be their
first home. She had been amazed and delighted by the
sheer size of the trees that grew in the rich soil, and as
they traveled slowly with no determined destination it
became a passion with her to seek out the largest trees
and to pace around their majestic trucks. Some of the
sycamores were as large as a settler's log cabin. When
Ah-wa-o discovered one monarch of the forest that had a
hollow at ground level as big as a room, a floor padded by
nuts dropped by generations of squirrels and softened by
the years, and an opening that could be covered by a
blanket, she said, "Here we will be dry and warm at
night."

"So, like the manitous of the forest, we shall live in a
tree?" El-i-chi asked. He preferred the open air. If it
rained, the canopy of a giant elm would give them shelter.

He could not deny Ah-wa-o anything within reason,
however, and so, for pleasant, lazy days they lived in the
hollow, sleeping on blankets spread over soft, green leaves
gathered by Ah-wa-o and swimming in a clear lake formed
by a huge beaver dam. In the mornings they could sit
quietly beside the lake and watch the bedraggled, comical
beavers at their work. For a great distance around the lake

saplings had been cleared by the animals, leaving the cone-topped, well-chewed stumps to stick up through bracken fern.

El-i-chi took a trout from the clear waters, spearing the fish with a well-aimed arrow. The trout was so huge that it gave them food for two days. There was another source of food, which even Ah-wa-o could tap. It was the time of migration for passenger pigeons, flocks so dense that their flight darkened the sky, and when they roosted at night, their weight broke tree limbs. The meat was tasty and pleasantly chewy. With such plenty around them, El-i-chi did not even have to leave their tree home to hunt, so that in that honeymoon period there was only Ah-wa-o, a font of laughter, love, and a closeness that El-i-chi had never experienced with Holani, the Chickasaw wildcat who had been his first bride.

It was easy for El-i-chi to understand why the white man coveted such country. The forest provided settlers with everything they needed. The trees gave them material to build homes, wood for fire, posts for fences, and handles for tools. For food there were game and fish and, in season, blackberries, raspberries, serviceberries, gooseberries, wild plums, and wild cherries.

For the Indian the forest was everything as well, and in spite of an age-old custom of setting fire to the forest to drive game, the Indian still did less damage than white settlers who, upon arriving in a virgin forest, immediately began to cut down the trees to clear ground for their fields. All that El-i-chi needed to live well indefinitely were his musket, his tomahawk, bow and quiver of arrows—the forest provided material to make new arrows—his knife, blankets, a small amount of salt that could be replenished at the licks, and a sack of corn that could be cooked or dampened to be used in bread. Later, he could trade skins and hides with the Indians of the area for more corn and for shot and powder once his supply was exhausted.

During this time, El-i-chi's thoughts were seldom serious, for his adoration for Ah-wa-o pushed away the memories of home and family. His love and happiness served to keep him content. His need to be with Ah-wa-o, to be one with her not only physically but spiritually, made all else unimportant. Never would he go back to the tribe and submit the woman who was his life to their disapproval. So it was that time stood still. The change of season had come when, returning from a nut-gathering walk near their tree home, Ah-wa-o found El-i-chi sitting on mossy ground, his head lowered, an expression on his face that she had not seen since they had left their home. For a long time she stood, unseen, watching him. He was deep in thought, and the thoughts were obviously not to his liking. She knew him well, and she knew that he was thinking of home, his brother, his mother, his people. She came to sit beside him.

"You were far away," she said.

"It is nothing," he said lightly, smiling and leaning to touch her.

"And yet your face was so sad."

He laughed.

"You have sacrificed much for me."

"No more than you for me," he replied quickly.

"Not so much. Had I married a man from, say, a Cherokee village at some distance, I would have left my home, for they are not like the Seneca, where the man takes the family of the wife."

"But you are Seneca and would never have married a Cherokee," he said.

"Oh?" She giggled. Her laugh was the sound of autumn leaves rustling in a wind. "Don't you remember that handsome one who came from the west and made it known that he wanted to pay court to me?"

"Until I let him know that no man but El-i-chi pays court to Ah-wa-o," he said fiercely.

"My love," she said, "would you go back?"

"And have you live forever in disgrace, an impure woman?" His face was dark. "Before I would do that—"

"You would give up seeing your brother, your mother, and your sister forever?"

"I have done what had to be done," he said, agitated by the talk.

She was silent for a long time. El-i-chi stared upward

into the canopy of the forest. Grapevines twined among the treetops, cutting out all sun, so that their glade was free of undergrowth, and parklike pathways wound among the huge trees. When he did look at her, tears were coursing down her cheeks.

"Here," he said, reaching out to take a tear on the tip of his finger and putting it to his lips. "I drink away your sorrow. I know that you miss your father and our people." His voice was low. "If you would go back—"

"No," she said. "These tears are not for me, for you are my world, Husband."

"Shed no tears for me, then," he said.

"I think of you, side by side with Renno, standing against the world—"

"Manitous," he whispered, for that had been the weight on his mind. *Renno*. He forced brightness into his voice. "Enough. I have considered traveling to the west, to seek new land and to find friends among the tribes west of the big river."

She was silent.

He mused for a long time. He had lost his brother, his people, his home. It was tempting to think of traveling far, of covering epic distances, as he and Renno had done in the west and in Africa; but to be among strangers forever was a burden that he could not face. One day, perhaps, they could rejoin the Seneca—not his own people, but northern Seneca—where the language would be his own, where the manitous would know of his presence.

"I think, little Rose, it is time we moved, time for us to seek a new home, for I have lived in a tree so long that I find myself thinking like a squirrel." He took one of the nuts from Ah-wa-o's pouch and bared his teeth, nibbled rapidly, and twitched his nose. Ah-wa-o laughed and clung to him, and for a time he was once again content.

Renno and Rusog were pacing the Spanish riverboat upstream. It was slow going, giving them plenty of time to hunt and rest. They followed the boat for three days, checking their back trail now and then to be certain that Dragging Canoe had not sent warriors upstream to protect—

or to steal—the boat. Each night the Spaniards had tied up on the east bank of the river. On the third night the officer aboard chose a snag—a huge tree washed into the shallows by some past flood and now firmly anchored by its weight—as a place to moor the boat. Below the river bluff a mud flat sloped down to a small cove where, out of the main current, the water was almost still. The boat was tied up about fifty feet out.

"We have waited long enough," Rusog decided as he and Renno lay side by side atop the bluff and looked down upon the river. It was twilight. The last rays of the sun made the western horizon glow red. Lanterns burned aboard the boat. The voices of the Spaniards could be heard clearly in the hush of evening. The crew was preparing its meal while the Spanish officer sat on crates of muskets and ate roasted fish with his hands, now and then tilting a bottle of wine to his lips.

"You understand their language," Rusog said. "What are they saying?"

"They talk of drink and women and of getting back to New Orleans," Renno said. "Nothing of import."

"Speak loud, Spaniards," Rusog whispered, "for soon your tongues will be still."

They withdrew, made a light meal of dried, moistened corn and honey-nut balls, and rested while a small moon rose and the night cooled. It was nearing midnight when Renno got up. Rusog was ready, seeing to his weapons. He followed Renno to the bluff. As the Spaniards had done on previous nights, they had left one lantern burning at the boat's prow.

"So they still feel safe," Rusog growled, "knowing that they are in the country of their Indian allies."

"The light will guide us," Renno said. "We will enter the water upstream and float down to the boat."

"The sentinel is mine," Rusog declared.

"He offers little challenge," Renno said.

The one guard was seated on the deck at the bow, leaning back against crates of muskets, and his snores could be heard all the way to the top of the low bluff. The officer and the rest of the crew sprawled around the open areas of deck. There were no living quarters on the bargelike riverboat—only small cargo spaces in the shallow hull. The Spanish officer had a choice location for his blankets, the hatch cover in the wide part of the bow.

"You from the bow, then," Renno said. "I will come over the stern."

"Take care not to slip in the blood of those who slumber in my path," Rusog warned.

"My brother is bloodthirsty tonight," Renno remarked.

Rusog grunted and led the way upstream. They found a spot where the bluff had collapsed in a dirt slide, then made their way to the water a hundred yards upstream.

"We will not risk getting muskets and powder wet," Renno said.

"Blades will be enough for this job," Rusog agreed.

They left their muskets, powder and shot, and Renno's longbow on the riverbank, waded into the muddy water, submerged themselves to the neck, and let the slow, bankside current take them downstream. A few yards before reaching the boat Renno signaled Rusog by touch. He pointed, then diverged from Rusog to make his way toward the back of the boat. Knowing that Rusog would already be in position, he reached up, caught the low gunwale, and drew himself up. The crew still slumbered peacefully. He waited for a few moments, memorizing the position of all the sleeping men toward the rear of the boat. When he saw Rusog reach up, knife in hand, and watched the flower of red bloom from the sleeping sentinel's throat, he heaved himself onto the boat, grasped his tomahawk in one hand, the stiletto in the other, and began a bloody business.

Death stalked the riverboat from stem and stern. The stiletto in Renno's left hand did its work silently and efficiently, and Rusog moved as quickly. Three of the men had died in their sleep before Rusog's bloodlust drove him to use his tomahawk on the skull of a sleeping Spaniard. The impact, a hollow thud, was loud enough to awaken the man sleeping next to the dead one. Before Rusog could shift his weight for another blow, a shrill cry of alarm created chaos on the deck as men jumped to their feet, shouting out warning. A musket blasted, firing at nothing. And then by the light of the one lantern the Spaniards saw the two shadowy forms and leaped into combat with sword, club, and knife.

Four of the crew converged on Renno. One, the officer, wielded a gleaming short sword. He led the way, and Renno had to parry a thrust with his tomahawk. The Spaniard's quick recovery revealed his skill as a fighter. Renno jumped to the side and lessened the odds by almost decapitating a crewman with a mighty swing of the tomahawk, then fell back before a determined attack by the officer. The white Indian was being encircled by the other two until with a backhand slash of the stiletto, he opened the belly of his adversary.

His two remaining opponents were more wary, having seen a pair of their number fall so quickly. The seaman lagged as the officer moved in, his short sword making gleaming feints in the lantern light. Renno, threatening with his tomahawk, saw the officer give way and slashed with the stiletto to feel it graze the man's clothing.

Rusog had killed one of the men facing him and was now engaged with a competent man with a sword. As he had promised, the deck was slick with blood.

"Fight, coward," the officer snarled to his crewman, who was backing away from the threatening steel in the hands of a man dressed only in a loincloth. The crewman reluctantly came to stand by his superior's side, holding his sword stiffly. The officer turned to his adversary. "I am Juan Revis." His eyes shone dangerously. "A savage should be told the name of the person who kills him." He lunged forward and sent his blade toward Renno's belly. Renno whirled, leaped, and came down with his tomahawk lancing in toward the Spaniard's head. The blow was solid, and the officer slumped to the deck, the sword clattering.

Now it was but a matter of seconds before the last man facing Renno died, his skull penetrated by the blade of the tomahawk.

The sachem, breathing hard, turned in time to see Rusog lunge and bury his tomahawk, blade turned horizontal, into the bridge of a man's nose, shoving broken cartilage back through the fragile nose cavities and into the man's brain. Rusog threw his head high and gave vent to a mighty yell of victory. His eyes were burning in the lantern light. He paced the deck, glancing at the dead, then leaned down to take a scalp.

"Let that wait," Renno said.

Rusog nodded, joining Renno, and with their blades they pried the lid off a crate. Inside the crate were a dozen fine, new muskets.

Renno began to toss the muskets into the dark river. "These will never be used against Americans."

Rusog opened another crate and followed suit. Their feet slipped on the blood-wet deck. One by one the crates were emptied. Then the heads of barrels of powder were smashed by the blades, and the black powder joined the muskets in the water.

"This is hot work," Rusog said, breathing hard. "I will look for the gold." He disappeared through the door that led to the cargo hold.

Renno looked at the moon and silently chanted a hymn of thanks to the manitous for his victory. He was still chanting when he heard Rusog call to him. The white Indian bent low and entered the cargo area. The Cherokee chief had broken the lock on a large chest and was throwing the lid back as Renno came near. The gleam in the dim light was not of gold but of silver Spanish coins.

"Enough to buy many guns and much powder and shot," Renno said.

"Or many items of value for the people of our villages," Rusog suggested.

"Then you intend to carry the chest on your back for a walk of several weeks?" Renno asked.

Rusog grinned. "We will carry some and hide the rest to be retrieved later."

"Fine," Renno agreed. He saw leather pouches stacked against a bulkhead. They held powder in quantity. He emptied the powder from a pouch and handed the bag to Rusog, who filled it with the coins.

"Perhaps we should be glad it is not gold," Rusog remarked, hefting the heavy pouch.

Leaving Rusog to that task, Renno climbed back on deck and looked around, checking to be certain that all weapons had been thrown overboard. A metallic gleam on the deck caught his eye. It was the short sword that had been used so skillfully by the Spanish officer. Renno picked it up; it had a good feel in his hand. He hefted it and slashed the air. It was well balanced, and the edges were keen. He moved forward to hold the sword in the lantern light and saw that it was made of the same fine Toledo steel as his stiletto. And it was similarly ornate, if not as richly decorated with jewels. The carving was the work of a craftsman. He was a man who lived by weapons, and his admiration for this fine piece of the weapons maker's art inspired an instant decision: The sword would be his. He bent to loosen the sash of the officer and removed the sword's sheath. "I thank you, Señor Juan Revis," Renno said to the corpse.

It was then he noticed the little pouch at the officer's waist, the kind used by the Spanish to carry correspondence.

Renno opened the pouch and removed its papers. In the light of the lantern, he read the curving Spanish writing. The letter was from Esteban Miró, governor of the Spanish Floridas. It was addressed to James Wilkinson, a name Renno knew, for Wilkinson was one of the most influential men in Kentucky. The letter spelled out an agreement: a promise of payment from Miró in return for intelligence from Wilkinson and for Wilkinson's efforts to secure the Ohio Valley for Spain and to ally Kentucky with Spain against the United States. It proved Wilkinson was a traitor. Renno realized that the letter would have to be shown to George Washington as soon as possible.

To be sure he had not missed anything, Renno went back to the dead officer, bent, and poked his fingers into the message bag. He was beginning to straighten when the officer, not dead after all, kicked him hard in the stomach with both feet, sending Renno crashing back against the bulkhead of the raised cargo space. Before he could move, the officer was on his feet, a fallen musket in his hand. Revis did not have time to aim but used the musket as a club when Renno bounced to his feet, the short sword in one hand, the letter that would prove a supposedly loyal American to be a traitor in the other. When he saw Revis readying for another swing of the musket, Renno dropped the letter and reached for his tomahawk.

As he watched, Revis looked around at the evidence of his failed mission: He was alone with the two Indians who had killed all his men. The flooring was slick with blood, and bodies sprawled everywhere. The deck was empty of the crates of muskets. Instead of attacking, Revis seized the lantern from its post and staggered to the open hatch of the cargo space.

As understanding dawned, Renno, horrified, switched the sword to his left hand, seized his tomahawk, and hurled it with great force. It sank into Revis's back just below the neck, severing the spinal cord. But the Spaniard had been in the act of raising the lantern. As he pitched forward limply, the lantern rolled down the four steps into the hold, spilling and splashing its oil.

"*Rusog!*" Renno bellowed as he threw himself to the deck. A mighty blast of wind sent debris whistling past Renno's head as the powder stored in the hold went up with a roar. The explosion opened the hull to the river, and the boat was settling rapidly, beginning to lean. Loose objects rolled on the deck as Renno shook his head to clear it.

"Rusog!" he cried again but could hear nothing, his eardrums deafened by the blast. Some rolling object struck him a blow on the shoulder, and the boat shifted ever farther. He pulled himself up, launched himself over the rail, which was at water level, and into the river. He swam strongly, wondering why he could not hear the crackle of flames from the boat's midsection or the smashing of things as the boat tilted.

Once clear of the sinking vessel, he treaded water and looked around. To his relief he saw Rusog's head, his face illuminated by the flames from the boat. Rusog's lips were moving, but Renno could hear nothing. He pointed toward the bank. The rapidly sinking boat disappeared

behind them, taking with it the silver in the chest and that
in the pouches as well. Renno had left his tomahawk
behind, but he had clung to the sword and its scabbard. It
would have to serve until he could get another tomahawk.

They walked along the mud flat and retrieved their
muskets and Renno's longbow. Rusog was talking, and
Renno slowly began to recover his hearing over a great
ringing in his ears.

"You are becoming a woman, Brother," Rusog said,
"unable to kill a man with just one blow."

"His head was as hard as the silver," Renno defended.
"Do you have a ringing in your ears?"

"Like all the church bells of the white man," Rusog
replied.

"And we have no silver," Renno said.

Rusog laughed wryly. "It was uncomfortably heavy,
anyhow. But I see that you didn't come away empty-
handed." He indicated the sword.

"I fancy it," Renno said, handing it to him.

"A fine weapon," Rusog agreed, "but it was of no use
against your tomahawk."

"It is a weapon for the left hand," Renno explained.

"Aha," Rusog said, returning the sword.

Renno strapped it to his belt in the place where he
usually wore his tomahawk.

"We are too far from home," Rusog complained.

"With the sun," Renno said, "we will begin to reme-
dy that situation."

And so the winds of change had blown Renno to the
Mississippi River. For one who believed that nothing
happened without purpose, there were many questions.
Had the manitous sent Rusog and him to Dragging Canoe's village for the sole purpose of destroying arms and
disposing of money that were intended for the enemies of
the United States? And why had the manitous put into his
hands evidence against an important man, only to wrest it
away immediately? He spoke of the matter with Rusog
during the journey home, but Rusog had no answers,

suggesting only that Renno's friend George Washington would accept Renno's word that *he* had seen the evidence.

"True," Renno agreed.

As they set a warrior's pace for home, the ringing in their ears gradually ceased, much to Renno's relief; for a time his hearing—and Rusog's—had not seemed as acute as it once was, but before they reached their home village, even that effect of the explosion had passed.

On his first night back, Renno spoke to Toshabe, Ena, and Ha-ace in Rusog's presence. "You, Ha-ace," he said, "senior warrior, pine tree of the Seneca, will be my voice while I am away."

Ha-ace nodded.

"You know that George Washington has asked for me twice now," Renno continued. "I can no longer deny him, for now there is new information that I must put into his ear. I will travel to the north, where there is war. I have been asked to observe, to learn the true feelings of those who now march along the path of war. You, Mother, will be Ha-ace's source of wisdom and advice."

"I would give this arm," Rusog said, lifting his left hand, "to be able to go with you."

"I will not even state why that is impossible," Renno said, "since you know as well as I."

Rusog nodded. With Dragging Canoe and the Chickamauga on the warpath, division threatened the Cherokee nation, and the news—gleaned from newspapers already months old—was grim: An American army had been defeated by the northern Indians, and war flared from the Georgia frontier to the Great Lakes. It was Rusog's responsibility to stay in his nation, to keep the main elements of the Cherokee at peace.

Chapter VI

Se-quo-i found Renno in his longhouse with Little Hawk and Renna. The white Indian had been giving Little Hawk a lesson in reading, and both father and son were a bit the worse for it. The teaching of the white man's words was, Renno had become convinced, woman's work. Reading the stupid thoughts of the white man was, to Little Hawk, a waste of time and energy. Renno seized upon Se-quo-i's arrival as excuse enough to put the book away.

"It is said that you will journey to the north," Se-quo-i began.

Renno looked at Little Hawk quickly. He had not yet told his children that he would be leaving them soon. Little Hawk showed interest but did not speak.

91

"That is true," Renno said.

"And from Rusog we have heard of the battle on the river and of how—" he paused, smiling "—the great Renno lost his tomahawk."

"Yes," Renno said mildly. "I suppose he would include that detail in his story."

Se-quo-i nodded. "If it pleases you, I would have you come with me."

"May I go, too?" Renna asked.

"I would have it no other way, Princess," Se-quo-i said, hoisting Renna onto his shoulders.

"It's fun riding Se-quo-i," Renna said, laughing, as they walked toward the Cherokee's log cabin. "He bounces up and down."

Se-quo-i looked at Renno and grimaced. He did not, of course, censure Renna for her description of the way he walked with the shortened leg. The spirits had willed it so; for as long as he lived, he would be crippled. It was up to him to accept the manitous' will.

Instead of going inside his cabin, Se-quo-i led Renno around to the back, where the young scholar had built an open shed. There sat a forge and an anvil. The anvil had caused much amusement when Se-quo-i had brought it out from Knoxville with the aid of a travois and a horse. Only Se-quo-i, the Cherokee, would labor so hard to move a heavy piece of iron so that he could sweat and strain over it like a demented white man.

Little Hawk immediately had to try out the blacksmith's sledgehammer, lifting it with straining arms to bring it down with a solid ring on the anvil. "One blow to the head with this weapon would take care of any enemy," he announced.

"That 'weapon' has a different purpose," Se-quo-i said. He unwrapped an object and extended it toward Renno. "To replace your loss. I pray that you find it worthy."

In Renno's hands now rested a war ax of such graceful design, of such beauty, that his heart soared. The blade was larger, by a small amount, than the blades of most tomahawks. The handle was of stout, well-cured oak and was as hard as iron. The blade gleamed almost as finely as the Toledo steel of Renno's stiletto and the short sword at his waist. And in the flat sides of the blade Se-quo-i had engraved the symbols of Renno's primary totems: On one side a bear reared, and a hawk soared, wings outspread, on the other. On the upper part of the handle were decorative inlaid lines of gold and silver.

Renno swung the weapon thoughtfully and found it to have perfect balance. He stepped to one of the wooden support posts of the shed and chopped a chip from the wood, then examined the blade to find its sharpness undiminished. He moved the tomahawk to his left hand and clasped Se-quo-i's arm. "No man ever had a finer weapon, my friend. I am in your debt."

"Never," Se-quo-i said. "It is a gift given freely. May it serve you well."

Renno, grinning wolfishly, made the air whistle with a blow of the war ax. "It is good."

Se-quo-i put his hand on Renna's head. "If you go to the back door and call out for my mother, I believe she will have something for you."

Little Hawk looked at Se-quo-i expectantly.

"And you, young warrior," Se-quo-i added.

Little Hawk and Renna ran to the house and were admitted. Se-quo-i leaned against the anvil and waited while Renno made a more minute inspection of the tomahawk and then shoved it into its place at his waist with a grunt of satisfaction.

"May I see the sword?" Se-quo-i asked. He accepted the weapon and examined it, turning it from side to side. He sighed. "However we try, the white man bests us in such matters."

"He has had centuries to develop such craft," Renno soothed.

"And we, my friend, will we try to catch up? Should we try to match him and come up with something second-rate, such as that poor blade that I fashioned for you?"

Renno jerked the tomahawk from his belt and sent it slashing a fraction of an inch over Se-quo-i's head. "Speak no ill of the weapon of the sachem of the Seneca," he said, only half-jesting. "For it was fashioned by a master craftsman, and is the finest blade to be had." He put the weapon away and faced Se-quo-i.

"Oh, it will do," Se-quo-i admitted. "After all, it's only an ax specially for chopping flesh, not wood, so it will serve its purpose." He limped over to stand a few feet away and spoke so softly that Renno had difficulty hearing what he said. "Whatever I do, Renno, I find it to be only adequate. I put my hand to the jewelry-maker's craft, and the objects I produce glint and glitter, but some white man in some European country centuries ago produced objects that make my creations look like the workings of a child." He turned suddenly and smiled ruefully. "Forgive me. I often think morbid thoughts these days."

"The women wear your jewelry with pride because it expresses not the life and taste of some white man in some European country but of Se-quo-i, Cherokee."

"Enough," Se-quo-i said, seemingly disgusted with himself. "You will leave soon?"

"Soon."

"Alone?"

"I have thought to take one man, maybe more, with me."

"Ah . . . ?" Se-quo-i said, looking as if he wanted to say more.

"I had thought to seek you out," Renno said. "I would have your opinion on something I am considering. This Tor-yo-ne—"

Se-quo-i grunted. "He is young and ambitious. He burns to prove himself, and it is my opinion that he is a true Seneca with the best interests of the tribe in his heart." He spread his hands. "And because he is ambitious and has the blood of sachems, he thinks that he has all the answers. If you are considering him, you would serve two purposes by taking him with you. One, you will remove a disruptive influence from the village. The young men are impressed by Tor-yo-ne. If your mission is long and he remained here, perhaps he would once again try to force the choice of a new sachem. Two, he is a mighty warrior, a good man to have at your side in a fight; and he has traveled through the north country more recently than you."

"I have thought the same," Renno said. "But it helps me form my decision to hear my thoughts echoed by one as wise as Se-quo-i."

Se-quo-i shrugged slightly. He patted his bad leg. "So this has reduced me to the status of elder."

Renno's voice had a trace of harshness. "It is unbecoming to Se-quo-i to revel in self-pity. There are many who have two legs, but there is only one Se-quo-i, for he alone can make a contribution to his people that will be far more important than any number of killings in the fields of war. He alone has the knowledge and the ability to give the Cherokee the tool that has contributed to the white man's power. He alone can give the Cherokee a written language."

Se-quo-i had lowered his head. He raised it, and when he looked into Renno's eyes, his own eyes were sharp, sparkling. "Thank you," he said.

Renno clasped Se-quo-i's arm.

"Travel with the spirits, my friend," Se-quo-i said, "and always speak to me frankly, as you have done, for you are right. I have been neglecting my work while mourning the passing of my leg."

Now that his decision had been made, Renno sought out Tor-yo-ne. The young warrior inclined his head in respect to the sachem. "Soon I will travel to the north," Renno said. "I have thought to have one warrior at my side."

Tor-yo-ne nodded.

"Your right arm is strong, your legs young, and you have most recently traveled in the lands to the north. If it pleases you, I ask you to accompany me."

Tor-yo-ne had difficulty covering his amazement. Then a wide smile took his face. "You honor me, Sachem. You have had my loyalty since your return, and now I pledge myself anew to you. My fighting arm will be yours. My heart as well. Forever."

Renno extended his arm. Tor-yo-ne took it in a firm clasp. "Prepare yourself, then," Renno said. "We travel fast and light."

*   *   *

As Renno walked away Tor-yo-ne's shoulders became even more proudly straight. He had more respect for the sachem than for any man alive, and after meeting Renno, he knew that he had done the white Indian a disservice by agitating to have a new sachem named in Renno's absence. If he had been asked, he would have said that Tor-yo-ne was the last man that Renno would want at his side. His head was held high as he knew a fierce elation, a surge of pride. Where Renno went, honor and fame followed, and now he, Tor-yo-ne, would have a chance to show his worthiness. Perhaps, in the future, he could be as great as Renno.

When considering a journey that would require months, a delay of a day, two days, even three, did not seem to matter. Renno spent the time with his children, taking them into the wilderness, swimming with them, watching proudly as Little Hawk used his boy-sized bow to put the meat of small game on the spit over the campfire. In the evenings he told the ancient legends of the Seneca to his children, with Renna cuddled in his lap. When it was finally time to tell them that he would have to leave them again, his heart was heavy.

"You know," he said, speaking primarily to Little Hawk, "that the League of the Ho-de-no-sau-nee was great and that the Seneca were not the least among them."

"I know," Little Hawk said. "And now the Seneca are scattered, some giving up their name when they moved to the west, calling themselves—or being called—Mingo. And we are here, a small tribe, among the Cherokee."

"You are wise beyond your years," Renno said. "What, then, will become of the Seneca, our tribe in particular?"

"I have counseled with many on this subject," Little Hawk said with great seriousness. "Some say we should remain as we are, but I do not think this is possible."

"Why?"

Little Hawk shrugged. "Because of the whites."

"But you are more white than Indian," Renno pointed out.

"I am Seneca," Little Hawk responded heatedly.

"I am Seneca, too," Renna piped. "But it was nice with Miss Beth in Wilmington, wasn't it?"

"So you remember her," Renno said.

"She was beautiful," Renna responded. "And she gave me pretty dresses."

"I have heard your words," Little Hawk said to his father. "And so I think that we must change, somewhat." He tried to look fierce. "We could fight, as the Indians in the north are fighting, and we would take many white scalps, but we are few when compared to the Americans, aren't we?"

"We are few," Renno confirmed.

"And you are a friend of the great sachem of the whites, and my grandfather fought with the whites. Seneca and American together can beat anyone at war, even England."

Renno smiled. "And so you realized that we must be allied with the Americans." Little Hawk nodded gravely. "And that we, as their allies, must do our part?"

"If you're trying to find a way to tell us that you have to go away again," Little Hawk said, "we understand. Don't we, Renna?"

"Yes," Renna said. "Grandmother Toshabe and Aunt Ena will take care of us." She looked up into Renno's eyes. "But you won't be gone long, will you?"

"Only as long as it takes," Renno answered.

"You could take me with you," Little Hawk suggested.

"Soon," Renno said, smiling warmly at the thought. "Soon you will stand at my side."

"Will you go to see Uncle El-i-chi and Ah-wa-o?" Renna asked.

When possible, Renno avoided thinking of El-i-chi. When his brother did enter his thoughts, it was always to the accompaniment of loss or anger. Just then it was swift anger, for of all the men he would want to be with him in times and places of danger, El-i-chi was the obvious choice.

The sachem's anger faded quickly, however. Little Hawk had bagged a yearling deer, and the roasting haunch of venison was sending out delectable aromas. Renno used the stiletto to cut the meat, and as they ate the juicy chunks with their hands, he looked at his pale-haired daughter, dripping grease on her buckskins, and told himself that soon he would have to find a way to accomplish what he had promised both Emily and Emily's mother, Nora Johnson. Renna especially was to have exposure to both worlds: She was Seneca and would learn the traditions and the life, but she was Emily's daughter, too, and would have the education of a white girl and would learn how to function in white society. How, he didn't know. Nora Johnson was dead. Beth, who had taught the children much of white manners, was the same as dead, gone from their lives.

At the first evening gathering in Toshabe's longhouse after Renno and the children had returned from their holiday in the wilderness, Renno announced his plans. Ha-ace raised one eyebrow when Renno said that his companion would be Tor-yo-ne.

Toshabe heartily approved, undoubtedly because she believed it was good that Renno should not leave the rascal in the village to stir up trouble. Then she saw An-da's stricken face, and her heart went out to the girl. The man she adored was going on the path of danger for a long time, and he was taking An-da's only family, her brother, with him.

"An-da," Toshabe said gently, "when your brother leaves, you will move in here, with us."

"Might as well," Renno said, winking at An-da. "You spend most of your time here anyhow."

Male smugness and ignorance of the hearts of women sometimes irritated Toshabe. Her eyes were daggers for Renno, but she spoke softly to An-da. "The longhouse has been empty since Ah-wa-o went away. It needs the sunshine of a young smile. Will you be part of us, a part of our family?"

"You are very kind," An-da said. "I will be honored."

Men, Toshabe was thinking. *When will this older son of mine wake up and see that this girl, this Sweet Day, is possessed by love for him and that she is the woman for him?*

El-i-chi and Ah-wa-o traveled to the north, avoiding the hillsides and stream valleys where the rank undergrowth was at times impassable, making their way through open areas among the titans of the forest where the dense canopy prevented the growth of brush. El-i-chi killed a young buffalo with his bow, and they feasted on the tongue and the hump. They remained in one spot long enough to sun dry the buffalo meat they could not eat immediately, and they worked together to clean and cure the hide. Winter would come, and a heavy buffalo robe would be welcome. The new beginning was well behind them. No longer were the hillsides turned to flame by banks of azaleas, delphinium, and rhododendron. The berries of spring that had supplemented their diet were gone, but there were berries of the summer, and soon there would be the fruit of autumn. The great bear in the sky would soon drip blood to color the leaves of the forest.

In that sparsely peopled wilderness it was easy to avoid the infrequent Indian villages, and El-i-chi's woodcraft and knowledge continued to prevent contact with hunters and, as they moved on toward the north, an occasional war column.

El-i-chi chose a rise of ground near a quiet beaver lake, hidden by dense thickets and sheltered by a huge sycamore, to build a longhouse. It was small but cozy. Around it they heaped huge piles of deadwood for the winter's fires, and together they stored food, drying flesh and fish in the sun and gathering nuts.

"So must have lived the Woman Who Fell from the Sky before evil was born," El-i-chi said as they lay, happy and warm, while a night wind bearing the scent of winter howled around the longhouse.

"Tell me," Ah-wa-o requested.

"You have heard it a hundred times, and from better storytellers than I."

"Never from one better," she began, nuzzling him coaxingly. "Tell me."

"A long time in the past," he began, "when all people, all Indians, lived in the sky, there ruled a wise chief who had only one daughter. The daughter became ill. A shaman told the chief that she could be cured only if she lay beside the great tree that produced corn, the only food.

'Place the girl beside the great tree,' the chief was told, 'and then you must dig up the tree.'"

"The shaman must have been a white man," Ah-wa-o said.

"Many of the people objected to the chief's destroying their only source of food—"

"I should think so," Ah-wa-o said.

"Are you going to talk or listen?"

"Tell me."

"One young man, angered, gave the sick girl a push with his foot, and she tumbled out of the sky through the hole that the chief had been digging to uproot the tree. The world she fell into was only water, and on that water swam a turtle and birds of many kinds. The birds, seeing the beautiful, ill girl falling, took pity on her and formed a downy blanket to break her fall. But then what was to become of her? The turtle said that he would care for her and let her rest on his back, but he soon tired of this burden, and so mud was brought up from the bottom of the waters and placed on the turtle's broad back."

"It was the toad who did this," Ah-wa-o interjected.

"Who is telling this story?"

"Well, don't leave out important things."

El-i-chi sighed, then continued. "Now there was a place for the girl who fell from the sky and for all the creatures that were to come after. It was the earth. The girl recovered from her malady and had a daughter of her own."

"Huh," Ah-wa-o said.

"I know, I know, no man," El-i-chi said. "It was the West Wind."

"You're nicer than the West Wind, and much more solid," Ah-wa-o said, seizing a strategic portion of El-i-chi's anatomy.

"That's another subject." El-i-chi grinned. "If you are more interested in that . . ."

"Tell me."

"The girl had a daughter," he continued. "The daughter grew and was beautiful, and she, in her turn, was with child. This displeased the mother, who had warned the daughter never to face the east while digging potatoes."

"Yes, I like our way much better," Ah-wa-o said, snuggling up to him.

"The breath of the West Wind had entered her, and she had twins that emerged into the world through the mother's armpit—"

"Only one of them," Ah-wa-o corrected. "And he did it to have the honor of being the firstborn."

"Since you know the story so well . . ." El-i-chi said, his hands busy with soft, rounded portions of girl.

"No, go on," she said.

"The first son was red and was called Othagwenda, or Flint. The second son was light in color, called Djuskaha, or Little Sprout."

"I think," Ah-wa-o said, sighing as El-i-chi's questing hands grew more and more impudent, "that you might shorten the story, after all."

"The Woman Who Fell from the Sky hated Othagwenda and loved Djuskaha, so she drove Othagwenda away to live in a hollow tree."

"Like our first home," Ah-wa-o said.

"I think I *will* shorten the story," El-i-chi said. "The two boys began to make the creatures. Othagwenda made a mosquito so large that it could topple saplings by punching its bill through them, but Djuskaha caused the mosquito to become small—"

"Thank the manitous," Ah-wa-o said.

"Djuskaha made slow, fat animals, easy to take in the hunt. He made the maple tree flow with syrup, and the sycamore trees to bear large, sweet fruit. But Othagwenda was jealous, so he caused the maple to have only sweetened water and the fruit of the sycamore to be small and inedible. So they fought it out"—he was talking fast now, for his mind was on other things—"and Othagwenda was killed, but the maple still does not pour syrup, and the sycamore fruit is still not good to eat, and the fat animals became bears and wolves and—"

"Enough." Ah-wa-o sighed.

El-i-chi pretended to misunderstand and removed his hands from her and pulled away.

"Enough of *words*," Ah-wa-o protested.

"Agreed . . ." El-i-chi said.

El-i-chi had lived many winters in the south. He knew that the northern winter would be longer and more difficult, so he and Ah-wa-o had done all that was necessary to prepare for it, with plenty of time to spare.

But the summer days were still long. Having little to do, El-i-chi turned his thoughts often to serious matters. They could not live in isolation forever. Ah-wa-o would eventually have children, and a midwife would be needed. Moreover, man was not intended to live in total seclusion, far from friends, family, and tribe. More and more El-i-chi considered the future, and at last he decided that with the new beginning he would take Ah-wa-o to the north, to the land of the great, roaring river, to find the main remnants of the Seneca.

Meantime, he set himself to work. He was a shaman, keeper of secrets large and small, secrets as simple as sleight-of-hand magic and as deep as the proper call to the manitous. Unlike Renno, El-i-chi had rarely been able to initiate direct communication with the spirit world, although the manitous had called to him occasionally. He envied his brother the frequent contact he was able to instigate with the manitous and set about trying to emulate Renno's gift.

Ah-wa-o, fascinated, begged El-i-chi to teach her simple magic; but he, with mock sternness, told her that a woman could only be a healer, never a shaman. He would teach her all he knew of the healing arts, but strong magic was man's work. So Ah-wa-o sat quietly and listened as El-i-chi practiced all the charms, prayers, and incantations that had been taught to him by Casno. El-i-chi had agile hands, and his sleight-of-hand delighted Ah-wa-o and occasionally startled her when, for example, he used a combination of dexterity and suggestion to produce a coiled rattlesnake on the floor next to Ah-wa-o's feet.

The mystery of suggestion was, even to El-i-chi,

inexplicable. Ah-wa-o, he found, was very susceptible to it. He could make her see and believe things to a degree that had been beyond his ability in the past. Such power, he felt, was dangerous but could prove useful if it could be used against an enemy. Since the willingness of the subject of the suggestion was generally required, it would be, he felt, a bit chancy to seek the cooperation of a warrior coming at him with a tomahawk in hand.

El-i-chi's continued attempts to contact the manitous worried Ah-wa-o, for he fasted during his efforts. Worse, no amount of fasting and chanting produced the desired results.

"You must stop this," Ah-wa-o pleaded, running her finger down El-i-chi's protruding ribs, "or you will waste away."

She did not intrude too often on his meditations. Instead Ah-wa-o busied herself making new garments from the deerskins supplied by her husband's hunting. With the new beginning, they would have a complete new wardrobe.

For three days and nights El-i-chi fasted, sleeping little, and filled the longhouse with his muttered prayers and supplications to the manitous. On the fourth night Ah-wa-o was on the bed, snuggled under robes, feeling lonely and wishing that he would cease the effort and join her, when a figure began to materialize in the flickering light thrown by the fire. She sat up, chills of fear running up and down her back.

El-i-chi's eyes were gleaming in awe and triumph as a warrior formed across the fire from him and stood silently, looking down. The spirit wore the ancient, traditional clothing of the Mohawk tribe. His visage was noble, his eyes striking.

"My son," the manitou said in a powerful voice, "you have pleased us. You have gained through your devotion the three dual principles preached by the great Dekanawidah: You have health of body and, just as important, of mind; you respect the peace among not only the Six Nations but between individuals; your thought and your conduct have been nothing but proper."

El-i-chi, who still felt guilty for having gone against the ruling of his tribe, bowed his head in silent gratitude.

The spirit continued. "You have a great respect for the rights of the individual, and you have proven yourself worthy, with much strengthening of that spiritual power that is within you, orenda."

"Who are you, manitou?" El-i-chi whispered.

"You know me," the spirit said. "I am the messenger of Dekanawidah, the prophet of the Great Peace. I am the disciple of Dekanawidah. It was I who first lighted the Fire of Great Peace under the Tree of Great Peace."

"Hiawatha," El-i-chi whispered.

"You have said." The manitou's head bowed, and his face became grave. "I heard the words of Dekanawidah, and in my canoe I traveled the great waters, going to the tribes who fought among themselves. Together we overcame the forces of evil and were at peace. Now evil rules once more, and the Great Peace is no more."

"What will come, manitou?" El-i-chi ventured.

"What will come will come because of the few, for all are not possessed by the spirits of evil. You will use the knowledge that has been entrusted to you by the wise men of the Seneca—the storehouse of good that comes as a gift from those who have gone to the Place Across the River before you. Work, my son, this autumn and winter, to develop the skills of the shaman of the Iroquois, drawing from the power of the Master of Life."

The manitou, with a gesture of respect, disappeared. For long moments El-i-chi sat enraptured, awed, wondering just what he was to do.

"I saw," Ah-wa-o whispered. "I heard."

He looked at her, startled.

"Yes," she said, nodding her head. "Your virtue and your power were so strong that I, too, heard and saw."

"There is much to be done, and I am unworthy," El-i-chi told her.

She sprang from the bed and threw herself into his lap. "You are most worthy," she said strongly. "You are El-i-chi."

Naked, warm in his arms, she clung to him and tried

to kiss him, but El-i-chi turned his face away, for there was a feeling of charge in the air, the same feeling he had known before the appearance of the manitou. He chanted a prayer, and old Casno came to them, smiling, looking down, his face showing fondness and pride.

"Man and maid together," he said. "That is the strength, the hope."

Ah-wa-o was trying to hide her nakedness.

The manitou laughed. "Be not modest before me, child."

But Ah-wa-o, still nervous in the presence of a spirit, scampered to the bed and covered herself.

"You have done well," the spirit of Casno said to El-i-chi. "You have pleased us. But I sense in you a conviction of strength that may mislead and endanger you. You have worked well, but you are not ready."

In the far corner of the longhouse a thing of darkness appeared, its face hidden by a wolverine cowl. The hissing voice of Hodano came to El-i-chi, causing the hair to stand up on the back of his neck. He heard a scream of terror from Ah-wa-o, and then the dark one, Hodano, was gone, and Casno looked down at his student with concern.

"Draw heavily upon the force of good," Casno warned. "Be not impulsive. Time, my son, time is needed."

"Hodano is the enemy?"

"He is strong with the forces of evil, and those forces are strengthened by his knowledge of the dark powers of the voodoo masters of Haiti and Jamaica."

"How, then, shall I face him?" El-i-chi asked.

"When the time comes, in the fullness of time, you will find the power that you need. For now, be content with this. I give you this gift, the Sight. You can see with the eyes of a hawk. And, if your spirit is pure, you will see the future in time of need."

The manitou waved one hand. El-i-chi felt nothing.

"Use the gift with great care," the manitou urged.

The spirit and the charged tension in the air vanished, leaving just the sighing wind and the glowing fire. After a few minutes El-i-chi joined Ah-wa-o in bed and held her close, but his thoughts were to the north. He did not know the working of this new gift from the manitous, the Sight, but as he concentrated, he saw dimly, in his mind, the dark form of Hodano amid warriors from several tribes. The vision did not allow him to determine Hodano's exact location, but he knew that the evil shaman was not far away, only a matter of a few weeks' easy travel.

"I know my mission now," he told Ah-wa-o.

"I fear that evil one," she whispered, shuddering.

"He is somewhere to the north," the young shaman continued. "There I will meet him. We will go north, but not to join the Seneca. All that has happened has been the will of the manitous, brought about for this one purpose—to bring me face to face with Hodano. For this we left our families and our people."

"Not I," she whispered, remembering the horribly scarred face of the vision of Hodano.

"Yes," he said, "for you are a kindness from the manitous, to give me courage and love and the strength to do what must be done."

He knew then that he would be ready with the new beginning.

The artist Ezra Ames had painted a portrait of the Mohawk war chief Thayendanegea, called Joseph Brant. The picture showed Brant as stern and full faced, with a high forehead sloping back to an Iroquoian topknot. The sides of his head were shaved, and he wore voluminous robes of fine fabric, a necklace of beads, and a kerchief at his throat. He had been called king of the Mohawk by British newspapers. As the driving force behind the Iroquois who fought on the side of the British during the War for Independence, his depredations on the frontiers of the northern states had earned him the name "monster" from colonists. Of the Indians who had fought for King George, the most savage and the most cruel had been the Iroquois, with their fine military tradition. Joseph Brant was the living symbol of the wartime outrages that had once enabled an Iroquoian war party to come within sight of New York City.

Brant, educated at the Lebanon, Connecticut, Indian

School, had visited England twice, there to be lionized as a war hero by the bishop of London, James Boswell, the prince of Wales, and George III himself. In England he had been awarded the honorary rank of colonel. Newspapers in the United States referred to him as Captain Joseph Brant of the British army. Soldier, diplomat, translator of the Prayer Book and St. Mark's gospel, Brant had received recognition and fame primarily through British sources, so his name was well-known both in England and the United States.

There were those—George Washington among them—who acknowledged Brant's influence, in spite of his exile in Canada following the war, but felt that Renno deserved more fame than the Mohawk. Renno's missions, undertaken on behalf of the United States, went unpublicized, however. If Washington had been forced to choose between Renno or Brant as his friend and ally, the President would have suffered no hesitation in choosing the Seneca. During those terrible days following Harmar's humiliation north of the Ohio, it irked Washington to have to agree to attempts to appease the Indians and to authorize his people to seek out Joseph Brant in an effort to bring the remnants of the League of the Iroquois solidly on the side of the United States.

Indeed, Brant was a much-sought-after man. In those months after Harmar's ill-fated expedition, Brant accepted an invitation to talk with Colonel Bramford Waith, the hawkish British commander in the northwest who was willing to take his nation to war, once again, against the upstart colonists. Brant journeyed to Fort Niagara for the conference with Waith, traveling with a dozen Mohawk warriors who had fled to Canada with him. He was not too optimistic about written promises from Waith to restore the lands of the Iroquois; he had heard British promises before. In London, he had heard expressions of sympathy for the lost hopes of the Indians and promises of British loyalty from lords, princes, and a king; but still he was an exile, and the westward expansion of the United States continued.

Now Brant was dressed in white man's clothing when

he dined with Colonel Waith at Fort Niagara, and he waited until the white man opened the subject of events that were taking place in the northwest.

"Colonel Brant," Waith began, "I think you must agree that now is the time for a new blow. Your brothers Little Turtle, Blue Jacket, Blackhoof, Red Pole, Captain Pipe, Black Wolf, Cat's Eyes, and Tarhe the Crane are in the field against our enemy at this very moment."

"Where then," Brant asked, "are the redcoats?"

"I assure you," Waith said, "that this war has the full approval of the Crown."

"How many Indians must die before the redcoats take to the field?" Brant persisted.

"Perhaps English involvement will not be necessary," Waith said. "The allied tribes are strong with your many warriors and with excellent arms provided by us."

Brant snorted. "If, with the full alliance of the League of Six Nations and many others, you could not beat the Americans, how in the name of God do you expect them to be beaten by a loose confederation of broken and displaced tribes?"

"I don't think you fully understand the situation, Colonel," Waith said, shifting uncomfortably under the steady gaze of the Indian. "The United States was unified under one capable man—an Englishman, mind you—during the war. Now they are disunited, at odds among themselves. They have no army. You saw what happened to the force led by Harmar."

"I saw what happened many times during the war, when I myself won numerous battles. I saw the strength of the Americans grow, and I saw a reluctance from England to commit its full power to the war. This, I think, will happen again. The Indians will win the battles and lose the war, and then you British will pull yourselves snugly back behind the Canadian border and say, 'I am sorry, my friends, that so many of you have died for nothing, but that's politics, you know, and our prime responsibilities are in Canada and at home.'"

Waith outwardly kept his composure, but his face

reddened with anger. "Surely you are not considering fighting on the side of the Americans?"

Brant waited a moment before answering. "At the moment, sir, I am waiting to see what the British government will do."

"There are Britishers in the field with the fighting warriors," Waith reminded Brant.

"No more than thirty Tory Rangers," the Mohawk retorted. "Outcasts, renegades, and diehards who have never forgiven the United States for the loss of property during the war. Show me redcoats, sir, in number, in great files, marching at the side of the Miami, the Shawnee, and the others, and then Joseph Brant will give you his answer regarding the participation of his people and those additional tribes to whom his name means something!"

The Reverend Dougald McKleven had journeyed to the frontier, at Marietta, ostensibly to convert the heathen to the light and to bring the message of God to the settlers who, in McKleven's mind, were often more ungodly than the savages. There was a further purpose to his trip, for even a man of the cloth who had given his life to the Church and in service of others had needs. McKleven was no longer a young man. Soon he would have earned the right to retire to some nice, seaside town in his native Maryland and partake of the rewards for a lifetime of service. The problem was that the rewards cost money, and in those days of debased currency and very limited opportunity, the collection plate held little, whether it was passed in McKleven's own church or under a brush canopy on the frontier.

Thus McKleven had recognized opportunity when it came. He was now a silent minority partner in a land company that had set its sights on the newly opened lands north of the Ohio. Thousands of veterans held chits for land promised by the Continental Congress. Most of them did not wish to risk their scalps in a war zone, and thus, in his travels, McKleven had been slowly and carefully buying up the chits for ten cents on the dollar. Already he had accumulated enough chits to exchange for thousands of acres if ever the savages were conquered. Once peace came and settlers felt safe beyond the Ohio, those thousands of acres bought up by the land company at ten cents an acre could be sold for a dollar an acre, probably more.

So it was out of self-interest as much as for the love of God that McKleven was in Marietta raining fire and brimstone upon the heads of any who visited his brush tabernacle. In the vicinity of Marietta were some few Indian villages, populated mostly by women, old men, and children, for the warriors were with Little Turtle and the other war chiefs. It was to one such village that McKleven traipsed, led by a creaky-jointed old Miami man, to speak the truth to the heathen. His sermon was heard by most of the village. He had a splendid voice, and Indians liked men who could make the leaves shake on the trees with their oratory. The sermon over, McKleven partook of Indian food, found it to be quite disgusting, as usual, and continued his efforts to convert the old man who had guided him to the village.

After a few moments of listening to the way of salvation, the old man found an opening and spoke in a rich, deep voice. "Brother, I know not what to believe. Years ago, a good man came here and convinced me that there was only one way to assure my soul's salvation. My old faith, the faith of my fathers, my ancestors, was of no use. I deemed that this good man, being educated, knew more than an ignorant Indian, and so I joined his church. I was a Methodist. Then the good man went away, and in his place came another who could talk the birds out of the trees, so I became a Presbyterian. Now you come, my brother, and say that I should be Episcopalian."

"We all worship the same God," McKleven said impatiently.

"Once I believed in the Master of Life," the old man explained, "and I worshiped Him in my own way, in the way of my ancestors. I have come to believe, my brother, that you white men who have books and education merely have a different way of speaking to the Master of Life, and I wonder if my poor words, without the eloquence of the educated men who have come to me, were not heard."

"You are confused," McKleven said.

The man held up his hand imperiously, and McKleven stopped speaking.

"You have the books; you have the knowledge; you have the education. I would think that you should know exactly what to do and how to live, but I see no two of you in agreement. Therefore I now pray to the spirits of my ancestors and to the Master of Life."

In disgust, McKleven left the village and went back to Marietta, where he happened to meet a disgruntled veteran with chits for acreage. The going price was ten cents on the dollar, and the man snapped up the opportunity to sell his right to land in the bloody Ohio valley.

In a small clearing, not more than three acres, the rich soil was producing corn as tall as a man's head. The land had been cleared laboriously by a young man of twenty-two years who had moved his young wife and three children aged three, two, and four months, west from New York City. The head of the household had ventured out from the clearing that morning in the hope of bagging a deer to put fresh meat on the table, leaving his family in the cabin with strict orders not to venture outside. Since there was no water in the cabin, and since the sanitary facilities consisted of an open space between the bushes of the enclosing forest, that order was impossible to obey.

The young wife went out holding the three-year-old girl by the hand and carrying the baby in her arms. She was squatting behind bushes when she saw the first of the Shawnee warriors dash across the yard on silent feet and seize the two-year-old boy, who was standing by the cabin door, by his hair. The toddler cried out in terror as he was lifted. A whoop sounded from the woods, and three more warriors ran across the yard. The three-year-old started to whimper, and the woman pinched her hard and hissed at her to be quiet. She managed to rearrange her clothing and to crawl, dragging the girl, to a place of better concealment.

She looked back in time to see a warrior lift her toddler by his heels and, with a great whoop of laughter, swing the boy hard so that when his head smashed against the end of a log in the cabin's outer wall, his fragile skull opened to splatter his brains across the side of the cabin.

The warriors went into the cabin, and soon the family's possessions were being thrown out the door. A strong warrior came out, wearing her bonnet and her only shawl, and whooped and danced to great laughter from the others.

And then the baby whimpered. The woman clamped her hand over his mouth, and he gasped and tried to cry. In desperation she bared her breast and thrust it into his mouth, but perhaps sensing the woman's terror, still he tried to cry. She crushed the baby's face into her full breast, smothering his attempts in softness. Beside her the three-year-old girl was white-faced and shocked into silence.

For at least a half hour the warriors amused themselves with items from the cabin, and carrying what they wanted, one still wearing the woman's shawl, they departed, but not before the cabin was ablaze. The woman let her baby's head free from her full breast. She looked down to see that the little face was purple, the baby dead.

Stumbling wide-eyed around the ruins, she managed to find some dried venison and picked up a few grains of corn from the ground where it had been spilled. She waited in the wreckage throughout the day and then into the night, drawing close to the stinking embers of the burned cabin for warmth.

With the dawn she and her girl set out in the direction of Marietta. She found her husband tied to a small tree not three hundred yards from the house. His genitals had been cut off and thrust into his already mutilated mouth.

Chapter VII

~~~~~~

Renno and Tor-yo-ne ran side by side. Although they were traveling light, each had his burden: Renno carried the short sword, stiletto, tomahawk, shot bag, powder horn, longbow, and quiver all in their places. He ran with his musket in his hand. On his back a small pack held a set of buckskins for the chill, northern nights ahead. Also in the pack were paints, for no true Seneca would ever travel into war without being properly emblazoned, and a small amount of dried corn, a few nutritious nut balls, and some dried venison. The food was for emergency use, for a time when it would be impossible to hunt. Tor-yo-ne was similarly armed, except for the short sword, and his Seneca bow was slimmer and shorter than Renno's English weapon.

It was a matter of some skill to be able to carry such an assortment of weapons and equipment without having them clank or jangle as the men's legs pumped tirelessly across the miles. At first Renno had fallen into that effortless rhythm known as the warrior's pace, and Tor-yo-ne had matched it.

When, in the heat of the day, Renno dropped the pace to a walk, a surge of pride coursed through Tor-yo-ne. He was not even breathing hard, and the mighty Renno had called a rest. In the late afternoon Tor-yo-ne began, gradually, to draw a step, then two, ahead, pushing the pace just a bit harder than Renno's choice.

Renno's warrior's pace had carried him over a lot of ground, and it was somewhat of a jolt to change that well-known rhythm. Still, two were on this journey, and if a slightly faster pace suited his companion . . . He pulled even with Tor-yo-ne. They wasted no energy in talk. The miles passed, and they made camp, hunted with the last light, and ate freshly roasted rabbit. Their conversation consisted of comparing memories of the route they would follow: across the Cumberland River into Shawnee country, and then turning slightly northwest to the lands of the Miami and Illinois, skirting around the main settlements in Kentucky.

Renno felt a healthy fatigue, but it was all right. His muscles flexed well, and his heart, rested after the day's march, beat strongly and very, very slowly. His belly was pleasantly full but not overstuffed, for he had stopped eating before his hunger was fully satisfied. He lay down with his feet pointing toward the flickering fire.

"Sachem," Tor-yo-ne asked, "will you have me stand the first watch?"

They were still in Cherokee lands, far to the east of the range of any hostile tribes. Renno, however, did not mention that obvious fact to Tor-yo-ne. "We will have to stand watch soon enough. Sleep well."

On the next day, Tor-yo-ne again pushed the pace. It satisfied his young pride to think that he was more man than the sachem—stronger, with greater endurance. It pleased him to see that with each increment of speed, Renno at first fell behind and then slowly caught up alongside. By the time the sun was at the zenith, Tor-yo-ne had increased the pace in stages until it was no longer that mile-covering, steady, flowing movement that could carry a body of warriors forty miles in a day and leave the men with enough reserve to fight at the end of the journey. Tor-yo-ne, in his youthful pride, was running a race.

It was not Renno's way to reprimand a warrior. A good leader led by example, and so for the balance of that day he matched Tor-yo-ne's pace and derived enjoyment from it, for there was no feeling to match the one that came when the body began to call upon its reserves. Still, the pace could not be kept up indefinitely; they had barely begun a journey to be measured in hundreds of miles. So it was that Renno, who would have counted running among his greatest joys, decided to make his point subtly but emphatically.

On the third morning he did not wait for Tor-yo-ne to increase the pace but started out with an initial rush that left Tor-yo-ne behind for a few moments. And then, as the sun climbed toward noon, he ran as if he were a messenger carrying vital news, a messenger who had fifty miles to cover in a day. And he did not slow when the sun's heat brought a river of sweat that cascaded down their bodies and drenched the headbands across their foreheads and seeped down into their eyes. He ran into that plateau of pain, then past it steadily, grindingly, punishingly. In the afternoon he could hear Tor-yo-ne's breathing becoming more labored. Slowly Tor-yo-ne began to lag while the sun was still high. But Renno pressed on.

He turned his head once to look back. The young war chief, seeing that gesture, pushed hard, and for some time he maintained the same pace as Renno, before, once again, he fell back.

With the sun low in the west, hidden behind the trees, Renno halted by a small, clear stream and used a considerable amount of willpower to keep from falling onto his stomach to guzzle water. Tor-yo-ne had fallen far behind, and when he finally came into view among the trees, his breathing was ragged. Without looking at Renno, he ran directly to the stream and, laying his musket aside, fell to his belly. He drank greedily and would have continued had the sachem not put his hand on his shoulder.

Tor-yo-ne looked up.

"Easy," Renno advised.

"Yes," Tor-yo-ne said.

Renno still had not had water. "Rest here. I will hunt."

Tor-yo-ne started to protest, then looked away, embarrassed.

Renno killed a small doe within two hundred yards of his chosen campsite and came trotting back under the burden of the carcass. Then and only then did he lie down on the mossy bank and drink sparingly. Tor-yo-ne had recovered well enough to assist in butchering the doe, and Renno took a haunch to roast over the fire. There would be considerable waste, even though the deer was quite small.

"The scavengers will feast," Renno said, "but we will not waste all. We will cook an extra portion so tomorrow we will not have to stop to hunt."

Tor-yo-ne nodded, unable to meet the sachem's eyes.

"And now that we have stretched ourselves to the limit, thus strengthening our bodies for the long journey ahead, the warrior's pace will seem easy tomorrow," Renno remarked benignly.

The young war chief looked up quickly. "Yes," he said, then grinned ruefully.

It was clear to Renno that his companion realized he had been given a lesson but allowed to keep his pride. They ate in silence, then hung chunks of the deer from tree limbs out of the reach of animals.

"I thank the manitous that we are still in safe lands," the white Indian said, "for I will sleep soundly tonight."

"I, too," Tor-yo-ne said in all truth.

Sleep they did—the sleep of total exhaustion, the sleep of restoration that, upon awakening, had erased the efforts of the past day. Renno rekindled the fire and went to the tree where he had hung the chunks of venison in preparation for their morning meal. He halted just short of the tree and examined the ground. Tor-yo-ne, alerted by Renno's sudden tenseness, came to his side. One of the best cuts of deer meat was gone.

"So we had a visitor during the night," Tor-yo-ne said. "A sly one. A bear?"

"I would have heard a bear," Renno said. He pointed. In the soft floor of the forest detritus, was half the imprint of a moccasin.

Now and again even a superbly confident and skilled warrior can be taken aback by events. Renno looked around, his hand on his war ax, and for a few moments he condemned himself for foolishly exerting himself to the point of exhaustion, merely to make a point to Tor-yo-ne, which caused him to sleep through a raid on his camp. Had the visitor been an enemy, both he and Tor-yo-ne might well be scalpless corpses on the forest floor.

He moved off, Tor-yo-ne at his shoulder, searching for further sign. The trail was plain, as if whoever had left it did not care, and the tracks were small. Renno began to feel more relaxed. The tracks were, perhaps, those of a boy who, unable to find his own game through lack of experience, had filled his belly with the meat of another's hunt.

The trail led first away from the stream and then back toward it, upstream from Renno's camp. The sachem moved soundlessly through a thicket, letting the brush close quietly behind him, and halted again as the aroma of cooking meat wafted to his nostrils. He motioned Tor-yo-ne to approach the source of the aroma from above, while he himself pushed on through the thicket. The smell was stronger now, and it was mixed with wood smoke. He heard a voice, humming an old Seneca chant in praise of the manitous.

Tomahawk in hand, he parted leafy branches and peered into a little mossy clearing beside the creek to see a girl in the dress of the Seneca kneeling beside a fire, a haunch of venison on a spit. A girl! So that explained why this one had not done her own hunting but had resorted to stealing another's catch. He stepped into the clearing, intent on reprimanding her and discovering why a girl was alone in the forest, but stopped in his tracks when she said, "You're just in time. It's almost ready."

"An-da?" He gasped, recognizing the pleasantly musical tones.

An-da looked back over her shoulder. "And you can tell Tor-yo-ne to come out now. He has been making as much noise as a herd of buffalo crashing through the brush."

With his jaw hanging slack, Tor-yo-ne pushed through branches into the clearing to look at his sister.

"Well, sit, both of you," she invited. "I imagine, after that exhibition of arrogant manhood yesterday, that you're both very hungry."

The shaman Hodano maintained two shelters. One, in a Miami village on the banks of the Ohio, was his public house, where he met with and advised chiefs and warriors engaged in the sacred war to halt white advancement at the river. The other, hidden deep in the forest, the paths to it protected by charms and by overt warnings in the form of skulls, was his private place, where he communicated with the forces of evil. It was here that he added to his power by swallowing the spirit of some dying captive that he took from the warriors as his due. For two days he had kept a white woman, taken in a raid, alive. When she had passed away late in the day and he had eaten her spirit in that last eerie, obscene ceremony, he had carried her mutilated body far from the lodge and had left it for the scavengers. Then he had slept well until, in the misty predawn hours, he had been awakened by a premonition that had been coming to him with regularity.

He rose, lifted his arms to his spirits, and called upon the powers of darkness. At first a vague uneasiness came over him. Something was wrong, but he could not understand what it was. Hodano added wood to the banked embers of his fire, and as the blaze soared he cast the white woman's scalp—her hair had been pale blond—into the blaze. As the stench rose toward the smoke hole in the roof, he sent an enchantment with it by dancing around the fire, hissing words.

And then he froze in midstride for he finally saw it—the reason for his unrest, the reason for that premonition of danger.

"You!" he grated as he clearly saw a vision, the face of a man who had beaten him not once but twice. He saw Renno and a strong, young Seneca warrior running... running... running inexorably toward him. He tried to focus on their whereabouts, but he could only determine that his enemy was nowhere nearby. He chanted the charms he had learned from the voodoo master of Jamaica and soared, in spirit only, seeking but not finding. As he rejoined his body after a long search, he concluded that Renno was still too far away.

Tor-yo-ne, a wide grin on his face, now sat across the fire from An-da. Renno sat between them, trying to understand the girl's presence. He had seen An-da bid her brother good-bye back in the village four mornings past. She had been standing with Toshabe and Ha-ace, waving, when Renno took one last look over his shoulder just before the two warriors had disappeared into the encircling forest. For three days he and Tor-yo-ne had set a fast pace and, on the third day, a killing pace.

"You must be sleepy, my sister," Tor-yo-ne teased, finishing the last of the venison, "staying awake half the night to steal our meat."

"Nonsense," An-da retorted. "You were sleeping like two hibernating bears before it was dark enough for the crickets to chirp."

"You risked death by coming into our camp," Renno said, mildly angry, for it was not wise for a maiden to be alone. She would have to return to the village, and escorting her home would cost them time. "Had you stepped on one small twig, I might have killed you in the darkness before I realized who you were."

An-da looked up at him, eyes huge, limpid as the eyes of a young doe. "But I didn't. And you didn't." She looked at Tor-yo-ne pleadingly, then glanced shyly at Renno. "I could not stay alone in the village."

"You will, of course, go back," Renno said.

"Must I? Please let me stay," she begged. "I want to be with my brother, for he is my only blood."

"It is not possible," Renno said.

"Yes," Tor-yo-ne said gently, "you must go back, even though you have matched more than a warrior's pace for three days, traveling alone, following our trail, and managing to steal from us to cook our breakfast." Unseen by Renno, he gave her a sly wink, then glanced at Renno's stern face.

"I, too, recognize stamina and bravery when I see it," Renno said. "You have performed well, An-da."

"There was a joy in it, wasn't there?" she asked, gazing at him openly. "It was good to use my whole body, to push myself yesterday. There were times when I wanted to stop, to give up, because you were traveling so fast, but then my body told me, 'No, you will not quit,' and—" She paused. "There are times when I go into the forest alone and try to catch the wind or to outrun a fleeing deer, and it is then when I can feel the life in me keenest."

Renno looked at the girl with appreciation. She had expressed his own feelings about running, using words that he himself could have never found.

"She cooks well," Tor-yo-ne observed. "And I hesitate to send her back unescorted. During these past three days she has been, I imagine, near enough to call to us for help had she encountered danger."

"We will have to escort her back," Renno said.

Tor-yo-ne groaned.

"A warrior's pace four days back, then four more days to return us to this spot," he said. "I have traveled with my sister, Sachem. She has been at my side on many long hunts, and never did I have to slow my pace to wait for her."

It was not unheard of, Renno knew. Three women had accompanied the expedition to the far west: Beth, Ena, and Holani. One had not returned. Still . . . he mused.

With the journey under way it was against his nature to waste eight days in taking An-da back to the village.

"You would have to tie me up," An-da warned, "or I would follow you again. And when they loosed me, as they eventually would have to, I would still follow."

A sound like soft thunder approached slowly. A vast flock of passenger pigeons came over them, darkening the sky visible over the creek.

"Tonight we eat well," An-da said, pointing up. "There is a way of roasting those birds in hot embers, with their breast cavities stuffed with wild onions—"

"It is for you to say, Sachem," Tor-yo-ne said, "but she would be no handicap. Instead, she would be an asset."

Renno noted that An-da had brought a bow and a quiver of arrows. They lay near the fire atop her blanket. "Can you use that?" he asked, pointing.

"My brother taught me," An-da answered.

Renno pondered.

An-da cast a blazing smile of hope at her brother. Men, she thought, were easily convinced in some matters, if not in others. But now she would have months with Renno—alone except for her brother—in which to demonstrate that she was a desirable woman to have around for reasons other than her cooking ability. She said a silent prayer of thanks to the manitous as she cleared the camp, scattering the fire and positioning her pack and the bow and quiver.

As the day's journey began, she ran behind Renno and Tor-yo-ne when the way through the forest was congested and narrow, and she matched them stride for stride in an open meadow, her long legs lifting strongly and gracefully. True to her promise she baked pigeons encased in clay in glowing embers, and the wild onions gave them so delicious a flavor that Renno and Tor-yo-ne each ate one bird too many, groaned in satisfaction, and slept soundly.

For some time there was a sameness to the days, although their way led them through new beauty, across unfamiliar streams, and up and down unfamiliar slopes.

The warrior's pace carried them almost fifty miles on most days. Traveling through Kentucky required extra precautions, but then they swam across the Ohio River, pushing their gear ahead of them on small rafts made of driftwood, and were beyond the area of white settlement, moving through a no-man's-land that was also devoid of Indian villages. Most of the villages just north of the Ohio had been attacked and burned by Kentucky militiamen.

Soon, however, Renno began to see signs of travel— the evidence of warriors and war parties. Now the three-some moved in silence, always alert. An-da did not slow them. She exhibited a knowledge of woodcraft that gained Renno's respect, and he treated her as if she were a young warrior. He had seen her use her bow to good effect, for occasionally she assumed responsibility for the hunting. As small as she was, as shapely and frail looking as she was, he saw her hoist a half-grown buck to her shoulders, carry it back to camp, and begin the butchering.

Late one afternoon, after Renno had chosen a camp-site, An-da assumed her place among the list of women who had earned the sachem's full respect. It was to be another night of eating An-da's delicious pigeons, in a lovely clearing only a few feet from a clear spring with a rich, mineralized taste, overhung by a huge sycamore that would give shelter in case the lowering clouds made rain during the night. The girl had left the camp, gathering a handful of sticks for hurling, making her way toward the noise of a flock not too far away. Meanwhile, Tor-yo-ne and Renno had gathered an ample amount of dry wood, and Renno was building the fire. Tor-yo-ne went to search the stream for suitable clay in which to encase the roasting birds.

These tasks completed, the two warriors were lounging on the ground when a small sound caused Renno to jerk into readiness. But it was An-da, slipping into the clearing.

"Miami," she whispered, gesturing behind her, her eyes wide, a look of agitation on her face. "They follow our trail."

"How many?" Renno asked.

"There were six," she said. "Five in the main body, one scout."

Renno failed to notice the significance of the word *were*. His weapons leaped to his hands, short sword in the left, the tomahawk made for him by Se-quo-i in his right. Tor-yo-ne's face was grim as he armed himself.

"How far?" Renno whispered to An-da, but before she could answer, war cries rang out, and garishly painted faces seemed to spring from the enclosing greenery. The late-afternoon light flashed on raised enemy blades.

An-da leaped back toward the creek as she reached for an arrow from her quiver. Renno, snarling like a bear, crouched to meet the assault of two whooping Miami warriors. Tor-yo-ne came to stand at his back, and he faced three men who were closing rapidly. Out of the corner of his eye Renno saw An-da string an arrow, just as he parried a blow from a war ax with the sword and sent his own tomahawk flashing. He prayed that the girl, in her excitement, would not try to use the bow and accidentally hit him or Tor-yo-ne by mistake.

The Miami rapidly closed in, whooping and yelling in a high falsetto. Renno heard the clash of metal at his back and for a fleeting moment wished that El-i-chi were here, but then he heard the solid thud of tomahawk on skull and a triumphant whoop from Tor-yo-ne. Satisfied that his back was protected, Renno settled into his work. A surge of fierce joy coursed through him when he saw that the adversaries facing him were seasoned warriors, both skilled with the tools of their trade. He allowed one Miami in close, tomahawk at the ready.

The white Indian thrust forward with the short sword, and the warrior danced to the side, directly into the horizontal swing of the tomahawk. The blade sliced through flesh and tendon, leaving the warrior's head supported only by the thin spinal column as he fell.

Renno backed up before a furious charge from the survivor and stumbled over the body of Tor-yo-ne's first victim. The Miami, recognizing his opportunity, leaped to the kill; but Renno let the momentum of his fall carry him to the ground, where he rolled and came to his feet with the short sword thrusting upward, burying itself in the Miami's belly. He caught the downward hack of the dying man's tomahawk with his own blade. As he straightened, Renno saw that Tor-yo-ne had sent a second enemy reeling, blood pouring from his chest.

One-on-one, Tor-yo-ne loosed a Seneca cry of victory as he moved forward, and for a moment there was a tableau of death as the enemies circled.

The man with the huge slash in his chest, moaning his death song, attempted to attack Tor-yo-ne from the rear. Since Tor-yo-ne faced only two men, Renno had taken the opportunity to assess his companion's battle skills. Now the sachem raised his tomahawk to throwing position, but before he could fling the weapon, an arrow pierced the hollow of that Miami's throat and the man gurgled his way to death, first on his knees, then on his face, breaking the arrow with his fall. Renno glanced at An-da to see fierce pride lighting her face.

Tor-yo-ne whooped and danced the ritual of death for the last Miami, toying with the warrior, slashing one shoulder and then the other before he crushed the Miami's skull.

A stunned silence prevailed in the glade, but Renno was still on the alert. Even the birds had ceased their evening chirping, perhaps shocked by the swift and deadly encounter.

"You said six," the white Indian told An-da as he looked around.

"I said," she replied as she plunged into the forest, drawing her knife.

Renno glanced at Tor-yo-ne, who stood, breathing hard, over the fallen five, scalping knife in hand. Then the white Indian followed the girl, wondering what she was doing.

He found her bent over a body, and as he came up behind her, her knife deftly lifted a Miami scalp. One of her arrows was lodged in the man's throat in the exact spot she had put the other, back in the glade. Moreover, the Miami's body had been dragged off the game trail and hidden in the bushes. An-da straightened, dangling the bloody scalp from her hand.

"I told you there *were* six," she explained. "This was the scout."

Renno moved forward for a better look. The arrow had been driven all the way through the man's throat to sever the spinal cord at the rear. "Well," he said, straightening, looking at An-da with a warmth and pride he had not felt previously. "My sister, Ena, was also a warrior maiden."

An-da blushed and lowered her head at this high praise. "I have never killed a man before." Suddenly she was shaking violently.

Renno went to An-da quickly, put his arm around the girl's shoulders, and led her back to the clearing and her brother.

"We can move camp easier than we can move these," Tor-yo-ne said calmly. He had not scalped, nor had Renno; as he looked at the scalp in his sister's hand, his eyes went wide.

"There were six," Renno explained.

Tor-yo-ne lifted his tomahawk and bowed a warrior's salute to An-da. His grin was proud and wide. "So my little sister has fangs, like the rattler."

Renno took a good, solid, steel-bladed tomahawk from one of the dead Miami warriors. Then the threesome moved their camp a mile away, taking great care to hide any trace of passage in case the war party had more members in the vicinity. For safety, they had a fireless night, nibbling on jerky and parched corn.

An-da's shivering had stopped almost as suddenly as it had begun, and now she sat quietly until, with a sigh, she arranged her blanket and lay down, closing her eyes.

"You had said that she would be an asset," Renno told Tor-yo-ne. "Now I travel with two strong Seneca warriors."

An-da heard and smiled.

The next morning Renno affixed the Miami's toma-hawk to An-da's sash. "The bow is a good weapon," he said, "but it is not always enough."

"I know not the use of this weapon," An-da said. "And I have not the strength in my arm that a man has."

"When the blade is keen, as this one is," Renno explained, "finesse is often the equal of strength. Tonight, before we sleep, I will show you."

There was no running that day. Deep in enemy lands, they moved with silent care and crossed the trail of a large war party heading toward the Ohio. During the day's march Renno found himself looking, quite often, at An-da. She was young, a girl-woman whose summers were counted only in the teens, but never had he seen or known a more proper Seneca maiden. Beautiful she was, an extreme pleasure for the eyes. And he now felt an intense pride for her, for she had proven herself—she could match the fastest pace set by a warrior, and she could take a scalp. Truly, this Sweet Day was an extraordinary creature.

Love or the mere thought of love was not in Renno. As always in the wilderness, he had thought occasionally of Beth, for their love had flowered during their long and dangerous trek southward from Québec. And often something would remind him of Emily, who, as his first love and the mother of his children, had her special place in his heart. To him Emily seemed more alive than Beth, for Emily's spirit had visited him, assuring him that when it was his time to come to the Place Across the River, she would be waiting.

It was natural for Renno to compare An-da with the two women of his life. An-da was smaller than the graceful Emily but, of course, of darker coloring. She was not as flamboyantly beautiful as Beth of the flame-colored hair, but she had dignity and grace.

That evening, with Tor-yo-ne hunting their dinner and with the fire made, Renno began An-da's first lesson in the use of the tomahawk. He stood at her side and, with a flick of his wrist, sent his war ax to bury its blade in the trunk of a sycamore. An-da's first attempt sent her tomahawk spinning past the tree, a wide miss.

"Don't throw like a girl," Renno chided, having retrieved the tomahawks.

"I am a girl. . . ." she said, giggling.

"I have noticed that," Renno said with a wry smile. "But you must put your arm and shoulder into it, thus." He put one hand on her shoulder, the other on her hand holding the tomahawk, and positioned the weapon.

She tried again. The tomahawk bounced off the tree. "No," he said in a kindly tone. "You looked as if you were waving good-bye to a friend." He put his arm around her lithe, slender waist, palm on her flat stomach, brushing against her from behind. He lifted her arm and positioned the tomahawk behind her head. "Now make a whipping motion with your arm, bringing it straight down and forward."

She followed his instructions, and the blade of the tomahawk almost stuck in the tree that time.

"Good, good," he approved, "but you tried to do too much with your upper body. It's all in the arm. Don't twist your shoulder so much." He put his hands on her shoulders and showed her how she had twisted her torso in the act of throwing. When his bare arm pressed against her firm young breasts, he repositioned himself immediately.

An-da was still practicing when Tor-yo-ne returned with a brace of hares, and then she set about her cooking.

The nightly lessons in the use of the tomahawk continued. Often, when they camped near a suitable stream, the instruction took place after An-da had gone off alone to bathe. Her clothing would be wet, for she rinsed them whenever possible to remove the day's dust and perspiration. She chafed when they made camp in a place where it was not possible for her to cleanse herself. After a bath in a stream her damp hair had a fresh, clean smell, and her wet clothing clung to her narrow waist and outlined her breasts. She drew Renno's eyes more and more often.

The threesome continued to move through the lands of the hostile tribes. One day Renno had An-da and Tor-yo-ne guard his rear while he crept forward to spy on a large encampment of warriors and a few followers. He counted the dress and paint of six Indian nations and no fewer than a hundred and fifty warriors. And that was only the first of several war parties, all making their way toward the Ohio, that he reconnoitered as they moved slowly northward. Under such circumstances, being in very dangerous lands where carelessness might pit three against a hundred or more, it was natural for Renno to be particularly alert.

As the days passed and he journeyed farther to the north, however, the tenseness that surrounded him was noted by both An-da and Tor-yo-ne. It was a restlessness unlike his normally deliberate, calm behavior. He did not speak of it, for there was, he believed, no logical explanation for the dread that unexpectedly came over him.

As Renno drew closer to Hodano's whereabouts, the evil man, while soaring, had seen the sachem, who was still far to the south. Although many miles separated them, Hodano, in spirit, hovered over his enemy quite often. He noted the lithe girl-woman, but it was the strength of her life force, not her beauty, that attracted Hodano. She would be an excellent weapon against Renno and a tasty morsel before the main meal—the sachem himself.

The evil Hodano did not know that his own restlessness and perceptions of danger had been triggered by the presence of the shaman El-i-chi in the northern forests. Emanations of El-i-chi's growing power had been responsible for alerting Hodano's evil spirits, but Hodano had passed over Renno's brother.

While in his spirit form, Hodano sent evil cascading down at Renno, only to find that it was repelled by the very purity of the Seneca sachem. And despite repeated efforts, the girl proved to be shielded from Hodano's evil influence because she thought only of her love for the white Indian.

In the mind of Renno's companion, Tor-yo-ne, however, Hodano found an aperture of receptiveness; although there was honor in Tor-yo-ne, there was also lingering envy for the sachem. Through that small hole in Tor-yo-ne's armor of honor, Hodano inserted kernels of thought. Although he could not directly affect Renno, it pleased Hodano to see that his presence through the young war chief made Renno increasingly restless and apprehensive.

In the night the voices that came to Tor-yo-ne identified themselves as his ancestors and harangued him with tales of white greed and cruelty. The voices keened for the numerous eastern tribes that had been exterminated by the whites or forced away from their homelands forever. They spoke of the sacred pledges made by the tribes making a stand at the Ohio and praised their wisdom and bravery while chiding Tor-yo-ne for having sided with the whites, who bred like maggots and cared nothing for the rights of the red man.

So, as the little band moved ever northward toward that point where they would turn to the east and enter the United States at Pittsburgh, Hodano, through the night voices, told Tor-yo-ne that the way of all Seneca lay with their brothers along the Ohio, that leaders such as Little Turtle were true Indians, unlike the sachem of the Seneca, who was the white man's lapdog.

Tor-yo-ne had never traveled so far west. He had seen magnificent lands in his traditional northern hunting grounds and on his trip to join the southern Seneca, but he had never seen more beautiful country than that of the Ohio Valley.

"This land would provide any tribe with a sweet home and good hunting grounds," he remarked one evening.

"It is a good land," Renno agreed.

"If the whites are victorious," Tor-yo-ne said, "they will cut down every last tree to clear acres for their fields. The land will be denuded, then gutted with the iron plow."

"There is much land," Renno said. "Perhaps enough for all."

"And the animals that make their homes here will be slaughtered," Tor-yo-ne continued, not aware that he was voicing Hodano's thoughts. "The animals that are food for the Indian will be no more, and those that are not killed by the flood of white settlers will be forced to the west, to new ranges. There will be nothing for the Indian but a field of corn . . . if the whites leave him that."

Renno knew that what Tor-yo-ne said was true. He

had long been convinced that the age-old luxury of having immeasurably vast hunting grounds could not last, for the Indian would be forced to share the land with the Europeans and their children and their children's children into the end of time. "You speak the truth," he said. "But the winds of change will not cease to blow."

"Perhaps we fight on the wrong side," Tor-yo-ne suggested. "Perhaps the Miami and the Shawnee and the others are right, and we, the Seneca, should be at their side."

"The manitous chose my course long ago," Renno said, "even before I was born."

"Sachem," Tor-yo-ne said, "we cannot be far from the camp of Little Turtle. What harm to visit there, to speak with him?"

"What good?" Renno responded. "I have counseled with Little Turtle and found him to be an honorable man, firm in his convictions. He would not be moved by my arguments now any more than he was when I was in these lands once before. Nor would I be swayed by his."

It was time to turn toward the east. It was true— Renno had made firm mental notes of numbers, tribes, and weapons—that the entire northwest was up in arms and that serious raids were a distinct possibility. It was time to take his information to George Washington, along with the warning that James Wilkinson of Kentucky was a traitor, in the pay of the Spanish.

Chapter VIII

~~~~~~

The mighty Ohio River outlined the eastern frontier of the lands for which the consolidated northern tribes were fighting. It flowed southwestward, then westward and northwestward, and then again west from Pennsylvania's westernmost settlement at Pittsburgh. The territory had been penetrated by individual settlers in an arc extending outward from Pittsburgh down to the newly established village of Cincinnati, on the Kentucky border near the westernmost reach of the territory. Lesser rivers flowed southward into the Ohio, including the Muskingum, the Scioto, and the Great Miami. In the northwestern corner the Maumee flowed southward from upper Canada. Marietta lay at the junction of the Muskingum with the

Ohio. Diagonally opposite, in the north, the British still maintained an establishment at Fort Miami, on the Maumee, an installation that could, at any given time, be reinforced rapidly from Detroit.

General Josiah Harmar's ill-fated army had marched northeastward from Fort Washington, near the site of Cincinnati. The army, made up mostly of militiamen, had been low on supplies when they started the march. Unknown to Harmar and to the American government in Philadelphia, most of Kentucky's surplus provisions, which could have helped the army, were being sent down the Mississippi by James Wilkinson to Spanish markets. This lack of provisions, plus the bitter rivalry between militia units and the few regular units in Harmar's army and Harmar's underestimation of the Indians' strength and strategic ability, had resulted in disaster on the upper Maumee.

The Ohio River served as the main line of communication between the small garrison at Fort Harmar, near Marietta in the east and Fort Washington in the west. Only a couple of scouts, Roy Johnson one of them, penetrated the width of country between the two forts. Here, in the depths of the forests, the Indians ruled; and it was into this country that Renno's threesome ventured, trekking all the way north to the juncture of the Licking and the Muskingum before turning back to the southeast toward Marietta on the Ohio.

Wearing the war paint of a Seneca, Renno spoke directly with roving bands of warriors, always keeping An-da hidden lest the enemy wonder why a man on the warpath was bringing a woman with him. Everywhere he heard the same words spoken—words of determination with a hint of desperation: The line would be held at the Ohio; the greedy whites who were encroaching into this final stronghold of Indian independence would be killed or forced back across the river.

Near the great river, Renno, Tor-yo-ne, and An-da encountered several abandoned homesteads where the settlers had either been killed by war parties or were too fearful to risk staying. Most likely they had gone back to the east, away from flames and blood and swinging tomahawks. When the main Indian offensive was launched, as many as three thousand warriors would take the field.

"I have learned all that I am going to learn," Renno told Tor-yo-ne and An-da one night as they sat in a dry and fireless camp. The area of their encampment was often crisscrossed by roving hunting and war parties. "Tomorrow we will march south toward Marietta. Perhaps we can find river transport to Pittsburgh."

"Unless the whites at Marietta shoot us on sight," Tor-yo-ne grumbled.

"I have these," Renno said, patting a pouch in which he carried the two letters from George Washington.

"I have no wish to travel among the whites," Tor-yo-ne grated. "An-da and I will go to the village we saw, two days north, where there are many Iroquois, and we will await you. Perhaps we can gain more information."

Renno waited, thinking that Tor-yo-ne would say more.

Instead it was An-da who broke the silence. "I have no wish to winter with strangers. Come with us, Tor-yo-ne. You can learn much with Renno as our guide in the lands of the whites."

"I know all of white manners that I care to know," Tor-yo-ne said with disdain. "You are in my care, Sister. You will come with me."

"No, I will not," An-da said. "You have changed, Brother. Your temper has sharpened, and...I do not think you are speaking true to your sachem."

Tor-yo-ne's eyes narrowed. "You will not question my decision," he said nastily.

"Each must answer the call of his own spirits," Renno said.

Tor-yo-ne snarled, and his hand was on his tomahawk.

An-da leaped to her feet, drawing her own weapon. "Are you mad, Brother? Do you dare raise your blade against our sachem? If so, you will fight two."

Renno was puzzled by this sudden turn of events. He had, of course, noted Tor-yo-ne's growing sympathy for the cause of the northwestern Indians, but he had not doubted the young man's loyalty. Tor-yo-ne had sworn an oath that his fighting arm and his heart would be his sachem's forever.

"There will be no more talk of fighting among brothers," Renno said evenly. "I sense a desire in you to join in this war."

"No, no," Tor-yo-ne lied.

"I pray, my brother," Renno said, "that your stay among the enemies of the United States will open your eyes. We have seen numerous tribes with many warriors gathering, and it is understandable that you would be impressed by their numbers and their determination. Let me say this: It will be a hard war, and many white soldiers will die. But many more Indians will die, and in the end the tribes will face total humiliation and lose any chance they now have of keeping great portions of this rich land by treaty."

"I have not said that I will join their war," Tor-yo-ne insisted. "I merely do not want to travel in white man's country, to be looked down upon and insulted."

"If you will have me, Sachem," An-da said, "I will be at your side."

"Go then," Tor-yo-ne said heatedly. "Our blood obviously means nothing to you."

"Our blood means much to me," An-da responded. "You are my only blood, my only brother, and it grieves me to be parted from you." She hung her head. "Yet, as Renno says, each must follow the call of his own spirits, and I must go with Renno."

The parting next morning was a silent one. An-da and Renno turned their faces toward the Ohio and Marietta. Without a backward look, Tor-yo-ne lost himself in the forest, his route leading toward the west.

Alone in the wilderness, Tor-yo-ne felt closer to his ancestors, for they came to him nightly, forcefully whispering in his ear. Their spirits appeared to him by day in the form of wolves, dark and sinister, appearing and disappearing, so he knew that he was being guided by spirits. His path took him not toward the village of many Iroquois but far west, deeper into the woods, until he penetrated a wilderness so rank, so overgrown with grapevines and other creepers that the forest floor was devoid of vegetation and he walked over the soft accumulation of centuries of fallen leaves.

In that dark, gloomy place he felt apprehension, but the voices pushed him onward until he stood in a dark, dank glade in front of a Seneca longhouse and knew that he had arrived at the destination pointed out by the spirits. He was not surprised when a tall, sinister form, face hidden by a cowl of wolverine fur, emerged from the longhouse.

"Come," the figure hissed, motioning Tor-yo-ne into the longhouse.

Inside, in the flickering light of a fire that burned even though the day was warm, Tor-yo-ne saw the visage of the shaman Hodano for the first time. The young war chief drew back, shocked by the skeletal face, the scars, and the dead, white eye. Tor-yo-ne's heart lurched when Hodano spoke, and the slit tongue darted in and out of the twisted mouth.

"Drink," Hodano invited, handing over a tin cup that held a bitter liquid. It burned Tor-yo-ne's mouth, but he drained the cup.

"You have decided wisely," Hodano hissed. "This potion will give you strength and will make you mightier than our enemies."

Tor-yo-ne felt a listlessness come over him. He sank weakly down to sit on the edge of a pallet. The shaman towered over him, his one good eye gleaming redly as it reflected the light of the fire. "Now you will learn," Hodano hissed. "Now you will hear your orders, and they will not have to be repeated, for they will be a part of you. You are to be my good right hand, Seneca. You will hear my voice at a distance, and you will do exactly as I tell you. Soon, soon, your blade will drink the blood of the one called Renno."

For a moment Tor-yo-ne wanted to protest. Killing Renno had never been his wish. But there was a peace in him, a feeling that at last he had come home. "I hear, Shaman," he whispered.

Hodano put out a hand, his fingers clawlike, and pushed lightly on Tor-yo-ne's shoulder. Tor-yo-ne fell back on the pallet, his eyes closed in a drugged sleep. A shrill laugh echoed in the longhouse and went out through the smoke hole in the roof to startle a solitary bird that was winging through that dark, forbidding part of the forest.

The white Indian and the girl ran together, weaving their path through forest monarchs that had been large even before the days of Ghonka, sachem of the Seneca, adopter of the great Renno. They ran lightly and joyously, arms scarcely moving. Renno could not help but admire her. His face turned often to her to see her head high, lips drawn back in a smile.

"You run well, little one," he told her at the end of a day.

"With you," she said, "I could run into the sunset forever." She blushed mightily, but Renno smiled.

On the morning before approaching the settlement at Marietta the white Indian painted his face in the patterns of an emissary and colors of peace, hopeful that the frontiersmen would be familiar with Indian lore and allow him to travel unchallenged. He nonetheless approached the town with great caution, and when he first saw a white man, he raised his hand in the sign of peace. An-da and Renno were watched warily as they were led to the town's leaders.

"I am Renno, sachem of the Seneca. I have been scouting for George Washington."

A few men laughed. Renno produced the letter that asked him to go into the Ohio territories.

"I'll be hornswoggled," the town's mayor said. "He's not lying." He handed the missive back to Renno. "You'll want to talk to the soldier boys over at the fort."

"I will want, if possible, water transportation to Pittsburgh," Renno requested.

"Might be a flatboat goin' upriver soon," a grizzled frontiersman said. "Reckon you'd make better time afoot, though. Injuns been jumpin' most of the riverboats lately."

"We'll give you a ride across the river," the mayor offered. "So's you can talk to the soldiers."

"Thank you," Renno said.

"Might want to talk to that feller that's scouting for General St. Clair, too," the old frontiersman said. "Name of Johnson."

Renno jerked his face around to look at the old man. "Would his first name be Roy?"

"The same," the old man confirmed. "Nice feller. Bit crazy, though, takin' off into them woods all by his lonesome."

Renno concealed his excitement as men rowed An-da and him across the river to the fort that had been built on the other side of the Muskingum. His eyes searched among the soldiers who watched the boat's approach. If possible, he would speak with Roy first and get an idea of what sort of men were at Fort Harmar before divulging any of his information to them. His intelligence was primarily for Washington, but if responsible officers were stationed at Fort Harmar, he would apprise them of what he had seen and heard.

A sloppily dressed sergeant met the boat at the landing and looked at Renno and An-da with evident disapproval. "'Nother one of them, huh?" he asked the boatman.

"Better be nice to this one, Sarge," the boatman advised. "He totes a letter from old George Washington hisself."

"Is Roy Johnson in the fort?" Renno asked.

"What do you got to do with Roy Johnson?" the sergeant demanded.

Renno's voice was steely. "Sergeant, if there are any questions for me, I will give my answers to your commanding officer. Now I have asked you a question."

The sergeant's face darkened, but after a moment he said, "Reckon you'll find Johnson in the officers' mess with General St. Clair."

"Would you be so kind, Sergeant, as to detail a man to take us there?" Renno requested.

"Take you myself," the sergeant grumbled. "I got to see what makes you so highfalutin', Injun."

As it happened, it was not necessary to go all the way to the officers' mess, for Renno saw the tall, lanky Roy Johnson walking across the compound, headed for the gate, even as they followed the sergeant into the fort. Renno, hiding a smile, did not call out. Roy's attentions were elsewhere, and it was not until he was even with Renno and An-da that he glanced at them and froze in his tracks.

"Roy," Renno said, "I thank thee that thou are well."

"Renno?" Roy's voice came out in a squeak and then in a roar, "By God, Renno!"

The sergeant looked on in distaste as white man and Indian embraced and then clung to each other in the warrior's greeting, hands clasping arms. "What in the world?" Roy asked, looking now at the beautiful maiden. "Is this little An-da?"

"I thank thee that thou are well," she said in Seneca.

"It is An-da! And prettier than ever," Roy exclaimed. Then his face softened, and he looked at Renno, obviously making the assumption that since they were together, so far from home . . . "Renno, my congratulations. You couldn't have picked a better wife."

Renno, starting to speak, glanced at An-da, who was blushing furiously.

"No," she said. "It is not that way."

Roy shook his head. "Excuse me," he said quickly. "Tell me, how are my grandchildren?"

"They were both well when we left," Renno answered.

"Good, good." Roy's eyes narrowed. "Are you here for the reason why I think you're here?"

"I would imagine," Renno said. "There is a general in the fort?"

"St. Clair, the governor himself," Roy said. "I'll take you to him."

"Not just yet." Renno turned to the other man and said, "Thank you, Sergeant. We won't need you any further."

The sergeant glowered. Roy nodded and motioned

the sergeant to go, then he put a hand on Renno's shoulder. "You been out among 'em?"

"We have," the white Indian confirmed.

"Old St. Clair can be hardheaded," Roy said, "but I think he'll want to hear what you have to say."

"First, a private talk," Renno requested.

"I have a little room over there," Roy said, pointing. He led the way, chattering questions about Little Hawk and Renna, asking about El-i-chi, and shaking his head sadly when Renno told him of his brother's disappearance. Roy had a pot going on a wood-burning stove, and the coffee was strong and bitter. An-da sat quietly as the two men brought each other up-to-date on personal matters and then turned their talk to the war. Roy imparted all he had learned about the dignified St. Clair during reports to him both at Fort Harmar and at Fort Washington over on the Kentucky border.

"Little Turtle's no fool," Roy said. "He sucked Harmar into a trap easily. Now that St. Clair's got his wind up and will be going in, Little Turtle will try to do the same to St. Clair's army. I've been out there, Renno. 'They's a heap of Injuns in them woods,' as a frontiersman would say, 'and they's mean mad.'"

"The belief among them is that the manitous are on their side this time," Renno said. "They take their spiritual guidance from Hodano."

"I heard as much myself," Roy said. "Friend of yours, right?" He grinned.

Renno grinned in return. "They can put well over a thousand warriors into the field at any given time—three thousand if given some warning."

Roy whistled low.

"And there's hardly a warrior who does not carry the latest British musket, with plenty of shot and powder," the sachem added.

They talked for a long time, and then Roy sent a messenger who returned quickly with word that General St. Clair would see them. An-da stayed behind in Roy's quarters.

*　　*　　*

Arthur St. Clair had been a well-respected officer in the Pennsylvania line during the War for Independence. Since his appointment as governor, Roy explained as he and Renno walked across the fort, St. Clair had spent a lot of time setting up local governments at Cincinnati and Marietta and planning the future settlement of the area.

Renno was greeted by the distinguished-looking St. Clair, who wore his hair full and ear length. Even in so distant a place as Fort Harmar, he dressed in the splendid white and blue uniform of a Revolutionary War senior officer, two stars on the tasseled shoulder boards of the coat. He had a long, strong nose and eyes permanently squinted into a near smile.

"General," Roy said, "this is my friend Renno, sachem of the Seneca nation."

"I greet you, Sachem," St. Clair said frostily. "And whom do you represent? Have you come here on behalf of the Seneca? I must admit that I do not know your name."

"Before you go jumping to conclusions, General," Roy cut in, "you'd better have a look at Renno's credentials."

Renno handed St. Clair the letter from President Washington. The general read quickly, looked up, and raised a questioning eyebrow. "Impressive, indeed. I apologize for my ignorance."

"General," Roy said, "Renno has been out in the territory for a few months, and because he's Seneca he could do something I can't do, which is talk with the Indians." He nodded to Renno.

Renno spoke in a brisk manner, using perfect English with an American accent. First he outlined the dimensions of the territory he had covered, then he listed the tribes he had seen represented. Using St. Clair's map, he pointed out the locations of large concentrations of Indians— villages peopled by women and children as well as warriors. St. Clair listened with his full attention, and when Renno finished, the general was silent for a moment.

"I thank you for this information," he said at last, "but I'd like to caution you before you go on to Philadelphia, if I may."

Renno nodded.

"I, too, know this territory," St. Clair said. "And I feel that you're greatly overestimating both the numbers of warriors involved in this uprising and the strength of their convictions. While it is true that they have scored a victory over General Harmar, that was merely a skirmish involving relatively few troops. I'd hate for you to go into Philadelphia and convince President Washington and the secretary of war that we're facing a force such as you describe. If they believed that, they would prevent me from ending this uprising quickly, which I intend to do."

"General," Roy said, anger creeping into his voice, "I know what you're thinking. You're discounting Renno's information because he is an Indian."

"I assure you, sir," St. Clair said, "that I will consider this sachem's report very carefully."

"And since he's an Indian, he is prone to some exaggeration," Roy went on. "You're convinced that there are only a few hundred braves out there and that you can whup them with a force of militia."

"My men will give a good account of themselves," St. Clair retorted. "One of my men is worth three Indians."

Renno, who had been coldly silent, spoke. "Of this I am certain, General: If you march into the heart of the territory with fewer than three thousand well-trained men, you will meet with a disaster that will make Harmar's defeat seem like a party."

"Nonsense," St. Clair fumed, his face darkening.

"Little Turtle is one of the finest strategists who ever led men into battle," Renno insisted. "He will have the warriors of the Shawnee, the Miami, and the other tribes fall back before your advance until he finds you splitting your forces or until he leads you into just the right position for ambush. And then he'll cut you to pieces."

St. Clair's face was grim. "I will hear no more of this nonsense." He stood, dismissing Roy and Renno. Renno rose with dignity and was out the door when St. Clair called, "Sachem, I did not intend to insult you. We happen to disagree with regard to your assessment. I do, however, offer you employment as a scout—full pay, and you will work closely with Colonel Johnson."

Renno turned to face the general. "Thank you, but I must decline. I make it a point never to enter into a battle I have no hope of winning."

St. Clair strode angrily to the door and closed it in Renno's face.

Back in Roy's quarters An-da was curled on Roy's bed, sleeping soundly. They spoke quietly so as not to awaken her.

"Roy," Renno said, "he's going in, and pretty soon, isn't he?"

"Looks that way. We'll be heading back to Fort Washington in a day or two. That's where the army is being put together. They're trying to get as many Kentucky volunteers as they can."

"There is a man from Kentucky," Renno said, "who, if he is involved, needs watching." He told Roy what he had learned about James Wilkinson.

Roy nodded. "Pretty common knowledge that Wilkinson has the ear of the Spanish governor and can trade with the Spanish in New Orleans even though the Spanish confiscate the goods of everyone else who tries it. I've warned St. Clair about him, but he refused to believe me. Said James Wilkinson has proven himself in raids against the Indians north of the river."

Renno snorted. "Against unprotected villages where he fought only women and children."

"You'll be speaking with Washington about him, I guess." Renno nodded.

"Before you leave, much as I hate to write, I'll do a letter. You don't need corroboration with Washington—he knows you well and trusts you—but maybe a letter from St. Clair's chief scout will carry some weight with some of the other Philadelphia bigwigs."

"It would be even better if you accompanied us," Renno said. "Then two will speak."

"Oh, I reckon I'll hang around here and see what happens," Roy said with a grin.

"You risk your life to the keeping of fools," Renno warned.

"I guess I just want to see how bad it can get," Roy said lightly. "Most of the time I won't be with the army—I'll be out front, where one man can find a lot of hiding places. If worse comes to worst, I can run like hell for Kentucky."

"For the sake of Little Hawk and Renna, be careful," Renno said.

"Oh, sure, you bet," Roy said. "When will you be leaving?"

"With the sun." Renno looked at An-da, still sleeping soundly on Roy's bed. "Are there people here that you know and trust, people with whom she could stay until I return?"

"There are some good men who have their families with them. Yes, if that's what you want."

Roy watched as Renno gently awakened An-da for the evening meal. Roy wanted to ask Renno about the girl, but a man did not pry into another's personal affairs. He hoped that the look he saw in Renno's eyes meant what he thought it meant. The grandchildren needed a mother, and An-da was a fine young woman. During the meal Roy got a little bit of the picture: how two had left the Seneca village and, with An-da, had become three and then two again when Tor-yo-ne decided to stay in Indian country. Roy did not ask about Tor-yo-ne's reasons, but he got the idea that neither Renno nor An-da approved of the young war chief's decision.

"An-da," Renno said, "you will remain here, in this fort, with friends of Colonel Johnson's. I will be traveling fast, very fast. You will be safe here, and you will be spared a rigorous journey."

"Is Renno ashamed to take a Seneca woman to see the great white chief?" An-da asked.

"Ashamed? Don't think that. That is not the reason. I think only of you."

"I will do as you wish, Sachem," she said demurely, but there was a glint in her eyes that made Roy hide a smile behind his hand.

* * *

There had been too many leave-takings in Renno's life, and now he suffered another. He gripped Roy's arm and looked into his eyes. "My children have only one grandfather."

"Don't you worry about me," Roy said.

An-da seemed little concerned. She told Renno good-bye almost casually. It had been decided that she would use Roy's room after Roy accompanied St. Clair back to Fort Washington and would take her meals with the family of a sergeant on permanent garrison at Fort Harmar.

As it happened, St. Clair had advanced his schedule to leave Fort Harmar, so Renno was heading east even as Roy and the general, with a guard of soldiers, were boarding a flatboat to go down the Ohio.

Renno was soon in the lands of Virginia, moving at the warrior's pace to the northeast. He had decided not to try to travel up the river by boat, thus alleviating the need for him to go all the way to Pittsburgh. He would go through western and northern Virginia and enter Pennsylvania from the south on the way to Philadelphia.

The sachem was not surprised when An-da walked into his camp on the second night out from Fort Harmar. It was almost as if he had been expecting her, for he had cooked more meat than he could eat. He had heard a small sound, like that made by a tiny animal, and then as he had waited alertly, she had stepped from behind a large tree, her face lowered.

"Eat," he invited.

"Thank you," she accepted. "There is a nice stream. I will wash first."

He was gnawing a bone when she came back, freshened, and sat opposite him.

"You left a plain trail," she remarked, helping herself to food. "Did you expect me to follow?"

He was startled to realize that he almost said, "I had hoped you would." Instead he said, "I am not surprised."

"Please don't be angry. I would not have been happy among strangers."

He was not angry. To his puzzlement, he was pleased.

"We travel into the mountains soon and then into Virginia."

"All right," she replied.

At Wheeling, site of Fort Henry, Renno used some of his meager stock of gold coin to buy a jacket, shirt, and breeches for himself, and a dress and cape for An-da. Two Indians dressed in white man's clothing drew little attention in that town, for it was on the frontier and had been the site of fierce battles with the Indians during the War for Independence. Its citizens now traded with the Indians in uneasy peace.

The white man's clothing would make them less conspicuous as they traveled into more densely populated areas beyond the mountains. The dress and cape did not make An-da look like a white woman, however.

They had traveled only two days from Wheeling through heavily wooded hills and valleys and were making camp on a clear mountain stream when Renno left An-da to gather wood and make the fire. He, meanwhile, ran back along their trail to secure the evening meal, small game if he saw it first, a deer if not.

An-da went about her chores. Soon a fire was burning merrily, and its warmth was welcome in the chill of the evening. A bed of coals was building up when she heard a twig snap and looked up, thinking that Renno had returned. Instead, she saw a bearded white face, then two more, as three men emerged from the trees and stood, weapons in hand, gazing down at her. She had put her weapons aside; after all, they were traveling in the lands of the United States, far from the marauding war parties of the Ohio Valley. But silent threat emanated from the three raggedly dressed, dirty white men. She lunged for her tomahawk, and three muskets pointed quickly at her breast.

"You just take it easy," a white man growled.

"Whar's that buck yew travelin' with?" another asked.

"He will be back soon," An-da said, fingers touching her tomahawk, which was on the ground.

"Hank," said the biggest man, "you and Charlie go out in the woods and watch fer that buck."

"Who says you're first, Jake?" the one called Hank asked.

"I say. You want to make somethin' of it?"

"Well, hell," Hank muttered.

"You just take it easy, girl," the big man said again, moving toward An-da with his musket pointed at her. "Drop that there ax now, afore I have to hurt you." He grinned, showing tobacco-blackened teeth. "I ain't aimin' to hurt you none."

An-da began to back away, edging herself along the ground, lifting the tomahawk.

"Hurry up," Hank urged from the trees.

"You're supposed to be watching fer that buck," Jake growled.

"Well, you hurry," Hank said, moving to stand behind An-da as she inched away from Jake's advance. The big man made a feint toward her, and she swung the tomahawk.

"Regular little hellcat," Hank said, moving to hit An-da lightly with the butt of his musket. The blow dazed her. Her hand went limp, and the tomahawk fell to the ground. After leaning his musket against a tree, Jake loosened his clothing and knelt beside her. She tried to rise, but he slapped her, knocking her to the ground. She felt rough hands at her throat, ripping the dress. When she heard fabric give under the strain, she tried to scream, but no sound came.

Renno took a big mountain hare with one clean shot from his longbow and trotted back up the trail toward his camp. When he neared, he made the sound of a cooing dove and paused to wait for An-da's reply. When no answer came, he cooed once more, and still not worried, he moved on. Perhaps he was farther away than he had thought. Soon he was just across the creek from the camp and could see the fire through the leaves. He heard a harsh laugh, then, "Hurry up, damn you."

Renno dropped the hare, checked the prime of his musket, loosened the longbow on his shoulder, and crept closer, moving fast, for the laugh came again, and he knew that at least two men were in his camp. He separated leaves and peered through. In the last light of the day he saw something that made him abandon caution. Rage flooded his heart and sent him splashing across the shallow, rocky stream, the angry roar of a bear reverberating among the trees.

Two white men, one leaning on his musket, stood near two struggling forms on the ground. One lifted his musket with a shout of warning as Renno charged across the creek. A ball whistled past not an inch from his ear; but he was closing rapidly. The interloper who had been leaning on his musket raised his weapon, but Renno threw his tomahawk on the run and the well-balanced war ax flew deadly true to smash its keen blade into the white man's forehead. His companion was frantically trying to reload, but because Renno was too near, the intruder took his musket by the barrel and swung it like a club.

The white Indian ducked under the wild swing and buried the short sword deep into his enemy's belly, jerked it out almost in the same movement, and threw himself toward the third white man, who was leaping to his feet, his breeches down around his knees. The sword swung with all the strength of Renno's arm. Only skin and a bit of bone supported the big man's head as he fell.

Renno looked toward An-da. She was scrambling to cover her nakedness. There was not enough of the dress left to cover her properly. Her face appeared ashen, and blood ran from her head and her mouth. Renno, his heart hammering in rage, saw the darkness of her loin patch, her lithe, long legs, and full, young breasts. She managed to sit up, the remnants of the dress clutched in front of her.

"An-da . . ." He could not find words. "An-da—"

She rose. Tears ran down her face as she walked past him. She was naked at the rear, her full rump moving with her walk, her slim waist graceful. "An-da?"

"Leave me alone, please," she said.

He did not know whether he had arrived in time or too late. Her tears and her behavior concerned him. He followed her to see her hurl the torn dress forcefully into the brush, then wade into the cold, swift waters of the stream and lift handfuls of white sand to scrub her body thoroughly.

She was sobbing. A great sadness closed down over him. He walked back to the camp, examined the three white men to be sure they were dead, took An-da's buckskins from her pack, and walked back to the stream.

"Here are your clothes," he called.

She was still scrubbing her body, although her skin had been reddened by the harsh sand. "Don't look at me, please," she said, choking. "I am not worthy."

He was, at that moment, on the brink of marching to the west and joining Little Turtle, ready to kill white men until either he was dead or there were no more. But even in his rage and sadness, he had to admit to himself that, thank the manitous, not all white men were like those dead ones back in the clearing.

Chapter IX

Renno stepped into the stream, took An-da's hand, and led her to the bank. She was shivering. He handed her her buckskins, and she held them in front of her wet body as he led her to the fire. He added more wood until there was a nice blaze. She was standing as he had left her, the clothing clutched to her breast. The fury was still roiling in him. Death had been too swift for the men—still lying here in the clearing—who had taken her by force. He went to her and examined the knot on her head. The cold water of the stream had stopped the bleeding, and she had rinsed the blood out of her hair.

"Does your head ache?" he asked.

He turned her until the fire lit her face, bent to look

at her split lip, and said, "*Ummm,* not bad. It will heal. Now you must get dressed. It's cold."

She fumbled with the deerskin tunic. He positioned it for her and held it as she put her arms through. His eyes quickly scanned her exposed body. He saw a red spot that would become a bruise on one breast, a scratch on her flat stomach, and bruises on her legs. Nothing serious. Only the damage to her spirit would not heal quickly, he thought. He covered her with the skirt and fastened it.

"Now rest," he said, spreading her blanket and lowering her onto it.

He turned to the unpleasant chore of disposing of the corpses. He did not want to leave three dead white men where they might be found, to cause a hue and cry about hostile Indians east of the Monongahela, and he certainly did not want to have to explain to the American authorities why it had been necessary for him to kill the men. He dragged the bodies one by one to a small gully, dumped them in, then covered them with loose rocks, leaves, and dirt kicked down from the banks. When he went back to the fire, An-da was sitting just as he had left her.

"We will move camp," he told her.

She rose and began to gather her belongings while he doused and scattered the fire. Renno led her across the creek, retrieved the rabbit, found a place upstream, and started another fire. An-da had cleaned the rabbit, and soon it was roasting, sending off good aromas. She had not spoken a word while the meat was cooking, and she shook her head when he offered her a juicy, well-cooked hind leg.

"Eat," he urged. "You will need your strength tomorrow."

She took the meat, but it was evident that she had no appetite.

"It is only small consolation," he said, "but no one need know of this except you and me, if that is your wish."

"For that, at least, I am grateful," she said.

"And you must not let it rot your spirit," he said softly. "I hold myself responsible. If I had forced you to go home when first you joined us—"

"No!" she said fiercely.

"Or if I had made you stay at Fort Harmar—"

"You must not," she said, shaking her head.

"And if by some decree of fate the white bastard's seed takes root in you—" He almost never used such words, but his fury was still great.

"No," An-da protested, but he went on.

"—there are women who can do certain things with a turkey quill—"

"No!" she said loudly, her face flushed. "That did not happen. He did not—"

Renno looked at her wonderingly. "He did not?"

"No, no, no!" she shouted.

"Then why, in the names of the manitous—"

"You must not think you have failed me," she said, tears coming. "It is I who have failed you, letting three such sorry men surprise me and overpower me. Ena would not have—"

Laughter roared out of him in a vast unloosing of emotion, in total relief. "Are you telling me," he said, gasping, "that you are so upset because you were unable to kill all three of them by yourself?"

"Yes!" she shouted. "And don't laugh at me!"

Renno fell backward and roared with laughter. He had thought that she had been dishonored. And then his laughter stopped, startled by the depth of his relief. He sat up, his eyes squinted as they looked into the beautiful, tearstained face.

"An-da," he whispered.

She tilted her head in question.

"An-da," he repeated, for he knew, then, that this girl, this Sweet Day, had inched her way slowly but surely into his heart. He looked at her for a long time in silence.

"You spoke my name, twice," she said at last.

He nodded.

"And I've never heard you say it just so."

"Perhaps not," he agreed, rising. "I thank the manitous that you have only a bump on your head, a split lip, and some bruises." He opened his belt pouch and pulled out a handful of gold and silver coins. "Perhaps this event, too, was guided by the manitous, for now we have the white man's money for winter clothing and for our fare when we reach that area served by the coaches."

"Money?" She rose, came to stand beside him, and looked down at the coins. "You took it from them?"

"They have no further use for it," Renno said. "When the white man takes the Indian's land, he sometimes pays him in gold. Let us say that this is partial payment for white men having stolen a small portion of your pride."

"Not enough," she grated.

"Come, we'll finish our meal," he said. "And stop blaming yourself. Even the mightiest warrior—or maiden—cannot be fully alert at all times."

"Teach me," she said, "so that I will never be surprised by an enemy again."

"You are a foolish young girl," he said, but the words were softened by his tone, "to think that I would blame you for something that could have happened to anyone, something that would not have happened had *I* been more careful. I had thought that we were safe from attack here in the peaceful land of the United States. I will not make that mistake again."

George Washington had received a letter from General Rufus Putnam, judge of the Court of Common Pleas in the Northwest Territory. The President was discussing the contents of the letter now with his secretary of war, Henry Knox.

"Are General Putnam's figures accurate as to the strength of Fort Harmar?" Washington wanted to know.

"I'm afraid so, sir," Knox said grimly. "Just more than a score of men there, the rest being with St. Clair at Fort Washington. If they could gather the two-hundred-eighty-some men that the general speaks of to bear arms, I think they'd be scraping the bottom of the barrel, sending out old men and young boys."

Putnam had written that the danger along the frontier was discouraging new settlers and that the number of settlers was in fact dwindling, not increasing. After Harmar's disaster, the tribes, feeling encouraged, had begun to direct their attacks on settlements under the direct protection of the national government, and river traffic on the Ohio had been brought to a virtual standstill.

"Is St. Clair ready?" Washington asked. "We must be certain of success this time."

Knox mused for a few seconds. "Sir, the Congress has made available a considerable sum, $312,686—"

"How very like Congress," Washington said wryly. "I will not even attempt to ascertain how they arrived at the final eighty-six dollars."

"Nor I," Knox admitted. "Obtaining even that sum was almost impossible. As you must know, sir, there are those—especially in New England—who believe that people should stay at home and not push into the land of the Indians."

Washington waved a hand, dismissing such sentiment. "Is St. Clair ready?"

"General St. Clair's last report to me indicated that he had just over eighteen hundred effective men."

Washington raised his brows.

"Sickness, sir, and, of course, desertions."

The President exhaled a deep sigh. "Then perhaps we should consider advising the general to move now, before his force dwindles to nothing."

Roy Johnson, moving easily at the warrior's pace, was making his way back to Fort Washington after a scouting penetration to the north. He ran through a light, spattering, chill rain, mindful of his back trail and on the alert for ambush. He was wet and smelled like a drenched animal when he was escorted into St. Clair's office at Fort Washington.

"They're out there, General," he reported. "I can guarantee that you won't have any trouble at all finding Indians if you're bound and determined to go looking for them."

"Can you be a bit more exact, Colonel Johnson?" St. Clair asked coldly.

"If you're asking me if I counted noses, the answer is hell no. I'm blasted lucky to have come back with my scalp. They'll let you make the first move. It's not their way to gather all their warriors in one big hive while they're waiting, General. But the minute your advance guard leaves the gates of this fort, it'll be seen; and when the main body goes out, the Indian runners will be pounding trails all over those woods, and the tribes will begin to gather."

"Good," St. Clair declared. "That is exactly what we want, Colonel. We want them all in one place so that we may smash them once and for all."

Roy was aware that St. Clair, like Harmar before him, was having supply problems. While he was expending great effort to keep his army together, there were frustrating delays in the arrival of the troops and equipment promised to him by the federal government. Furthermore, the Kentuckians still seemed to think that in view of the success of—or at least the lack of opposition to—their transriver raids against Indian villages, the frontiersman himself was more qualified than the so-called regular army to deal with the Indian problem.

So it was that St. Clair's march to the north was greatly delayed. At last he halted the unopposed advance— the Indians were following their usual tactics of wait and see, of falling back until just the right opportunity—to build forts, which would guard his supply lines.

He arrived at the headwaters of the Wabash River, still far short of General Harmar's deepest penetration. In addition to sickness and desertion, men left behind to man the rearguard forts had lessened his army to fourteen hundred troops. And now the snows came. They were not yet the deep snows of winter, but they were enough to cover the ground and make life miserable for the soldiers.

Roy Johnson left the sprawling camp in the darkness of a cold, November night. Not a quarter of a mile from the pickets he began to smell and see the campfires of the Indians. He would have given a lot to have known where Little Turtle and his war chiefs were camped and to be able to hear them talking; Roy had a feeling in his gut that Little Turtle wasn't going to wait much longer. He valued his scalp too much to try to go any farther, however. He had seen what he had come to see: The main body of the Indians was gathered and was uncomfortably near St. Clair's army.

Making his way back to camp, he walked within ten feet of a sentry who was leaning against a tree, bundled into his clothing, face hidden, trying to keep warm. Roy went directly to St. Clair's tent and bellowed, "Hey, General!"

St. Clair's aide came running out the tent next to St. Clair's and hissed, "You crazy, Johnson? It's the middle of the night!"

"You'd better wake him up," Roy protested.

"I will do no such thing," the aide said.

"Well, then," Roy said, pushing the half-dressed aide aside and bending to lift the tent flap, "I'll do it myself."

St. Clair, awakened by the bellowing and the talking, had pulled on a warm overcoat and was standing. "I take it, Colonel Johnson, that you have something of import?"

"We have company," Roy said, waving his arm to indicate a half circle around the camp. "The main body."

St. Clair frowned. "You've been out there?"

"I have," Roy confirmed.

"And what makes you think that they have come together?"

"I can smell 'em," Roy said.

St. Clair snorted in disgust.

"The smoke of many fires," Roy continued. "It's a still night out there, General, so the smoke hangs."

"You have awakened me to tell me that you have smelled the smoke of campfires?"

"I've awakened you, sir, to tell you that Little Turtle's out there with only God knows how many warriors, and your army is huddled here trying to keep warm, with sentries asleep at their posts and—"

"Thank you," St. Clair said. "If there is any truth to that last statement, I will see to it that men are shot."

"Maybe you'd better save them for shooting at Indians."

"Is that all, Colonel Johnson?"

"General," Roy said, "by God, sir, I pray that you alert this camp, right now, before sunrise."

"We've had these little alarms before, it seems to me," St. Clair replied. "Thank you. And now, if you don't mind, I'd like to get back to sleep."

Roy shook his head, came out of the tent into the cold, dark night, and looked around. Fires were burning over a large area. Men were wrapped in anything that was available for warmth. It was about two hours to dawn. He found the officer of the guard and told the man that he had been able to slip back into camp right under a sentry's nose and that it might be a good idea to make the rounds and awaken the sentries. The officer of the guard, who had already made the rounds of his area twice on that cold, dismal night, thanked Roy kindly and went back to stand beside the fire.

As Roy returned to his tent, he hoped that he was wrong, that Little Turtle, seeing how the army was blundering around in the woods like a blind hog, would bide his time and wait for St. Clair to stumble into a good spot for ambush. Once inside and wrapped in his blanket, Roy did not feel like sleeping. He went back outside, found a good fire, and stood there with sleeping men all around him. He listened to the night sounds of an encamped army: the soft rumble of snoring men . . . coughs . . . horses stirring in a supply park not far away.

Little Turtle struck at daybreak. The outposts and sentries died quickly, many never realizing they were in danger as warriors of many tribes moved soundlessly over the snow-covered ground to assault the first line of defense.

Although it was beyond his scope of responsibility, Roy was awakening men and giving advice to junior officers as they positioned the troops on an inner line. In the growing light Roy saw the first line crumble, and then the Indians, with their fine English muskets sending a deadly hail of fire, overcame the second line of defense and swept toward Roy's position.

"Either we hold 'em here," Roy told a young lieutenant, "or we'll have to run all the way back to Fort Washington."

The morning dissolved into smoke and war whoops

and the eerie wails of the dying. Roy was fighting for his life in a battle that became hand-to-hand combat. He had attached the bayonet to his rifle and used it as he fell back.

Men rallied to his side, recognizing his battle experience. For a while the group around Roy halted at the artillery park. The guns here stood silent, the gunners having fled with the growing panic. When the gathered soldiers had to fall back, the artillery and all the stores were lost, and the ground was littered with muskets and equipment thrown aside by fleeing troops. It was a rout.

Roy had never been involved in a total panic before. He found himself running with the others, hearing the muskets and the howls of the victors behind him. He ran not because he was afraid but because he wanted to live to say "I told you so" to someone. He had promised Renno that he would run like hell if that was what it took to keep Little Hawk and Renna's only grandfather alive. And run he did until there was no longer the sound of musket fire behind him.

He rested. He thought that Renno had been more accurate than anyone in his estimate of the Indians' strength. The army encampment had been about three hundred and fifty yards in length, and it had been almost entirely surrounded, with masses of well-armed enemy coming in on all sides.

"Well," a soldier said to Roy, "I guess we been whupped bad."

It occurred to Roy that it would be some time before anyone could begin to imagine just how badly the Army of the United States had been beaten.

"Son," Roy said, "it could be worse. The only reason you and I are alive is because they're back there now sharing the spoils and maybe having a little fun with the wounded and captives instead of chasing us."

Once again An-da wore the clothing of the whites. The coat that Renno had purchased for her, she said, was not nearly so warm as a good buffalo-hide robe and not as comfortable as buckskins, but she wore it, sitting by his side on a stagecoach bumping its way over the roads leading northeast toward Philadelphia. By then she had become accustomed to odd looks from whites—something that seemed not to bother Renno in the least. She was impressed with the way he talked with white men. He could initiate and maintain conversations easily and, without seeming to pry, make remarks or ask "innocuous" questions that inspired a stranger to divulge information so personal that he probably would have hesitated to share it with his closest friend.

On the early stages of their journey through the so-called civilized areas, the people had been of a sort familiar to An-da: down-to-earth frontier types, if not overtly friendly at least tolerant of an Indian girl dressed up in white man's clothing. Occasionally An-da joined in conversations with fellow stage riders, mostly answering questions from curious women about her life in the wilderness. As their journey took them into Pennsylvania and the density of the white population increased, however, An-da began to notice that more and more people looked at her oddly.

Only two days' ride out of Philadelphia, An-da got her first real taste of white prejudice. She and Renno had changed coaches. Their companion passengers were a bewigged and powdered man dressed in velvets and a heavy-skirted woman of regal bearing. The elegant couple was already ensconced on the seat facing forward when Renno lifted An-da into the coach and followed her. The prosperous-looking white man had been sitting with his feet stretched out in front of him, most probably to ease the tightness of his breeches over a fully distended paunch, and An-da stumbled over his feet and almost fell.

"I say," the man grumbled, "have a care there."

"I beg your pardon," An-da said. Seated, she looked across at the white couple to see a look of shock on the woman's face. Renno, arranging his and An-da's belongings, did not notice.

"Jonathan," the woman whispered in a voice that was easily audible to both Seneca in the close confines of the coach, "how could you allow such a thing?"

The man was silent, but his face was set in grim lines

as the coach jerked into motion and started pounding and rocking its way north.

Renno caught the man's eye and said, "Good day, sir. At least the roads seem to improve the nearer we get to Philadelphia."

The man grunted and looked away. His wife leaned close to whisper, "Jonathan, I will not travel in the company of a squaw man and his savage. If you won't protest to the driver, then I will."

An-da felt Renno tense a moment, then relax.

"Are you going to do something about this?" the woman demanded in a louder voice. "How can you expect me to stand the stench?" She glared at her husband.

The man shifted uncomfortably; after all, he sat with his knees almost touching the knees of a strong-looking young man with a knife and tomahawk at his belt.

An-da stiffened. Renno, seeing that her dander was up, seized her wrist and pulled her toward him as she leaned forward to speak to the insulting woman. He looked at her and smiled, but his eyes were steely. When he spoke, she hardly recognized his voice, for he was affecting the almost effete accent of a certain type of upper-class Britisher.

"Mustn't allow the natives to puzzle you, Princess," he advised. "After all, there is a price one must pay for independence, and part of that price is to be cut off from civilizing influences."

The regal woman's face blazed red.

Renno smiled first at the man, then fixed his cold eyes and humorless smile on the woman. "I assure you, dear madam," he intoned, "that I do not speak of a lady such as you, but of those semibarbarians back at the station who had no way of knowing, bless them, that this is Princess Shining Gold, daughter of the very king of all the Indians and, because of his vast and rich holdings, perhaps the richest man in North America." He sighed elaborately. "Ah, but how could they know that the princess has been summoned by the President himself to negotiate for peace on behalf of her very important father?" He turned and patted An-da on the hand. "Never mind, Princess. Soon we will be met by Mr. Washington's personal coach, and you will find yourself traveling in much more comfort."

There was a silence. The paunchy white man cleared his throat. "I say, sir, do I detect a British accent?"

Renno smiled icily, thinking, *I should hope so, unless I've forgotten how.* He nodded. "But I am American, sir, as American as you yourself."

"Yes, yes," the man said, intrigued, looking at An-da with new respect. "You seem, sir, vaguely familiar. Far be it from me to pry, but could I inquire your name?"

"I am John Smith, sir," Renno said. "Just John Smith." He sighed again. "For, alas, out of respect for my father—although he and I disagreed, of course, about my coming here to fight against our cousin the king—I have become a new man and assumed a new identity, divorcing myself from my background entirely."

A glint of interest came to the woman's eyes as she studied Renno's face. He suppressed a smile, for she obviously was convinced that she saw nobility there.

"And, although I do miss my old home, with its comforts, I have found myself here, sir, in my new country. I must admit that I have found interesting work and have made some good friends."

An-da, having recovered from her surprise at the change in Renno's manner of speech, had begun to realize that he was having fun at the expense of the white couple. She decided to join him in the ruse. "I do so look forward to meeting the President's wife."

Renno looked at her, and now his eyes twinkled. "A splendid lady," he said. "And you'll find that she sets a lavish table, my dear."

"And you, sir, were commissioned to escort the, uh, the princess?" the paunchy man asked.

Renno raised one hand, looked around, and put one finger to his lips. "I committed an indiscretion, sir, in divulging that fact. I must ask you, please, to respect my secret."

"Of course, of course," the man hurriedly assured him.

The white woman's face had altered into a simpering

smile. "I have heard that the President serves the finest of wines at his mansion in Philadelphia."

"True, true," Renno said.

"And that he has terrible trouble eating because of his false teeth," the woman said, leaning forward eagerly.

"Well," Renno evaded, spreading his hands.

"And have you actually been out in the territories, where those savages—uh, those wild Indians are committing so many atrocities?" the man asked.

"Oh, there's a bad element in every society," Renno said. "Even in ours, you must admit."

"True, true," the woman said. She reached down for a basket under her feet and opened it. "I have some lovely blueberry tarts here, Princess. May I offer you one?"

"If it pleases you," Renno told An-da as she glanced at him. "I'm sure that this dear lady runs a very clean kitchen."

"I think not," An-da said, lifting her nose. "One cannot be too careful while traveling in a foreign country, you know." She leaned back. She was tired.

"I think," Renno said, "that the princess is fatigued and will sleep." And with that he put an end to the conversation by closing his own eyes.

At the next change station the white couple who had ridden with Renno made it a point to tell one and all that the powerful-looking bronzed man was a secret emissary from the government and that he was escorting a very, very important Indian princess whose goodwill was vital to peace on the frontier. When she had a chance, when they were alone, An-da asked, "Are they all so bigoted and so gullible, these Americans?"

Everyone was very solicitous when Renno and An-da boarded the stage again, and this time, with new traveling companions, they were given the seat facing the front.

They were not, of course, met by George Washington's coach. Renno hired a carriage to take them to the presidential mansion, where they found the door to be stoutly guarded. The guards looked with disdain at the commonly dressed couple and told Renno that the President did not see anyone without an appointment. Renno produced Washington's first letter.

"Take this to someone in authority, if you will," he requested.

"I told you, friend," the guard said, "that the President is busy. Now get along with you."

"Can you read?" Renno asked coldly.

"Of course," the guard answered.

"Then look at the letter."

The guard read, his lips moving. He looked undecided for a moment, then went to the entrance and called someone. In a few moments a liveried servant was showing Renno and An-da into an ornately furnished waiting room. To the amazement of everyone who saw, George Washington walked briskly from his office into the anteroom, halting for only a moment before he advanced, arm extended. Washington did not shake hands with any man, but he gave his arm to this one in a Seneca clasp.

"My friend," he said warmly, "it is good to see you. Come. We have much to discuss."

"This is An-da," Renno said, "who has come with me."

Washington seemed to notice the girl for the first time. "Ah, yes. Do you desire her to be present as we talk?"

"I think, sir, that she would appreciate a bath and a room in which to rest."

Washington snapped his fingers, and a servant sprang forward. "Please ask my wife to join us."

A few minutes later, Martha Washington, looking somewhat plain even though impeccably dressed, entered the room. "My dear," Washington said, "would you take this lady in hand? Her name is An-da, which, if I remember, means Sweet Day. And so she is aptly named."

An-da looked pleadingly at Renno. He smiled. "Go, rest. I will speak with you later."

An-da, looking back over her shoulder doubtfully, followed Martha Washington away. Renno returned a short bow to Washington and preceded him into the President's office.

"I had wondered," the President said, "if you had received my letters."

Renno was not a man to make excuses. "I answered your request when I could."

"Then you came up through the territory?"

"I did."

"If you don't mind, Renno," Washington said, "I sent word to Henry Knox, my secretary of war, when I learned that you were here. He'll join us within minutes. I don't want you to have to repeat your observations and information. In the meantime we'll have some tea."

"Very well," Renno said. He had acquired a taste for it during his time with Beth.

A servant entered, carrying a tea tray. The brew was of the finest leaf and very enjoyable. In answer to Washington's questions Renno told briefly of his trip to Africa and spoke of conditions in England.

And then the portly Henry Knox entered the room, taking a chair to one side. General Henry Knox had a long, strong nose, which was a bit red on the tip, and a double chin.

"So this is Renno," he said with enthusiasm. As commander of the Continental Army Artillery during the war and a longtime friend of Washington's, he had heard Renno's name mentioned more than once, although he had not met the white Indian.

Now, upon Washington's request, Renno launched into an account of his travels through the Northwest Territory. He spoke briskly and concisely and was interrupted only occasionally by a question from the two men who listened with rapt attention. Finished, he lifted his teacup and drank.

"By the Good Lord above," Knox said, "if he's right, Mr. President, and if Little Turtle can field two to three thousand warriors, well armed—"

"He can," Renno said. "You haven't asked my advice, General Washington. . . ."

"Only because, knowing you, I thought you'd volunteer it," Washington said, with the nearest thing to a smile that ever appeared on his face.

"I don't mean to speak ill of General St. Clair," Renno said, "but he seemed determined to march. It is my opinion that he is premature, that any invasion of Little Turtle's heartland should be postponed until the army is more ready."

"General," Washington said to Knox, "your opinion?"

"I am under the impression, sir, that you put total confidence in this man," Knox said, glancing at Renno.

"I do, sir," Washington agreed.

"If then we accept his appraisal of the overall situation, we have only one choice—to order St. Clair to remain enforted."

"Thank you, General," Washington said. "You confirm my first opinion. Will you see to it, sir? Send the orders immediately."

Knox rose, bowed to Renno, and left the room in a hurried, portly waddle.

"General," Renno said when they were once again alone, "there is one other matter that I did not mention previously."

"For my ears only, eh?"

"Yes, sir." Renno told of his and Rusog's adventure on the Mississippi and recited, almost word for word, the letter from the Spanish governor Miró to James Wilkinson of Kentucky.

For some few seconds Washington rubbed the bridge of his nose as he sat in silence. When he spoke, he did not immediately address the subject. "Renno, there are times when I long for the old days, uncertain as they were. In war, a man can be honest. There is only one objective, to win. There was a time when I had only to state my wishes, and men gave their all to bring them about; when I had only to ask to get agreement, for, by God's will, even though I often felt unworthy, the fate of the country was on my shoulders."

He poured tea, lifted his cup, then looked at the ceiling. "There were those who wanted me to be president for life—a king, as it were—but that is not why we fought, is it, my friend?"

Renno knew that an answer was not expected.

"For better or for worse we have entered into an era of experimental democracy, where, in theory at least, every man has a voice. I have found myself on unfamiliar ground, on the battlefields not of honest war but of politics." He looked at Renno. "For some time now I, and others, have known that James Wilkinson draws a permanent pension from the governor of Spanish territories."

"Then why is he still alive?" Renno wanted to know.

Washington shrugged in resignation. "At first, he was needed to counterbalance the efforts of George Rogers Clark to form an army and take New Orleans. We could not risk war with Spain; we were too weak. Now, he is needed to secure the goodwill of Kentucky. He has great influence there. With Clark in disfavor—deemed a madman by some—Kentucky listens to James Wilkinson. We need Kentucky's long rifles in the fight against the Indians."

The President rose, put his hands behind his back, and paced. "You're getting a lesson in advanced politics, my friend. Not only have we not hanged Wilkinson as a traitor, we have given him the commission of lieutenant colonel commandant in the federal army because, you see, we were too craven to support Clark's plan to open the Mississippi to trade and too weak to raise a proper army to allow General Harmar to defeat the Indian-English alliance in the northwest." He turned to face Renno. "We are buying time. To keep Kentucky, and perhaps other areas of frontier settlement from going to Spain or England for protection, we placate Wilkinson—while keeping him a bit off balance with such honors as his commission in the army."

"I think the quickest solution to this problem is a musket ball to Wilkinson's head," Renno suggested.

"I would gladly pull the trigger," Washington said. "Once I would have given the order for a firing squad as quickly as I could have spoken the words." He spread his hands. "Now I must walk a razor-thin line between war with one of the great European powers and dishonor, between my honest feelings and politics." He halted and looked down at Renno. "Don't judge us too harshly, my friend, for we do truly value your friendship. Heaven knows, we need all the friends we can get." He brightened. "Enough of that. Can you stay in Philadelphia for a time?"

"I had thought to go home quickly," the sachem said. "The snows will be deep in the mountains."

"That is true," Renno agreed.

"You and your charming companion will be our guests at a dinner in your honor tonight. Now, I suspect that you, too, would like to freshen yourself. If there is anything you need, you have only to ask one of the servants."

Renno had not seen a bathtub since his trip to England. He luxuriated in hot water, and when he came out he found that Martha Washington, always efficient, had organized fresh clothing for him, formal evening wear that fit perfectly, including the fine shoes. When he was summoned to dinner by a servant, he followed the man along a hall and down the stairs to find the President, in a fine velvet suit, in a sitting room. Renno had only time to greet his friend when Washington said, "Ah, here are the ladies."

Renno turned. Martha Washington and An-da were descending a sweeping flight of stairs side by side, the older woman wigged and powdered, dressed regally. But Renno's eyes were for An-da. She was in white, and her dark hair had been piled atop her head in a gleaming, raven mass. Her skin was a beautiful contrast to the gleaming white of the gown.

"My word," Washington breathed.

Renno was speechless. He offered his arm to An-da, and she took it as if she had lived all her life in such surroundings. Washington and his wife led the way into the formal dining hall, where the dinner guests awaited. To a man, and a woman, they stood as the President entered, their eyes going first to the velvet-clad Washington and his wife, then to the radiant An-da.

Chapter X

A t first An-da was awed by the distinguished and glittering company at the President's dining table. She knew none of the people except George and Martha Washington. Martha had been very kind and warm during the preparations for the evening and had seen to it personally that An-da was properly dressed and coiffed. In violation of accepted etiquette but for the girl's comfort, she had seated An-da next to herself, just across the table from Renno, who sat at Washington's right as guest of honor.

Renno had trouble keeping his eyes off An-da, and for a time his concentration was so affected that he did not always hear all of the conversation, mainly carried on by the men at the table—Washington, Henry Knox, Thomas

Jefferson, and Alexander Hamilton. He was pleased that An-da did not seem overtly ill at ease. She sat straight in her chair, head high, and followed Martha Washington's example in the correct choice of eating utensils as the meal progressed.

Seeing An-da in the beautiful white gown showed Renno a new aspect of her character and her charm. He got the impression that, in time, An-da could adapt to the new situation and be as ladylike as anyone; but, thank the manitous, this artificial world of stiff manners and affectations was not for her—or for him—on a permanent basis. Seeing An-da thus convinced him of one thing, however. She was as beautiful as Beth and as his beloved Emily. In her eyes was a look that penetrated deeply into his heart, an adoration that made his spirit sing. For the first time he realized the tremendous appeal that she had for him, and this led to speculative musings that distracted him until the President requested that he give a brief summary of his report for the benefit of Hamilton and Jefferson.

Martha Washington sniffed. "My dear," she said, "must we speak of war at table?"

Washington chuckled through closed lips. "You're right, my dear. It can wait."

But now Renno became involved in the table talk. He answered questions from Jefferson, and his first impression of the man was that here was an old-fashioned aristocrat, a bit standoffish. He warmed more quickly to Hamilton's personality. Now and again his eyes would stray back to An-da, and when Martha coaxed the girl into speaking of life in a Seneca village, he listened with pride as she told of hunting for fresh greens and berries in the spring and of the closeness of family life.

"I am curious," Hamilton said to An-da, "as to just how you came to make such a long and dangerous journey. All the ladies of my acquaintance would faint at the mere thought of having to walk ten miles, much less several hundred."

"She came to make the journey out of pure hardheadedness," Renno said. "This one has a will of her own and would not be left behind." He told of how she had

matched a warrior's pace for three days and of her participation in the first clash with hostile Indians. Ladies gasped
and covered their mouths with their napkins. The men
looked at An-da with respect.

After dinner and in privacy, Washington had Renno
brief Jefferson and Hamilton and told them of his and
Knox's decision to send orders to St. Clair to delay his
invasion of the Indian lands for a time.

"Mr. Hamilton," Washington said, "it appears that we
might have to go back to Congress for more appropriations
to field an army that will ensure success."

Hamilton groaned.

Jefferson smiled. "Once more into the lion's mouth,
Mr. Hamilton. I can't say that I envy you."

Renno revised his opinion of Jefferson slightly when
he learned in conversation that Jefferson had grown up
close to the Virginia frontier and was not ignorant of the
problems there. And then, as the three cabinet members
took their leave, Jefferson took Renno's hand and said, "It
would please me if you and your charming friend would
accept my hospitality for dinner. There is much I'd like to
know about the lands west of the mountains, and it seems
you've seen more of them than most."

"My pleasure, sir," Renno said.

He, too, made a move to take his leave of President
Washington after the cabinet members had retrieved their
ladies and left the mansion, but Washington waved him
back into the office, abandoning Martha and An-da to chat
or to retire as it pleased them.

"Are you still determined to make a winter journey to
your village?" Washington asked.

"There is unrest there as well," Renno replied.

"Only in the west," Washington said. "Relations are, I
understand, excellent between the main body of the
Cherokee, your people, and the Cumberland and Knoxville
settlers."

Renno did not respond.

"I understand how you feel, however," Washington
said with a sigh. "I must confess that once the war was

won, my one desire was to go home to Mount Vernon; but that was not to be."

"You have a better chance of bringing peace to the frontier than any man I know," Renno said. "The tribes will fight you, but they have respect for you. They know that your word is true."

"The problem, my friend, is that under our system of government, my word has to be backed up by Congress."

"We, too, listen to the elders of our tribes," Renno said, "but if the sachem says we go to war, we go to war."

For another hour the two men sat in Washington's office, and the talk turned to the War for Independence, to good times and bad. Then, once again, the President stated his desire to go home. "That I cannot do, my friend." He fixed Renno's eyes with his commanding stare. "Nor, I fear, can you."

Renno raised an eyebrow in question.

"For some time now I have been contemplating a change in command of the army; my request is that you remain with us for a time, at least until some decisions are made here in the capital." He paused, and a twinkle came to his eyes. "You see, I am determined to save that beautiful young girl from a long march through the winter snows of the mountains."

Renno thought for a moment, his heart aching, knowing that to agree would keep him away from his children for an indefinite period of time. "I respect your wishes, sir."

The room that had been assigned to Renno was on the opposite side of the house from the bedrooms of the Washingtons. He made his way there without the help of a servant, waving the man off, running lightly up the stairs and walking down the long hallway with his mind preoccupied. He opened the door. The room was lit by a lamp turned low, leaving the bed and furnishings in dark shadows. He began to remove the confining formal wear with a gusting sigh of relief, then tossed jacket and shirt onto the back of a chair. Although he had not worn weapons to the dinner, when a soft sound came from the shadows on the other side of the testered bed, his hand went automatically to the spot where his tomahawk usually hung.

The sound came again, a soft rustling. He moved on cat's feet past the end of the bed. In the soft light he saw An-da seated in a large chair. His face softened into a smile.

"A small, quiet mouse has crept into my quarters," he said.

"Forgive me."

"There is no need," he said, still speaking English. "I am pleased to see you. I wanted to tell you that you made me proud with your poise and your beauty."

She hung her head, but she was smiling happily. "Now you will not be proud of me, for I am a foolish girl."

"And why are you foolish?"

"The servantwoman offered to help me," she said.

"Help you?"

"I felt that I could undress myself," she said, her voice a childlike whisper. "But I find that these garments have been fashioned by puzzle makers."

Renno laughed. "It is true that the whites are ingenious at making fasteners to defy the wits of anyone. Perhaps I can help."

"Please," she said. "I was too embarrassed to call for the woman once I had sent her away." She stood and presented her back to him.

He fumbled with snaps at the neck of the dress, found the combination, and soon had the dress open down the back. "There," he said.

She shrugged off the dress, gathered it, and placed it carefully on the bed, then stood before him in soft, lawn underthings. "The shoes defy me as well."

Renno lifted her, sat her down on the edge of the bed, and knelt to unbutton the shoes. His eyes traveled up her legs, their shapeliness emphasized by hose. Her eyes were full of him.

"Now that I am undressed," she whispered, "how will I get back to my room without being seen by someone?"

"Wrap yourself in a blanket."

"And then the servants would say, look, the Indian has reverted to her native state."

Renno chuckled. "I will wrap myself in a blanket with you, and if we see a servant I will give a war whoop and frighten him away."

She giggled. During the exchange their eyes had been locked together, and Renno's entire body was warmed by her eyes and her smile.

"I had thought to sleep here, with you," she confessed.

"A highly improper suggestion," he said with a smile, "in the house of the great sachem of the United States."

"I will sleep very quietly, on the floor," she offered. "That huge room where they have put me is empty and lonely."

"An-da," he said in mild reproval. "Is this the maiden who ran alone for three days and who has killed her enemies?"

She slid off the high bed to stand before him. "It is so strange here." She was leaning toward him, and as if they were pulled by an unseen force, their bodies touched, and Renno's arms went around her. He felt her warmth through the undergarments. Then, for the first time, An-da was introduced to that odd, white custom that involved mouth-to-mouth contact. The force of his kiss sent a trembling wave of weakness through her. She clung to him and was supported by his arms.

When he lifted his lips from hers, she whispered, "That is the way of love between whites?"

"Some of their customs are interesting," Renno said before he covered her lips with his once more. His hands explored her back and her firm, rounded, lower lines, then he gently pushed her away. "The blanket," he said.

"No," she whispered.

He had not been ready for commitment to this girl-woman and had told himself that in the future, when things were less uncertain, perhaps he would speak to her of love and a possible union. But with the heat of her in him, all caution and all doubt were swept away. He found himself loosening her remaining garments, and the results of that were inevitable.

* * *

For a time—a few heartbeats? a lifetime?—she lay totally uncovered. The winter chill of the unheated room caused her smooth, young skin to form goose bumps, but the inner fire of her love vanquished the cold. She could feel her body become more sensitive to the heated knowledge that her maidenhood was shortly to come to an end. She had loved the man for so long! A melting sensation inside her lower stomach was followed by the awareness of a natural flow of juices. This embarrassed An-da. She thought to reach down to cover the offending area, but the expression on Renno's face left her helpless to move.

An-da had experienced the odd yearnings of her developing body, but true Seneca maiden that she was, only her own hands had touched the places where now Renno's fingers played lightly in exploration. Never had she felt the heat of a man's lips on her bare skin. Never had she been totally possessed by a storm of emotions so powerful that they left her breathless as Renno's head lowered to place his warm, soft lips on the taut plane of her stomach.

As for Renno, he was surprised by the passionate desire that An-da's slim body had aroused in him. He was concerned for a moment that this little one would be frightened or alienated by his savorings of her. He was ten years older than she and had been the husband of not only Emily but of Beth, a sophisticated woman from a land where making love was elevated to an art form. It had been a long time since he had said good-bye to Beth, and Renno felt himself shivering with his need, for he was young and strong.

There was something different about An-da because she was Seneca. He approached her young, lithe body with an attitude of near worship. With Beth and Emily, there had been white, soft skin, not the rose-dusk complexion of his beloved people, and his desire to couple with her was both physical and symbolic. But first he needed to possess her, experience her with his senses—his taste and his smell.

Thus it was that An-da, modest Seneca maiden, first knew the soft, wet kiss of Renno's lips and gasped as she realized with shame that his mouth was encountering the liquid expression of her passion for him. But a new sensation caused her to expel her breath in a long, pleasure-ridden sigh. And his heated kiss became even more intimate and engendered in her an instinctive motion, the rocking, giving-and-taking, hip-swiveling expression of a woman's total commitment.

She cried out in awed surprise as his mouth caused odd little inner contractions, and then her breasts were wet with his kisses. At last she opened herself to the painless penetration that made her a woman, Renno's woman.

She lifted and tried to turn herself inside out to take more of him. She pulsed around him as she accepted his seed with another vast upheaval of pleasure and little cries of gladness and surprise.

And then the storm subsided, and they lay entwined, still joined, as their hearts slowed and their breathing became normal.

"With this act I make thee mine," Renno whispered.

"I give myself gladly."

"I feared that my great need would frighten you."

"No. You could never frighten me," she promised, clinging to him. And then she went stiff and emitted a small cry.

He lifted his head and looked at her anxiously. "Are you in pain?"

"No," she replied, but she was unable to meet his eyes.

"We are one," he assured her. "You are not regretting what has happened . . . ?"

"Oh, Renno . . ." she said, beginning to weep.

He held her close and coaxed her to tell him what was bothering her.

"I have been told that the first time is difficult and painful for a maiden," she said. "And it was neither for me, and so you must think that you are not the first."

When, at last, she confessed, he chuckled and rolled onto his back, bringing her atop him.

His amusement surprised, then angered her. When she began to beat on his chest with her fists, he begged her to stop and reached for the oil lamp. He held it over the bed to show her a few spots of dark, fresh blood. "I did not need that proof myself," he told her fondly, still grinning, "but since you do, here it is."

She looked down into his musing smile, then rolled to rest beside him, propped on one elbow. "And you said that my sleeping on the floor would be improper behavior in the home of the great sachem of the United States."

"You have bewitched me, my Sweet Day," he said.

"I have dreamed of this," she whispered. "Not knowing how it would be, I was a bit frightened at the very thought." She pinched him on the flat stomach. "But you are not so fearful, after all." Her hand began to smooth its way downward. "You are like the small boys who swim naked in the streams, but more—" She blushed.

"You are not like the small girls," he said, his hands finding her breasts. "You are woman, and beautiful." His face went serious. "We are one, An-da. I pray that that pleases you, for it is my wish to be one with you forever."

Tears of joy sprang into her eyes, and she threw herself onto him, clinging fiercely. "The manitous are indeed kind."

Sleep was the last thing in their thoughts. Instead there were mutual exploration, soft talk, and long kisses. And then, in the early hours of the morning, replete with love but unwilling to part even in sleep, she asked drowsily, "Will we live in your longhouse across from the longhouse of Toshabe and Ha-ace?"

"If it pleases you. If not, I'll build you another."

"It pleases me," she said. "I long to be there, but I fear what Little Hawk will say. I think Renna will be pleased."

"They will both be pleased," Renno assured her. "Although, as he feels his approaching manhood, it might be necessary to discipline the boy now and again."

"Let's go home," she urged.

"There is nothing I'd rather do," he admitted. "There will be feasting and dancing when we celebrate our union with our people." And he was praying that somehow El-i-chi would be there to perform the ancient ceremony of union. "But not just yet," he went on. "I have told General Washington that I would stay here for a time."

"No matter," she said. "As long as I am with you."

He laughed. "Then we must do something to prevent the servants from seeing one or both of us creeping around the hallways wrapped in blankets."

He spoke with Martha Washington at breakfast, explaining to her that he felt it would be a good omen for all if he and his An-da were united in marriage with a Christian ceremony in the mansion of the President of the United States. Martha was delighted. She started making elaborate plans and talked nonstop until Renno held up a hand pleadingly.

"Please, please," he said. "We are not accustomed to the pomp of your life. A small and very private ceremony will make both of us very happy."

And so it was that Renno and An-da were married in the manner of the white man by an Episcopalian minister. In attendance were George and Martha Washington, who acted as the legal witnesses. The wedding feast was for five. A proper Seneca ceremony would be performed later, when events allowed.

In the days that followed, the newlyweds strolled together down the streets of Philadelphia. Renno treasured each moment alone with An-da and longed for the time that they could be away from the mansion, from the city, and alone in their own land. At his suggestion they chose not to attend the Washingtons' almost nightly dinner parties, for the white Indian knew that those occasions were used by the President for political purposes and that the presence of two Seneca, however well dressed, could be distracting.

They did dine in the bachelor home of Thomas Jefferson, and Renno was pleased to find himself among the type of men with whom he was most familiar—military men and frontiersmen. The talk was mainly about the conditions along the frontier, and Renno's observations and opinions were listened to with great respect. Jefferson's always questing mind produced inquiries that pleased Renno, giving him an opportunity to express his great concern for the future of all Indians and to describe the magnificence of the country through which he had traveled. Jefferson was especially interested in Renno's venture beyond the Mississippi.

"We fight now," Jefferson said, "for that relatively narrow band of land between our mountains and that great river, thinking only vaguely of the even vaster stretches between the Mississippi and the Pacific Ocean. If I were a young man and without responsibilities, Renno, I would ask you to show me those lands. Together we would set off into the setting sun and go until the ocean lay before us."

"Thomas," said one of the military men, "you know you couldn't run off and leave your growing Democratic-Republican party."

Jefferson frowned. "If I could not get to heaven but with a party, I would not go there at all."

In the general laughter, Jefferson smiled. "I do long to see the expanses of this continent, but, alas, I suppose I never shall. It will be to men like you, Renno, to explore it and, I hope, to claim it for the United States."

"I think, sir," Renno responded, "that the Comanche and the Apache and the Indian nations of the plains might have something to say about such an idea."

It was in December when, returning from a walk on the city streets with An-da, Renno was told that the President wanted to see him in his office. When he entered, Washington was pacing, grasping a piece of paper in his hand.

"Please sit down, Renno," Washington said.

Renno sat and waited. The President continued to pace, then paused at last, his face set in grim lines. "When I was a much younger man and only a few wild-eyed dreamers harbored notions of an independent nation on the North American continent, I marched with General Braddock against Fort Duquesne. I was a lieutenant colonel in the Virginia militia. We had fourteen hundred British regulars and our seven hundred provincials. Edward Braddock led us into an ambush sprung by no more than a thousand Frenchmen and Indians, but we lost just over seven hundred men, killed and wounded. For many years, I had the dubious distinction of having participated in the worst defeat ever inflicted by Indians on this continent."

Renno felt a chill of warning, but he said nothing.

"Now I can no longer say that." Washington held out the letter, looked at it, and threw it violently onto his desk. "General St. Clair was on the march even before we sent him the order to desist. He reached the headwaters of the Wabash River. There was no ambush, no trickery on the part of Little Turtle. He simply sent his warriors into the army's camp at sunrise."

Renno waited patiently, for it was evident that Washington's words were spoken with great pain.

"He lost almost nine hundred men," Washington continued in a soft voice. "All his artillery, all his stores. A complete and total rout."

Renno's thoughts were for Roy Johnson. He prayed that his father-by-marriage had distanced himself from the main battle.

"For all practical purposes, the Army of the United States has been destroyed," Washington said. "Now nothing stands between the Indians and the frontier settlements."

"Now would be an excellent time to strike a counterblow," Renno suggested. "It is my guess that the tribes, elated by the victory and rich in loot, will have dispersed to their respective villages to celebrate and tell tales of their bravery."

"Yes," Washington said, "so it seems. I suppose the whole thing could have been worse. They could have mopped up the entire army, piecemeal, as they fled, throwing away their weapons."

"That is not the Indian way," Renno explained. "I guess that they stayed on the field instead to loot weapons and material, to take scalps—"

"To torture the wounded and the captured," Washington said. "There were women among the camp followers, Renno. Some thirty of them were found, afterward." He looked up. "Oddly enough, it was our, uh, friend James Wilkinson who took a small force to the battlefield to bury the dead. He found the women impaled, through the female orifice, on stakes."

"General, if you're asking me to defend or condemn the way of the Indian, I will do neither."

"No, no, Renno, nothing of the sort. There have been cruel acts on both sides. I've heard it claimed that the white man invented the custom of scalping."

"Yes," Renno confirmed. "Taking the scalp proved that an Indian was dead in order to collect the bounty put on the Indian's head by some of your earlier settlers."

The men were silent for a moment. Then the President spoke.

"You mentioned that now would be a good time to strike back. The problem is, you see, that we can't. We'd have trouble raising a regiment now. I shall have to go to Congress and ask for more money—a prospect I am not looking forward to. I'll have to come up with an explanation as to why this worst defeat in the history of American arms came to pass."

He paced again, rubbing his mouth and face as if his teeth hurt. "I will have to appoint a new army commander. And I'll need information, my friend. Will you accept a commission directly from me, as chief of scouts in the Northwest Territory? You will not answer to or take orders from any military man. I may ask you to advise and consult with St. Clair's replacement. I know of no man more eminently qualified than you. The future of your Seneca—both in Tennessee and in the north—will be affected by what happens in the Ohio lands. I don't think you'd want to live under the rule of Spain or of England."

Renno was moodily silent. *Little Hawk ... Renna ...* At length he said, "I will do all that is within my ability, General."

"I am very pleased," Washington said gratefully. "I'll have the papers drawn up, but I think it would be a good idea for you to remain here in Philadelphia until we can get a grasp on the altered situation."

The situation proved to be chaotic. Swiftly messages from the frontier began to come to President Washington. Governor Mifflin of Pennsylvania wrote that Pittsburgh could not be defended if the Indians launched a serious attack and that the fall of Pittsburgh would expose all of western Pennsylvania to raids. The Virginians of Ohio County wrote, telling of fifty dead from Indian raids and warning that the Indians were attacking with increased confidence following St. Clair's defeat. From the south came word that the Creek were more actively warlike.

To make matters worse, a new Spanish governor had arrived in New Orleans just in time to hear of the St. Clair disaster. Hector, baron de Carondelet, immediately recognized the opportunity. He sent entire armies of Indians carrying Spanish arms against American outposts.

All along the frontier the war parties re-formed even as the sachems and chiefs hurried from conference to conference in their continuing effort to build a united Indian front. Dragging Canoe had rushed to consult with the Creek McGillivray, saying, "Now is the time." Only the Chickasaw and the main body of the Cherokee nation, under Rusog, prevented an uninterrupted front of war from Lake Erie to the Gulf of Mexico, and it seemed likely that all white settlements would be swept from the Ohio and Mississippi valleys.

During the long months of a northwest winter, El-i-chi had practiced his magic and strengthened his orenda by contemplation and appeals to the manitous. He and Ah-wa-o had made their longhouse a place of comfort and, because of their love, a place of happiness. With the new beginning, the trees and other growing things were not the only evidence of new life, for Ah-wa-o's stomach was huge. Her time of birthing was near. For weeks El-i-chi had shown her great consideration. In fact, he had earned some initial displeasure from Ah-wa-o when he insisted on cooking and doing other chores that were ordinarily woman's work.

"This does not befit a great warrior and a shaman," she would protest.

But he would laugh and wave away her objections. "We are but two alone," he said, "and it gives me pleasure to save you from the work." He patted her protruding belly.

When the initial warning came in a flood of water, El-i-chi was ready. He had a great stack of firewood gathered and a store of food. He sat with Ah-wa-o as the labor pains began, holding her hand and talking to her softly. Even when the pains were great, Ah-wa-o did not cry out. She clenched her teeth tightly and clung to El-i-chi's arms with a strength that left fingernail marks.

As shaman of the tribe he had blessed births, and he had observed. It seemed to be a simple, straightforward process, but in the last moments he began to worry, for the pains racked her, and nothing much seemed to be happening otherwise. He berated himself for not having taken her home or to an Iroquois village where she would have had the services of a midwife.

Then he saw the emergence of a small, delicate head with a thick thatch of black hair, and with one mighty effort and one extended grunt of strain from Ah-wa-o, the baby slid forth into his hands. Only the ceremonial cutting of the cord and the cleansing of the newborn remained to be accomplished.

"A boy," he whispered, holding the baby close for Ah-wa-o's inspection.

"Of course," she said.

"You yourself are the greatest gift of the manitous," El-i-chi said. "But next in rank is this gift from you, this son."

Outside, a spring storm, heralded by a roaring wind, ripped through the treetops and whistled around the longhouse. Thunder crashed overhead, and lightning slashed across the dark skies.

"He came with the wind," El-i-chi said. "He shall be called Gao, the Wind."

"As you wish," Ah-wa-o agreed.

*   *   *

The baby was immersed in the clean, clear waters of the lake, and his father chanted the old words over him in this ceremony of welcome to an uncertain world. And now El-i-chi's life was complete—or nearly so, for he had long since reconciled himself to his and Ah-wa-o's situation. He was glad that he had abandoned his plans to join the Seneca in the north. He felt that he had more work to do, that the manitous were directing him to stay here, in the wilderness with Ah-wa-o and Gao, until he was called.

So, for sweet weeks he was content to watch his son and to marvel at Ah-wa-o's quick recovery from the birth.

He had not been successful in his recent attempts to contact the manitous, but he accepted his failure, secure that when the manitous had something to tell him, they would appear. He spent a great deal of time using the Sight, the gift of the spirit of old Casno. It was, El-i-chi had found, both frustrating and awesome. At times he seemed to be able to look far away. For example, he once had a dim vision of his home village and saw there the activities of his family. It was also possible to sense the movement of living things in the area directly around him, but only at unpredictable times.

"If your Sight were consistent," Ah-wa-o said, "it would make you the greatest of hunters, for you could know the location of every deer."

Of course, he would never abuse the gift for such mundane purposes. He was capable of supplying the needs of his family without magic.

On a day when Gao was just over two months old, El-i-chi hunted early, made his kill—a yearling buck whose soft skin would give Ah-wa-o material with which to fashion blankets and garments for the boy—hung the dead animal to drain off the strong, reeking blood so that the meat would taste sweeter, cleaned the carcass, and slung it across his shoulders for the trip back to the longhouse. He was in a range of forest that he knew well, and eager to be with his family, he moved at a swinging trot under a canopy of green. When he came to a small rill, he halted,

drank deeply, washed himself, and was about to lift the
carcass once more when his vision blurred momentarily.
The Sight came to him: Before his eyes, in an eerie
silence, a force of warriors from several tribes was swooping
down to the attack. He saw oddly uniformed white soldiers
turn to meet the onslaught, saw men—red and white—
fall, and then, so clearly that he gasped, El-i-chi saw the
face of his brother. Renno's lips were pulled back in a
fighting snarl, his strong arms wielding a tomahawk and an
odd, short sword. Fear enveloped El-i-chi, not for himself
but for Renno, for his brother was surrounded by
overwhelming numbers.

The vision faded as quickly as it had come. El-i-chi
knelt on the mossy bank, imploring the manitous for more
information, for clarification; but he was answered only by
the calls of birds and the rustle of a squirrel searching in
the leaves of the forest floor for a buried tidbit.

As El-i-chi was swinging along at a steady pace for the
longhouse, he made a decision. The swift, incomplete
vision of the Sight had been so disturbing, he knew he
would have no peace until he was moving.

Ah-wa-o did not question him when he told her that
it was time to travel to the north, to find Renno. In
preparation, she had already made a carrying pouch of
deerskin so that Gao would sleep comfortably on his
mother's back during the march. It was only a matter of
gathering a few items before she was ready.

The night before they left the longhouse, El-i-chi
abandoned sleep to implore the manitous for guidance.
The rising sun found him vaguely uneasy but determined
to move northward.

Rumors of war came to the Cherokee-Seneca villages
through newspapers brought from Knoxville by long hunters and wanderers. Throughout the late winter and early
spring young men returned from hunts to speak of signs of
large war parties of Creek traveling through Cherokee
lands toward the north and west. Although Rusog felt that
it was safe enough in the eastern ranges of the Cherokee
lands, he sent runners to all villages to warn of the

presence of Creek and to caution warriors against rashly joining with Dragging Canoe.

The feast of the new beginning had come and gone in the Seneca village. That year's celebration was notable for the presence of a new and surprisingly young member of the False Face Society, Little Hawk. There was no question in anyone's mind that he would be the future sachem of the Seneca. Not a day went by that he was not reminded of that in some way—by Ha-ace and other senior warriors who saw to his martial training and woodcraft, or by Toshabe, who coached him in Seneca traditions and the responsibilities of a sachem. So it was that the boy, wearing a gruesome mask fashioned by the talented Cherokee Se-quo-i, took part in the dance of the false faces and sat in attendance, far to the rear, when the elders of the village gathered in council.

With the spring, as usual, women and children fanned from the village in search of edibles, especially the prized pokeweed, whose tender shoots added tang to any dish. On a day blessed by the manitous Ena took her two-year-old twins and joined a group of laughing, chattering women and children guarded—as a precautionary measure—by Cherokee and Seneca warriors. She had Renna to help with the active twins and her own personal guard in the form of the "warrior" Little Hawk.

The sky had the beauty of summer, with tall, fleecy clouds outlined against brilliant blue. It was neither too hot nor chilly, so Little Hawk quickly shed his buckskin tunic and tied it at his waist in order to feel the warm kindness of the sun on his back. Ena, never one to seek out the company of large groups of women and children, slowly diverged from the group, going her own way. "Do I not have a warrior to guard me and my children?" she asked, for Aunt Ena knew well how to massage the pride of a boy.

Little Hawk preened and put on a show of alertness, looking to all points of the compass as Renna led the twins ahead, searching for a choice spot. They crossed a creek and found a nice patch of pokeweed on the far bank. Ena began to pick the tender shoots.

"Renna, don't let the twins get in the water," Ena called out just before Ho-ya made a waddling dive and splashed mightily into the shallow stream. Ena sighed in resignation. Renna plunged into the water and pulled Ho-ya to his feet. Renna was deluged as We-yo flopped on her stomach in the water.

Little Hawk climbed to a rotting stump and gazed all around, examining the tree line across the creek and the brush on their side of the stream. The small animals of the forest, as if realizing that the human objective for the day was limited to gathering greens and berries, went about the business of spring with verve and daring. Squirrels made furry lines of motion up and down the trees in the ritual of courtship and competition. Birds chirped and searched for bits of nesting material. A pair of red foxes came to the stream, leaped it lightly, and disappeared in a flow of graceful motion.

Ena was humming a spring song softly when Little Hawk caught a hint of motion about a hundred yards down the creek, just where it began to make a bend. He waited for a repetition of the movement while telling himself that it had been only a squirrel or that a bird's weight on a branch could cause it to bend. But then he saw the bush move again.

"Aunt Ena," he said softly, "at the bend of the stream, on our side, just past the largest sycamore . . ."

Ena didn't jerk her head to look. She finished the motion of plucking and placing the shoots in the pail and then moved on her knees so that without making it obvious she could look toward the spot. "Where?" she asked after a few moments. Then she caught her breath, for she had seen the glint of sun on metal among the lush greenery. As she continued to pluck the shoots, she said, "Go to the stream. Get the younger ones across to the other side."

Little Hawk did not question her. He walked slowly to the stream, acting, if anything, a bit too casual. He looked up at the clouds and the treetops but not once down the stream. He waded into the water, dodged a splash from the twins, and told Renna, "Take them to the other bank, now."

Renna was alerted by the edge of imperativeness in her brother's voice, and she grasped the hands of the twins and pulled them, protesting and splashing, to the other bank.

Little Hawk looked back. Ena was standing, her hands at her back, stretching, giving the impression of feeling as safe as if she were surrounded by a thousand warriors. Then she started toward the stream, swinging the bucket.

The boy went tense as he saw a figure hurdle the stream, down near the bend. He recognized the dress and the war paint, for that had been an important part of his continuing education. Creek. But he continued to act as if nothing were happening.

As Ena neared him Little Hawk said in a low voice, "A Creek warrior is now on the other side of the stream."

As if to confirm the boy's observation, a flock of mourning doves took flight from the brush not thirty yards away.

"Now we have fresh greens for the cook pot," Ena said loudly. "Who would like to play a game?"

Renna and the twins answered in unison.

"It's to be a race," Ena explained. "We will see which of you can first reach the others, there." She pointed unnecessarily, for, from a distance, came the shrill voices of the children with the main party. "Go now, like the wind."

Renna and the twins started running, the twins' chubby legs pumping. Renna slowed her pace to stay behind them. "You, also," Ena told her nephew. "Get them to the warriors, quickly."

The boy splashed through the stream and disappeared into the trees. Ena walked slowly, all senses alert. She saw two more Creek warriors cross the stream down from her, and she prayed that, as she suspected, the interest of the Creek was in her, not the children. They would have been away from their women for a long time to be so far north, and a solitary female in the woods would be tempting. She crossed the stream and entered the trees, pail in hand. She had not walked ten paces when, with the suddenness of which any warrior is capable, three war-painted Creek stepped into the trail to block her way.

"I greet you, Creek brothers," Ena said calmly, "and welcome you to the land of Rusog, Chief of the Cherokee."

"You are polite, woman," said the largest of the three, standing in front of the other two. "Perhaps you will be generous, as well."

"There is food for those who come in peace," Ena said, bending to put the pail with its content of fresh greens down in front of her.

In any language there is a play on words similar to the English regarding *peace* and *piece*. In the dialect used by the Creek in their next exchange with the Seneca woman, their meaning was as clear, and as offensive to Ena, as they would have been in English.

"So you have come to insult the wife of Rusog?" Ena asked, drawing her tomahawk.

The Creek laughed and accused her of lying, saying that the wife of a chief as great as Rusog would not be alone in the woods. They laughed, too, at her belligerent stance, her fine legs spread and tomahawk at the ready. One said to the leader, "Since it was you who first saw this choice one, it is you who should have the pleasure of disarming her."

Ena stood her ground. "At least you have the manhood to come at me one at a time." Actually, she felt a surge of fierce joy. For too long she had been performing solely as a wife and mother, letting her warrior skills go unused. The children were safe, far ahead now, most probably near the main body, where there would be Cherokee and Seneca warriors.

"I will have your weapon, woman, and then I will have you," the Creek said.

"Come and take that which I am willing to give gladly," she invited, tensing, poised to strike as he drew near.

A scream of surprise and pain turned the warrior's head. One of the two warriors behind him staggered, and blood was spurting from his right leg. A small boy with a bloody tomahawk smaller than a man's weapon was standing at the ready beside a tree.

Ena realized that Little Hawk had crept quietly into the clearing, and, with his tomahawk, its fine blade made by Se-quo-i, had cleanly slashed the tendons at the back of the warrior's knee. The warrior howled with anger.

"What kind of people are these," he asked harshly, "who send a boy and woman to do their fighting?"

"We have not been sent," Little Hawk said. "We are Seneca, and we choose where we will fight."

The warrior tried to use his leg but almost fell. He started hopping toward Little Hawk. "I do not kill boys," he growled, "but this once I will make an exception."

"Run, Little Hawk," Ena called, but the boy stood his ground.

The big warrior turned his attention back to Ena. "Your weapon, woman. Otherwise I will have to hurt you."

He moved forward, intending to knock the tomahawk from Ena's hand, but she sidestepped the blow with an agility that caught him by surprise—a surprise from which he never recovered, for Ena's blade slashed in under his arm and opened his stomach with the sound of a ripe watermelon being sliced. He clutched at his falling intestines, and his slump toward the ground became a nerveless collapse as Ena's tomahawk crushed his skull.

The third warrior, dividing his attention between what he expected to be the death of a small boy and the conquest of a woman, yelped in anger and leaped toward Ena. He was a man of skill, and she backed away from his assault.

"Come, Creek," Little Hawk said to the warrior hopping toward him. "Why do you not walk on two legs like a man?"

With a roar of rage and pain the warrior slashed down at his small target with enough force to cleave Little Hawk's head from his shoulders. But the child danced aside and then darted in to slash at the man's already useless leg. The warrior yelled out, fell, then made one desperate attempt to cut Little Hawk's legs from under him, swinging from his prone position on the ground.

Little Hawk jumped over the swing of the tomahawk and sent his own blade crashing down, both his hands on the handle. The Creek warrior knew no more as the blade of a boy buried itself in his skull.

Ena, by that time, had discerned the pattern of attack used by the Creek facing her. She parried a blow, steel on steel ringing out, and sent an underhand blow upward into the Creek's breechclout. Horror was in the scream of the warrior, and a great torrent of unbelievable pain made him weak, helpless to evade the horizontal slash that opened his throat. Ena stood over the fallen Creek.

"I came as quickly as I could," Little Hawk said. "As soon as I had hidden the small ones in the forest."

The woman's eyes gleamed hawklike, full of pride and the excitement of battle. "You are truly your father's son, heir to Ghonkaba, Ja-gonh, and the great Renno."

She drew her knife, bent, and deftly sliced off the scalp of her last victim. And then she lifted the scalp to the skies and whooped a cry of victory. Little Hawk joined in, throwing his head back and dancing around the body of his fallen enemy. Then he pulled his own knife and, wondering where to start, began to saw and slash at the scalp of his victim. He looked up, startled, when Renna, having come to stand behind a tree, remarked, "I think you're doing it wrong. Aunt Ena did it so easily."

"So?" Little Hawk said, trying to start a cut with his knife.

"I believe you begin at the front," Renna said.

"Perhaps you will come and show me how," Little Hawk said.

"Ugh, no thank you," Renna responded.

Ena, two scalps in hand, came to stand and watch. "Start at the front," she suggested.

"I told you," Renna said.

"Where are the twins?" Ena asked Renna.

"Here," the two-year-old twins piped as one.

"You were told to join the others," Ena said.

"We hid," Renna said. "We knew you and Little Hawk could handle just three Creek."

Now the warriors guarding the main body, having been alerted by the whoops of triumph, were arriving on the run, only to stop short and look at the bodies. Little Hawk had managed to separate at least most of the scalp from his victim's skull. He held it high.

"Let it be noted," Ena said, "that on this day the son of the sachem Renno has counted coup, has conquered his first enemy, and has taken his first scalp in proof."

Chapter XI

Never had Renno stayed so long in a city. Never had he lived so long in a fine house. During his stay in Philadelphia he learned more about the operations of the new government of the United States than he really cared to know. He saw the venality of men and the influence of personal ego on matters of vital importance not only to the United States but to the Indian. As the weeks passed and still George Washington asked him to stay, Renno seemed to feel a slow but steady stifling of his spirit. Only An-da's presence made it bearable.

Philadelphia insiders began to think of Renno as a member of a shadow cabinet—a man who had the President's ear but did not abuse that position; a man who, it was said, was often alone with Washington in the President's study after hours.

Renno did not concern himself with the day-to-day disputes of government, the petty rivalries among the thirteen states or the disputes of Congress, although he was aware that significant events were taking place. The war along the western frontier was, he well knew, but one aspect of national crisis. Congress had voted, for example, to admit Kentucky as a state, and James Wilkinson had been given the rank of general. Furthermore, Congress and the press harbored open sentiment against the western settlers. Many in the east said that it was not proper to have to pay higher taxes to benefit the land companies, which grabbed property at every opportunity, and the Indian haters who were "a violent and unjust race in many respects, unrestrained by law and consideration of public policy."

For lack of might, the federal establishment, long intent on appeasing the western settlers lest they cast their lot with Spain or England, now tried to appease the Ohio Indians.

One of the reasons for Washington's request that Renno remain in Philadelphia became evident when some fifty elders of the Iroquois came to that city. Among them was Cornplanter, a sachem who had Renno's respect, and the two men quickly found the opportunity to separate themselves from the others for a private discussion.

"I fear that many of our delegates have come merely to see the sights," Cornplanter began, "to eat and drink their fill, to receive presents, and to display their oratory in conference."

"But not you, Sachem," Renno said.

"You know that I have long counseled against war," Cornplanter said. "Today the tribes of the Ohio bask in victory, but you and I know that there is a vast population of Americans. For the moment they are reluctant to fight. They seek to avoid further war by offering terms—"

"Which," Renno said, "Little Turtle and the other war chiefs are not likely to accept."

"True," Cornplanter agreed. His face was impassive,

but there was humor in his tone. "Of course, we do not doubt the Americans' sincerity when they pledge to make no further territorial demands on Indians lands."

Renno was silent for a moment. "Then you, too, Sachem, realize that our traditional way of life cannot go on forever."

Cornplanter looked away, and his eyes misted.

The Iroquois delegates, well fed and carrying many gifts, returned to their homes, leaving behind a promise to remain neutral; and then came the Mohawk Joseph Brant, who had not accompanied the Iroquois, lest, some felt, his treatment be not as lavish as he felt he deserved . . . which was nothing less than the welcome that would have been accorded to a European chief of state.

"How soon people forget," Washington grumbled to Renno on the night before he was to meet Brant. "Only a few years past this man was called a bloodthirsty, inhuman monster. He called himself Thayendanegea. Now he is Captain Brant of the British army and king of the Mohawk."

Washington arranged a private meeting between Renno and Brant, who appeared in traditional Mohawk dress. He was resplendent in feathered headdress, necklaces, flowing garments, wampum belt, and armbands that gathered the loose sleeves of his shirt above the elbow. Renno was wearing the day clothes of a white man, for he felt no need to impress his Indianness on Brant.

"Has the sachem of the Seneca become a white man?" Brant asked as an opener to the conversation.

Renno laughed. "No more than Thayendanegea when he visits England."

Brant, too, laughed, easing the tension. "I know of you, Sachem. You, too, had certain English ties once."

"And my great-grandfather once astounded the English court with feats of arms." Renno straightened, and his face became serious. "But we are not here to remember the past, Thayendanegea, however pleasant."

"I have already heard the words of the president of the United States," Brant said. "What does Renno of the Seneca wish to add?"

"I cannot hope to influence a man who has led his people bravely in war, a man who has his own reasons for his thinking and for his position in this situation. I say only that centuries of war have not benefited the Indian. This war, if continued, will be the greatest disaster to befall the Indian."

Brant nodded. "*If* George Washington is able to mobilize the people of the various states behind him. *If* England does not take an active part in the war."

Renno was silent.

Soon Brant spoke again. "My friend, these whites think that anything can be purchased with gold. I have been offered twice the amount that I receive from the English"—he spread his hands—"for services rendered. I have been offered the equivalent of twenty thousand English pounds if I arrange a peace with the tribes of the Ohio." He chuckled. "Perhaps I will not turn down the money; I have my people to consider. But these whites overestimate my influence, as you well know."

"When Thayendanegea speaks, others listen," Renno said.

"As they listen to Renno of the Seneca," Brant responded. "We make our mistakes, do we not? I have made mine. My biggest mistake was in trusting the words of any white man. Looking back, I feel that we should have listened to the sachem of my own nation who took it upon himself to promise the delegates from the Continental Congress that the League of the Ho-de-no-sau-nee would not take sides in the White Man's War. But we did not pay attention to his example. You chose to fight at the side of the continentals, while I cast my lot with the British. What have either of us gained?"

Renno leaned forward, and his blue eyes gleamed with an intense light. "We must learn the rules of the white man's game, Thayendanegea. We must learn to play it with a skill equal to his."

"To become white men, Sachem?"

"No. But to strike a balance or gradually cease to exist."

"Both are the same," Brant said. "There are still

places in Canada where we can continue to observe our traditions and continue to live by the hunt." He laughed suddenly. "Fortunately the white man does not like the cold of the Canadian winters; thus the settlement of that area does not proceed as quickly as that of more gentle climes."

"That is nothing more than postponement of the inevitable," Renno pointed out.

Brand nodded solemnly. "But before it comes to an end there, I will have long since joined my fathers in the Place Across the River."

"I assume," Renno said, "that you stated such intentions to Washington?"

Brant smiled. "I am a true Indian, and true Indians cry 'Peace, peace,' while secretly praising the victories we have enjoyed in the northwest. Have I given you the impression that my mind is made up about this affair? If so, you misunderstand." But he was smiling.

Thayendanegea had had, Renno believed, his fill of war. He would continue to use his reputation and his influence to gain support and money for his tribe, but the Mohawk would not march the warpath with the tribes of the Ohio. That knowledge was sufficient for Renno. He would do nothing and say nothing to damage Brant's chance of continued bribes from both the British and the Americans.

"Farewell, my friend." Brant rose. "I don't think we will meet again." They exchanged the Iroquoian arm clasp, and his hand tightening, the Mohawk said, "They all will gather at the forks of the Auglaize and the Maumee at the time of the council of the harvest moon—the elders of the Ohio tribes, the southern tribes, the Canadian tribes, *all* of the nations gathering—but I will not be there."

"For this information, I thank you," Renno told him.

"Walk with the manitous," Brant said.

"In order to reach the forks of the Auglaize and the Maumee in time," Renno informed Washington, "I must leave within the week."

"There are facts you should know," Washington said.

"Two peace envoys have been killed. The man McGillivray, who fancies himself to be king of the Creek, has signed a treaty with Governor Carondelet in New Orleans on the promise of enough arms and supplies not only to harass the frontier but to regain lost lands."

Renno nodded.

"One result of this is favorable," Washington added. "There is no longer any danger of the western settlers going to Spain for alliance. It is more evident than ever, though, that a very clear understanding exists between the courts of London and Madrid—an understanding calculated to check the rapid increase, extension, and consequence of the United States. The British have proposed to make the Northwest Territory a neutral area, with the Indian boundaries guaranteed by both England and the United States. Of course, we cannot accept this. I must warn you that war with England is a very real possibility, even though England is preoccupied with France. Mr. Jefferson, who has spent considerable time among the French and English, tells me that war is a certainty between those two countries."

Renno was grateful that Washington had shared that information. He had been warned that to be on the side of the United States might mean, in the worst of futures, being a defeated tribe under the dominion of the British; however, Ghonkaba had taken that risk, and such a possibility would not affect Renno's convictions.

"At this time, my friend," Washington went on, "I am unable to inform you of the name of the man who will be commanding the army in the Northwest Territory. I would like to see my fellow Virginian, Light Horse Harry Lee, in the position, but he is junior to many other officers. After you have attended this great Indian conference, please journey back to Pittsburgh. I'm sure that the military situation will be better in hand by then. When a new commander is appointed, he will have a letter from me explaining your position and qualifications, with my firm recommendation that he listen to you closely."

*   *   *

Rather than submitting to the rough-riding coaches, Renno and An-da opted to ride on strong, well-trained horses on loan from the army for the trip across Pennsylvania to the west. Left behind was the fine clothing that they had worn while they were guests in the presidential mansion. Both now wore buckskins. Renno's one concession to being still in the United States was to refrain from donning his paints; but as the miles were paced off and the larger towns left behind, the white Indian knew a feeling of relief and freedom. He looked forward to leaving the white man's land completely at Pittsburgh, and An-da, too, seemed to blossom even though the days were long and hard.

Compared to Philadelphia and the other, older towns of Pennsylvania, Pittsburgh seemed a poor place, a scanty collection of hovels, dirt streets—that were either quagmires or dust pits, depending upon the weather—and a few unpainted-board storefronts. Ubiquitous hogs and chickens roamed freely, and the ladies of the night, who made up a disproportionate percentage of the local female population, enjoyed a steady business with river men and the hardy types who still penetrated beyond the Ohio to hunt, gather furs, and trade with the Indians.

Neither Renno nor An-da was interested in lingering in the frontier town. A flatboat was due to head downriver to Marietta and Cincinnati, so Renno left the army horses with the small garrison of regulars at Pittsburgh, and he and An-da took passage on the flatboat westward to the big bend of the Ohio. They disembarked at the point where the river turned sharply southward.

Around them the wilderness was teeming with life. All traces of white civilization seemed so remote as not to exist, and Renno felt his blood surge with joy. All his senses became more acute. Ahead of them lay two hundred miles of unmapped forest and rivers never charted by the white man. But there was also danger: members of half a score of Indian nations, all of whom would be more than happy to slay a friend of the white man. Renno and An-da alternated running and walking, eager to put even the river, that last link with the United States, behind them. When they rested to roast and eat a young deer

Renno had hunted, tempting aromas wafted out from their small clearing. This meal marked the final transition from the life they had led for months among the whites back to something that, to them, resembled paradise.

The manitous smiled upon them in many ways: with good weather, clear trails made by game animals, and an absence of hostile encounters. War parties were operating on the frontier and along the rivers, but it was as if the manitous had given Renno and his woman that vast, trackless forest for their own Eden. Their schedule and steady pace allowed them to enjoy a more leisurely journey than their trek north had been. There was time for swimming in the clear streams and beaver lakes, time to sit atop a hill, arms entwined, and watch a sunset, and to speak of home. They talked about Renno's children and the children that he and An-da would have together. It was, in short, a honeymoon. And in those blissful weeks the girl-woman who was now all woman wrapped herself around Renno's heart with her obvious adoration, her cheerfulness, and her limitless youthful vitality.

In Renno's heart there was only An-da, although, in his mind, memories of Emily and Beth existed. His love for An-da managed to relegate both women to the past, where they belonged. There were no more bittersweet recollections of the time he had spent in the wilderness with Beth. And although Emily, the mother of his children, would never lose her place in his esteem, An-da eased the last, lingering remnants of the pain of Emily's loss.

The leaves had begun to turn when Renno and An-da struck the Maumee River south of the western end of Lake Erie. The twosome encountered others who were journeying toward the great council, some of whom traveled for months to attend. On the final days of the trek they saw representatives from more Indian nations than had ever been gathered together before, including a contingent from as far away as the Floridas. The white Indian and his bride built a temporary shelter on the banks of the river, joining a small village composed of travelers.

Renno sought out representatives of the Iroquois. All
of the Six Nations were represented, and Cornplanter was
among them. The Seneca sachem was pleased to learn that
the Iroquois were in agreement: They would advise peace.
Renno became a part of that group, sitting with them
when the great conclave began and listening to the oratory
of men from scores of tribes.

Little Turtle saw Renno among the Iroquois and
singled him out, for he remembered Renno from their
encounter years before. They spoke only in generalities,
exchanging wishes for health and long life. Both would
have their say in council. One face, for which Renno was
constantly searching, did not appear—the scarred visage
of Hodano; but for reasons Renno could not explain, he
felt that the evil shaman must be near.

One after the other the orators spoke of war—of a
great Indian confederation linking north and south and
pushing back the white man. When it was time for the
Iroquois leaders to speak, Cornplanter set the tone.

"Brothers," he began, "the League of the Ho-de-no-
sau-nee has experienced victory as well as defeat in our
many wars with the whites. Hear me. There are those
among you who have murdered the envoys who came to
you from the United States to talk of peace, and yet the
great sachem in Philadelphia would listen to you if you
cared to talk of peace, not of war."

Hoots of derision began to sound from the assembly.

Cornplanter maintained his dignity. "Still you accept
the counsel of fools who care not how many warriors die,
who either ignore or are ignorant of the vast numbers of
the white man."

The loud taunts almost drowned out Cornplanter's
rich, deep voice.

"Remember the words of one who has fought,"
Cornplanter urged. "You think that the white man is
craven. You think that he does not want to fight, that he
will continue to try to buy you into peace and allow your
raids on his women and children to go unavenged. It is not
so! He will rise up, and his vast riches and his sea of
soldiers will bear you down by sheer weight of numbers—"

Cornplanter could speak no more. He stood silent, his head high, as the jeers rose to a roar. And each Iroquois speaker, following Cornplanter's example to advise peace, received the same treatment.

Little Turtle rose after the last Iroquois had given up his attempt to shout over the rebukes of the war advocates. "There is one who has not spoken. Renno of the Seneca, how say you?"

Renno, simmering over the rude treatment given his fellow Iroquois, rose and let his steely blue eyes play over the seated delegates for long moments, seeking out individual faces, marking them, causing more than one warrior to shift his eyes from his burning intensity. When he spoke, his voice was purposely low, and those at the rear had to strain to hear.

"There was a time," he began, "when your inexcusable rudeness toward these brave warriors of the Six Nations would have been silenced with the blade."

A mass intake of breath was followed by a stirring among the delegates.

"I will not advise you to avoid blood in this council of brothers, for you are men, and you know your own hearts. I say only that I have heard reason from men like my brother Cornplanter. As for me and mine, we walk the path of peace."

He stood silently, looking at the delegates from many tribes, as if daring any one of them to challenge him; and then he strode away. At his temporary shelter he told An-da to prepare to travel.

For a few days Renno pushed the pace, but An-da matched him step for step. He was constantly on the alert, especially for pursuit on their back trail. When, at last, he felt that it was possible to set a more leisurely pace, he began to enjoy again being alone with the woman he loved. But throughout their travels the white Indian felt a twinge of urgency because he knew that war was inevitable.

"I feared for you when you defied all of them," An-da said one evening when they had halted their march early to bathe in a cool, clear lake. "But then, you are Renno."

"I grieve for them," he replied frankly. "There was much truth in many of the things they said."

"Why is it that the white man thinks that money is the answer to everything?" An-da asked. "It's true, isn't it, when the delegates say that money is of no value, that the Indian provides for his women and children from the very land that the white man wants to buy?"

"It is true. To make it otherwise would require vast changes."

"Would it not be sensible, then, as I heard it suggested by Little Turtle, that the United States take the vast sums of money they offer the Indian for his land and give it instead to the settlers, who are so poor that they must brave the dangers of this northwestern frontier of war and death? If they did that, the settlers could live in peace and comfort in their own lands."

"But if things were so simple," Renno said, "then it would be necessary to make the same argument to the British and to the Spanish, who also want the land."

"I will never understand," An-da said, cutting slices of steaming venison for both and tearing into her portion hungrily.

Renno smiled as he watched her eat. "My little one is hungry."

For a moment An-da was silent, and then, watching him closely for his reaction she said, "Perhaps that is because I eat for two."

Renno gasped. "Is it true?"

She laughed delightedly and nodded.

He went to her and placed his hand on her flat stomach. "You are certain?"

"I last bled not long after we left the Ohio," she answered.

He held her, grinning, and then his face became serious. "We will turn south. I will take you home."

"You'll do no such thing."

"An-da, I have spoken," he said sternly.

She nuzzled her face into his neck, and her soft lips brushed his skin as she said, "I hear only the rustling of leaves in the wind. Don't ever ask me to live without you, for I would shrivel and die of my loneliness."

A feeling of foreboding came to Renno. A ripple of coldness went up his back, and he looked around hurriedly. The autumn evening held no threat. But for a moment he had found himself trying to imagine life without this little one, this Sweet Day, and the momentary desolation in his spirit was more than he could bear. He put that feeling away, lost it, and destroyed it by taking her into his arms.

For as long as George Washington dared, he proposed that his fellow Virginian Light Horse Harry Lee be appointed to replace Arthur St. Clair in command of the Army of the United States. But too many powerful men opposed Lee's appointment because of his lack of seniority. Northern senators and congressmen felt resentment toward all aristocrats from Virginia—except Washington and possibly Jefferson. Many meetings were held in the presidential mansion, and many nominees were advanced. When Washington first proposed Anthony Wayne as a possibility, his three principal advisers—Jefferson, Hamilton, and Henry Knox—maintained a polite silence until the discussion passed on to the name of another candidate.

It was, perhaps, with some desperation that Washington again put forward the name of Anthony Wayne. St. Clair had come back to the east, demanding a court of inquiry to clear his sullied reputation, and now the United States was represented in the west by General James Wilkinson. The President did not like the thought of having Wilkinson as senior military officer in the west; he was definitely in the pay of Spain and, possibly, of the British.

Jefferson, reluctant to speak ill of any man, said, "I have heard that Wayne's health is poor."

Hamilton added, "He's far too impetuous. A cool head will be needed for this task."

The men were at a stalemate, so the conversation turned to Jefferson's proposal that a fleet of vessels be built to command the waters of Lake Erie.

"Thomas," Hamilton said, "I know of no surer way to provoke war with England." He turned to Washington. "Have you considered, sir, my proposal to build a line of forts all along the frontier to shield it from attack?"

Washington, perhaps more than any man alive, knew the futility of trying to maintain a purely defensive position. "Mr. Hamilton, had I enforted myself during the War for Independence, we would still be singing 'God Save the King.' Perhaps we should return to the matter of most immediate importance. I know that people call him Mad Anthony."

Jefferson stiffened.

"He was mad, I suppose, at Stony Point on the Hudson in 'seventy-nine, but he was successful in taking the position, gentlemen." Washington mused for a moment, remembering. "Only two men thought it was possible to take that British stonghold," he went on. "One was myself, the other Anthony Wayne. Do you know what he told me when I asked him if he could do the job? He said, 'If you plan it, General, I will storm hell.'"

"Mr. President," Henry Knox responded, "we all know that Wayne was a capable commander during the war."

"Next to General Green, the best commander I had," Washington said.

"But he's an aging man," Knox pointed out. "As it has been said, his health is poor."

"He has failed at everything he has tried since the war," Jefferson said. "I am told that he is horrendously in debt, with creditors hounding him constantly."

"Even his election to one of the Georgia seats in Congress is tainted," Hamilton said. "There is an ongoing battle about it, with his opponent in the election claiming unfair—if not criminal—election tampering."

Washington, having abandoned his wish to have Lee named commander, was remembering more about the harsh but often glorious years of battle. Wayne had come to his attention early in the war, when General Benedict Arnold's invasion of Canada failed. It had seemed that Arnold's retreating army would be cut up and destroyed.

Wayne, then a young regimental commander, had marched north in sharp order to aid Arnold in his retreat. After Arnold's treachery became known, it had been Wayne who took his men on forced march to safeguard West Point, preventing its being handed over to the British. He had fought well, with one star on his shoulder, at Brandywine, and at Germantown; and he had done a sterling job against the British-backed Creek after being dispatched to Georgia.

The President sighed, then spoke: "Well? No one has yet accused Wayne of being overly fond of the bottle."

Knox laughed. "If so, General, he wouldn't be the first military man with that failing."

"Gentlemen, I shall propose General Anthony Wayne to the Senate to be appointed major general in command of all American armies." He twitched his lips without opening them. "All of our great and glorious and well-armed armies."

Henry Knox nodded. "He did have a fine record in the war. Perhaps, in spite of his obvious faults, Wayne is the man of the hour."

"Heaven help us," Jefferson muttered. "You're going to have a devil of a time getting him through the Senate, Mr. President."

A devil of a time it was, and Washington had to use all of his considerable influence to overcome the many objections; but one last obstacle was removed when the Congress ruled that yes, Wayne had won the Georgia elections through illegal dealing, but his campaign manager had acted without Wayne's knowledge.

Washington himself handed Mad Anthony Wayne his commission as "major general and of course commanding officer of the troops in the service of the United States."

Meanwhile, Congress had passed "an act for making further and more effectual provision for the protection of the frontiers of the United States." The new army would consist of four regiments of infantry, dragoons, and artillery, and a suitable staff of officers. The force would be called the Legion of the United States. Each regiment would be a sublegion. On paper it was an impressive force.

The forty-seven-year-old man who inherited this paper army had not been treated kindly by the fates since his successes during the war for independence. Old war wounds, in combination with a persistent and recurring fever that he had contracted in the swamps of Georgia, had ravaged a once impressive constitution. Moreover, his left leg often swelled alarmingly—a condition for which the doctors could do nothing but say "gout," and shrug helplessly.

Estranged from his family and a failure in business and politics, Wayne seized upon this command as a godsend and his last opportunity for redemption; and inside his ravaged, overweight body his spirit flared up with new vigor. He knew himself. He knew that he was in his proper element when it was time to form and then execute a plan of battle. He had supreme confidence in his ability as a military commander, as evidenced by his instantaneous acceptance of Washington's offer.

He was in great pain as he mounted for the ride across Pennsylvania to Pittsburgh, and in more pain when he dismounted on a dusty Pittsburgh street and came face-to-face with the daunting task. But no aching war wound, no amount of feverish vomiting, and no swollen leg would keep him from his moment of redemption.

Only a few of St. Clair's veterans were left, gathered into the wilderness forts along the Ohio. They were poorly armed, often hungry, and almost never paid. Desertion was so common that it was standard procedure to pay frontiersmen a bounty of forty dollars to track a fleeing man through the wilderness and bring him back, dead or alive. Army conditions were so terrible that the few new recruits came from one of four places: prison, hospital, poorhouse, or gutter. And the ghosts of the men who had died with Harmar and St. Clair haunted the frontier, making everyone skeptical of this new army and its new general.

For some time Wayne stood on his swollen, aching

leg, gazing across the river and thinking of the enemy—a
vast army of strong, young warriors who were better
armed than any Indian force in history. When he turned
away and limped about his duties, he found a few sad-
looking recruits, a handful of the sorriest-looking soldiers
he had ever seen. The American army in the height of
winter at Valley Forge had looked more soldierly than
these.

Wayne had orders not to initiate hostilities while
peace overtures were being made to the Ohio Indians. It
was, he felt, laughable, for the only hostility of which
these men were capable was an occasional fist- or knife
fight in one of Pittsburgh's taverns.

The few officers were not much better than the men.
Wayne determined quickly that the greatest challenge of
his life lay before him, and immediately he set about
putting a stop to the drinking, the scandals among the
wives of regular-army sergeants, the gambling, and even
occasional duels. He moved his command away from the
temptations of Pittsburgh and built a fortified camp, which
he named Legionville, twenty miles downriver.

His detailed orders from Secretary of War Henry
Knox included a warning: "Let it therefore be again, and
for the last time, impressed deeply upon your mind, that
as little as possible is to be hazarded and that a defeat at
the present time, and under present circumstances, would
be pernicious in the highest degree to the interests of our
country."

Defeat was not even a consideration to Wayne. He
took extreme precautions against surprise attack, and he
seized his slowly growing army in an iron fist, determined
to teach some soldiering. He based his entire strategy on
two elements: never to be surprised by the enemy and to
take any battle with the Indian to close quarters as quickly
as possible, for, like many who had fought Indians, he
knew that the red man hated the bayonet more than any
other weapon.

Throughout the winter Hodano had been filled with
fury. He had seen golden opportunity evaporate because

of the traditional greed and fecklessness of the Indian nations. He had exhorted them to follow up the destruction of St. Clair's army with concentrated and powerful raids on white outposts such as Marietta and Pittsburgh. Had they listened to him, there would now be no whites west of the Ohio River.

To show his disgust, he had decided not to attend the conclave on the Maumee, and this decision became a gnawing, festering lesion in his spirit when he heard that his archenemy, Renno, had been there. Thus he, too, had missed an opportunity. He had been so involved in his fury over the inaction of the tribes that he had failed to sense it when his enemy had passed, with only a woman at his side, through the northwest to and from the council on the Maumee.

But now, once again, with the coming of spring, the war dances were filling the forests with chants and the sound of drums, and the warriors were taking white scalps. He sent his minion Tor-yo-ne to visit the various tribes and to report back to him. At each opportunity Tor-yo-ne spoke the urgent words of war that his master had put into his mouth: "Now! Now!" was Hodano's message. "Now, before the whites can raise another army."

To Renno's pleasure, An-da's stomach had begun to swell as they neared the Ohio River. Her pregnancy did not slow their travel. If anything, she seemed to be stronger, and Renno was continually amused by her appetite. He teased her, telling her that no game animal would be safe with her around, and she bantered back, telling him that if she bore a son, he would be a great warrior, a great sachem, and a fine eater.

During the last leg of the trip, Renno received word that the new commander of the army had established his base below Pittsburgh. The sachem and his woman took to the river on a flatboat being poled upstream.

Renno was not impressed when he saw the new rawness of Legionville. The only sturdy building was the log fort. Around it, in neat rows, were army tents, and a few hastily constructed log cabins sat on the outskirts.

The sachem's first concern was for suitable lodging for An-da. He asked for Roy Johnson and once again clasped arms with the man who had been his father-by-marriage and always a firm friend. Roy had built himself a cabin, more sturdy than most, well chinked against the winter winds that would come, he predicted grimly, before *this* army was ready to march. He welcomed An-da and Renno to share the cabin with him.

"Maybe, you can come up with something halfway edible," he told An-da jokingly. "The army cooks and I sure can't."

They enjoyed a good evening of comparing notes. Roy listened with interest to Renno's account of the journey to the conclave the autumn before and grinned when An-da interrupted to tell how Renno had dared the great gathering to hoot at him as it had done to the other Iroquois. And then Renno inquired about the new army commander.

"You'll meet him tomorrow," Roy replied. "He looks like he's on his last legs, but don't let his appearance fool you. He's a fire-eater. He's a good man, and if the government will give him the tools, he'll get the job done."

"He must be a good man if Washington chose him," Renno said.

"Only one fly in the ointment," Roy said. "His second in command is none other than General James Wilkinson, of Kentucky."

Chapter XII

Anthony Wayne's linen was as stiff and white as that of any staff officer fresh from his toilet in Philadelphia. His great, double-breasted coat was spotless, all buttons gleaming, the gold braid at his shoulder boards looking as if each tassel had been individually combed. He was a man who hated long hair, and one of his first demands for the new army—the legion—had been the hiring of a barber for each company. And so, his own hair well trimmed and unpowdered, he stood proudly erect when Roy and Renno entered his crude but tidy office at Legionville.

As Roy had forewarned, Wayne looked to be a very unhealthy man, carrying too much weight, his face seeming red and mottled, but in his eyes was a look that held Renno's. There was, Renno felt, a real man behind those eyes.

Wayne stepped forward, favoring one leg, and extended his hand. "Sachem, I have heard much of you."

"And I of you, General," Renno responded.

"Not too long ago, down in Georgia, we heard about a spirited little war involving the Spanish-led Chickasaw and a Seneca chief who turned the Spanish guns back on their owners." He laughed as he motioned both Roy and Renno to chairs. "That sounds like something I might have accomplished back in my salad days."

Wayne limped to his chair behind a plank table that served him as a desk and lowered himself with a grimace. "You come to me with some high recommendations, young man," he continued, "but there is one thing that troubles me." He fixed his eyes on Renno's, and his voice was firm. "Your commission from the President says that you are responsible only to him and not to be under orders from, and I quote, 'any military officer.'"

Renno nodded.

"That simply won't do," Wayne said. "I will not have a chief of scouts who can pick and choose his actions at his own whim. I have, therefore, drafted a letter to the President telling him that I must reluctantly deprive myself of your services."

"I understand," Renno said, standing, feeling a mixture of anger and a growing joy. So easily was he relieved of his responsibility, and not as a result of his own request. Now he and An-da could go home.

"Now hold on a minute, General," Roy put in. "I think you're making a big mistake here." He put his hand on Renno's shoulder. "Renno, I, too, can see the general's point of view." He was speaking for Wayne's ear as much as for Renno's. "You and I know that President Washington wrote that into his letter to protect you against men as stupid as a certain general we both know who wouldn't listen to either one of us and consequently got a lot of men killed. General Wayne, here, doesn't realize how Washington feels about you, so maybe you ought to give him a chance to explain his problems a bit further."

"I have said that I am reluctant to lose so valuable a scout," Wayne reiterated.

Now Roy addressed Anthony Wayne. "Renno told St. Clair that he never entered into a battle unless he felt there was some chance of winning. General, Renno and I both have seen a lot of incompetent officers—American and British—and Renno doesn't know you."

"Is he, then, to be my judge?" Wayne asked, his face darkening. He sighed. "On the other hand, gentlemen, I, too, have seen my share of incompetent commanders. My position is this: I simply cannot have a chief of scouts on whom I can't depend in time of need. You two were correct in advising St. Clair not to march against Little Turtle. But I intend to be the man who makes the decision when this army is to march—not a committee of politicians in Philadelphia. This army will not march until it is ready, until I am certain that no force that the Indian can put against us will result in our defeat."

Renno's hope of going home was fading rapidly.

"The President has advised me to listen to you, Sachem," Wayne went on. "That I am willing to do, for I agree that you are in a unique position to advise me on Indian ways—although I've had some little experience there myself, with the Creek. But a chief of scouts will not make decisions of strategic importance in this legion, whether they have to do with his own actions or the actions of myself or my men."

Renno sat down. Roy, grinning, followed suit.

"I have no desire to command this army," Renno assured the general. "The uniform of an officer is too confining."

Wayne leaned back and laughed. "I think we can work together. Hell's bells, if I can keep men like Colonel Johnson here, who's half-horse and half-grizzly, under control, I just might be able to keep one Indian scout from taking over my command." He wiped his face with a bandanna and shifted in his chair.

Renno was in the process of learning that Anthony

Wayne was a prolific user of profanity and that he was constantly in discomfort and often pain.

"But if your main purpose here is to be a spy for George Washington, I will soon know," Wayne said. "And that, too, I will not tolerate."

For some time, Renno was tempted to walk out of Wayne's office to commence the journey homeward. Perhaps, he decided, he was restrained by the look of confidence in Wayne's eyes. Or perhaps it was the way Wayne roared in laughter. Then, perhaps it was simply that he knew, deep down, that he had to be a part of the history-altering events that were to come.

Wayne concluded their first meeting by saying, "Gentlemen, I'm going to depend on you to be my eyes and ears while I build an army. Do you have any reservations about working under this chief of scouts, Colonel Johnson?"

"None," Roy said.

"Good. I don't care how you divide the responsibilities, just so you don't let a bunch of savages sneak up on this camp while I'm trying to turn the dregs of the nation into soldiers. If you need more men, get them. If you need equipment and supplies, you have access to all that we've got. Just don't be too damned wasteful, because Congress is tighter with money than a virgin with her favors. But I want a constant flow of information about Indian movements over this whole bedamned wilderness."

Renno nodded.

"Good, good," Wayne said, standing, shaking hands with both in dismissal.

"Well," Roy said as they walked toward his cabin, "that's a mighty big order."

Renno was thinking of El-i-chi. Where was he when he was needed? And he was wishing for perhaps half a dozen Seneca from his village in the south, warriors he could trust.

"I have about four scouts," Roy remarked. "Two Shawnee and two Miami."

"Are they to be trusted?" Renno asked.

Roy shrugged. "They take the money; they eat the food; they go when I tell them to go; and so far they have come back."

"We cannot, of course, cover the entire territory," Renno said.

"No," Roy agreed.

"When next we meet, we will tell General Wayne that we will provide a safe zone for him around the camp but that building a network of scouts to cover larger areas will take time."

In spite of the fact that Little Hawk had gained stature among the Seneca by taking his first scalp in a deadly battle, he was, after all, only a boy. He was a bit large for his eight years, much more coordinated than the other boys, and so independent that Toshabe often wondered what was to become of him.

"You must not roam the woods alone," she was constantly reminding him.

But Little Hawk recognized an iron-clad order when he heard it and could distinguish a wish from a command. Thus he knew that his grandmother only wished for him to act more like an ordinary boy, to play with his fellows, and if he went into the woods, to go in company with others.

There were times when he enjoyed being with other boys. On such occasions he never took advantage of his station as son of the sachem, bullied, or boasted of his superior prowess with bow and tomahawk. Instead he did his best to encourage the other young ones to practice the skills of warriorhood and, most of the time, hid his displeasure when the boys tired of drills that so closely resembled work and opted instead for play—whooping in chase of a chipmunk or dashing off to spend an afternoon swimming in the stream.

Quite often, however, Little Hawk merely slipped away to be alone in the forest depths. Here he practiced with his bow until his arms ached. His targets were inanimate, for he would not kill except for food or in defense. He left many gouges on the trunks of trees and saplings as he threw his tomahawk repeatedly until he could hit a target of inches from a distance of twenty paces. And he tracked, remembering the teachings of his father, following a wary deer until, in total silence, he found the animal grazing or resting in a dense thicket. The boy would also trail a hunting party that had passed by days before until he was certain of their direction.

Not wanting to cause his grandmother concern, he made a point of returning to the village before nightfall. At mealtime he would question Ha-ace about the habits of animals and men and listen respectfully as Toshabe taught again and again the traditions of the Seneca and the Iroquois.

Renna would ask, often, "When is our father coming home?"

"When he has accomplished that which he set out to do," Little Hawk would say. He missed his father, of course, and his uncle El-i-chi; but he would question neither the actions nor decisions of the two men he respected most in the world.

On one particularly beautiful day he left the village just before dawn, setting as his goal the top of a hill to the west. He practiced the warrior's pace, his young legs pumping easily.

At the top of the hill there was a splendid view from the outcrop of rocks. Miles away he could see the smoke of the cook fires in the village. To the west he saw the forest, mysterious, tempting. For the first time Little Hawk experienced the sensation that was so familiar to his father: the urge to run as fast as he could, to travel as much ground as his strength allowed, and to see what was there, far off to the west, behind that ridge and beyond the next.

He ate meat left over from Toshabe's dinner with a slab of cornbread, washed them down with water from a sparkling spring, and lay back to watch the antics of a squirrel that had become accustomed to his presence and was playing a game with himself—leaping to the trunk of a tree, whirling to spring back to the ground, there to dash around in a tight circle as if chasing his own tail. The sun was warm, and Little Hawk was pleasantly tired from his run. He closed his eyes.

A sound in the brush brought him to instant alertness. He seized his bow and readied an arrow. The sound came closer, and he heard a bleating cry that he did not recognize. He sought concealment behind a tree and watched as the brush parted, and a bear cub, not long from its mother's winter den, pushed into the little clearing.

A smile of pleasure lit up the boy's face. "Ho, totem of my clan," he whispered.

The cub nosed around, bleated once, found the crumbs of Little Hawk's cornbread, and sniffed them, its red tongue lapping out, searching.

Little Hawk eased from behind the tree. "Brother, you are hungry."

The cub reared onto its hind legs and looked around nervously, not yet having seen Little Hawk.

The boy took a careful step forward. "Here, Brother," he invited, removing a cube of cooked venison from his pouch and tossing it to the cub.

The cub turned, ran a few steps, then stopped. Its nose twitched, and it came back to gobble the meat.

Little Hawk sat cross-legged on the ground and tossed another small bit of meat. The cub was suspicious but, tantalized by the smell, moved to eat that morsel. The process became a game. Inch by inch Little Hawk lured the cub closer... closer... talking softly and calling the cub his brother, until he could smell the cub and almost touch it. He held out a cube of meat in his fingers.

"You will have to come and take it gently," he said.

The cub rocked back and forth in indecision, then made a sudden lunge and a snap of its teeth. Fortunately, Little Hawk had dropped the meat into the open mouth and jerked his hand away.

"I am not sacrificing my fingers to your appetite," the boy said, offering another piece of meat. "If you snap, I will not let you have it."

At last the cub learned to trust its benefactor enough to take a bit of meat from Little Hawk's fingers without snapping. The boy, pleased, reached for more meat but found that the pouch was empty. "Well, we will have to do something about that," he announced, standing.

The wary cub backed off.

Little Hawk walked a few paces to a rotting log, turned it, and found fat, white grubs underneath. The grubs satisfied the cub as well as the venison had, and for an hour Little Hawk scoured the hillside for rotting logs and grubs, with the cub tagging along, bleating piteously if the interval between grubs was too long.

The sun was sinking. It was past midday, time to start back for the village. "Brother," Little Hawk said, "I must leave you. Go and find your mother."

He set off. Once, he glanced over his shoulder to see the cub lumbering after him. The boy stopped and spoke severely. "Go. Go to your mother. Leave me."

The cub, startled by the loud words, turned into the brush. But when Little Hawk looked back again, the cub was following, a furry, fat butterball moving with a rolling motion.

"What am I to do with you?" he asked.

He assumed a pace that was faster than the warrior's jog and left the cub behind; then, winded, he slowed to a walk. Soon he heard the bleat of the cub behind him. It was, Little Hawk decided, quite a predicament. He rolled over a log and found grubs to placate the cub while he delved for a solution. Had the cub's mother met with some natural disaster? Had she been killed by some hunter who was not a member of the bear clan?

"Are you, too, alone?" he asked.

The cub bleated and came to sit down, with a fat plunk, beside Little Hawk, nosing his hand in search of food. "I can do nothing more for you."

In frustration for having created the situation, Little Hawk ran with the wind, hiding his trail in a stream for perhaps two hundred yards. As he came to within a half mile of the Seneca-Cherokee village, he looked to see no sign of the cub. He wanted to cry for the motherless animal, but a warrior did not weep. He settled into a trot and reached the village quickly, then went to Renno's longhouse to wash and change clothes before the evening meal.

Little Hawk joined Ha-ace, Toshabe, and Renna as the meal began. Ha-ace spoke of a report that had come from a group of warriors who had scouted far into the west. In talks with a Chickasaw hunting party, they had been told that the Creek were almost on a total war footing in the south and that the Chickasaw were being pressured to join the war against the whites.

"Our father will win this war, and then he will come home," Renna said.

Little Hawk waited patiently for his opportunity to tell of his interesting encounter with a motherless bear cub. When Ha-ace fell silent, the boy started to speak, but from outside a chorus of frantic barking from the village dogs stole everyone's attention. The barking came nearer, then a yelp of canine pain. Ha-ace rose and started toward the door but halted in amazement when a bear cub waddled in, walked past him with total unconcern, and plopped down beside Little Hawk. He bleated to be fed.

"What in the name of the manitous ... ?" Toshabe gasped, backing away.

Little Hawk grinned guiltily. "I was just going to tell you."

"Now what have you done?" Toshabe demanded.

"I did nothing. I only fed a motherless cub," Little Hawk replied.

The dogs' barking was a constant din. Ha-ace stepped to the door, waved his arms, and yelled. Then he picked up a handful of loose stones from beside the doorway and threw it. His reward was a yelp of pain. The barking dogs retreated.

"Well," Toshabe said, "totem of our clan or not, motherless or otherwise, this is no place for a bear cub. You will take him back into the woods, now."

"As you say," Little Hawk agreed meekly. He gathered food, coaxed the cub out with tidbits, and led it down the street toward the woods. The dogs barked but kept a respectful distance. Indian dogs were not bred for hunting or fighting. Occasionally, one would be eaten if other food was scarce, but usually they served only as noisemakers, yipping at the slightest movement, as scrap eaters, and as playmates for the young.

Little Hawk had coaxed the cub to the edge of the village and was wondering how to convince it to stay away, when he froze at the sound of an angry, roaring growl. He whirled to see a huge bear coming at him, with what seemed to be the speed of a racing deer. *"Aiiiiii,"* he whispered. The cub had not been motherless, after all.

Little Hawk's first impulse was to run back to his own house; this was a very big and a very angry bear, and he was only a boy.

His feet had wings. He ran full speed, arms pumping, and he could hear the bleating of the cub behind him all the way.

"Go to your mother!" he yelled.

The dogs were barking in panic now as two bears, one of them huge, thumped down the spaces between houses. A few curious faces were poked out from doorways only to be withdrawn hurriedly as a female bear making bloodcurdling sounds thundered past.

"Ha-ace!" Little Hawk was screaming.

A dog, yelping in excitement, ran in front of Little Hawk. The boy sprang to jump over the canine, but the dog leaped at the same time, and they rolled, entangled, in the dust. The cub caught up and bleated. The bear sow was so near that Little Hawk could see the huge teeth bared. He jumped up yelling, *"Ha-ace!"*

Ha-ace came charging out of the longhouse, tomahawk in hand, elbow bent for action. Behind him, Toshabe peered out and saw her grandson leading a parade of bears. She voiced an angry oath—quite unlike her.

With the cub on his heels and the mother only feet behind, Little Hawk dove for the longhouse door, contacted Toshabe's legs, and sent her tumbling. He rolled and made frantic shooing motions at the cub, which was beside him on the floor.

And then, with a roar of outrage, the bear sow entered, knocking down one doorpost as she swung in

through the opening. She reared to fill the longhouse with
angry sound.

"A *big* one," Renna called out from her bed. She was
kneeling and clapping her hands. Toshabe scrambled on
her hands and knees and leaped into bed with Renna.
Ha-ace, yelling and waving his tomahawk, entered behind
the bear, which crashed into a support pole, causing a
section of the longhouse roof to collapse atop her. She
batted the debris aside easily. Little Hawk was crawling
just ahead of the bear's advance.

"Brother," he squeaked. "Brother, I meant you no
harm."

"She's a sister," Renna yelled. "She's a mama."

"Sister," Little Hawk croaked.

The cub started toward Renna, and the sow landed a
blow with her front paw that would have stunned an adult
man. The cub bleated. Ha-ace was shouting, trying to
draw the bear away from Little Hawk. Just then a dog
entered the house, barking hoarsely. The bear turned,
roared, and with a rolling charge smashed through the
rear wall of the longhouse, leaving a gaping hole. The cub,
bleating, followed her. The barking of the dogs faded as
they chased the bears.

A silence came to the longhouse. Toshabe was examining flowering bruises on her legs.

"My father talks to bears, and so does my brother,"
Renna announced proudly.

"Your *brother*," Toshabe said, menace in her voice.
"Your brother!"

Ha-ace still had his tomahawk raised as he looked
around, stunned. His longhouse was a shambles. Cook
pots littered the floor. The evening meal had been spilled
and scattered. A great patch of sky was visible through the
fallen roof, and an evening breeze came in through the
back of the house where the bear had exited.

Little Hawk sat on the floor, legs crossed, sneaking a
wary look at Toshabe. "I am sorry if I hurt you, Grandmother."

Toshabe tried to speak, but only odd sounds came.

She closed her mouth and fought to regain her dignity as she stood, brushing her skirt.

"We can sleep in my father's longhouse tonight," Little Hawk suggested.

"Well," Ha-ace said, "we will not lack for work around here."

Toshabe was nonplussed. Her shin hurt. Her pride was damaged, for she had scrambled, panicked, before the bear on hands and knees. "We will sleep in Renno's longhouse tonight and until the work has been done," she declared.

Little Hawk breathed a sigh of relief at her calm tone.

"And with the morning," Toshabe continued, pointing at Little Hawk, "this one who brings 'motherless' bear cubs into my house—"

"He didn't bring the cub, really," Renna said, coming to Little Hawk's defense. "The cub followed him, Grandmother."

"When I want your opinion, young one, I will ask for it," Toshabe said. "This one who talks with bears, who feeds 'motherless' bear cubs, will clean up this house, cut the material for repairing the damage, and fix it."

"I think that's only fair," Little Hawk agreed.

Toshabe's eyes flared, then softened. "Yes, it is fair."

Little Hawk, eager to atone, was hard at work shortly after sunrise. He carried the debris of the fallen roof outside and started a fire to burn it. Dogs had sneaked into the house during the night, so there wasn't much of the evening meal to clean up. He replaced fallen items on their pegs, swept the floor with a broom made of twigs, and, the place tidied, decided that five saplings for poles would be enough to fix the roof and to form a framework for the repair of the hole in the wall. Little Hawk walked to the woods, selected a sapling, and began to chop. It was hard, hot work, made more difficult because his tomahawk was not a man-sized tool. He had only the first sapling cut and trimmed when Ena came, a tomahawk in hand, the twins trailing behind her. She started to work without speaking.

Little Hawk said, "The work is mine, Aunt, but I thank you for offering."

Saying nothing, she continued to chop.

"Please," Little Hawk said. "It is my work. It is my punishment from my grandmother."

"I will handle your grandmother," Ena said. "Come. Trim the small branches away while I chop down another." She looked at her nephew. "Renna said that you spoke to the bear and that it promptly left."

"Through the back wall," Little Hawk confirmed ruefully.

"Why did you not stop and speak to it when you were running like a deer through the village?" Ena asked with an odd little smile.

"I wasn't sure the bear was in a mood to listen to oratory," Little Hawk replied.

Ena grinned. "It is said that you ran with a speed that would have bested the fastest warrior."

"I don't doubt it," Little Hawk replied, chuckling. "At my heels she looked as big as a settler's wagon."

Ena laughed, doubling over, and the twins giggled, too—not because they understood, but because the sound was so infectious and because their mother was having such a good time. "I would have given much to have seen it." When Ena's mirth had been reduced to rippling giggles, she stood up straight. Tears of laughter streamed from her eyes. "Perhaps you will go into the woods and find another motherless cub so that I will not again miss the excitement."

"I don't think, Aunt, that I could stand such excitement again—at least not so soon."

"Well, then," she said, wiping her eyes, "to work, tamer of great bears."

For a radius of fifty miles around Legionville the forest was empty of Indians. Renno, returning from a scouting mission, made his report to Anthony Wayne and then hurried to the cabin that he and An-da shared with Roy. An-da's pregnancy was nearly full-term, and Renno had cut his trip short, wanting to be present when the infant was born. Pregnancy had enhanced An-da's beauty. Her skin seemed to glow. She had not gained weight except in her stomach, and her off-balance load caused her to walk with her head back and her legs wide.

Upon entering the cabin, Renno held her for a long time, looking into her eyes. Then nothing would do but for him to feel the baby's lusty kicks through the taut skin of his wife's belly.

Roy had not returned from a trip to the south, scouting along the river with two of his Indians. The cabin was theirs for the night, and they talked far past An-da's usual bedtime. Renno told her of the forests, and she described her day-to-day activity, including her friendship with Floral Anderson, the wife of a sergeant. Mrs. Anderson had birthed six children of her own, four of them living, and she would be in attendance as midwife when it was An-da's time.

Renno voiced his approval of Floral Anderson. He knew Sergeant Rufus Anderson. The man was a good soldier, one of Wayne's drill officers who worked every day trying to whip the legion into shape.

It was late before An-da said, "I have forgotten. There is a letter for you."

She produced the letter. "Actually, I didn't forget," she confessed with a shy smile. "I wanted you to myself for a few hours and not with your mind on the war and other matters."

Renno recognized the handwriting immediately as George Washington's. The sachem sat near a lamp and read, scowling, while An-da watched him anxiously. She remained silent when he rose to pace the small cabin.

"You will tell me what is bothering you so when you are ready," she said at last.

"It is nothing," he told her. "At least nothing to do with us—only a dispute between the white generals and politicians."

"If it has nothing to do with you, then why are you concerned?" she asked.

"Go to sleep, my darling," he said.

"In your arms or not at all."

He smiled, and putting the letter out of his mind, he complied with her ultimatum. The missive was not mentioned again, nor did Renno reread it until Roy Johnson returned late one evening, tired and dirty, with a crusted wound on his left arm where it had been grazed by a musket ball.

An-da cleaned the wound and applied a new bandage.

"I suppose I will have to keep the grandfather of my children under my wing," Renno said, "if he insists on letting himself be damaged."

"Sure could have used you," Roy grumbled. "I got a little careless. I was pretty far down south and in a hurry to get back. I ran right into a war party of Shawnee." He smiled. "I don't know who was more surprised. I lit out of there, but not faster than the ball that nicked me."

"Where?" Renno asked, bringing a map to lay on the table in front of Roy. The older man pointed out an area south and west of the big bend of the Ohio.

"You were farther than fifty miles from Legionville," Renno remarked.

"Well, it was pretty country. I wanted a look."

"How large was the war party?"

"Didn't take time to count. Six, maybe eight. I circled around later, but I couldn't find more signs. I figured maybe there was a push on toward the Virginia frontier, but there was no sign of that."

"I talked with both Miami and Shawnee warriors when I was in the territory," Renno said. "The feeling is that the war chiefs will wait to see what the new commander of the army is going to do."

"I envy you the ability to pass as one of them," Roy said wryly. "I have to do it the hard way. They probably believe that one more big defeat will win the war. Could that be why they're not trying to hit established places like Pittsburgh or Marietta?"

Renno shrugged. "If Wayne marches the army into a defeat like Harmar's or St. Clair's, there will be no more war, for there will be no whites west of the Ohio to fight."

"That's the way I see it, too," Roy agreed.

After Roy had eaten, Renno produced the President's

letter. The old man read through it. "I'll be damned," he said, looking up at Renno. "In my opinion, he's putting too much on your shoulders, Renno."

"I, too, have difficulty with this," Renno said.

"Politics." Roy snorted. "Politicians will be the death of this country yet. So old Wilkinson has started the same kind of poison-pen campaign against Wayne, writing to congressmen and other politicians in the east that he used to such good effect against Clark."

"There are those in the east who will believe him," Renno said.

Roy grunted in disgust. "Take my advice, Renno: Stay out of this. If you start hinting to the general that his second in command is a traitor and is trying to get his job, Wayne might get ornery."

"This is one trail that I shall follow with great care," Renno promised.

Chapter XIII

The days that Renno spent with General Wayne's army were good and productive. One by one the sachem had added reliable men to his force of scouts, by depending mostly on displaced Iroquois. Some of these warriors had come to the Northwest Territory with intentions of fighting, only to be dissuaded by the advice of such men as Cornplanter at the great Indian conclave on the Maumee.

Renno had assigned the best of the recruited scouts to Roy Johnson and had told them in no uncertain terms that the life of his father-by-marriage was dear to him and that it would go badly for anyone who allowed harm to befall Johnson in the wilderness.

Renno's happiness was increased because of the vast,

virgin territory to be explored and because of An-da's presence. The peace Renno felt was unlike any he'd ever known; it was as if the manitous were extending permanent blessings as a reward for his having chosen a Seneca wife.

Renno would forever remember the day his strong son was born—a baby who took his dark skin coloring from his mother. "Now this one," Renno said happily, holding the baby in his hand, "is a true Seneca."

"He has your nose, your lips," An-da observed.

"A fine boy," declared Floral Anderson, a buxom, red-haired, motherly woman who had become very fond of An-da.

For long, pleasant evenings they delayed naming the boy, each making numerous suggestions. An-da wanted him to be called after one of Renno's great ancestors, and the white Indian was indeed tempted to honor the memory of either Ghonkaba or Ja-gonh, but finally he decided against that.

"To name him after either my father or my grandfather," he told An-da seriously, "is to burden him, for those are the names of warriors, men who followed the old traditions. This one comes into a changing world. In fact, one day, like Joseph Brant and many others, he might well take a white man's name."

"There will be no white man's name thrust upon the head of my son," An-da protested.

"No, no, not yet," Renno agreed.

So it was that after long discussion the boy was named Ta-na-wun-da, a Seneca name, meaning Swift Waters. It was a traditional name, a name that had a pleasant, murmuring sound.

The time came when Anthony Wayne felt confident enough of his army's ability to commence his penetration of the Indian heartlands. For months he had weathered the criticism of such men as James Wilkinson for his so-called inaction when, in fact, Legionville had been a beehive of activity. He had drilled and trained his troops constantly and with a severity that was also criticized by some. General Wayne believed that only disciplined troops could hope to win against warriors as determined and as skilled as those the Ohio tribes would field. He knew that in a wilderness battle, he would suffer losses, and only troops with a pride instilled by discipline and training would stand against such losses and move forward to put into effect his second principle of battle against the Indians, to bring the fighting to close quarters, hand to hand, as quickly as possible.

The army he loaded onto flatboats for a trip down the Ohio to Fort Washington, near Cincinnati, included new recruits among the well-trained men. Wayne was still far short of the promised five thousand men, the target strength of the Legion of the United States. The general had been counting on having a force of mounted Kentucky riflemen with him, but those men were preoccupied with a new effort by George Rogers Clark to sweep the Spanish from the Mississippi.

When the army began to move, Renno was faced with a decision. He had no desire to leave An-da and the baby in Pittsburgh, but to take her home would require months.

"Bring her and the baby along, Renno," Roy suggested. "This is one fine army. Look at those men."

Indeed, the legionnaires were impressive. Due to Wayne's unrelenting pressure on Congress—he believed that a well-uniformed soldier was a better soldier—the legion was, to a man, resplendent. A bearskin hat with a feather topped off each man's neatly trimmed hair. The sublegion to which each man belonged could be discerned at a glance by the color of his plume: white for the first, red for the second, yellow for the third, and green for the fourth.

The long-tailed uniform coats were reminiscent of those worn by continental soldiers in the War for Independence: buttoned only at the top to reveal a neat, matching waistcoat underneath; crossed at the breast by white leather belts supporting a backpack. The trousers were tight on the lower leg, had a striking stripe down the outside seams, and were secured by straps under the soles

of fine boots. At each man's throat was a bunch of white
lace.

Some of Wayne's requisitions sent back to the east
were considered frivolous by some, for he had ordered
color standards for each battalion, plus many decorations
so he could immediately honor individual soldiers when
the war finally started, and an official standard for the
legion as a whole.

"Yep," Roy reiterated, "it's a fine army, probably the
finest ever fielded. Old Mad Anthony has drilled them
and chewed on them and run them and marched them.
Those men have burned enough powder in target practice
to fight a small war, and they're so damned tired of drill
and training that they'll welcome a spirited fight. Yes, I
think the safest place you could find for An-da and the boy
is with the army."

Renno was aware that Floral Anderson and her two
young teenagers were going with the army, as were many
other wives and children. The camp followers would fill
more than a few flatboats for the drift downriver.

During the troop movement, Renno and Roy worked
together, ahead of the flatboats, to make certain that the
woodlands along the river did not hide ambushers. During
the trip they did not encounter hostile Indians, but they
saw plenty of signs.

"We're being watched closely," Roy said. "They know
we're on the move."

The vagaries of nature complicated the landing, for
the river was in flood, and the flatboats had to be pushed
through partially submerged treetops to a landing place.
Fort Washington, with its log palisades and quarters for a
small garrison, was far too small to house the legion.
Wayne put his men to work building a fortified camp
similar to Legionville. He named the camp Hobson's
Choice, since the flood had forced him to choose from
among several equally undesirable alternatives. And he
immediately resumed the seemingly interminable drills.

Now Wayne sat astride the invasion route that had
been followed by both Harmar and St. Clair. Although the
army was ready, if still undermanned, orders from Phila-

delphia were to sit tight, for peace negotiations were still under way.

"Are they going to have us idle away another year?" Wayne stormed to Renno and Roy. "At this moment representatives of the United States of America are creeping— *creeping*, mind you—to Detroit to beg the savages for peace. The Indians have killed our peace representatives before, and they may murder these. Then, by God, we will move." After he paused to consider his statement, he waved one hand. "No, no, by the Almighty, I certainly don't wish that to happen. But how do they expect me to maintain an army indefinitely? Hell's bells, I can't even keep up communications with Philadelphia because of the damned yellow fever. I've got hundreds of men on sick call, and the longer we delay, the more desertions we'll have to endure."

Perhaps because Renno and Roy were not of the military establishment, or perhaps because they were good listeners and held their tongues during his tirades, Wayne had formed a habit of talking freely to his two main scouts, using them as a sounding board or just to vent his spleen.

One thing bothered Wayne more than anything else: The legion was being supplied out of Kentucky by a firm of private sutlers, and shipments were always late to arrive.

"The damned suppliers," he thundered. "Can't depend on them. I've raised holy hell all the way to Philadelphia, and those bastards who are responsible for getting me the food for my men, our powder and ammunition, tell me to be patient. Well, I'm tired of being patient. I detect the fine hand of my second in command in this."

Roy sneaked a look at Renno, who had decided that it was not his place to tell General Wayne that the Kentuckian might well be a traitor.

"The man's hated me from the beginning," Wayne went on. "He's used every opportunity to blackguard me. And now he's deliberately interfering with my supply line, and I'm at the end of my patience." He paused to turn an anger-reddened face to Renno and Roy. "Boys, I need someone I can trust to go down there—not in an official capacity—and nose around a little."

Roy spoke up. "I know the way to Kentucky. I'd be happy to oblige, General."

"Good, good," Wayne said.

"I, too, will go," Renno offered.

Wayne frowned. "Hate to have both of you gone."

"The tribes will not attack you here," Renno assured him. "You are too strong. They will wait until you march."

"Well, I guess you're right," Wayne agreed. "Two heads are better than one, and all that. What I want you to do is find out just where the hell the holdup is in getting me my supplies. Find out who's responsible, and I'll do some ass kicking so that the bellows of pain will be heard all the way back to Philadelphia."

Renno took his leave of An-da and held his son for a few moments. Floral Anderson was present. "Don't worry," she said. "I'll keep an eye on 'em for you."

Two buckskin-clad frontiersmen were not out of place in Kentucky. Roy's skin was burned almost as bronze as Renno's, and neither looked any more like an Indian than any other frontiersman. Renno's bow might have attracted some attention, but only because it was of English make; the Indian tomahawk was considered to be a useful tool by many frontiersmen. Roy himself carried one.

A new spirit of vitality was evident to the men as they passed through settlements on the way to Boonesborough, headquarters of the firm contracted to supply the legion. The citizens were proud that Kentucky had been the second state, after Vermont, to be added to the original thirteen.

Twice they met wagon trains moving north toward the Ohio carrying supplies for Wayne. They halted to speak with the drivers and guards. Roy, with sudden inspiration, asked some men about the prospects of employment with the company.

"I reckon they might need some men who know the

woods," they were told. "Man to talk to is Vance Tuller, at Boonesborough."

Boonesborough had grown considerably since Roy had passed through on his way north after Nora's death. He and Renno asked for directions to the buildings of the sutler firm and soon were standing in the office of a harried little man who very quickly responded, "Yes, gentlemen, we do need good men for several purposes. How would you feel about making a trip downriver to New Orleans?"

"Well, sir," Roy said dryly, "I have no desire to spend the rest of my days in a Spanish prison."

Tuller waved a hand. "No worry about that. Our firm has trading rights with the Spanish. The pay is good. Vessels are loading right now."

"I think, sir," Roy said, "that we'd prefer to stay up here. Thought you might need men to work on the supply trains going up to Wayne's army."

"Very well," Tuller grumbled, obviously disappointed. "But there won't be a train leaving for several days. Meantime, however, if you don't mind work, we can use you in loading wagons."

"Well, my boy," Roy said to Renno as they joined a gang of workers lifting crates into wagons, "I think we're doomed to learn what it means to do what they call an honest day's work."

One by one wagons rumbled off toward the Mississippi. Some were laden with crates heavy enough to inspire Renno's suspicions. When the last wagon of the day was loaded, he and Roy strolled toward a boardinghouse.

"What did you think were in some of those long crates?" Roy asked.

"I have been thinking that we might take a walk in the night and find out."

"After those last wagons?"

Renno nodded.

They followed a rutted road west of Boonesborough after consuming a hearty meal at the boardinghouse. The wagons that had left the supplier's establishment during the afternoon had not traveled far, and four of them were drawn just a few miles from the sutler's warehouses. The drivers and guards were settled within the circle of the wagons; the horses were tethered in a group nearby. Because it was still relatively early when Renno and Roy came upon the encampment, they waited until the moon was high and the sound of snoring drifted to them. One guard had been posted, but he was far from alert. He sat on the driver's seat of one of the wagons, a pipe glowing in his hand.

Renno motioned Roy toward the rear of the wagon. He himself glided silently through the night, avoiding patches of bright moonlight, until he was within a dozen feet of the wagon. The sentinel was on the verge of falling asleep, his head falling down onto his chest to be raised with difficulty. It would have been easy and safe to silence the guard permanently with one quick slash of the stiletto, but Renno, thinking that the man might be merely an innocent workman earning an honest dollar, did it the hard way: He eased up to the wagon, put one foot on the hub of the front wheel, and then in one fluid motion he rose, his hand closing over the man's mouth, to jerk the man off the seat. After a brief struggle Renno applied the flat side of his war ax to the man's skull, and then all was still.

The others slept on. The sachem moved swiftly to the back of the wagon, where Roy was already slitting the ties of the canvas cover with his knife. Luckily, one of the long crates was positioned at the back of the wagon. Renno climbed up, gesturing for Roy to keep an eye on the sleeping men. He used his tomahawk to pry open the lid, lifting it slowly and pausing when the nails, releasing, made a creaking sound.

Finally the lid loosened. Renno lifted it and dug into the packing material to feel the unmistakable shape of a musket. He removed the gun and handed it down for Roy's inspection. Roy stepped into the moonlight, brought the musket close to his eyes, nodded as he read, then handed the weapon back up to Renno, who replaced the gun, pushed the lid onto the crate, and then retied the canvas cover.

A couple of hundred yards up the road, as they headed back to Boonesborough, Roy halted. "Those were legion muskets, intended for Wayne."

"No doubt," Renno said.

"That's why Wayne's not getting his supplies," Roy fumed. "Someone's sending them south, to New Orleans. I wouldn't be surprised if in a few months those muskets are in the hands of Creek warriors."

Renno started walking, and Roy paced him. "What do you think we ought to do, Renno?"

"Find out who is responsible for diverting Wayne's supplies to New Orleans."

"Heck, we know that: Wilkinson's the only man who can send shipments down the Mississippi without having them confiscated by the Spanish."

"We must know that without a shadow of a doubt before we make such a charge," Renno said.

"Easy to say," Roy grumbled. "You have any ideas?"

"One."

"Want to tell me what it is?" Roy asked after they had walked for some time.

"Vance Tuller," Renno replied.

They reached Boonesborough in the predawn hours. The town was quiet, with even the most boisterous celebrants having given in to sleep. Only the dogs were awake, and their lonely barkings sounded from different quarters of the town. The false dawn created a dim light to guide Renno through the back garden of a neat log house near the sutler's buildings—the home of the firm's manager in Boonesborough, Vance Tuller. The Seneca paused, standing in the moonlit yard amid flowers that testified to a woman's touch.

"Remove your tunic," he whispered to Roy.

Roy hesitated only for a moment, until he noticed that Renno had his small kit of paints in hand.

Vance Tuller was having difficulty breathing. He tossed in his feather bed, and his eyes opened. In the light of the moon coming in his window he saw a nightmarish face of horror, an Indian in full war paint. The intruder's hand was over Tuller's mouth, so that his efforts to scream amounted to nothing more than muffled moanings.

"Be silent," the Indian hissed.

Tuller looked at his wife. She stirred beside him uneasily. Another man put his hand over her mouth, and her eyes snapped open.

"Just take it easy," that man whispered. "You won't be hurt."

Now the man hovering over Vance Tuller spoke menacingly. "I am going to remove my hand from your mouth. If you cry out, you will die."

Tuller felt the sharp edge of a tomahawk against his throat. He nodded, eyes wide. The hand was removed.

"It's a pleasant night, Mr. Tuller, a nice night for some friendly conversation."

"What do you want?" Tuller asked, his voice quavering. He felt disoriented; his attacker looked like an Indian but spoke with a British accent. "Don't hurt my wife, please."

"Neither of you will be hurt," the British savage said, "if you will speak freely about the legion guns that are on their way to the Mississippi and New Orleans."

Tuller gulped. "I don't know anything about any legion guns except those we sent to General Wayne."

"I wonder," the Indian said musingly, looking across at the fearsomely painted face of his companion, "which would make him more eager to speak the truth: a little pain for himself or for this lovely lady?"

"I think he might be a bit selfish," the companion remarked. "He might let his wife suffer before he'd talk."

"So," the one with the accent said. "Shall it be an ear?" Tuller felt the sharp blade of the tomahawk next to his ear. "Or a nose?" The blade was moved accordingly.

It was the woman who spoke. "Please don't," she begged. "I told him not to get mixed up with those men. Please don't hurt us."

"What men are those, Mrs. Tuller?" she was asked politely.

"James Wilkinson," Mrs. Tuller answered, "and his man, Reuben Reynolds."

"Do you know, ma'am, why guns intended for the legion are on wagons heading toward the Mississippi?" the British Indian asked.

"No, please, I just know that I didn't like Mr. Wilkinson and Mr. Reynolds," the woman said.

Tuller's assailant turned to him. "My friend," he said, putting pressure on his blade until Tuller could feel a fine cut across the bridge of his nose, "it seems that you will have to tell us about these men."

"I know nothing," Tuller claimed. "I just work here. I take orders. The owners tell me to load such and such for the river, such and such for the wagons going north."

The British savage looked to his companion. "Would you please remove one of Mrs. Tuller's rather nice ears and place it ever so gently into Mr. Tuller's mouth?"

With wild eyes Tuller saw his wife faint. The other Indian positioned his knife at Mrs. Tuller's ear. Tuller knew he could not let this go on.

"Don't do it, please!" he begged. "It's Wilkinson. I am not blind. The firm is supposedly owned by Mr. Wilcox and Mr. Mayer, but when General Wilkinson comes around, always wearing civilian clothes, Mr. Wilcox and Mr. Mayer do everything but bow and scrape. Most of the time, though, it's Mr. Reynolds who brings the orders." He paused, swallowed, and looked fearfully at the man who was still holding a knife at his unconscious wife's ear.

"The muskets . . . ?" Tuller was asked.

"They come over the mountains from Virginia," Tuller said. "Either Mr. Wilcox or Mr. Mayer tells me how many to, uh, lose—I mean, by falsifying the records so that many muskets are not accounted for. Those are the ones that go to General Wilkinson's river vessels for shipment to New Orleans, along with other durable goods intended for the army."

The British savage smiled approvingly. "You're a good conversationalist, after all. Is there evidence of a deliberate slowdown of supply shipments to the legion?"

Tuller nodded. He felt perspiration rolling into his ears. "I've heard Mr. Wilcox tell the drivers to be gentle with the animals—not to push them, to give them plenty of rest. He laughed when he said it, and I got the impression that he was ordering the drivers to be slow."

"Tell me more about this Reynolds."

"All I know is he works for Wilkinson," Tuller responded.

"Doing what?"

"I don't know," Tuller admitted. "I did hear him say, only a few days ago, that he wouldn't be around for a while, that he was going on a trip up north."

Tuller saw that his wife had revived. She was weeping piteously.

"Let's go," the Indian next to her said. Tuller thought he heard remorse in his voice. "We've heard enough." He patted the woman on the shoulder, and she cringed away. "Forgive us, Mrs. Tuller. And the next time, be a bit more insistent in your advice to your husband in regards to his associates."

"I am in no hurry," said the man with the British accent. "I think I'll linger awhile in the gardens to enjoy Mrs. Tuller's flowers and, incidentally, to put an arrow through anyone who cries out after we leave."

The men backed out slowly. Renno stood in the hallway for a moment or two. He heard the sound of the woman weeping from the bedroom. Then he and Roy were moving away from the house, with no outcry being raised behind them.

Renno pushed hard on the trip back to Fort Washington and the camp at Hobson's Choice, causing Roy to complain for a few days, but then he seemed to take pleasure in matching Renno's pace. Their first stop was at their cabin, for a brief reunion with An-da and the baby, and shortly thereafter they were standing in Wayne's crude office.

Wayne listened to the report in stunned silence. "I knew the man was ambitious, but I thought him to be only after my command." He rose, and his voice thundered,

"Well, by all that's holy, we'll put a stop to his outright theft. I don't care how important a man he is in Kentucky or whether I lose that state's goodwill by my actions!" He called out in a loud voice for his new aide, a young officer of rigid stance. His name was William Henry Harrison, a Virginian who had enlisted as an ensign in the First Regiment at Fort Washington in 1791. He had come to Wayne's attention quickly and now wore the insignia of a lieutenant. He had a long, powerful nose; wide-set, piercing eyes; and the affectation of a lock of hair falling down over his forehead.

"Mr. Harrison," Wayne grated. "I have an assignment for you. Do whatever is necessary to take over the movement of the supplies for my army. If those thieving sutlers in Booncsborough give you any trouble, have them shot."

"I think," Roy said, grinning at Renno, "that the general has the situation well in hand."

Harrison asked one or two well-phrased questions to get a clear idea of the general's wishes, saluted smartly, and left.

"Do you know of a man named Reuben Reynolds?" Renno asked the general.

"I've met him," Wayne answered. "As a matter of fact, he was through here not long ago, traveling upriver."

Renno told Wayne what the manager of the sutler firm had said about Reynolds, then about Reynolds's intentions to travel to the north.

Wayne pondered for a moment. "So Wilkinson's man is traveling north, is he? I wonder how far. General Wilkinson is probably still trying to play both ends against the middle, not content with his pay from his Spanish friends but now trying to dip into the treasury of the British Crown as well."

"That's my guess, General," Roy said.

There was a look in Wayne's eyes that revealed the satisfaction of a man who had stood just so much and was ready to take action. "Gentlemen, these months, while I've been forced into inaction by those who cry peace, by those who do everything but crawl to the Indians, to the Spanish bastards, and the British, I have held my tongue.

Meanwhile Wilkinson has deliberately interfered with my lines of supply and accused me of feeble and improvident arrangements. He has written to the secretary of war saying that my entire operation is a tissue of improvidence, disarray, error, and ignorance. Fortunately I have a friend in Henry Knox, and once he realized Wilkinson's perfidy, he has kept me informed. While I have been held here by the politicians, Wilkinson has accused me of being overly cautious and, God help me, of possessing thoughtless temerity. Now I can take being called a liar, drunkard, fool, and a hypocrite, but when that man calls me a coward—"

He sat down and thought for a moment. "If Reynolds is indeed acting as Wilkinson's agent to the British, where would he most likely go?"

"Detroit," Renno guessed.

"Or, depending on his mission, maybe Montreal or Mackinac," Roy added.

"Since he went north up the river from here," Wayne said, "he would most probably enter British territory at Niagara. I shall have my eyes open for this man Reynolds, and when he comes south again—" He smiled, as if in anticipation, then straightened. "In your absence, my friends, our scouts have reported some activity"—he rose and jabbed a finger at a map"—here. Since you can move freely among them, Renno, it is for you to go up there and see just how many warriors are gathering." His flabby face relaxed into an ironic smile. "That is, sir, if you will consider that a request, not an order from a military man."

"General," Renno said, returning the smile, "I have not yet seen anything to make me disagree with your orders."

"Well, bless my ass," Wayne said, still smiling.

It soon became evident that something was astir in the territory. Once Renno had reached the Miami River and started northward, he found traces of war parties everywhere. He had not far to go before he encountered large encampments of warriors. Wearing the war paint of the Seneca, he mixed among the warriors of many tribes and learned that a council had been called. He knew that after he had stated his views at the grand conclave, it would be dangerous for him to appear at a council of the Ohio war chiefs; but he traveled north until he found the temporary encampment where the chiefs were gathered. He moved about casually, and as luck would have it, the first man he recognized was the Miami Little Turtle, who was, in effect, the field marshal of all the Ohio tribes. Little Turtle was standing alone, looking out over the river, oblivious to the talk and noise of the camp. Renno approached and made the sign of brotherhood.

The Miami's eyes widened for a moment, then his face returned to impassivity.

"I thank thee that thou art well," Renno said.

Little Turtle returned the greeting, in good Seneca, then switched to English. "There are those here who would lift the blade toward you on sight, Sachem."

"Life is ever uncertain. I pray that my brother Little Turtle is not among them."

"I thank the spirits that you are here," Little Turtle confessed, "for I am troubled. I have seen the Legion of the United States, my friend. I stood, so"—he crossed his arms and raised his head—"and looked down from a hilltop to see an ocean of men in blue. Their marching was that of trained soldiers."

"This is an army," Renno confirmed.

"It is not fear for myself that troubles me," Little Turtle said. "The man who says that should be prepared to defend himself."

"The courage of Little Turtle is beyond question," Renno told him.

"I have heard from a Shawnee who was in the pay of the white general St. Clair that you, Sachem, once told the white general that you did not enter into a battle when there was no hope of winning."

"I believe in that," Renno replied.

"And the words of Cornplanter ring in my ears," Little Turtle continued. "'They will bear you down by sheer weight of numbers,' he warned us, and for that he was jeered at and shamed."

"Little Turtle is wise to remember Cornplanter's words."

"And so, my friend, I am here to counsel peace, to tell my brother war chiefs that it is time to negotiate seriously with the whites, and to take what they can be forced to give us."

Renno nodded.

"Knowing, all the while, that they will not listen," Little Turtle went on. "For the blood is hot in the eyes of Blue Jacket and Blackhoof and Tarhe the Crane and all the others."

"One can only speak his mind," Renno said.

"Once again we have been betrayed by the white men," Little Turtle said. "Where is the promised support from the British? I see no redcoats. Where are the Iroquois, who, the British assure us, will appear under Joseph Brant? I see only scattered Iroquois, and I do not see Brant." He looked into Renno's eyes. "If you are present, you will hear my words."

Renno was present. He mixed inconspicuously with the warriors who listened to the oratory of the war chiefs, and he listened as Little Turtle, obviously full of emotion, voiced his doubts. And he heard Little Turtle's arguments derided by the others. Then Little Turtle suggested to delay, at least, the coming battles by prolonging negotiations with General Wayne.

Renno watched with interest as the war chief Cat's Eyes stood and did everything but brand Little Turtle a coward.

Little Turtle kept his composure. "Judge my courage, Cat's Eyes, by standing beside me in battle or, if you cannot wait, by facing me now."

Black Wolf spoke. "We honor you, Sachem of sachems," he said, nodding his head to Little Turtle. "You have led us to great victories. And now all Indians want just one more victory—the *final* one—and we pray that you will lead us with your wisdom. I have traveled from the north, and close behind me comes the support that you have sought, Little Turtle. A powerful force of militia from Detroit will be at our side when the white general

marches his prettily dressed soldiers into our ambush.
Many white men will fight at our side, in addition to the
Detroit militia."

"Trappers, squaw men," Little Turtle said scornfully.
"A handful of Tory Rangers. What will be their numbers,
including this Detroit militia? Two hundred? Three?" He
spat. "We could do as well without them. To face this army
of General Wayne's, we need the ranks of redcoats with
their disciplined volleys of fire, not a handful of white
renegades and young men from Detroit out for an adventure."

And so it went. They were still debating when Renno
slipped quietly away and headed back for Hobson's Choice.

In Renno's absence, Wayne had moved the legion
north. He had begun construction of another fortified
camp, called Fort Greenville, about seventy miles up the
Miami. He had sent smaller bodies of troops ahead of him
to garrison a log fort near St. Clair's battlefield, Fort
Recovery.

Wayne had told Roy Johnson that by manning Fort
Recovery he was hoping to force the Indians into action;
he was still under orders to observe the peace while one
last attempt was being made to negotiate a settlement.
And there he sat . . . waiting . . . exercising a patience that
was not in his nature.

Renno had traveled back southward, away from the
Miami River, and he went all the way to Hobson's Choice
only to learn that the army had moved. He followed their
trail through muddy tracks and arrived at the site of Fort
Greenville. He found An-da and Ta-na-wun-da settled in a
hastily built cabin. General Wayne was very interested in
the report that Little Turtle, principal war chief of the
Ohio tribes, was having second thoughts.

"Perhaps I should send envoys," the general mused.
"We might avoid a hell of a lot of bloodshed."

"He will fight," Renno said, "but his heart will not be
in it. No, General, you will have to defeat the Indians in
the field to end this war."

"So be it," Wayne said, then told the white Indian
that Roy Johnson had gone north, to Fort Recovery, with a

supply train under the command of Major William MacMahon.

Due to the muddy conditions, the sachem knew that the train would be making poor time. Renno had a feeling that the impatient war chiefs had been held in check as long as could be expected. He also recognized that by erecting Fort Recovery near the site of St. Clair's defeat, Wayne was telling the Indians: "Look, here we are, back again, in the very heart of the lands you claim."

Feeling glum, he slogged through the mud to his family's shelter and told An-da of his plans to join Roy.

"Renno," An-da said, "you are almost always away. Can't you stay with us for just a few days? Roy told me that this was a routine operation and that the supply train is well guarded. There are soldiers at Fort Recovery."

"When this war is over," Renno said gently, "then we will all be together—this new son of mine and Little Hawk and Renna with us."

"Then you must go?"

"I must, little one." He took her into his arms. "But not until the morning." As she pressed herself to him, Renno whispered, "I think that our son is lonely and would enjoy the company of a brother."

"Or a sister?" she asked.

"Or a sister."

"Then, warrior," she whispered, "there is work for you, for such desirable things do not come merely as the gift of the manitous."

Renno was preparing to leave next morning when a runner summoned him to Wayne's office. The general was beaming, and he paced the office as if his leg did not pain him at all.

"By God, Renno," he said with enthusiasm, "I've got the bastards. My men caught Reuben Reynolds in Pittsburgh, on the way south. We have evidence that he has been dealing with the British on Wilkinson's behalf while posing as a deserter! We have a witness who saw him with redcoat officers in Detroit." He clapped his hands together and rubbed them. "Yes, sir, I've got him now."

Renno nodded.

"Of course, the slippery bastards will deny everything, so I have to be sure before I make a move." His mood changed suddenly. He looked at Renno, his eyes bright with eagerness. "First let's kill us some Indians. They're getting nervous, Renno. They keep waiting for me to move into an ambush, but I don't move. They'll have to do something soon, or their warriors will begin to melt away. Do you agree?"

"It is the nature of the warrior to want to fight or be at home—not to wait endlessly for action," Renno told him.

"By God, if only the politicians would say go," Wayne said. "I've got the army now. It's ready. We're past the season of winter illness, and there's no pox or fever in the territory. Hell, we can whip them without the Kentuckians, if they'll just turn me loose."

"I'm going up to Fort Recovery today," Renno said. "I'd like to have a look around up there."

Wayne grinned. "Still looking after old Roy, are you?"

"He can look after himself," Renno said.

"Of course," Wayne agreed. "Well, I think it's a good idea. If you can, scout on north a bit. I have a hunch that those eternal peace negotiations are going to come to a halt soon and that we'll be on the march. Somewhere up there we'll meet, Little Turtle and I, and maybe not too far north of Fort Recovery."

Soon Renno was following the deeply cut tracks of the supply wagons at the warrior's pace. For a while he encountered patrols from Fort Greenville, and then he was alone, his feet eating the miles steadily. He ran through a heavy rain, then back into sunlight, which dried his clothing. On the second day, after only two hours' travel, he heard a horse's complaining neigh and the creak of wheels that needed oil.

Renno looked down from a wooded ridge to see the supply train strung out on the muddy track. Mounted dragoons lolled in their saddles as their horses walked slowly to keep abreast of the wagons. When he spotted

Roy Johnson riding down and out of the woods, guiding his horse toward the lead wagon, Renno ran down the hill, overtook the rear guard, waved greetings to men whom he recognized, and soon was standing beside Roy's horse.

"Miss me that much?" Roy asked, grinning. "Or are you just out on a sight-seeing trip?"

Chapter XIV

From the time the supply train for which Roy Johnson was scouting had left the legion's new fortified camp, it had been under the eyes of Indians. One of them, a muscular young Shawnee in his midtwenties, was called by his followers Chief of the Beautiful River. His name was Tecumseh, and he had good reason to hate all whites. From his teens he had been fighting against white encroachment into the land north of the Ohio, and he had seen his father and two older brothers fall in the continuing struggle.

Tecumseh was not, in actuality, a sachem, nor did he claim to be. He did, however, have a certain following, and he had shown his bravery many times in battle. He was alone when he shadowed the supply train to the north, and when he was certain that its destination was the insulting installation called Fort Recovery, he ran northward to join an encampment of warriors, among whom was his brother Tenskwatawa, the Prophet. Tenskwatawa joined with Tecumseh, to run through the forests until they stood before Little Turtle.

"This is an opportunity to strike a blow at the white man without serious risk of loss to the tribes," Tecumseh said. "The supply train is guarded by only ninety soldiers. I can take it with three-score warriors, Sachem."

Little Turtle mused. "I have been told that the tribes want only one more victory," he said. "But the only victory that will matter is a decisive one. This raid on a supply train would serve no real purpose."

"It would fill bellies," Tecumseh said, "for the wagons carry corn and bacon. And I counted sixty-four horses."

It was the food that helped Little Turtle form his decision. He nodded and lifted a hand. "Go then."

Tecumseh and the Prophet circulated among the warriors, and when the force was gathered, Tecumseh counted just fewer than fifty, including himself and his brother.

"We will be outnumbered," the Prophet grumbled.

"We will have the advantage of surprise," Tecumseh reminded him.

"We need at least ten more warriors—twenty would be much better," the Prophet argued.

Tecumseh was about to respond, but instead he remained silent as a thin figure appeared as if by magic in the shadow of a large tree. Tecumseh smelled, or imagined he smelled, an odor of rank decay emanating from the cloaked and hooded shaman.

"Go," urged Hodano in his hissing voice. "The spirits will be with you. I will be with you."

Roy, dismounted, led his horse as he walked beside Renno. The road to Fort Recovery was well traveled. The creaking wagons bumped and jerked slowly through mud and deep ruts. Renno was telling Roy of his last talk with Little Turtle. Roy agreed that although Little Turtle was experiencing doubts, he would have to fight. No sachem, even one with as much honor as Little Turtle, could stop something that had been building toward a climax for so long.

"How was the family?" Roy asked after they had walked awhile in silence. He had just returned from scouting around the flanks and the front, so he felt that he could relax a bit before going out again. He had two good men—one Oneida and one Mohawk—scouting the woods on either side of the newly cut road.

"They are well," Renno replied. "I am thankful that An-da has such a friend in Mrs. Anderson, for she—" He stopped speaking suddenly, halted, and cocked his head. He had heard nothing, but something had intruded into his awareness.

Roy, too, halted. "Hear something?"

A teamster bawled a curse at his horses. A whip cracked. The creaking of the wagon continued as Renno stood, all senses alert, to let the rear elements of the supply train pass him. The rear guard rode past with a jangle of metals.

"What do you think?" Roy asked uneasily.

"I don't know," Renno said. Around them the forest pressed in. As the sounds of the train diminished Renno heard a crow call, to be answered by others.

"Think we ought to go out and take a look?"

Renno nodded.

"Let's catch up with the rear guard. I'll leave my horse with them," Roy said. "If there are Indians around here, I don't want to go crashing through the brush on a horse."

A few minutes later Roy was handing the reins of his mount to a dragoon, then he told another man to ride forward and inform the officer in command that he and Renno were going out on the flank. The dragoon kicked his horse into motion to do Roy's bidding.

"Split up?" Roy asked.

"No," Renno said, pointing toward the eastern side of the trail. "We go together."

Only a few feet from the road they were in virgin

forest. Any trace of the white man's ambition seemed far away. Renno took the lead, his eyes on the ground. He saw tracks.

"Just one warrior, keeping an eye on us. . . ?" Roy ventured.

"Perhaps." Renno would not have been able to explain to Roy why he felt apprehensive. He had heard nothing, had seen nothing, and yet it was as if subliminal alarms were sounding inside him. He could feel the presence of a threat.

Following the single Indian's tracks, he led the way at an easy run, wending through the trees, with Roy at his heels. They had come abreast of the supply train and could hear its sounds. Then they ran past the slowly moving train and were approximately two hundred yards in front of it when Renno halted in midstride and drew his tomahawk. One of Roy's Indian scouts lay sprawled in his own blood, his scalp lock missing, his bowels opened in mutilation.

"Let's alert the soldiers," Roy said grimly.

They turned back toward the supply train, but before they had run twenty yards a great whooping erupted, followed by a blazing barrage of musketry.

"Oh, my God!" Roy cried out. "I should have been out front myself."

"One man cannot do all," Renno told him. "Come."

Fewer than fifty warriors howled down upon the supply train from the front and the west, muskets firing. They closed in so rapidly that the dragoons, not yet blooded, were caught by surprise, and only a few lifted their weapons to return fire. As the Indians rushed in, their war whoops making it sound as if five hundred and not fifty were attacking, the mounted guard broke and fled.

In its first test in battle, Anthony Wayne's vaunted legion proved itself to be no better than the soldiers of Harmar and St. Clair. Some men fell from their saddles, blood staining the elegant uniforms, and the others retreated. Teamsters leaped down from their wagons and joined the rout, running back down the muddy road, into the woods to the east, to escape the horde of screaming, death-dealing warriors swarming from everywhere.

When Renno and Roy burst out into the road, the altercation was almost over, so quickly had victory come to Tecumseh's small force. Renno saw that two officers had rallied a group of men, and from the cover of a wagon they were firing intensely on the attackers.

Roy took in the situation at a glance: There were no mounted riflemen, but thirteen men were in the group making a stand. "We can fight our way through to help the men by the wagon."

"They are dead men," Renno said.

"I'm going," Roy argued. "This is my fault."

Renno seized Roy's arm. "If it is fighting you want, there is enough for all." He pointed: A dozen warriors had moved away as a group from the main force surrounding the supply train's surviving guards. One noticed Renno and Roy, whooped, and led the rush toward them.

Two muskets spoke almost as one, and two warriors crumpled in midstride to sprawl in the mud. The others ran on. Roy coolly clicked his bayonet into place and assumed a fighting stance. Renno put his musket aside to stand with the war ax in his right hand, the short sword in his left. The sword had not been tested thoroughly in combat, but as ten warriors closed on the pair, he knew that it would be thoroughly tested this day.

Roy drew first blood, lunging to impale a warrior. He jerked the bayonet out, swung the butt of the musket, and smashed the forehead of another warrior.

Renno waited for the charging enemy to come to him, parried a downward slash with his sword, and almost severed the man's neck with a vicious swing of his toma-hawk. He lunged aside, thrust with the sword, and felt the two-edged weapon sink into softness, bounce off a bone, and emerge bloodied.

A second warrior died on Roy's bayonet, but the blade became caught between ribs, so when Roy thrust mightily, the weight on the blade caused it to snap. Desperately seizing the musket by the barrel, he lashed out so that the butt smashed through his enemy's skull.

Roy positioned himself to stand back-to-back with Renno as the warriors, made wary by the deadliness of the white men, circled cautiously.

The short lull in the battle to the death was, Renno saw, going to end quickly. The thirteen men who had made a stand with the wagon train were dying one by one, freeing their assailants to join those Indians surrounding Renno and Roy. Two warriors moved in concert to slash at Renno with their blades. The white Indian ducked one mighty swing, driving his sword under it, into the man's gut.

This was, Renno believed, his last fight; already the odds were too great, and within seconds he would be facing twenty or thirty of the enemy. He fought on, pleased with the performance of the short sword. It would be, if he lived through this battle, a valuable addition to his small arsenal of weapons. Unlike some of the weapons he had used in the past, such as the spirit knife, the great war club of his ancestor, and the spirit ax, it would not vanish with the spirits.

The second man, having seen his companion fall so easily, tried to retreat, but he was not swift enough to avoid Renno's tomahawk.

Now at least fifteen Indians surrounded Roy and Renno. Only the warriors' eagerness to count coup and to kill these two who had proven their bravery and weapons skills prevented it from ending quickly. The warriors got in each other's way, which gave both Roy and Renno a momentary advantage. Renno leaped forward to kill with both hands, and Roy sent another warrior to the Place across the River with a crunching blow to the skull.

And then, penetrating the din of howls, shouted orders, and whoops was a hissing voice. Renno looked past the circling warriors to see Hodano standing at the edge of the woods.

"Cannot so many kill but two men?" Hodano challenged. "Don't fight among yourselves for the honor of killing them."

"Hodano," Renno called. "Why do you not take up the weapons yourself?"

"I want that one taken alive," Hodano hissed, stabbing a bony finger toward Renno. "The man who kills him will suffer my displeasure."

"Friend of yours, huh?" Roy grunted as he bent low under a killing swing of a tomahawk, then lashed out to elicit a howl of fatal pain.

The enemy closed, the strongest warriors having pushed the others to the rear. These muscle-corded warriors presented a solid front of blades and death-hungry eyes. It was, Renno knew, only a matter of how many he would take with him to the Place across the River, for he would never allow himself to be taken alive.

Renno had faced unfavorable odds before, but never such hopeless ones. As the ring of warriors closed around him and Roy, he allowed himself only one moment of regret. He would never see Little Hawk and Renna again, would never again know the joy of holding An-da in his arms, would not watch his new son, Ta-na-wun-da, grow up. But such thoughts were not long with him. He bellowed his fighting call, and the sound of a great bear was so realistic that it startled a warrior facing him. Renno took advantage of that opportunity, and one more body twitched at Renno's feet.

Only two or three soldiers were still alive at the wagons, but their fire was keeping a portion of the enemy busy. Hodano stood in the shadows on the edge of the woods, watching intently, and there formed in Renno an intense desire to smash that scarred face, to send Hodano to his evil spirits before he himself tasted the final slash of a blade. The white Indian told Roy to stay at his back, then he began to hack and slash toward Hodano's position. Hodano, seeing Renno's intention, drew his huge, oversized tomahawk, and a leer that might have been a smile exposed his slitted tongue.

"Come to me, Hodano," Renno called. "Or do you let others do your killing?"

"Alive," Hodano hissed. "I want this one alive."

It was evident, however, that the warriors facing Renno would not heed Hodano's words. Faced with the most awesome enemy of their experience, those nearest the white Indian were eager to end the battle, to prevent themselves and others from falling before Renno's two-handed attack. To the amazement of the overwhelming number of adversaries, it was one man who was in command of the fight, not desperately defending himself but edging over fallen bodies toward the hissing shaman who stood at the edge of the woods.

When Renno heard Roy grunt, he stole a quick backward glance to see that a blade had drawn blood on Roy's upper left arm. Renno, sounding his war cry, renewed the fight with fury. He was feinting a slash with his tomahawk and lunging with his sword when he heard the distinctive whistle of an arrow. Directly to his front, a warrior fell, an arrow driven through his neck. Again came the whistle, and another warrior went down. Then Miami, Shawnee, and Mohawk shouted with surprise, turned this way and that in a futile attempt to locate this new opponent, and went down to his arrows.

Roy grunted again, dodging a tomahawk, and slashed to cut the biceps muscle of the attacker, disabling him. "We're not alone."

An arrow thudded into a warrior's breast, and then a bronzed warrior leaped from the shadows of the woods, yowling the war cry of the Seneca.

El-i-chi! Renno's heart soared, and he felt new strength surging in his arms as he smashed and slashed his way inexorably toward Hodano. Now his beloved brother was at Roy's side, having seen that the man needed aid, to deal swift death with tomahawk and knife.

"We go, Brother," El-i-chi said, "into the woods."

"Hodano," Renno gasped.

Although the three were still outnumbered greatly with the addition of the warriors who had killed the last men by the wagons, the addition of one more deadly fighter had caused their opponents to withdraw momentarily.

"This for Hodano," El-i-chi said, stooping quickly to scoop up a fallen tomahawk and, with one fluid motion, sending it winging directly toward Hodano's shadowed face.

The shaman hissed in alarm and, using his power, soared, disappearing to the eyes of all.

"Now!" El-i-chi shouted, killing a Miami who was too eager to end the fray. The Seneca shaman took Roy's arm and jerked him toward the woods. Renno had no choice but to follow. The last of the soldiers was dead, and a band of at least fifteen warriors was storming up the road toward them. Renno fought his way past three warriors and followed El-i-chi and Roy into the shadows of the dense forest. Here he halted and loosed his bow. The first two men to follow, whooping, met stout arrows, driven with a force more powerful than they had ever seen, from the English longbow.

"Quickly," El-i-chi urged.

Renno ran a few paces, turned, and once again a man died. Thus it continued: seven arrows from Renno's bow, and seven warriors dead or dying.

Two Miami warriors at the forefront of the pursuit paused, looking down at a warrior whose heels were drumming a tattoo of death. An arrow was lodged in his heart.

"There is magic here," said one. "Did you not see that the one who came from the woods forced even Hodano to flee?"

"When faced with magic," said the other Miami, "it is best to be cautious."

El-i-chi reached a small glade in the forest shortly before his brother. When Renno arrived in the glade, longbow in hand, El-i-chi opened his arms and clasped his brother to his heart. Neither could find words.

"When you two get through with your tearful reunion," Roy said, "I could use a little help. I'm bleeding like a stuck pig."

"Brother," Renno whispered, moving back to clasp El-i-chi's arms. "Your appearance was most welcome."

The Seneca shaman went to Roy, cut away the slit sleeve of his buckskin tunic, and saw that the cut on his upper arm was deep. He took Roy's bandanna and wrapped it around the wound tightly.

"That'll hold it for a while," Roy said, satisfied. "Let's make some tracks."

Ah-wa-o was well concealed, about a quarter mile off the road to Fort Washington, in a cluster of rocks that formed a small cave. El-i-chi alerted her to his coming with the coo of a dove. She answered in kind.

"I thank thee that thou art well," Ah-wa-o said, bowing her head to her sachem.

Renno returned her greeting formally. She ducked back into the cave, and when she emerged, Gao was in her arms.

"This is my son," El-i-chi announced proudly. "He is named for the wind that blew as he was coming into this world."

Renno took the boy from Ah-wa-o's arms, looked at him, and then hoisted him high and began to chant a song of praise to the manitous. Gao smiled happily and squealed.

"He will be a great warrior, Ah-wa-o," Renno foretold, handing the boy back to his mother, "and he will have a companion, for I, too, have a new son."

El-i-chi whooped with joy.

"Don't you think it might be a good idea to be just a little quiet?" Roy asked, looking around nervously.

"When there is great happiness," El-i-chi responded, "one does not worry about the small things."

"A bunch of warriors on our tail isn't a small thing," Roy said. "We'd better get back to Fort Greenville and tell the general he's out one wagon train and some men and horses."

"Now we are together," El-i-chi said as he walked at Renno's side, Roy and Ah-wa-o behind them, Gao strapped snugly to his mother's back. "You have made this your war?"

"So it seems," Renno said.

"Then it will be mine, also," El-i-chi declared.

Roy's wound reopened as they began the trip back to Fort Greenville. El-i-chi looked again at the wicked-looking cut. "We will halt here for a time," he said. "Ah-wa-o, I will need wood for a fire."

Ah-wa-o began to gather dead branches, and soon a fire was crackling. El-i-chi waited, chatting easily with Roy, until a good bed of coals had built up. Renno, who had been making short scouting sorties, returned in time to see El-i-chi using his razor-sharp tomahawk to whittle a short section of sycamore limb into a flatness about a quarter of an inch thick. Roy was lying on a mossy slope, his eyes closed. Ah-wa-o was nursing Gao.

"I take it we are still alone. . . ?" El-i-chi asked as he thrust his knife into the coals of the fire.

Renno nodded.

El-i-chi removed the knife. Two inches of the tip of the blade glowed white hot. "You will hold him," he said to Renno.

"I don't need anyone to hold me," Roy objected, sitting up.

El-i-chi raised one eyebrow at Renno, who nodded. Then El-i-chi held out the flat piece of wood to Roy. The older man set it between his teeth and bit down solidly as El-i-chi removed the blood-soaked bandanna.

Roy locked his arm to his side and looked up at the sky. Beads of sweat were popping out on his forehead in anticipation, and he squeezed his eyelids tightly shut. But when El-i-chi, with one swift, definitive motion, pressed the flat side of the white-hot knife into the gaping cut on Roy's arm and the rank odor of burning flesh and blood surged up, the frontiersman's only reaction was a knotting of the muscles in his jaw. The piece of sycamore wood cracked with the force of his bite as he endured the pain. Roy, smelling his own burned flesh, gagged. El-i-chi took the knife away.

"Oughta hold it," Roy said, looking down at the cauterized wound. He started to rise, but El-i-chi put a restraining hand on his shoulder.

"We will rest for a few minutes more," El-i-chi said.

Roy wiped perspiration from his face and grinned. "Well, if you young sprouts are tired—"

"I can see," El-i-chi said, "that my nephew Little Hawk carries the blood of more than one warrior."

Roy grinned crookedly at the compliment and closed his eyes against the continuing pain.

They had to lie low to avoid a clash with a war party of some thirty Ohio-tribe warriors not more than five miles from the fort, then they entered the patrol area and were escorted into the encampment by none other than Sergeant Rufus Anderson, whose wife, Floral, was An-da's friend.

"What happened up there?" Anderson asked.

"Well," Roy said, "I hate to say it, but most of your boys ran. I don't relish the idea of being the one to tell the general."

Wayne had already heard that there had been an engagement. He was pacing in front of his office. When he saw Renno and Roy, he came to meet them, a question on his lips.

"We'd best talk about this inside, General," Roy suggested. "First, I want you to meet Renno's brother, El-i-chi."

Wayne offered his hand. "Have you come to join us?"

"I have come to join my brother," El-i-chi replied.

"Another independent-minded one, is it?" Wayne said, rolling his eyes.

Before Renno followed the others into Wayne's office, he pointed out An-da's cabin and told Ah-wa-o to go there and wait.

"A few stragglers have come in here," Wayne began, "telling of an attack in great force."

"General, you want to sit down?" Roy asked.

"No, by God, I don't want to sit down. I just want to know what in blazes has happened."

"Well, you've lost a supply train."

"Everything?"

"Every horse, every slab of bacon. And you can bet the Indians will carry off enough pieces of the wagons to make them useless, then burn the rest," Roy said. "You've lost two good young officers. Lieutenant Lowry and Corporal Boyd. Eleven men stayed to fight, and—"

"Eleven men?" Wayne exploded. His face flushing, he held up one hand to silence Roy. "What in the name of hell are you saying, Johnson?"

"He's saying," Renno cut in evenly, "that most of the soldiers fled at the sound of the first war whoop."

Wayne used every expletive in his vocabulary.

"He's got a talent for it, hasn't he?" Roy asked Renno out of the side of his mouth.

"Harrison!" Wayne bellowed, and Lieutenant William Henry Harrison stepped smartly into the room.

"Sir?"

"I want you to round up every man who ran from that fight. Give me their names and their ranks and then start assembling firing squads."

"Yes, sir!" Harrison barked, although his long face had paled.

"Now git." Wayne went behind his desk and sank into his chair as Harrison left. "I will have no cowards in my legion," he whispered. "I will make examples of all who ran." He wiped his face with a slightly soiled handkerchief, then looked up. "An attack in force?"

"No more than fifty warriors," Renno answered.

Wayne's face went almost purple.

"Just take it easy, General," Roy advised.

"Fifty?" Wayne croaked.

"If that many," Roy said. "I'm afraid I have to take responsibility for this, General. They were on us before we knew it. I should have been—"

"He had just returned from scouting," Renno said. "The enemy moved in fast behind him. One man cannot be expected—"

"I know Johnson's a good man," Wayne said, waving off the defense. "And I know that we've been surprised, just like Harmar and St. Clair. By God, I want to know why."

"Because you're up against one of the finest military minds in the world," Renno said. "General, your troops were green. They'd never been under attack before, and

the surprise was total. Your losses are not serious. Most of
the men escaped."

"We'll hunt them down as deserters," Wayne vowed.

"And they were not legion," Renno reminded the
general. "They were dragoons."

Wayne's face brightened. "You're right. Give me good
infantry every time. Give me a man in a smart uniform, a
man who is proud of his unit and of himself, a man with
cold steel on the end of his rifle." He sighed. "All right,
gentlemen, I am calm now. Tell me all you can about this
skirmish."

He listened without comment, making notes, as Roy
and Renno spoke; then he looked at El-i-chi. "And how did
you happen to arrive just in time to get into the fight?"

El-i-chi smiled enigmatically. "It was just the will of
the manitous," he answered.

Five men, selected at random from those who had
made their way back to the fort, were shot for cowardice in
the face of the enemy. The legion stood at attention as the
muskets roared, and the lesson was firmly implanted in
their minds: If a man had signed on to fight with Anthony
Wayne, he had better be willing to fight.

An-da and Ah-wa-o had enjoyed a tearful but joyous
reunion while waiting for their men to come home. The
friends had compared notes on everything that had happened
since they had left the Seneca-Cherokee village separately.
They laughed happily while comparing stories about their
completely superior children. In the meantime they had
prepared a fine meal of roasted chicken, sweet potatoes,
and corn bread.

Gao got much attention from his uncle Renno and
Aunt An-da and "honorary grandfather," while Ta-na-wun-
da was bounced on the knee of his uncle El-i-chi as Aunt
Ah-wa-o looked on. The family enjoyed being together,
until Roy, at last confessing that his arm smarted a little,
went off to bed.

While the women nursed the boys and put them to
bed, Renno and El-i-chi strolled outside. The encamp-

ment was settling down for the night. Fires burned in front of some tents and shelters where most of the camp followers lived. El-i-chi asked Renno about their mother's reaction to his elopement with Ah-wa-o.

"She and the others will forgive," Renno replied.

"I will not have Ah-wa-o and my son subjected to scorn," El-i-chi warned.

"When it is time, we will all go home," Renno said. "Those who speak ill of you, your wife, or my nephew will answer to me."

"It will be good to be home," El-i-chi said.

"Yes."

The brothers watched a bat dart down and up, and their eyes were led to the stars and the rising moon. Each was silent for a long time, content to be once more in the other's company.

"So," El-i-chi said at last, "we fight an old enemy."

"If he only *would* stand and fight," Renno snarled.

"Eventually he will," El-i-chi replied. "This I promise you."

Renno detected something different about his brother— something, perhaps, in his voice or in his stance or just in the way he looked. El-i-chi had always been the eternal youth, in spite of his position and his responsibilities; but this was no boy who stood at Renno's side now and spoke as if he had the knowledge given by the spirits.

In Philadelphia, these new events added to the already crushing burdens of George Washington. He had a well-trained army in the field in the Northwest Territories but no assurance that victory would come. Meanwhile, the old European powers were once again engaged in war, and in Canada, Governor Dorchester had assured the Ohio Indians that they had the support of the British. Moreover, Dorchester had told the Indians: "I shall not be surprised if we are at war [with the United States] in the course of the present year." Dorchester had returned to Canada from England just before making that statement, and so it seemed that England was determined to go to war. As if to emphasize Dorchester's threats, the British had begun construction of a fort in the heart of the northwest, on the Maumee River. Called Fort Miami, it was garrisoned by British regulars, and the gunports were filled with British guns. Worse, the British navy was seizing American trading ships, impounding the cargo, and impressing the crews.

It was a time, Washington knew, for careful study and for negotiations. He knew that his young nation could not, at that moment, survive another war with England. He asked Chief Justice John Jay to be his personal emissary to the British court and, with Jay under way, turned his attention to trying to prevent Congress from making the situation worse with panicky acts aimed directly at England. The house passed a bill forbidding any contact with England, and bills were being introduced willy-nilly to establish arsenals, to enlarge the army, and to hoard naval stores.

Henry Knox came to meet with Washington in private. Knox, as secretary of war, was as aware as Washington of the nation's weakness.

"In view of the present situation, Mr. President," he said, "is there any alteration you would like me to make in General Wayne's orders?"

Washington was silent for a long time. "There will be no change in General Wayne's order to secure United States territory in the northwest." He sighed. "Henry, if we surrender there, we might as well scrap the Constitution and apply for reentry into the British Empire."

Chapter XV

~~~~~~

Toshabe was worried. She had hoped that her remaining years would be spent with her children and her grandchildren around her, with peace and prosperity the rule. But the world was changing. Now only one of her children, Ena, remained in the Cherokee-Seneca village. Two of her grandchildren were motherless and, at least temporarily, fatherless; and her second son had violated one of the most sacred taboos of the tribe and was, in effect, lost to her forever. As if this were not enough of a burden for the manitous to place on her, it was evident that war was closing in on the peaceful community where Seneca and Cherokee lived side by side as brothers.

Toshabe prayed constantly for Renno's return. Ha-ace

was a mighty warrior and a good man, but he did not have Renno's skills when dealing with people. Rusog was... Rusog. He was a great chief, and he had the loyalty of most of the scattered bands of Cherokee, but it was beyond his diplomatic talents to convince Dragging Canoe to cease his war against the whites. As a result, others were now joining in that war that boiled and exploded in isolated incidents up and down the entire frontier of the United States.

Over an evening meal with what was left of the family, Toshabe voiced her concerns:

"At Muscle Shoals thirteen white men are dead."

Rusog looked up quickly at Toshabe. This was news to him; he had only just learned of an attack on a flatboat carrying several white families. "Toshabe, do you have spies everywhere?"

Toshabe ignored the half joke. "White women were captured. Those who attacked and killed and took white women prisoner were Cherokee."

"Renegades," Rusog grated. "The leader of that party of renegades calls himself Chief Bowl, but he is no chief."

"He is, however, Cherokee," Toshabe pressed on, "and that is my concern. We know, Rusog, that those Cherokee who fight against the United States are not the majority; but the white man remembers only Cherokee war paint when he buries his dead. When a small band of Cherokee warriors goes into Virginia to kill and loot, the Virginians do not discriminate between renegades and the Cherokee nation as a whole."

"You speak wisely," Rusog admitted. "These things I know, and I, too, am concerned. I have sent emissaries with messages of peace, urging the village chiefs to control their young men. There is a Cherokee called Doublehead who also defies the wishes of his elders. Since you know so much, Toshabe, know the rest: Doublehead has raided along the Wilderness Road into Kentucky, and isolated houses have been attacked almost within sight of Nashville. Yes, I, too, fear that the United States will perceive these isolated attacks as the acts of the Cherokee nation."

"The truth is," Ena said, "that many of the attacks

blamed on the Cherokee are made by Creek traveling north to join the great war there. The Creek influence our young men with promises of glory and loot, and there are always inexperienced warriors who long to establish a reputation, to count coup, and to take their first scalps."

"And when the whites, in all their maggotlike numbers, rise up and smite us in punishment, will the guilty be distinguished from the innocent?" Toshabe demanded.

Rusog respected his mother-by-marriage's intelligence. "Toshabe, our lands are wide and our people many. Would you have Cherokee fight Cherokee?"

"That is for you and the elders to decide," she replied.

Rusog nodded. "I have not been idle. For the past months I have sent bands of warriors into the field with orders to drive Creek war parties from our lands. Indeed, one such war party was apprehended within twenty miles of Knoxville itself, and had we not intercepted them, they would surely have attacked settlers there."

"This I had not heard," Toshabe said.

"I do not want to inflame our warriors against the Creek," Rusog said. "Nor do I want the peace that exists between us and the whites to be sullied with blood. Thus, when my men captured the leader of the Creek war party, we turned him over to the white authorities in Knoxville."

Ha-ace sucked in his breath. He was old-fashioned enough to be shocked that one Indian would turn another over to the whites, regardless of tribe. "Why did you not simply kill the Creek?"

"Because now we have established that it is Creek, by and large, who are on the warpath," Rusog explained. "If a Creek war party should evade our warriors and attack Knoxville or settlers near the town, then the whites will know that it was not Cherokee."

"And when word reaches the Creek nation that the Cherokee betrayed one of theirs to the whites?" Ha-ace demanded.

"Then I hope that Ha-ace and the Seneca will stand by my side and, if necessary, take a few Creek scalps to show that our lands are not to be violated," Rusog said.

"The Seneca will do what is necessary to protect the lands that we share," Ha-ace assured him.

To Little Hawk, it was a somewhat murky situation. He did not like thinking that Cherokee was to be pitted against Cherokee, that Creek might be fighting Cherokee and Seneca. He had listened to his father long enough to think that the Indian was not the Indian's enemy. But if that was true and if the white man was not the enemy of the Seneca, then who was the enemy?

As he approached his tenth summer, Little Hawk was already as tall and well formed as some of the smaller warriors of the tribe. Although his boyhood was not entirely behind him, he had learned to use his time wisely. In addition to his continual but solitary practice with bow, tomahawk, and knife, a portion of each day was devoted to study. His teacher was Se-quo-i, and the subject was mainly the English language: reading and writing. At times his brain felt ready to explode with all the knowledge that people wanted to cram into it. Toshabe drilled him in Seneca lore; Ha-ace and other warriors worked with him in weaponry, battle strategy, and woodcraft; and Se-quo-i seemed intent on teaching him everything that the talented Cherokee had learned himself.

Renna had taken to following Little Hawk to his reading and writing lessons with Se-quo-i, and he was proud that she seemed able to absorb the lessons.

So much time had passed since Renno and El-i-chi, the two most important men in the lives of Little Hawk and Renna, had left the village. Sometimes it was difficult for Little Hawk to remember what his father looked like, how he talked, and the manner in which he had shown his great love for his children. But Little Hawk could remember Renno's teachings. Not once did he ever doubt that the sachem would return. He continually reassured Renna of that certainty and reminded her of the good times they had enjoyed with their father and their uncle. Still, the boy missed his father terribly, and often when he was alone in the forest, he would send his pleas to the manitous to bring Renno back safely and quickly.

He knew that his standing in the village was unusual and that he owed his status to his father, his grandmother, and his ancestors. The blood of sachems was in him, but that was often a nuisance—when, for example, he would have preferred swimming with the other boys instead of taking his daily lessons with Se-quo-i. But it was also a great honor—one that he would not neglect.

So it was that Little Hawk was included in the joint council when a Creek delegation came to the Cherokee village. The Creek demanded an explanation for Cherokees' having turned over a Creek war chief to the whites to be hanged. Little Hawk, as usual, was seated far to the rear behind the least senior of the elders. He remained silent as the Creek delegates spoke in haughty words of the perfidy of the Cherokee and then urged Rusog and the Cherokee nation to remember their blood, to join their brothers, and to help throw the white man back into the east beyond the mountains.

Rusog responded in a calm manner, telling the Creek visitors that they were being led into danger by men who did not understand that the time to fight the white man had long passed. He spoke eloquently, for Rusog; he was more a man of action than oratory. When a Creek rose to refute everything he had said, Rusog's face darkened.

The Creek looked around, and when his eyes fixed on Little Hawk, he added, "But then what can be expected of a people whose council includes a mere boy and who harbor in their midst traitors to the once-proud Iroquois League, traitors who fought against their own during the great white man's war?"

Little Hawk had to restrain himself from leaping to his feet to challenge the Creek.

But Rusog spoke in a voice no longer calm. "It is only the sanctity of the council that prevents you from feeling my blade," he told the delegate.

"Perhaps you will have the opportunity to test my blade on the field of war," the Creek challenged.

Se-quo-i rose. "Brothers," he said, "in these trying times it is often difficult to know the proper path, but it is surely not war between Creek and Cherokee. My Creek brothers, hear me."

"Now we must listen to a cripple," a Creek said in loud disgust.

An angry stirring rippled among the Seneca and Cherokee warriors.

But Se-quo-i raised one hand and continued: "This war will end as all past wars have ended, with the white man victorious."

The Creek hissed.

Se-quo-i was not to be deterred. "Not because of lack of courage and fighting ability on the part of the Creek, Shawnee, Miami, or any other tribe, but because of the strength and numbers of the soldiers of the United States. And when it is over, the white man, remembering his dead—the stolen women and mutilated children, the scalped soldiers and settlers—will exact his revenge. This, as you know, always takes the form of land for blood."

"So says the cripple," a Creek taunted, rising. "Our brave brothers to the north have won great victories—so great that the white chief who now commands the Army of the United States cowers behind his palisades. He knows that to march would result in defeat. Now is our great opportunity to regain that which was once ours. The whites do not have the stomach for a fight, and if we rise now, together, we can thrust them back. Once again the Indian will be able to roam his hunting grounds as he has since the dawn of time. Those who refuse to join in this great war will be considered less than dogs when the final Indian victory is won. The Chickasaw, who were once mighty fighters, are dogs of the white man. Will the Cherokee also learn to bark and beg at the white man's bidding?"

The council ended as it had begun, in acrimony. The Creek hurried away, watching their backs, and Toshabe, speaking to Ena alone, said ominously, "The whites will forget that some Indians did not rise against them. When they have crushed the criers of war, they will forget that only a few Cherokee renegades fought them, that the

Seneca and Chickasaw honored their treaties, and that the Choctaw, too, stayed in their lodges and kept the peace. They will lump us all with those who shed their blood, and only the manitous know what a terrible price we shall pay."

Roy Johnson's wound had turned septic in spite of the cauterization that El-i-chi had performed. Now and again the cut had to be opened and drained. The frontiersman suffered from fever and weakness. An-da and Ah-wa-o tended him with great concern and affection. Renno delayed leaving Fort Greenville until Roy was past the fever and the wound was healing solidly; and then, with El-i-chi, the sachem went north. The brothers reached Fort Recovery without incident.

It was June. The spring rains that had made movement difficult were over; the roads were drying. The legionnaires at Fort Recovery were in high spirits. They were dressed smartly; discipline was firm. Some soldiers had been on the frontier for two years, and they were ready.

Some who knew Renno voiced the main complaint of the legionnaire: "When's the old man going to move?"

On 30 June 1794 Wayne's patience and attention to detail was proved worthwhile. Renno and El-i-chi had slept in the fort and were planning to scout to the north. Renno could almost feel Indian eyes on the fort from the surrounding forest, and he knew that the enemy scouts were there. The shaman, eager to be outside the walls, was told that they would wait until late afternoon, since Indian activity was concentrated in the early morning. El-i-chi grumbled, saying that they would lose the opportunity to shut some of those spying eyes forever.

A supply train that had been unloaded at Fort Recovery was being made ready for the trip back to Fort Greenville. Renno and El-i-chi watched the train creak through the gates, and just as the wagons were pulling onto the road, hordes of Indians materialized out of the trees and the brush. Seeing that they were hopelessly outnumbered, the escort dashed back to safety.

"No," Renno said, seizing El-i-chi's arm as the younger man made for the gate. "We will fight from the fort this time."

The attack was in force, and a storm of musket fire came from the Indians. El-i-chi found himself a loophole and began firing as rapidly as he could reload. Renno stood and watched. So intense was the fire from outside the walls that now and then a man would fall, wounded or killed by a ball coming by chance through the small loophole. But another legionnaire would immediately take the place of the victim. The veteran troops extracted a severe toll from the attackers, remaining steady and disciplined all the while.

Renno went to peer through a loophole, but he left the fighting to the legion. It was not his manner of fighting to kill men from a relatively secure position behind log palisades. Instead, he took note of the paint and dress of the different tribes and was surprised to see so many white men among the attackers. He recognized the dress style of Tory Rangers—bitter men still fighting the Revolution; but even more chilling was the presence of three red-coated British officers. Rather than taking a direct part in the fight, they stood at a safe distance, arms behind their backs, consulting now and then with the Indian war chiefs who were directing the assault.

The attack was repelled with heavy loss to the Indians. Bodies littered the approaches to the palisades. Inside the walls men began to take care of the wounded and to remove the small number of dead. Legionnaires shouted their triumph. Anthony Wayne's army had come of age.

Renno spoke to the senior officer at the fort. The officer had also seen the redcoats advising and observing, and he included Renno's written remarks with his own report when he sent gallopers to inform Wayne of the attack.

"When we march," the officer said, "we may just be marching right into the rifles of a British army."

When Renno and El-i-chi left the fort at dusk, the bodies of the dead attackers had been removed by their

fellow warriors. As Renno led the way into the forest, he
halted to allow his eyes to become accustomed to the
gloom. Moving in silence, alert to every night sound, the
Seneca brothers traveled a full mile from the fort without
encountering an enemy. A moon was rising, and its dim
light filtered down through the leaves. Renno and El-i-chi
crossed a small rill, and ahead was an area that had once
been cleared but was now showing second-growth brush.

"This is an evil place," El-i-chi said, the Sight flickering,
showing him nothing definite.

"Here Little Turtle smashed St. Clair's army," Renno
told him.

"Let us pass it quickly," El-i-chi suggested, uneasy. It
was as if he could feel the light touch of spirits brushing
against his arm, spirits of evil. And as the Sight flickered
weakly he could hear the screams of agony and smell fresh
blood. For a moment he envisioned the battlefield immediately after the fight . . . saw Indians scalping the fallen,
tormenting the wounded, torturing women.

The brothers stepped gingerly into a nightmarish
field. Animals had unearthed the remains of St. Clair's
dead. Although James Wilkinson had led a force to the
battlefield to bury them, the task had been accomplished
in haste, perhaps with Wilkinson nervously looking over
his shoulder, fearing the return of the mighty army that
had wrought such devastation.

A smell of death and rot pervaded the air. Skulls
stared up at them with hollow, dark eyes. The moonlight
revealed rotting uniform pieces and skeletal remains to
which dried, blackened flesh and muscles still clung. And
over that charnel field floated a shadow of threat and a
feeling of chill dread. El-i-chi stopped abruptly and grasped
his tomahawk.

Renno, too, felt the presence of evil. A low growl
came from his throat as he turned slowly, peering in all
directions. He could see only the moonlit remains of the
dead and the shadows of new brush. But he knew that
they were not alone. He had felt that presence before. He
threw his head back and roared, "Hodano!"

His voice echoed back from the surrounding forest and faded slowly into silence.

Hodano stood deep in the forest's shadows, thanking his evil spirits for this gift, for they were here, the two men he hated most in life. They were here where, on a glorious day, he had flitted from dying man to dying man, inflicting mutilation on those who still had strength or quickly killing those who were close to death. There had been many casualties and much strength to be gained. For the first and only time he had sucked into himself enough life force to sate even his greed. As he felt his strength grow and expand until it was almost bursting out of him, he had chanted and praised the forces of darkness.

And now they were here, his enemies, in the place where his power was greatest. He would have them both, and even as he despised them he gloried in the knowledge that the spirits of the brothers would be the most potent power that he had ever absorbed. He would become invincible.

He would not make the mistake of underestimating them. He was confident that here, on this field, his power would prevail; but he would do nothing to risk having Renno and his brother escape him again.

Hodano lifted his arms and sibilantly whispered the chants, the incantations of evil. He would send an army against the brothers to weaken them, and then they would be his!

Renno stood in the center of the site of the massacre. El-i-chi was at his back, and both men held weapons at the ready. An eerie silence engulfed them, strangling the night sounds. That silence was invaded by a rustling sound, like dry leaves blowing in a breeze. As the rustling became louder, the earth seemed to move. The bones of long-dead soldiers clacked and rattled.

Hodano's shrill voice accompanied the rustlings, tappings, and clickings.

"Hodano . . ." Renno called.

A shape leaped up in front of El-i-chi, a death's-head,

a white skull that gleamed in the moonlight. The arms and legs of bone were covered with ribbons of blackened, desiccated flesh and remnants of a uniform that hung in decayed threads. All around them the ground was giving up its dead. Headless figures marched toward them.

El-i-chi cringed back. "Manitous," he whispered, recovering to swing his tomahawk as a spectral figure rattled and jerked toward him.

When his blade made contact, the bones and the skull flew apart, struck the ground, and rolled.

Renno's fear was cold and tangible, for he and El-i-chi faced an army not of flesh and blood. The sachem felt his brother pressing against his back. Even the shaman was fearful; but why should he not feel fearful?

A skeletal form launched itself at Renno, and he responded instinctively, bringing his tomahawk down into the skull. The crunch of breaking bone was strangely loud, but the spectral presence pressed onward.

The stench of rot and decay hung heavy in the air as El-i-chi smashed his blade into a bony chest. The skeleton fell apart, forming a heap on the ground. But the spirit army was closing, closing.

Renno's heart beat wildly. He felt it leaping in his throat and throbbing in his temples. Then, suddenly, he remembered. "This has been foretold," he told El-i-chi. "The manitous have said." He remembered the beautiful form of Emily and felt somewhat comforted. "The manitous have said that when these came against me, I would not be alone. I was not to perish at the hands of spirits of evil."

"For this I thank the manitous," El-i-chi said, smashing out at an approaching form.

Hodano's shrill laugh rang in Renno's ears as he battled against a foe unlike any he had ever faced. They floated or jerked forward in clicking, rustling groups, advancing in a tide of death to be smashed and broken by sword and tomahawk. Now and then he would feel a touch—nothing of great force, for the army of the dead had no weapons and no muscle to put strength behind the action. And yet with each touch pain gave birth to excruci-

ating agony from deep within. Even the fallen, broken
bones separated, to writhe and crawl over the brush to
touch his feet and his legs, causing the internal pain to
creep slowly throughout his body.

"Brother," El-i-chi said, gasping, the torment straining
his voice, "we are being pecked to death from within."

Renno did not answer. He saved his strength to beat
and push the eerie spirit warriors away from him.

"Casno," El-i-chi whispered. "Adviser, friend, teacher, we are in need."

Renno did not speak aloud, but he, too, was praying
to his manitous, for despite Emily's assurances, this was an
enemy beyond his strength, an enemy that was eroding
his life force from within with each light touch. His arms
were weakening. He had to concentrate hard to raise
them, and he had to put his whole body behind a blow to
smash the enemy's bones.

"Spirits of my ancestors," El-i-chi chanted. "Come to
me."

The sachem heard it first—a wild call to battle, a
swooping, reverberating, rising cry, the voice of a Seneca
warrior with blood lust in his eyes. Then the dim moonlight illuminated other forms, insubstantial and misty. His
heart soared as they took on the appearance of flesh and
blood. Renno answered the cry with the roar of a bear, for
he saw a bronzed warrior with Seneca topknot, his face
painted in symbols that meant death to the enemies, his
strong legs pumping, and his tomahawk raised. The warri-
or slammed into the rear of the circling spirit forms, and
the sound of his mighty ax brought new hope to the white
Indian.

"We are not alone," Renno said, his energies re-
stored, for the newcomer who was hacking his way forward
to stand at their side was their great-grandfather, the first
Renno.

"There!" El-i-chi said, pointing with his tomahawk.

"Father," Renno whispered, slashing out with renewed
strength. "Ghonkaba."

Then it was Ja-gonh arriving, and, following Ja-gonh,
a tower of strength, a symbol of all that was good, old

Ghonka roared a war song. He, too, worked his way through the bizarre ranks of the dead.

"Casno," El-i-chi whispered as another form joined the fight. "You, as well?"

And so they fought, Ghonka roaring; the great Renno fighting silently, a smile on his face; Ja-gonh and Ghonkaba side by side; and Casno, no longer elderly, doing his share with whoops of joy.

No longer did the agonizing inner pain drain them. El-i-chi yelled out in pure elation. The Sight was with him. He seemed to be looking down on the scene as if from a great height. He saw Hodano pacing in frustration in the shadows, his arms lifted and his lips moving in rapid supplication to his forces of darkness. And not far away, El-i-chi saw a huge male bear, poised, sniffing the air and cocking his ears at the sounds of the battle.

"*Brother,*" El-i-chi whispered, knowing that he was projecting a message the great totem could understand. "Come. Join us."

The bear rolled forward, pushing through low-growing brush, and within seconds he was lumbering out onto the battlefield to mix with the ghostly army that still pushed in great number toward the battling men and spirits. The great bear rose to his full and impressive height and with both forepaws batted away the rattling, rotting things, waddling ceaselessly toward the center of the fight.

It was evident to El-i-chi that the struggle was well in hand, with the spirits of his ancestors ranked beside him and his brother. "*Brother,*" he communicated to the bear, "*there is Hodano.*"

The bear turned, fell to all fours, and ran forward with surprising speed.

Hodano, watching victory being slowly stolen from him, did not notice the animal until its grunting, panting breath was near enough to smell. He looked down, the chant dying on his lips, and saw the bear only feet away, its great maw open. Hodano screamed in fright and soared. The bear swung a great, clawed paw that, as Hodano disappeared, left the leg of Hodano's buckskins in shreds.

Simultaneously the spirit army collapsed on the field

of death with a sound not unlike a hailstorm. Then there was silence.

For a moment the manitous stood close by: the great Renno next to Ghonka; Ja-gonh and Ghonkaba positioned back-to-back. Casno looked at El-i-chi and smiled in approval. Then the images became faint, until there was nothing. The old battlefield was as it had been before, with jagged bones and rotted uniforms protruding from the earth, exposed by scavengers. The stench of death was blown away by a gust of wind. An owl hooted from the woods.

"We will leave this place," Renno said.

"Gladly," El-i-chi agreed, shuddering.

From a safe distance Hodano looked down on the field as his two enemies trotted into the forest. The evil shaman screamed with rage and disappointment. He stopped his soaring, made contact with the ground, and, standing in front of his secluded longhouse, drew his huge tomahawk and raised it to the skies.

"You give me a taste of victory, and then you steal it away," he stormed. "You promise me much. I have given myself to you. I have obeyed you." He stuck out his tongue, and the two slit pieces wiggled. "This I have done at your instructions." He threw back his wolverine cowl, exposed his mutilated face, and turned his blinded eye to the sky. "This you did to me, and this price I was willing to pay gladly, and yet you abandon me in my time of need. You tell me you are all-powerful, and yet you allow me to be beaten again and again."

His rage drained out in a rush as a sudden coldness paralyzed his entire body. In his ears was a voice: "Tempt me not, Hodano. The struggle continues. You still have power and the tool with which to implement it."

Into Hodano's mind sprang the image of the Seneca Tor-yo-ne.

The shaman fell to his stomach and groveled in the dirt, for the coldness had brought incredible pain. "Yes!" he screamed, his voice moving toward the falsetto. "Yes!"

* * *

"It is good to be home," El-i-chi said to Ah-wa-o. He was holding Gao on his knee, and that small warrior was trying to pluck El-i-chi's knife from its scabbard. Roy Johnson, recovering nicely, had accompanied Renno to make a report to General Wayne.

An-da was preparing the evening meal. She looked up when El-i-chi called the cabin at Fort Greenville *home*.

This is not home, she thought. Her heart was heavy, for she knew that it would be difficult for El-i-chi and Ah-wa-o to go home to the southern village. She had always been fond of Ah-wa-o, but that affection had deepened as the young women waited for their warriors to return from their frequent trips to scout. An-da had come to love her friend; Ah-wa-o took the place in her affections that once had been reserved for Tor-yo-ne. It would grieve her terribly if, when the war was over, Ah-wa-o, El-i-chi, and Gao could not accompany her, Renno, and their son back to the south. Then she brightened, for Renno had declared that El-i-chi and his family would go home. If Renno said so, then it would be so.

She looked toward the door with a glad smile as it opened. Roy stepped in, followed by Renno.

"An-da," Roy said cheerfully, "you're going to have to feed me or shoot me." His appetite had returned full force, and the venison stew smelled good.

Renno went to pick up his son, who had been seated at An-da's feet, reaching up to tug at her skirts just to remind her that he was still there. Renno tossed the boy high, and Ta-na-wun-da laughed happily.

"Did the great general say when he would march?" El-i-chi asked Roy.

"The old boy has fire in his eyes," Roy reported. "I have a hunch we won't be here for long."

The venison stew was as good as it smelled. No one talked much during the meal. Roy finished last, sopping up the juices with a piece of corn bread. He rubbed his stomach. "An-da, if you weren't already married, I'd court you myself."

"If I were not already married, I would probably encourage you," she teased back.

"Yep, there's life in the old boy yet," Roy said, reaching for Ta-na-wun-da to place him on his lap. "Now, this boy here and I, we want to hear all about that battle you mentioned, El-i-chi."

Renno was not sure he wanted An-da to learn about the spirit battle. It seemed unreal now. When he and El-i-chi had returned to Fort Recovery, they had convinced the officers to send men to the field to rebury the partially disinterred remains.

"Yes, please," An-da said. "Tell us."

El-i-chi began. When he described the feeling of menace that he had known, Ah-wa-o shivered and drew close to him. And then Renno and El-i-chi alternated in the telling, for, in the end, the sachem loved tales as well as any other Indian. An-da's face was a study in horror as they told of fighting the long-dead soldiers. She swept Ta-na-wun-da into her arms and held him tightly.

"There is nothing to fear," Renno assured her. "We show no scars; we have no wounds. Now I am not even sure that it truly happened, for Hodano could have influenced our minds, causing us to see things that were not real."

"This land is evil," An-da said. "I wish that we could all go home right now."

"Soon," Renno promised.

"Real soon, An-da," Roy continued. "Once our army goes into action, it is going to end the war quickly. You'll be on your way back to the village before you know it."

"That is my prayer to the manitous," An-da said fervently.

"I wish I could have seen that fight," Roy said to El-i-chi. "I would have given my left arm to see those old warriors in action. You saw them all, huh?"

"All," El-i-chi confirmed.

"And the first Renno—how did he look?"

"He was Renno," El-i-chi said.

"Your descriptive powers overwhelm me," Roy said wryly.

"He was dressed as a Seneca warrior of long ago,"

Renno elaborated. "His head was shaved, save for a blond scalp lock. His face was painted for war."

"Sure wish I could have seen it," Roy repeated. "And you say, Renno, that even before you left Tennessee you saw what was going to happen in a vision?"

"I was told," Renno said.

Roy knew that he was on a touchy subject. He himself didn't quite believe that the spirits of the dead could visit the living. "The manitous?"

"Yes." Renno nodded.

"You see them, and they talk to you?"

"Yes."

"Who told you that when the bones rose against you, you would not be alone?" Roy asked.

Renno mused for a moment. Roy had asked; if the answer disturbed him, so be it.

"Emily."

Roy blanched.

"She used to read to me from the Bible," Renno said. "She came to me and told me of Ezekiel's Valley of Bones, and I remembered, for it is, you must admit, a good story."

"Emily came to you?" Roy's voice had an angry edge.

"She has come to me before," Renno said, guessing what Roy was thinking.

"Renno . . ." Roy, obviously disturbed, could not go on. His daughter was in a Christian heaven, not in the Place across the River, that misty, ambiguous place where Indian warriors went when they crossed the river of death.

"I'm sorry if that bothers you, Roy," Renno said sincerely. "She was a good Seneca wife. She accepted my ways and my traditions."

"But she read to you from the Bible," Roy pointed out.

"That is true. I never disputed her right to worship as she pleased," Renno said. "At first, she, too, was disturbed when I voiced the opinion that, perhaps, God is God and that we all worship the same God, if in different ways and with different names."

Roy forced himself to calm down. "Emily picked her own life. She chose to become more Seneca than white. If she is with her chosen people, then I'm glad. Maybe, as you say, Renno, God is God regardless of the name given him by different people. Then maybe after I die, I'll get to see Emily and Nora again." Suddenly he laughed.

"A joke to share?" An-da asked, smiling at him.

"No, honey," he said. "Just the musings of an old man. Nora, my wife, became bitter and unhappy after Emily died. She came to believe that God would eternally punish people such as Indians, who had never heard of Him. Wouldn't she be surprised to find that heaven had a place for an old savage like Ghonka." Roy chuckled, then looked around. "Anyone for a short walk before we sleep?"

El-i-chi rose and followed the frontiersman out the door.

They walked in silence for a while, making their way between the rude cabins thrown up by the camp followers.

"Was it real up there, El-i-chi?" Roy finally asked.

"The pain seemed real," the shaman replied.

"Can *you* hypnotize people?"

"There are times when I can influence people's thoughts."

"This old Hodano is remarkably powerful."

"He has the power of evil behind him," El-i-chi agreed.

"If he can appear and disappear at will, how will you ever catch him?"

"In spite of his powers," El-i-chi said, "he is a man. He is vulnerable to cold steel, just like any man."

"If we ever come face-to-face with him, I think I'll let you do the fighting," Roy said with a nervous laugh.

El-i-chi did not see the humor. "Yes, that is my task."

Chapter XVI

Because Anthony Wayne was furious, his cursing could be heard through the chinks, windows, and doors of his office as Roy and Renno approached. The legionnaire guards snapped to attention as the two scouts came up the log steps and were allowed immediate entrance. Harrison, the general's aide, was standing with his hands behind his back, his long face composed. He had become accustomed to his commander's outbursts.

Wayne was seated, with his swollen leg propped up. He waved a paper as Roy and Renno entered.

"Mornin', General," Roy said amiably. Renno nodded.

"Politicians," Wayne thundered, preceding the word

with several expletives of solid Anglo-Saxon origin. "Do you know what they've done?"

"Lately?" Roy asked. "Nope."

"They've allowed the state of Pennsylvania to occupy Iroquois land," Wayne said. "Moved into Presque Isle on Lake Erie."

Roy shook his head. "That doesn't sound good."

Idiots was the kindest description Wayne had for all politicians. He picked up another sheet of paper. "Just last year the Iroquois tried to mediate on our behalf, urging the Ohio tribes to make peace—and this is how we pay them back. I won't read the whole thing to you, but the Iroquois have come out solidly on the side of the Ohio tribes, saying that they will hold the Ohio River line. They warn that if the United States does not agree to the Ohio line, they will—and this is a quote—'determine on something else.' Here's another quote: 'You know, General Washington, that we, the Six Nations, have always been able to defend ourselves, and we are still determined to maintain our freedom.'"

"Sounds like an ultimatum to me," Roy said.

"General," Renno asked, "does the name of Joseph Brant appear on that paper?"

"No, thank the Almighty," Wayne answered. "But that doesn't mean much, does it? We know Brant's feelings. Now I face the prospect of marching not only into British guns but perhaps those of the whole Iroquois nation."

"General, I think not," Renno said.

"Well, at best hundreds, maybe a couple of thousand Iroquois warriors under Brant," Wayne complained.

"Thayendanegea will not march," Renno declared flatly.

Wayne raised an eyebrow. "I pray that you're right. Do you know something that I don't know?"

"I know that Thayendanegea, Joseph Brant, has no faith in the promises of either American or Englishman," Renno replied.

Wayne mused for a moment. "Gentlemen, I don't know who will line up against us, but face them we will.

We have delayed long enough. An army reaches a point when, if it does not march, training and morale begin to deteriorate. I have sent one last appeal to the Ohio tribes, asking them not to be deceived by the promises of the British. The British on the continent have neither the power nor the inclination to fight as their allies, so the Iroquois should accept the hand of friendship that I extend to them." He sighed. "I didn't expect them to submit, but at least I tried."

Suddenly Wayne's face brightened. He had clearly reached a decision. The general lowered his swollen leg to the floor, rose, and faced them. "But by God there's an *army* out there. Gentlemen, I want every scout you have in your service out in front of me, to warn me of any ambush, any gathering of the enemy."

"I take it," Roy said, "that we're going to move."

"Colonel Johnson, you take it rightly," Wayne said. "With or without the bedamned, procrastinating Kentuckians, we're going to get this thing done with."

Now Renno and El-i-chi were faced with deciding where their families would be most secure from the enemy. A garrison would be left behind at Fort Greenville, and it was unlikely that the Indians would risk attacking a position so secure as the fort. An-da, Ah-wa-o, and the two boys would be safe here.

"But, Renno," An-da objected when she realized that he was thinking of leaving her behind, "everyone's going." She pointed toward her friend, who was visiting the young Indian women. "Floral and her family are going. She says that the safest place to be is with the legion. She says that a wife should be near her husband, to give him a place to come back to after the battles, to tend his wounds, and to see that he eats well."

Floral Anderson, smiling and motherly, said, "You boys just might have to winter up there somewhere. 'Twould be a shame to leave these little girls alone for so long."

Ah-wa-o added her pleas. "Husband," she said to El-i-chi, "we came together through the heart of the

enemy lands. Now that we have the protection of this fine
army, why should we be separated?"

Renno was still undecided when, with a flourish of
drums and bugles, with much shouting and an undisciplined,
skyward discharge of firearms, the long-awaited volunteers
finally arrived in Fort Greenville, sixteen hundred strong
and full of energy, eager to fight Indians. James Wilkinson
strutted among his fellow Kentuckians with a self-satisfied
air. Although the legion had never approached the projected
force of five thousand men, in combination with the
Kentucky long rifles, it was an impressive force.

Renno, reluctant to be separated from An-da and his
son, agreed that his family and El-i-chi's would march
with the army. An-da and Ah-wa-o happily began their
preparations.

Two days after the arrival of the Kentuckians, the
legion began its northward march. The legion itself was
composed of regulars—a small army but without a doubt
the best-trained American force that had ever taken the
field.

The legion moved with clear intent but also with
careful deliberation. Wayne took the time to cut suitable
roads, and a screen of scouts and pickets always surrounded
the legion. Each night a halt was called early enough to
fortify the camp. Wayne was marching into the unknown,
facing the possibility of fighting Ohio tribes reinforced by
countless Iroquois and a British army out of Canada. To
further complicate matters, he was marching with an
order from George Washington to avoid attacking the
newly reconstructed English position, Fort Miami, on the
Maumee, at all costs save one—defeat. Defeat was un-
thinkable, even if to avoid defeat meant killing British
soldiers and, thus, risking a general war with England.

Renno, El-i-chi, and Roy were kept busy. With trusted
Indian scouts they roamed the forests all around the
legion. They saw the usual signs left by Little Turtle's own
scouts but had no encounters. Renno knew that Little
Turtle had watched Wayne's actions for two years, and he

was still watching, biding his time, waiting for just the right opportunity.

Indeed, to Little Turtle, who had led the tribes to many victories, Wayne's slow, deliberate advance was ominous. To test the alertness of the legion he sent out small, quick raiding parties to harass the troops. The Indians, however, were unable to penetrate the screen of pickets and scouts.

"The Americans are now led by a chief who never sleeps," Little Turtle told a council of war chiefs. "He is like a blacksnake—the night and the day are the same to him."

Little Turtle continued to retreat before the legion's slow advance.

Behind the army, strong points were left: Fort Loramie, Fort St. Mary's, and Fort Adams. Renno was on familiar ground as he scouted ahead of the army toward the union of the Auglaize and the Maumee. He stood on the spot where the greatest Indian council in history had been held, and it was he who advised Wayne on the location of still another strong point, Fort Defiance. Wayne devoted eight days to the building of the fort, while many of his officers chafed and grumbled.

Still there was no real contact with the Indians. Although El-i-chi brought back a few scalps, Roy did his best to avoid contact with the enemy, and Renno, supervising the entire scouting operation, met no adversary on his occasional excursions.

The white Indian was often with An-da, sometimes taking a couple of hours to march with her, carrying his son. Sometimes he spent the night with her in a temporary shelter. She had the ability to brighten his mood and make him forget for brief periods that soon, very soon, Little Turtle would be forced to make a stand.

In fact, it was becoming imperative that the legion go into action. Anthony Wayne, in spite of his knowledge of James Wilkinson's duplicity, still had to deal with Wilkinson as his second in command. Wayne's accusations against

Wilkinson had been made quietly, at the highest levels. To his disgust, nothing had come of the capture in Pittsburgh of Reuben Reynolds, Wilkinson's partner in treason, as Reynolds returned from talks with the British. Unfortunately there were the Kentuckians to consider: Wayne needed those sixteen hundred long rifles, so he suffered Wilkinson, although that man was becoming ever more vocal in his criticism of Wayne's actions.

Wilkinson was not alone in accusing General Wayne of incompetence. When scouts came to report the presence of a Miami village on the west flank, an ideal target for a surprise attack, Wilkinson and others—he had, of course, influenced the officers under his command against Wayne—were dumbfounded when the general refused to send a force to destroy the village.

William Clark and Meriwether Lewis, two young officers who had become friendly during their time in the legion, also questioned Wayne's intentions. Regarding the general's refusal to go off on a tangent and attack the Miami village, Clark wrote in his journal that he could not understand why Wayne did not "embrace so probable a means for ending the war by compelling them to peace."

On an evening when Renno, El-i-chi, and Roy were together with the families, the shaman said, "When will he fight? Are we to march around, letting Little Turtle stay just beyond our reach, until the winter snows come?"

Renno opened a map and spread it across his knees. "Little Turtle will fight, and soon." He traced the fifty-mile course of the Maumee River from Lake Erie. "Once, the villages of the Miami, Shawnee, Wyandot, and Delaware were scattered all through this territory. Now, for the safety of numbers, they have been concentrated in this valley."

El-i-chi nodded knowingly. "The valley of the Maumee is narrow, but on either side there are many cornfields to feed many people."

"Here are the towns of the war chiefs," Renno said, pointing on the map. "There is the town of Blue Jacket, of Tarhe the Crane, Black Wolf, and all the others. And here are we."

"You're right, Renno," Roy said, looking at the map from over the sachem's shoulder. "They'll have to fight. Old Wayne's put himself right in the heart of their stronghold. The legion could range out and destroy the corn supplies of whole nations and the towns of all of the war chiefs." He nodded grimly. "I see now why he named this place Fort Defiance. He's telling them that they have to fight or starve this winter."

Next day the three men scouted together. And, at the foot of the rapids of the Maumee, they stood on a densely wooded hill overlooking a fort that flew the Union Jack.

Renno was drawing a diagram of the fort, including the placement of the guns. It was a typical British wilderness fort, well built, and the guns were well placed. Although the garrison appeared to be small in number, the guns could be a severe threat to the attacking legion.

Blue Jacket, a sachem second in prestige only to Little Turtle, was addressing a council of war chiefs. He was not unaware of the legion's pressure on the tribes.

"We have allowed this white chief to push us to the northern limits of our land," he said. "Now the great lake and Canada are to our rear. This white chief sits arrogantly astride our lifeline, within a short march of our principal towns, where live our families and our people. With a sweep of his hand he can destroy our crops. And we have watched in idleness while he has built forts in our lands."

Others spoke in much the same vein. At last Little Turtle stood. The August day had begun brightly, with a warm sun and a gentle breeze. As the other war chiefs had spoken, a line of thunderclouds had begun to rise in the west, and as Little Turtle rose, the clouds towered to the zenith, dark and roiling, making for a subdued light. Distant but constant rumblings of thunder provided a background for Little Turtle's words, and lightning lit the ominous, churning clouds that continued to climb.

Little Turtle spoke for a long time, recounting the battles that had been fought and praising the courage of the chiefs and the warriors. The audience, accustomed to

long, rousing orations, sat in silence except to grunt in
agreement. Now Little Turtle was in accordance with the
others that the situation as it stood was unacceptable; the
time had come to fight.

"The fate of our people will be decided here," he
declared, "but we must not play into the hands of this
chief who never sleeps. We will not waste our young
warriors in a frontal attack on his fort."

"Where, then, will we fight?" asked Cat's Eyes.

"At a place of our own choosing," Little Turtle answered.

"This white chief does not march blindly into ambush, as did Harmar," Red Pole said. "Nor does he allow
surprise at his encampment, as did St. Clair."

"And if he does not give us an opportunity?" asked
Captain Pipe.

Swirling, dark gray clouds blocked the sun and threw
the council into shadow just as, with a snarl, the form of
Hodano emerged from the trees and stood amid the
seated war chiefs.

"Hear me," the shaman hissed, raising his arms and
tilting his head upward to the malevolent, seething clouds.
The wolverine hood fell back from his head to expose his
fire-ruined face. Several war chiefs uttered startled grunts
to see the man's massive scars, the useless, white eye, and
the burning, living eye.

"Hear me well, brothers," Hodano commanded, lifting
his arms higher. Then he lowered his chin and hissed a
chant, which became increasingly shrill until he was screaming incomprehensible sounds at the roiling, glowering sky.

A huge cloud mass rumbled, and forked lightning was
directly overhead. The air seemed to thicken and become
harder to breathe, and as the awed chiefs watched, the
lightning-laced cloud took on the color of a bruise and
lowered itself. As Hodano howled, the cloud changed
form, dropping a long, swirling funnel from its belly. Over
the continual drumming of the thunder, a rushing, roaring, moaning sound chilled all hearts.

The cloud's funnel touched the earth, and a sound
like that of raging rapids blotted out all else. Not more
than half a mile from the little hill where the chiefs sat in

council, the full violence of the tornado ripped through the virgin forest. Giant trees were torn from the ground, their root systems intact, and hurled away like straws. For an eternity the tornado ravaged the woodlands, and then, as suddenly as it had descended, the storm was past, and a heavy rain lashed the chiefs.

"Here you will fight," Hodano exhorted. "Here you will destroy this chief who never sleeps. Here you will secure the hunting grounds of our people for all time."

Little Turtle walked with the other chiefs over sodden ground. The heavy rainstorm was over. They inspected the area of the tornado's damage to find a position so strong, so impenetrable, that Little Turtle's heart expanded with hopefulness. The entire engineer corps of a great European army could not have constructed so strong an abatis. Both huge and small trees had been tossed into a defensive tangle of limbs, trunks, and dirt-covered roots. The barrier extended from the river to the wooded hills, a two-mile-deep fortification that would give the Indians the best of covers.

"*Here* we will fight," Little Turtle declared. "If the white chief attacks from the front, his mounted riflemen will be of no use to him. If his infantry attack, the men will be forced to break formation once they enter the fallen timbers and thus can be picked off easily by our own muskets. If the white chief chooses not to attack this position but tries to move along our flanks instead, he will be marching through dense forest, where we will have the advantage of mobility. We will pick off his soldiers one at a time and in small groups."

For the first time in months, Little Turtle felt optimistic. In spite of promises, there was no red-coated army at his side. The few British soldiers anywhere near the area were safely locked inside Fort Miami. Nor had the promised flood of Iroquois warriors arrived from the east. Even Joseph Brant had distanced himself from the struggle. But now! Now Little Turtle had the best fighting position he had ever imagined. He had two thousand brave warriors and several hundred white volunteers—traders, trappers, a contingent of the Detroit militia, squaw men, and the deadly, albeit small, group of veteran Tory Rangers.

"*Here* we will stand," he reiterated. "This I have spoken. This I will do."

Renno and El-i-chi moved northward at the warrior's pace through virgin forest, alert to the movement of each leaf. To their right flowed the Maumee River; to their left were vast distances. The game trail they followed showed the passage of many men, and as the tracks were joined by even fresher signs, Renno slowed his jog.

The brothers glided on silent feet through the forest, using every available bit of cover, moving so quietly that they did not disturb the nut-gathering squirrels or the birds. Now they heard the sounds of encampment and of many voices. They crept closer to look across a devastated expanse of earth from which all vegetation had been stripped. At first Renno did not understand; he could not believe that such a work had been done by Indians, who, whenever possible, avoided physical labor.

"Tornado," El-i-chi whispered.

Renno nodded, having come to the same conclusion. Before them was a stacked and entangled mass of trees, and the voices of the Indians emanated from within that obstacle. Slowly, carefully, Renno led the way in a circuit of the storm-damaged area, then looked down on it from a hilltop. The natural abatis lay on a diagonal from the bank of the river southwest to the wooded hills. If Wayne chose to attack, the assault would have to be made directly from the front, for there was no maneuvering room between river and hills and no good ground for the cavalry, except, perhaps, a narrow band along the banks of the Maumee. Renno made sketches of the position. It was evident to him, from the large number of campfires and the occasional sighting of warriors in and near the area of fallen timbers, that Little Turtle was there, and there he would fight.

The two brothers ran together back toward Wayne's encampment, once meeting an enemy scouting party of five warriors. Both groups were surprised. Renno drew his short sword and tomahawk and, growling a challenge, plunged into battle with deadly effectiveness. El-i-chi killed two warriors quickly with his tomahawk, and Renno dispatched the last enemy, who was trying to flee, by hurling his tomahawk to embed itself in the back of the warrior's neck. This encounter had delayed the brothers only momentarily, and they did not take time to remove scalps.

Renno went to report to Wayne, while El-i-chi continued on to the temporary shelter where An-da and Ah-wa-o tended their sons.

Renno marked the defensive position of the Indians on Wayne's battle map.

"This is the main body, then?" Wayne asked. "They're all here?"

"Yes," Renno said.

Wayne studied the map, which was not, Renno noted, altogether accurate. The general was tracing a finger around the western end of the fallen-timber area. "Can cavalry get through here to hit them from the rear?"

"It is not cavalry ground," Renno answered. "The hills are higher than shown on your map, and the hills are densely wooded, allowing for excellent cover and very little room to maneuver."

"But they could get through?"

"Given enough time," Renno said. "This is a very strong position, General."

"But we've got them all together," Wayne said. "We can end this war here and now. Keep your scouts out. I will hit the enemy at dawn."

"General, if I may...?"

Wayne nodded permission.

"On the eve of battle it is customary for the Indian warrior to fast," Renno said. "They will eat nothing until the battle is over tomorrow. If you should make a demonstration of strength, feigning an attack, then postpone the attack, they will eat nothing tomorrow, either."

"By God!" Wayne said. "Excellent. Excellent." He bellowed for Harrison, his aide, and issued orders.

* * *

With the morning the legion was on the move but not to attack. Wayne moved his army to the head of the rapids of the Maumee and began to build still another fortified camp, Fort Deposit, where he would leave his supply trains and baggage in safety. Here, in the enemy's face, he remained for three days, beginning each day with the threat of attack so that Little Turtle's warriors, always thinking that battle was imminent, continued their fast.

In their positions in the dense tangle of fallen timbers, the warriors sweated in the August heat as they fought the pangs of hunger, awaiting the attack that could begin at any moment. Now and again an alarm would be sounded, and great whoops could be heard from the dense cover; but the alarms always proved to be false as day followed day for three sunsets.

"Gentlemen," Wayne told his officers, General James Wilkinson among them, "for three days now I have chosen to allow our enemy to, uh, purify and strengthen himself with prayer and fasting." He chuckled. "I would guess that he is now as pure and as strong as he's going to be, and to wait longer would encourage him to break his fast; then we would be fighting well-fed men instead of half-starved ones. We attack at daybreak."

After the conference with the officers, Wayne called his three principal scouts to his office. They were given their orders as he sat, leg elevated.

"Gentlemen, I want all three of you with me during the battle in case I need to know something about the terrain as the situation changes."

Only El-i-chi looked disappointed to know that he was not to partake in the action.

"That'll suit me, General," Roy said, "just so long as you don't decide to lead the charge yourself."

Wayne chuckled. He seemed to be in a state of high excitement. He patted his swollen leg. "My days of leading charges are long past."

An-da, having seen the preparations being made, knowing in her heart that the time for battle was near, had cooked a special meal. She had learned from Floral Anderson how to fry sweet potatoes with brown sugar and molasses, and Sergeant Anderson had provided a choice chunk of beef, which she had roasted.

Roy appeared just in time for the meal, toting a jug of warm, fresh milk from one of the camp follower's cows.

"Whooo-ee," Roy said appreciatively, with his mouth full, "this is fine eating."

Later, in the darkness, Renno lay with his arms around An-da. Ta-na-wun-da slept peacefully nearby, snuggled into a blanket.

"You will fight tomorrow?" she whispered.

"Tomorrow," Renno confirmed. He kissed her. "You are not to worry. I have orders from the general to stay at his side."

"I'm glad. Let the white soldiers do the killing."

"You will stay here, with Mrs. Anderson and the others," Renno said. "You will be safe, for the general will guard his supply trains and baggage well."

"Yes," An-da agreed.

"And, if the manitous will it, by sundown it will be over, and then we will go home."

"Oh, yes," she whispered fervently.

He held her in his arms long after she had gone to sleep, smelling the clean, fresh goodness of her. He alternately felt sorrow for all those who would die before the sun had reached the zenith and joy to think that soon he and those he loved, his brother among them, would be going home.

It was after midnight. Preparations had been completed for the morning. The camp was silent except for the occasional barking of a dog and the challenge of a sentry as an officer of the guard made his rounds. Renno disengaged himself from An-da's arms, rose silently, fastened his weapons into place, and departed the camp by the main entrance, making his way toward the river.

A half-moon gave him enough light to pick his way among the debris of past floodwaters, trees, and clumps of brush. He was moving slowly, carefully, toward the river end of the fallen timbers, imagining himself to be mounted, marking in his mind a lane of travel for the cavalry. It was, he realized, an exercise in futility, for General Wayne, not he, would deploy the troops; but Renno could not have slept or even lain awake in the encampment.

His heart was heavy, for, with the sun, one more blow would be struck at those who had welcomed the white man to their shores so long ago, and there was the knowledge in him that after tomorrow the world of the Indian would never be the same.

He was back in the camp two hours before first light. He lay beside An-da and slept deeply until the sounding of orders and the movement of men woke him. Outside, Roy had a pot of tea brewing over an open fire. Renno drank gratefully, letting the hot liquid revive him.

Anthony Wayne's leg was more painful than usual that morning, 20 August 1794. He wrapped the swollen limb in flannel bandages, for that seemed to ease the pain, even if in the heat of the day the flannel would make the leg itch mercilessly. Harrison was nearby as he mounted, offering assistance, but Wayne shrugged him off, struggling into the saddle on his own. In a quiet voice he gave the order that sent the American legion marching.

Wayne's plan was straightforward. His forces were divided into six groups. At the fore, General James Wilkinson was in command of the forces on the right; Colonel John F. Hamtramck was in command of the legion units on the left. The legion cavalry was positioned behind Wilkinson on the right, and a reserve force was on the left, behind Hamtramck.

The Kentucky volunteers were at the left rear. It would be the task of the mounted long rifles to protect the legion's extreme left flank while the better-trained legion cavalry anchored the line at the river. The point of the advance was a selected battalion of the legion under Major William Price, who had orders not to engage but to inform Wayne immediately when contact was made with the enemy.

"Well, gentlemen," Wayne said heartily to Renno and

Roy, riding at his side, as they left the fort, trailed by his staff. "We will soon know, won't we?"

El-i-chi, who had been lagging behind, rode forward to pull his horse to a walk beside Renno's. "I would say, Brother, that this is not exactly a headlong charge."

Wayne, hearing El-i-chi's words, said, "Patience, my friend. We have miles to go."

It was evident to everyone who looked at the general that Wayne was in pain; but only he knew that not only his bad leg was giving him severe discomfort. He felt the onset of a bout of his recurrent fever, and he prayed that he would not, with battle to his fore, fall victim to one of the vomiting spells that often smote him. As the slow miles passed, he fought against his sickness, and when a rattle of musket fire came from the front, he forgot his pain and nausea.

"I told Price not to engage!" he bellowed as the rifle fire crested into a storm of sound. "Aide!" But Harrison had been sent off with instructions for Colonel Hamtramck.

"I'll take a quick look, General," Roy offered, and before Wayne could reply, the frontiersman had kicked his horse into a gallop.

For a few moments the musket fire reached a volume akin to distant thunder's, then it began to wane. It was half an hour before Roy came riding back. "Small skirmish, General," he said. "Price's battalion ran into a little ambush in the trees and grass. He started to fall back, but Wilkinson's infantry had pulled up too close behind him, and they got all mixed-up."

Wayne looked beseechingly toward the heavens. "I have said all I am going to say about General Wilkinson's ancestry, but when and if he ever gets home, I pray that his mother will run out from under the porch and bite him on the ankle."

"The Indians are falling back toward the cover," Roy added.

"And General Wilkinson?"

"Well, General," Roy said, grinning as he anticipated

an outburst, "he's ordering all the mixed-up troops to the rear for re-forming."

Instead of exploding, Wayne looked thoughtful for a few moments. "Gentlemen, we will ride forward and see for ourselves."

Renno and El-i-chi flanked the general, and Roy brought up the rear. They rode into a sparsely treed but grassy area to find the bodies of dead legionnaires. Then they came upon a fine view of the Indians' defensive position.

"Little Turtle has chosen his ground well," Wayne remarked. "Colonel Johnson, please ride back and tell my staff to form up in front of this area." He stood in his stirrups, wincing against the pain. "Would you say, Renno, that the enemy seems to be concentrated to our left?"

Renno narrowed his eyes for fleeting glimpses of warriors moving toward the wooded ridge. "I think they plan to put the greatest pressure on your left wing."

As the legion came up and began to position itself for the attack, Wayne ordered some of the Kentucky mounted riflemen to circle into the hills, make their way through the woods, and hit the enemy from the rear. The general took note that the white Indian, who had already warned that the mounted men would have great difficulty getting around that flank, said nothing. The hours were passing, and there had been only one relatively minor skirmish.

Wayne's officers gathered. He looked at Wilkinson, who was burning with anger over the mix-up of troops. "My men are ready, General, in position in front of the enemy," Wilkinson reported.

"Very well, General," Wayne said, "you may strike when you are ready. I want you to roust the enemy out of his cover at the point of your bayonets and deliver a close and well-directed fire upon his back so that he will be denied the opportunity to reload his weapons. I will be behind you with a second line of infantry."

"Sir!" Wilkinson barked, turning away.

"Close with him, General Wilkinson! Close with him quickly," Wayne called after the man.

* * *

It was a new kind of American army that moved to the attack. The men marched with a confidence and a precision that Renno had never seen before—not even when he had faced British regulars. A unit of mounted Kentuckians led the way as skirmishers, and the infantry of the legion, weapons at the trail position, followed. When the horsemen came near the fallen timbers, a storm of musketry broke out. Men fell, horses screamed in pain, and the Kentuckians broke and ran.

"By God!" Wayne shouted joyously as his infantry continued forward, merely opening their ranks to let the fleeing horsemen pass through. "Oh, by God!"

The legionnaires closed ranks, swung into attack position—exactly as they had practiced many times on the parade ground—and advanced on the fallen timbers, the multicolored plumes atop their homemade bearskin hats gleaming in the August sun.

The line of fallen timbers burst into smoke with the discharge of a thousand muskets, and the blast of their firing came to Renno's ears only after his seeing the smoke. The disciplined lines of the legion took the hellish fire without breaking. When men fell, others closed ranks and, still not answering the Indians' fire, charged into the fallen timbers with their rifles uplifted, the glistening steel of their bayonets sparking reflections of the sun.

"Cold steel," Wayne enthused. "Indians can't stand the sight of it. They're great and brave warriors, but they lack discipline. They'll run at the sight of the bayonets."

The firing from the fallen timbers had become sporadic, and from a distance the shouts of the charging legionnaires drifted back to Renno and the others.

"General," Renno said, envisioning the scene among the entangled trees, "the enemy will be driven now. They will fall back slowly for the two-mile depth of their cover, and then they will be forced into the open. If you send the cavalry there, along the river, you can take them from the rear."

Men with whom he shared common ancestors far in the past were dying in the dense, tangled gloom of the fallen timbers. His heart was heavy, but it would be better to end it here, breaking the power of the tribes forever, than to have the war be extended year after year.

"That's why I sent the Kentuckians—"

"The Kentuckians will not get through the hills in time," Renno interrupted.

"There will be the same problem for my cavalry along the river," Wayne pointed out.

"There is a way—a narrow path of open ground between the barrier and the river," Renno said. "I can guide them through."

"Go, then," Wayne said, turning to bark orders.

El-i-chi came to ride at Renno's side. The legion cavalry was ranged behind them. They rode through fields of corn along the narrow flatland beside the river.

Inside the maze of fallen, twisted tree trunks, roots, and limbs, the legionnaires pushed on, facing Indians who had discarded their muskets to fight with their traditional tomahawks and knives. And the warriors were, as Wayne had predicted, driven before the cold steel of the bayonets.

When the demoralized remnants of Little Turtle's army burst from the timbers into open ground, they met a charge of mounted men, the legion cavalry. As the tornado had swept through the forest, so did the cavalry sweep through the fleeing warriors of the Ohio tribes.

Renno, having led the cavalry into position, fell back as the riders charged into the backs of the Indians emerging from the fallen trees. El-i-chi, uncharacteristically weaponless, was at his side. They watched as the rout continued . . . as Indians died . . . as those who had escaped the bayonets of the legionnaires among the timbers were forced to run a deadly gauntlet of sabers and muskets.

Some Indians made it through alive and continued up the valley to swarm around the gates of the British fort, begging entrance. The gates remained closed and barred, although British gunners stood on the parapets, matches burning, waiting for the order to fire their cannon in defense of their Indian allies.

"Why do they not fire?" El-i-chi asked.

"Just as General Wayne had his orders to risk war but

not to begin it with the English," Renno explained, "so, I suspect, the English had much the same orders."

"I think I am beginning to understand for the first time, Brother, the things that you have said in the past. When I was younger, I feared for your courage when you counseled peace, when you said that we must ally ourselves with these Americans." El-i-chi brooded silently for a long time. "But my heart is heavy for those, our brothers, who have been used, once again, as soldiers in the cause of white men. I can wish, almost, that I had been there, at the side of the Miami, the Shawnee, the Delaware—all our brothers—for if I had fallen, I would not feel the great sadness clutching my heart now."

The Indians fled, realizing that no sanctuary would be offered by their British "allies." General Wayne arrived shortly thereafter, with the victorious legion in marching order. The American legion camped directly in front of the British fort, as if daring the British commander to open fire. For three days Wayne camped at the gate, exchanging notes that were anything but polite with the British commander who had betrayed his Indian friends. Either man, far from any opportunity to consult his government, could have started a new war, but *that* war was to be postponed for several more years.

Chapter XVII

~~~~~~

Hodano had rejoiced when Wayne's soldiers marched in orderly ranks directly into the muskets of the tribes. The evil shaman had seen the white soldiers break and run several times in the past, and he believed that this battle would be over almost before it began. It was not in his nature to admire the bravery and discipline of the legionnaires as they closed ranks when men fell to the murderous fire. Instead he screamed with anger and amazement at his evil spirits. So quickly had his dream ended!

At first, as the fighting closed to hand-to-hand combat and the bayonets of the legionnaires began to take a terrible toll, Hodano indulged himself, flitting from dying man to dying man to perform his obscene rite of spirit sucking; but soon Hodano found that he himself was also being driven before a surging wall of glistening bayonets. He watched as the brave warriors, armed with knives and tomahawks, died or fled.

In his anger he forgot his human mortality, and wielding his oversized war ax he leaped to meet two young white soldiers who were fighting side by side, pushing their way through the fallen trees. He surprised the first, taking him from the rear and smashing his skull; then, quickly, before the other could react, Hodano swung his huge blade with so much force that the legionnaire was beheaded on the spot. But then others were coming in great numbers, yelling and crashing through the limbs. With a snarl of desperation Hodano soared, escaping the scene of his greatest defeat.

From the safety of his spirit haven he watched the total rout. He saw Renno and El-i-chi lead the legion cavalry down the bank of the river and through the only small opening between the fallen timbers and the water, to fall upon the retreating warriors from the river. Tears of lost hope and anger blurred the vision of his one functioning eye. He knew then that it was over; not even his influence could gather the scattering survivors to face an army the likes of which had never been seen before.

As Renno and El-i-chi sat on their horses and watched the American victory, Hodano vowed one thing, and one thing only: Renno would die. Perhaps he would not be able to kill El-i-chi as well, but Hodano could accept that so long as Renno did not live to see the snows of winter. The shaman soared to his hidden longhouse, deep within the dark forest.

Hodano had not allowed his vassal Tor-yo-ne to partic-ipate in the battle. The shaman had become dependent on the young Seneca to do his chores: carry water, gather firewood, and prepare meals. Moreover, Tor-yo-ne, neces-sary for his final recourse against the enemy who had frustrated him for years, had to be protected for that important task. He called Tor-yo-ne to him, seated him, and spoke to him in his hissing voice.

"The white army will return to the fort at the head of the rapids of the Maumee," he said. "Renno of the Seneca will be among them. Your sister is there. Go to her. Tell her that you were wrong, that in the end, you did not fight against the United States. Ask her forgiveness, and she will give it to you, for you are her beloved brother. Before Renno returns, bring her to me. Her man will follow."

Tor-yo-ne traveled swiftly, reaching Fort Deposit while the legion was still face-to-face with British guns at the gates of Fort Miami. When the sentinels challenged him, he introduced himself as Renno's brother-by-marriage, come to visit his sister. "I am Seneca," he finished. "I do not fight against you."

For months Tor-yo-ne had had no will of his own. He had been kept in the depths of the forest, where Hodano's power was most potent. Now, among white men, with Hodano at a distance, stirrings of fond memories came to him, although they were swiftly passing and confusing. He understood his mission well, but as he walked through the habitat of the camp followers—the soldiers' families, the merchants, and the prostitutes—he could remember his sister, An-da, as a cheerful, uncomplaining young child who had accompanied him on the long journey to the south to join Renno's band of Seneca. The memories made his head throb. Under Hodano's close control, all love had been driven out of him. But now, nearing the reunion with An-da, the faintest hint of that emotion was fighting to reemerge in his mind.

He found his sister talking with a buxom, red-haired woman over cups of tea while a little boy toddled around them, begging sips of tea and charming them with winning smiles. When his shadow fell across her, An-da looked up into his face.

"Tor-yo-ne!" she gasped.

"My sister," Tor-yo-ne said, his head hurting frightfully as his love for An-da battled against Hodano's conditioning.

She rose. For a moment love won, and he moved forward and embraced An-da.

"This is my brother, and this is Floral," An-da said. She smiled with joy. "And this, Brother, is my son."

Tor-yo-ne studied the boy. There was a definite resemblance to Renno in the boy's face, and that was enough to restore Hodano's control, for Tor-yo-ne felt a surge of hatred engendered by the shaman.

"Now you must tell me all," An-da said warmly. "Are you hungry?"

"I have no hunger," Tor-yo-ne replied. "Where is Renno?"

"He's with the army, of course," An-da answered.

"But the fight is over," Tor-yo-ne said. "When will he return?"

"The word is," Floral Anderson said uneasily, "that the army will not return until they have destroyed the towns of the war chiefs."

An-da sensed that something had changed about her brother. "Why do you ask for Renno?"

"I must tell him that in my inexperience I wronged him," Tor-yo-ne said. "And I must tell him—and you: I did not lift my blade against the United States."

"But where have you been all this time?" An-da wanted to know.

He hesitated. Floral's eyes were narrowed in suspicion. "In my confusion I traveled far," he said, "and I was ashamed at my inability to decide the right course. I spent many months alone in the depths of the forest."

Tor-yo-ne's eyes were filled with the sight of his sister. She had matured and was rich in womanly beauty—a mother but still An-da, whom he had dearly loved. An-da, the last of his close blood. Rebellion grew in him against the malignant force that controlled him. Once he and his sister had been together, and that was as it should be.

He was uncomfortable here among so many people after having been alone—or with Hodano—for so long. He yearned for the peaceful solitude of the forest, and he envisioned that his relationship with An-da could be as it had once been—that they would be together, brother and sister against the world.

"Let me prepare some food for you," An-da offered.

"No, no," he said. "We must go."

"Go?" she asked, a little tendril of unease unfurling within her.

"We will go home, to the land of the Seneca," he explained. "You do not belong here, nor do I."

"I am the wife of Renno," An-da protested. "I cannot leave him."

Tor-yo-ne looked around. They were a hundred feet from any other shelter. No one was watching them.

"An-da," Floral said casually, "I'll be going now."

"Where do you go?" Tor-yo-ne demanded, madness in his eyes, moving to block her way.

"Time to start cooking, I guess," Floral said, struggling to keep her tone friendly.

Tor-yo-ne was hearing voices in his head. Hodano, knowing the woman's intentions were to summon help, was warning him.

"Stay!" Tor-yo-ne ordered harshly.

"No, I'd better go," Floral said. "Got things to do."

She turned her back to An-da, and Tor-yo-ne lifted his hand and plunged his knife into the woman's abdomen, just below her breasts, then drove the blade upward and twisted it. The blade ripped through Floral's diaphragm, paralyzing her, then penetrated her heart. Tor-yo-ne caught her as she started to fall.

"Floral!" An-da gasped. She had been distracted by her son, who had chosen that moment to investigate the abandoned teacups, and had not seen the fatal plunge of the knife.

"I think she has fainted," Tor-yo-ne said, lowering the body to the ground. He glanced around quickly. No one had seen. No one was looking.

But then An-da saw the blood seeping through Floral's dress. The young woman opened her mouth to cry out. Tor-yo-ne, moving with the speed of a striking snake, lifted Ta-na-wun-da with one arm and held his bloody knife at the ready.

"Silence," he ordered, and An-da's scream stuck in her throat. "You will walk quietly at my side. You will smile, and you will talk with me as we leave this camp. If you do not, and if we are stopped, I will kill this spawn of Renno's."

For a moment An-da was speechless. Then she swallowed and said in a voice that sounded almost normal, "I will gather some things."

"There is no time. Come now."

"Yes," she agreed. "I will do as you say. Do not harm my son."

They walked away from the shelter and made their way among tents and rude lean-tos. An-da, her heart pounding, nodded and spoke to people she knew, praying that someone would realize that something was wrong, while at the same time fearing that if someone did, Tor-yo-ne would hurt Ta-na-wun-da.

Tor-yo-ne spoke easily as they walked, his voice sounding natural. "Tell, me, Sister, when did you and Renno marry?"

She answered in kind, talking soothingly, humoring the madman. Thus they walked through the open gates of the palisade. No one questioned them. They were, after all, only two Indians; Indians came and went around the camp, as scouts or beggars.

"I will carry him now," An-da offered, reaching for her son as they crossed the cleared fire field in front of the fort.

Tor-yo-ne laughed. "He is not heavy."

Now they entered the forest, and soon no sounds from the fort could be heard. "Brother, I like this not," she said. "Where are you taking us?"

"I told you," he said. "We go to the east, to the land of the Seneca. There we will be as we were, brother and sister together."

"And my husband?" she asked.

A snarl issued from Tor-yo-ne's lips, for here, away from the voices and the presence of the whites, Hodano was regaining control.

"Tor-yo-ne," she pleaded, "I want to go back. You are my brother, and I have loved you, but now you have killed without reason. You must go far, perhaps to the west, to escape the vengeance of that woman's husband and the soldiers who follow him. Please go. I will tell them that I don't know where you are."

For a moment her words made sense, but then Hodano's mind closed on him in a dark cloud, and his orders were clear. The evil shaman awaited them and guided them to him. He turned from the easterly direction in which he and An-da had been traveling.

"Why do we turn to the south?" she asked.

"To confuse any who might follow."

Tor-yo-ne kept his knife in hand, always ready to strike, and An-da, a small, weaponless woman, concerned for the welfare of her son, could do nothing but obey.

That night, as Tor-yo-ne seemed to be sleeping, the boy clutched close to him, An-da crept toward her brother. In her hand she grasped a stout weather-hardened limb that she had chosen when gathering firewood. When she was near, she raised the makeshift club.

An evil laugh made her stop. She saw, with horror, that Tor-yo-ne's knife was poised at her son's throat.

"Sister," he said, "to me the boy is an encumbrance. It is only for your sake that I let him live, and it is up to you to keep him alive. Do not tempt me."

For three days they marched, and during that time they ate only once—a rabbit roasted over an open fire. Since it was the custom for Indian mothers to nurse their children until the children themselves stopped the feedings, An-da's rich breasts gave Ta-na-wun-da sustenance.

It was almost twilight on the third day when they penetrated a dark grove and approached Hodano's longhouse. The shaman stood outside, a dark figure radiating an evil that caused An-da to shrink back.

"You have done well," Hodano commended. "Give the boy to me."

Tor-yo-ne stepped forward and handed Ta-na-wun-da into the hands of his master. An-da sprang forward, crying out. Hodano met her with one swift blow; the back of his hand crashed into her mouth, sending her sprawling to the ground.

Dazed, An-da came to her hands and knees, shaking her head to dispel the dizziness. Blood had sprung up from a split lip. She spat out two teeth.

"He is his father's son," Hodano said, examining the boy closely in the fading light, his head cocked to put his good eye close to Ta-na-wun-da's face. "But his life force is small."

An-da could not even scream, so numbed was she by what had happened. Hodano seized Ta-na-wun-da by the heels with one hand and let him hang head downward. The boy gave a startled cry. An-da clawed her way on her hands and knees toward Hodano, crying out, "No! No!"

Hodano met her with a kick to her chest, and she was lifted to land hard on her back. Tor-yo-ne made a convulsive move to help his sister; but when Hodano's burning eye transfixed him, he stopped immediately.

"The time is not yet," Hodano said. He flung Ta-na-wun-da away, and Tor-yo-ne managed to catch the child before he struck the ground. "Bring the woman," he ordered, bending to enter the longhouse.

In the aftermath of the brief but fierce battle among the fallen timbers, Anthony Wayne moved the legion onto Miami lands. Here, at Fort Wayne, he initiated the actions that would complete his victory, while compiling the report that would be sent east to Philadelphia. He had routed the enemy at a cost of only thirty-three dead and one hundred wounded.

The will to fight had been completely destroyed in all but a handful of the Ohio tribesmen. The once-formidable Indian army had scattered, and the councils that were held following the battle were notable for the absence of many of the former leaders.

At one such meeting of lesser chiefs, Tecumseh rose. He, like many, had dreamed of a great Indian nation of allied tribes in the Ohio Valley, where red men could live in peace and equality with their white neighbors. Thoroughly

Indian in his outlook, he had not understood the European concept of nationalism and would never be able to understand how the soldiers of the legion had been able to march, shoulders almost touching, into the barrels of a thousand muskets and, as men fell, close ranks and march on.

"This is not the final defeat," he told the small gathering. "Before the white chief who never sleeps came, we were victorious. We will be victorious again. For did the Indian not fight well with the French, in days gone by, and with the British in the great white man's war? Did we not fight bravely against Harmar and St. Clair?"

"We have seen the end," intoned a grizzled old warrior.

"We must fight on," Tecumseh urged. "We must go to our friends, the British in Canada, for more guns and for their aid in renewing the battle."

"Can you not see, young one," asked the old warrior, "that the friendship of the British was nothing but a scheme to get the Indian to fight England's battles?"

"We must unite all tribes under one leader!" Tecumseh insisted, fire in his words. "Together we will have the strength to regain that which is ours."

One by one those who had been listening rose and, heads lowered, walked away. Tecumseh lifted his hands to the spirits. "This I pledge: I will not cease my efforts until all Indians are united and until this great Indian force has avenged those who have fallen here."

For six days Wayne's army raged along the Maumee, bringing fire and destruction to the villages of all the tribes that had waged war for so long in the Northwest Territory. St. Clair had been avenged. And Harmar had been avenged, for Wayne had built Fort Defiance near the site of the Miami settlements where Harmar had met defeat.

The general, unaware of the completeness of his victory, had ordered his team of scouts to guide legion units to the villages. In spite of the tribes' heavy losses, Wayne felt endangered by forces of Indians still on the loose. As a result he set about destroying the crops upon which the renegades would depend for food during the coming winter. Village after village was put to the torch.

Renno and El-i-chi witnessed only one of the punitive attacks. There was no resistance. Women, children, and old men ran away upon the approach of the soldiers.

"Brother, I like this not," El-i-chi muttered as they watched the burning of the settlement. "I do not war upon women and children."

Renno's expression was one of distaste. "It is time for us to go home."

"There is one enemy, still," El-i-chi remarked.

"Coward that he is," Renno acknowledged, knowing that El-i-chi meant Hodano. "He will not show his face, and we have been here long enough."

Roy was with another unit of the legion. Renno and El-i-chi, with their families, planned to meet him back at Fort Deposit. The brothers traveled swiftly, for An-da, Ah-wa-o, and their sons awaited them, as did the long trail to the south, which could not be covered before the onset of winter. When they reached Fort Deposit, they walked into a happy camp and were greeted with friendliness by men who knew them. The victory had been great, and the celebration was not yet over.

Ah-wa-o saw them coming and ran to meet them. "Thank the manitous you are here," she said, and the expression on her face brought a feeling of dread to Renno. He looked past Ah-wa-o, expecting to see An-da.

"She's gone, Sachem," Ah-wa-o said. "A warrior, dressed as a Seneca, came and talked with her, and she is gone."

It took some time to get the entire story out of Ah-wa-o. Floral Anderson had been murdered. Her husband had been sent for, and Rufus Anderson himself had led a body of men into the forest in search of the Indian who had killed his wife and stolen An-da and Ta-na-wun-da. The sergeant had not yet returned. Renno's face was taut with concern.

El-i-chi clasped his shoulder and said, "We go."

There was no hope of following the trail of the Seneca

warrior who had taken An-da and Ta-na-wun-da, but there were traces of the larger party that had been led by Sergeant Anderson. On the theory that Anderson may have cut the trail days earlier, they followed. At first the way led east, then swung to the southeast toward the heart of the forests. When the tracks of the army detail turned more southerly and then began a slow circle back toward the forts, Renno halted, puzzled.

"He would not turn back toward the army," El-i-chi said. For some time he had been trying to avail himself of his gift of Sight, but, as often happened, he saw nothing beyond the capability of his own human vision.

"We rest," Renno said, for he was at a loss about what to do and could not decide in which direction to travel.

El-i-chi hunted, and as the meat was roasting, Renno walked into the forest. El-i-chi, knowing that his brother was going to consult the manitous, did not speak or attempt to follow. Instead, he went into contemplation himself.

There was no time for Renno's usual fasting. He implored the manitous in vain, and with the dew of early morning on the leaves, he morosely made his way back to the camp to find El-i-chi sitting, eyes staring unblinkingly into space. Renno, respecting his brother's meditation, sat down quietly and waited.

In the darkness that preceded dawn, El-i-chi's face transformed, and a snarl of anger came from his lips. He shook his head as if awaking from a sleep and looked around. Seeing Renno, he leaped to his feet. "There is no time to lose. We have far to go."

"You have seen?"

El-i-chi could not bring himself to tell his brother what he had seen. He set out, running at near capacity, Renno at his heels.

An-da fought as she had never fought before, for she knew that she and her son faced deadly evil. When her own brother seized her and started to drag her toward the dark longhouse, she kicked, scratched, and tried to bite, but Tor-yo-ne, his will completely subjected to Hodano, jarred her head with an open-handed slap, and she was dazed for a time. When her head cleared, she was standing with her back against a post in the longhouse, her arms tied behind her around the post, her ankles bound. Ta-na-wun-da, thoroughly frightened, was shrieking, tears rolling down his cheeks, as he clutched at her skirt.

"Tor-yo-ne," she said. "Why?"

But her brother stood at the back of the longhouse, erect, arms dangling at his sides, face slack. Before her, moving wraithlike in the flickering light of the fire, Hodano danced without making a sound. His movements were slow, as sinuous as a snake's. He had thrown back the wolverine hood to expose his terrifying face. She looked around in desperation, and her eyes widened as she saw, ranged along the walls, scores of human skulls of various sizes.

Ta-na-wun-da continued to cry loudly as Hodano broke into song, his voice a quavering falsetto. The child clung to An-da's legs and by his movements showed that he wanted to be picked up. But the shaman seemed not to be bothered by the child. He continued his writhing dance, moving slowly around the fire.

"Tor-yo-ne," An-da begged, "help us, please."

Tor-yo-ne strained forward, but it was as if he, too, were bound. His blank expression remained unchanged.

Hodano's dance and chants seemed to go on forever. Night had come; the fire had burned to embers. No sounds came from the forest outside. It was as if Hodano's evil had warned away all living things. The shaman, still chanting, his tongue flicking in and out of his mouth, added dry branches to the coals, and the flames sprang up quickly. He undulated to stand directly before An-da, and his breath had an unearthly stench.

"I am helpless before you," An-da said bravely, "but Renno will come, and when he does, your death will be certain."

Hodano's mutilated mouth twisted in what might have been a smile. "The woman of the Seneca who is to die has spirit," he said. "It is time to see how courageous she is, for she will not die swiftly."

A knife seemed to materialize in his hand, and An-da caught her breath, thinking that her time had come. But Hodano used the knife to slit her tunic to expose her torso. Then the knife sliced through the band of her skirt and her sash, and with swift movements she was naked.

The shaman whirled, making complete circles, and then bent to take from the embers of the fire a ramrod that had been fitted with a leather strap. The leather was hot in his hand; the tip of the rod glowed with white heat. He came to An-da, his one eye shining, his mouth open, his split tongue darting in and out.

She tensed as the smoking metal came near her stomach. The woman prepared herself for the pain after a quick glance at her brother proved that he would be of no help to her. An-da sucked in her breath in a great, tortured gasp as Hodano began to brand a symbol of evil on the smooth, tight skin of her stomach. She would not give him the satisfaction of her screaming. She closed her eyes and called out in her mind for Renno. The agony continued for a long, long time. The pain did not cease as Hodano stood back, examining his work.

"Tor-yo-ne!" An-da called out as the shaman leaned toward her again, the white-hot ramrod pointed toward one of her upper thighs. "You allow this to happen to your sister?"

With a strangled cry of pain Tor-yo-ne broke his mental bonds and leaped forward. Hope flared in An-da's heart, only to be chilled when, with a raised hand, Hodano commanded him to halt.

Tor-yo-ne stopped as if he had run into an invisible wall. All his muscles strained, and his face was distorted with his efforts. Then, with a cry of despair he collapsed to the floor, writhed, then pulled himself into a tight fetal position and lay still.

"Thus I will control your Renno," Hodano said to An-da. "First he will be my slave, and then he will die even more slowly than you and your son."

Hodano bent himself to his work throughout a long night, applying maximum pain short of death by concentrating his attention on specific points of the human body, now and then kicking aside the child. Ta-na-wun-da, bruised and stunned, finally crawled into a corner and escaped into sleep.

An-da was still alive when dawn sent its light through the open door and down the smoke hole on the longhouse, although she had been praying to the manitous for death for many hours.

Hodano, pleased to find such strength in the woman, was looking forward to a day, perhaps even another night, of pleasure—and then there would be the boy. He was small and would not be capable of withstanding more than a fraction of the agony that was being dealt to his mother; but, after all, the son had the blood of Renno and was thus a tiny reservoir of Renno's strength and orenda. Fortified with the spirits of the white Indian's woman and son, Hodano would face his enemy with confidence.

Hodano sent tendrils of himself away into the forest in search of Renno and cursed when he detected nothing. When would they come? He was ready. Were the great Renno and his brother so helpless that they could not follow the trail? Was El-i-chi so inept that he could not hear the pulse of Hodano's heart?

The very fact that Hodano could not locate his enemies made him feel uneasy. He left his pleasure and walked into the dawn to stand in the clearing in front of his longhouse and cast his spirit into the wind, searching . . . wondering. El-i-chi's power had been great on the field of the dead. That memory of defeat rankled inside Hodano and became fear.

He hurried inside. He would cut short his enjoyment with An-da, for he had a feeling that something must be wrong with his ability to sense the brothers' whereabouts. He would fortify himself with the spirits of Renno's wife and son, and then, perhaps, he would be strong enough to find his enemies.

Throughout the torment An-da had not given up hope. In her agony she realized that nothing had been done to her that would not heal in time. Renno would come, and she would have relief. She would ask Renno's permission to visit upon the body of Hodano the same tortures that she was suffering. This hope, this hatred for the man who sent her body into silent convulsions of pain, kept her sane. She was whole—damaged but whole—and she would live to see Hodano die.

Hope died, then became despair, when Hodano returned from the out-of-doors. There was in him a determination she could see in his expression to end her life quickly. An-da firmed her jaw and met the sure knowledge that she was going to die with courage.

Hodano prepared himself for the ultimate pleasure, the climax of his long ceremony. He felt the spirit of the woman quivering, seeking escape from the mutilated, dying body, and braced himself to take that strength.

"Renno . . ." An-da whispered, and knew no more.

Hodano leaned forward, mouth gaping, to suck in her spirit. He screamed out in terror and anger when, with the sound of a hawk's wings, something thrust itself between his face and An-da's, and he felt the life force of the brave young woman leap free to be taken up . . . up . . . on soaring wings beyond his reach.

He bellowed his disappointment, and then a clear picture of Renno and El-i-chi sprang into his mind. Their tomahawks in their hands, torsos gleaming with the sweat of their exertions, they were running toward him.

He had been robbed. Once again the forces of light had frustrated him, taken from him the thing he needed most to face two powerful enemies. In desperation, he turned, lifted the sleeping boy, measured the strength of the small life force, and wailed, for it was not enough— even if combined with the spirit of Tor-yo-ne, still lying on the floor in a fetal position. The shaman El-i-chi would possess the power to penetrate Hodano's defenses. And El-i-chi, Hodano knew, was dangerously close, only minutes away.

Once more he screamed his anger at his spirits, knowing that he was beaten again, knowing that he could not face Renno and El-i-chi together.

He stood over Tor-yo-ne, hands spread, and muttered a spell. The young man stirred, then sat up. "Take the boy," Hodano ordered. "You will go here." And into Tor-yo-ne's mind he inserted instructions. "When you arrive, I will be waiting."

Tor-yo-ne carried the boy into the forest and was gone.

Hodano stood in front of his longhouse, thinking about his strategy. He had sent Tor-yo-ne to a place where the spirits were strong in his favor. He planned to have Tor-yo-ne lead his enemies there, and with the spirit of Renno's son giving him additional power, Hodano would, at last, even all scores. Hodano planned the moment of initial contact with the white Indian; he had his words ready. He intended to gloat a bit, and then to watch the pain on his enemy's face. Renno would burst into the clearing, Hodano expected, then halt to assess the situation.

Renno, detecting the smoke from Hodano's longhouse, increased his stride to push past El-i-chi. He burst into the clearing recklessly to see Hodano standing in front of the dwelling, arms folded, hood back, scarred, bony face fixed in a sneer. Instead of stopping, Renno put on a burst of speed that closed the gap between him and Hodano with startling swiftness.

Renno's arm drew back on the dead run, and sun reflected off the blade of the tomahawk. He whipped his arm forward, the blade whirling at the evil shaman's chest.

Hodano screamed in fear and soared just in time to prevent Renno's blade from smashing his breastbone.

Renno howled in frustration, slowed his pace, and halted at the door of the longhouse, for there was a stench coming from inside that was all too familiar—the smell of death, of burned flesh, of blood, of released intestinal contents. He was so overwhelmed with dread that for long moments, until El-i-chi was at his side, he was without the strength to enter the darkened doorway.

El-i-chi went past him, and from within the longhouse exploded a chilling outburst of rage. He tried to prevent Renno from entering, but the white Indian pushed him aside and looked at the thing that had once been An-da. He fell to his knees.

El-i-chi took swift stock of the room's interior. Renno's voice was hoarsely whispering a song of mourning. El-i-chi moved to his side and knelt, for a time joining him in mourning, but his mind was working. They had seen Hodano use the power of the voodoo masters to escape, but he had not been holding Renno's son.

El-i-chi rose and slipped out of the longhouse, leaving Renno to his sorrow. He began to cast around the clearing. When he saw fresh tracks, he followed them for a hundred yards, then went back to the longhouse.

"One ran just before we arrived. Perhaps he was carrying Ta-na-wun-da."

His words penetrated the haze of Renno's shocked senses. He looked up through glassy eyes.

"I will go," El-i-chi told him. "I will leave a trail that you can follow on the run."

The sachem nodded, and El-i-chi was gone.

In the eerie silence of Hodano's hidden clearing, the voice of mourning mounted, continued for half an hour, then faded. No bird sang. Not even a squirrel's chatter broke the stillness.

An-da had died a death more terrible than any Renno had ever seen. Not even in the past, when the women of the tribe offered a captured warrior an honorable chance to show his courage under torture, had a human being been so misused. And into the mourning came an anger so terrible that it shook his body.

He drew his stiletto and cut the bonds that still held her to the post, caught her body before it could hit the floor, and carried her gently into the clean, outside air. There would be time for mourning later. Now he buried her in the manner of the ancients, first wrapping her in tree bark. He dug the grave deep, to prevent her from being disinterred by scavengers, and sang the song of death as he lowered her and covered her with more bark and clean, fresh branches. He used his hands to push the earth atop her and marked the spot with a mound.

He stood, head bowed, trying to eradicate from his mind the sight of her as she had been in death, for that bloodied and mutilated thing of tortured flesh was not his An-da. An-da was in the Place across the River now, and he implored the spirits of those who had gone before to welcome her. He said his farewell to her in Seneca, speaking softly and slowly.

And then he was running...running. True to his word, El-i-chi had left an easy trail, slowing his own progress by breaking branches to point the direction. The vision of An-da's mutilated body relentlessly invaded his mind's eye. To inflict the same torment on Hodano—and on whatever monster had been Hodano's helper—would not lessen that memory; but it would, at least, cool the fire of hatred that gave him strength to run as he had never run before.

He caught up with El-i-chi with the last of the day's light.

"He leaves a good trail," El-i-chi said, "as if he wants us to follow. And yet, as swiftly as I move, he stays ahead of me. It is as if his feet are given wings by spirits."

Chapter XVIII

Sometimes the trail became obscured: Rain obscured the tracks of moccasined feet, the passage of small herds of deer along a game trail obliterated the traces; the trail became mixed with the tracks of others—small hunting parties, Indians making their way back to their villages after the battle in the north. While the trail was fresh and the brothers moved swiftly, it became evident that the warrior who had left Hodano's longhouse and, they prayed, carried Ta-na-wun-da was traveling due south.

Once, when the trail had been washed away by a strong thunderstorm and a full day of casting around had failed to turn up any trace, the brothers approached a camp of Miami Indians and gave the greeting of peace. After they were

offered a share of the evening meal, Renno inquired about
the passage of a single warrior with a small boy.

"I have seen such a one," said a warrior. "He passed
us two days back, moving swiftly. He had a boy of perhaps
four seasons strapped to his back."

"His tribe?" El-i-chi asked.

"He wore the paint of the Mingo," the Miami answered.

Renno, who had lapsed into silence, content to know
that Ta-na-wun-da was alive, looked up with attention, for
Mingo was the name applied to the Seneca who had
moved west into the Ohio lands. The warrior who had led
An-da out of Fort Deposit had been described as Seneca.
"A tall warrior, well formed?"

"That he was," the Miami replied. "He ran well with
long strides, turning aside for nothing."

For some time Renno had been entertaining suspicions. He could not envision An-da leaving the army camp
with a stranger—not even a Seneca, not even if that
Seneca had pretended to be Renno's messenger. More and
more he was becoming convinced that when he caught up
with his son's kidnapper, he would stand face-to-face with
Tor-yo-ne. The warrior who ran before them was capable
of maintaining a pace that would have pushed even a
superbly conditioned man like Renno. He had run with
Tor-yo-ne and knew Tor-yo-ne's capability.

For a day Renno set a killing pace. El-i-chi did not
complain. They followed a well-traveled track that, in the
end, would lead to the sites of the destroyed Shawnee
villages along the Ohio east of Cincinnati, for he had a
feeling that the kidnapper was making for the river.

His hunch paid off when they came upon a campsite
where the ashes of the previous night's fire were still
warm. The marks of the moccasins they had been following were around the fire, along with the imprints of small
bare feet. Renno set out immediately, for he knew he was
only hours behind.

Now the trail was fresh. It led them through sparsely
peopled rolling country. By the end of the day Renno
could almost smell his quarry. The kidnapper, who had

traveled so rapidly, was now slowing. In the late evening with the sinking sun casting dark shadows in the forest, the tracks veered away from the trail.

"He is looking for water," Renno said softly. "He will be camped there, below the ridge." He loosened his stiletto in its sheath and caressed the haft of his tomahawk.

The brothers moved slowly along a deer trail that wound toward the ridge. Renno held up his hand, halting El-i-chi, for he smelled wood smoke. Now they moved slowly, silently, slipping from cover to cover like ghosts of the dusk. The sun was down behind the ridge, leaving the sky to the west the color of blood.

Although the smell of smoke was strong, Renno could not see the fire. He soon discovered why: A dark opening in the ridge told of the presence of a cave. He moved to his left and, when he was directly in front of the opening, saw the flicker of flames just inside the cave's mouth. There could be only one approach to the entrance—directly from the front. Renno motioned El-i-chi to approach the cave from the right. He himself disappeared back into the forest and moved to his left, coming up to the slope of the ridge a hundred yards from the cave's mouth.

The sachem approached with great caution, then stood for long minutes near the dark opening, listening. He could hear the hiss and crackle of the fire but nothing else. There was no sign of El-i-chi beyond the cave. The silence seemed unnatural. Perhaps, he thought, the warrior was already asleep, or had ventured from his campsite to hunt. If the latter were the case, then Ta-na-wun-da should be alone, inside the dark opening.

Renno lowered himself to his belly and snaked his way through weedy growth laced with rocks. He crawled to a point where he could see directly into the cave, and his heart leaped with joy. Ta-na-wun-da, so small, so beautiful to his eyes, was sitting by the fire. He looked wan and had lost weight, so that his formerly rounded little form was gaunt. Of the warrior there was no sign.

Renno knew that it would be best to wait for El-i-chi. Ta-na-wun-da's captor might try to harm the boy when he realized that they had been overtaken. But Ta-na-wun-da

looked so forlorn, so helpless. . . . Renno, noticing a slight
movement of the brush to his right, forced himself to wait.

Moving like a shadow, El-i-chi appeared, fifty yards
away, crawling toward the entrance to the cave. Renno
could wait no longer. He gathered his legs under him,
leaped up, and in a silent rush ran into the opening,
thinking that he could be at Ta-na-wun-da's side so quickly
that even if the warrior was inside, Renno would have his
tomahawk between the enemy and Ta-na-wun-da before
the warrior could do anything to harm the boy.

Tor-yo-ne was crouched in a recess in the rock just
inside the cave, his tomahawk in hand. He had heard the
soft, running footfalls and had readied himself.

Renno shot into the cave running with all his speed,
and only the swiftness of his entrance saved him. Tor-yo-
ne's tomahawk grazed the top of Renno's head, but then
the sachem was past, whirling to crouch between the man
who had almost killed him and his son.

Tor-yo-ne, seeing that his ambush had failed, held up
one hand quickly. "Renno," he said, relieved. "It is you."

"Explain yourself," Renno said from between clenched
teeth as he moved slowly forward.

"Hold!" Tor-yo-ne said. "I did not know it was you.
There is your son, safe, for I have protected him."

"But you did not protect An-da," Renno raged, hatred
darkening his face. "You were there."

"I was," Tor-yo-ne confessed, "but I was a captive. I
could do nothing, Renno. Then, when I had the chance to
save your son, I took it and fled, for Hodano is more than a
mortal warrior can face."

Renno glanced up to see El-i-chi standing in the
entrance, listening to Tor-yo-ne's words but looking with
narrowed eyes at Ta-na-wun-da. Renno glanced briefly at
his son, suspicion awakened by El-i-chi's expression. The
boy was unaffected by his father's appearance. A blank
look rested on his little face.

"Speak, Tor-yo-ne," Renno urged. "My impulse is to
kill you swiftly. Tell me why you killed the white woman at
the army camp. Tell me why you took An-da to Hodano."

"You know his powers," Tor-yo-ne explained. "By the manitous, Sachem, I did not know what I was doing. I was under a dark spell of evil cast by Hodano. You must know that I would have died myself rather than—"

"Haven't you heard the old truth," Renno interrupted, "that Indians cannot lie convincingly to another Indian?"

"The spirits know that I tried, Sachem! But I was helpless before his magic. It was only when he was preoccupied with my sister that his hold on me weakened and I was able to take the boy and run."

"El-i-chi," Renno asked, "could Hodano so use his powers?"

El-i-chi nodded grimly.

Confused, Renno came out of his fighting crouch. "Where is Hodano?"

"Sachem, I don't know."

Renno turned his attention to his son. He knelt beside the boy and spoke his name. It was as if Ta-na-wun-da did not hear. He continued to stare into the fire. "El-i-chi . . ." Renno said, his voice revealing his distress.

"Keep an eye on Tor-yo-ne," El-i-chi said as he moved deeper into the cave, knelt, lifted Ta-na-wun-da's chin, and looked into his eyes. A dullness was there. He quickly examined the boy for injuries, but aside from a few scratches, he could find nothing.

"He has been this way since he heard the screams of his mother," Tor-yo-ne explained sadly.

"The boy is under a spell," El-i-chi said.

"My son," Renno said, laying aside his weapons to gather the boy into his arms. "Ah, my son." And as he embraced Ta-na-wun-da, he was remembering An-da as she had been, sunny and as sweet as her name. It was at that unguarded moment that Tor-yo-ne saw his chance. El-i-chi, in deep concentration, searching for a power that would break Hodano's hold on the boy, was distracted. Tor-yo-ne sprang with the swiftness of a panther, his toma-hawk sweeping down, aimed at the back of Renno's neck.

But El-i-chi caught movement out of the corner of his eye and swung his tomahawk instinctively, catching the Wolf in midleap. Tor-yo-ne felt the blade bury itself in his stomach. His momentum carried him onward, but the strength had gone out of him, and his blow whistled past Renno's shoulder. The blade of the tomahawk was driven into the soft earth floor of the cavern as he fell.

Tor-yo-ne felt the life force drain from the gash in his belly. Hands grasped his hip and shoulder and gently rolled him onto his back. El-i-chi hunkered down beside him, turned Tor-yo-ne's face, and bent his ear to the warrior's lips.

"I tried." Tor-yo-ne gasped. "Her pain was my own, but I could not. . . . I lay there hearing . . . him laugh. I saw her . . . blood."

"Where is Hodano?" El-i-chi probed softly.

"Sachem," Tor-yo-ne whispered, his voice faint. "I was so wrong. I should have . . . stayed with you." His eyes closed. His lips moved, and the name he spoke was his sister's. "An-da. An-da."

"Hodano," El-i-chi whispered fiercely.

"Kill," Tor-yo-ne whispered. "Make . . . death . . . long, Sachem."

"That I promise." Renno dropped to his knees beside Tor-yo-ne. "But first I must find him."

Tor-yo-ne's eyes fluttered open. His hand moved to clutch the bloody entrails sliding from the great slash in his stomach. He lifted his head, but no words came.

"Where is Hodano?" Renno asked.

"South. One day's march from the . . . Ohio. The ancient ones buried . . . dead," Tor-yo-ne managed. He opened his mouth to speak more, but only blood came in a gush, and his head sank back. A blackness came over him, and a desire to sleep. He tasted blood at the back of his tongue.

"Tell me," Renno grated, gripping Tor-yo-ne's shoulder. "Tell me where!"

"Great . . . serpent." Tor-yo-ne's words gurgled with blood. "Ser . . ."

With Ta-na-wun-da strapped to his back, Renno trudged southward in new sadness. The boy ate and drank and breathed, but otherwise he was as dead as Tor-yo-ne. His eyes stared into unfathomable distances. He did not utter a sound.

Hodano, Renno was repeating in his mind. *Hodano.*

In the charred remnants of a Shawnee village they found one old woman who had been left behind to die by Wayne's legion. She had been living on corn gleaned from the destroyed crops. She looked up from her bed of scorched, ragged furs to see two young warriors.

"Mercy," she whispered. "Show me your mercy and give me the gift of death."

"It will come, old one," El-i-chi said. "It will come."

"All dead," the old woman moaned. "All from this village are dead or gone away." She raised herself on one elbow. Her clothes were in rags, exposing her wrinkled, sagging breasts. "And our fine, brave warriors—are they also dead?"

"Many are dead," El-i-chi said. "The white man's army was victorious."

A wail came from the old woman's lips. "Then be kind and touch me with your blade, Sachem."

Renno opened his food pouch. "Here is meat, old mother."

In spite of the woman's wish to die, she seized the meat eagerly.

"Old mother," Renno said, "do you know of a place where the ancient ones buried their dead?"

The woman was ripping off a small piece of the well-cooked meat and putting it into her mouth. "There is such a place," she said, "but I beg you not to go there, for it is a place of the spirits of the long dead."

"Where is it, old mother?" El-i-chi asked.

"Across the stream," the woman answered, "walk due south, and you will see an area where the trees have climbed the curved mounds. If you walk these mounds, you will understand why the spot is sacred and filled with spirits. You would do well to avoid this place."

They left the old woman eating contentedly, but the brothers knew that her death would come soon, and by starvation.

* * *

They camped beside the stream mentioned by the old woman and, with the light of the new day, moved southward with caution. The mounds of the ancients were not visible until the brothers were quite near, for the forest was dense and hid its secret well. Then, directly in front of them, rose a huge mound of overgrown earth stretching into the forest on either side. The mound towered over their heads, and its extent was not discernible.

Heeding the old woman's warnings, they walked alongside the mound. Within a few paces it began to curve, forming a sharp loop. The going was difficult because of the dense brush. After trudging some distance, they reached another portion of the mound that curved sharply into a circle, then into a spiral.

"It is like the coiled tail of a snake," El-i-chi observed.

Renno was achingly alert, for since he had approached the mound he had felt a presence—or presences. Such a feeling had come to him before, in odd places, such as at the site of an Arawak massacre in Jamaica and in the City of Blood, old Benin, in Africa. It was as if hordes of silent spirits were trying to make contact with him but succeeding only on an unconscious level.

El-i-chi stood in the center of the spiral mound, the high dirt walls all around, fingering the handle of his tomahawk. "Here is only that which cannot be seen by human eyes," he said. "A very odd place."

Renno led the way out of the spiral and walked along the other side of the mound, going back in the direction whence they had come. He counted four convex, outward loops; three more inner loops, which were indented deeply; and then the men were walking along an almost-straight mound. Here the trees were not as thick, and the white Indian could see that the mound thickened at this end.

Renno ascended to the top and climbed a tree, where he found a vantage point in the fork. From here he could make out a double mound. This twin rise enclosed an open triangle of brush with what seemed to be another doubled mound beyond.

The sounds of the forest were reassuring—the coo of a dove, the caw of a crow, the hoarse chatter of a squirrel who sat on a high limb and repeated his claim to a particular little patch of forest. But there were other sounds, which were not so much heard as felt . . . a whispering that never rose to audible levels.

"The old woman was right," El-i-chi said, his head swiveling from right to left as Renno jumped down from the tree. He turned to look over his shoulder. "This place abounds with spirits. Do you feel them?"

Renno nodded. *Manitous,* he thought, *help me. Help me to find him.* The almost-heard voices were many and confused, and their odd words held no meaning for him.

The brothers walked carefully around the far end of the great mound, where they found a steep wall. They climbed to the top, there to see an oblate circle enclosed by the high, dirt mounds. The enclosed area, free of trees and brush, was covered by a low growing, dark green grass.

"This is the serpent's head," El-i-chi said, picturing the entire mound in his mind as they slid down from the wall. "This is a snake, tail coiled, body looped, the head and the brain enclosed by the high mounds. Tor-yo-ne used the word *serpent." And,* he thought, *the old woman said that we would understand the evil of this place when we knew the shape of the mound.*

From the carrying pouch on Renno's back Ta-na-wun-da whimpered, his first utterance since they had found him in the cave. Before Renno could react, the ground began to shake under his feet, and he almost lost his balance. El-i-chi braced himself by grabbing a sapling.

"Hodano is here," El-i-chi said.

As if to prove the shaman's words, a horrid growl was unleashed behind the brothers. They swung around as one, weapons at the ready, to see a huge creature out of a nightmare, half wolf and half puma. Its long yellowed fangs dripped saliva as it sprang, loosing another terrible growl. With no time to use his bow, Renno leaped forward, tomahawk lifted.

"Hold!" El-i-chi cried out, then pulled Renno back. He himself raised his arms and faced the beast. He chanted, his voice rising, and the beast, after making two bounds toward them, faded into nothingness with a whimper.

The wolves came next; Renno had faced Hodano's spirit wolves before and was ready to face them again, but once more El-i-chi chanted, and the animals faded to nonexistence.

Hodano, hidden among trees atop a mound, ranted in frustration. The great power in the form of his two enemies ranged against him, but he had countered by drawing from the depths of his own evil and staging the fight on turf that would enhance his abilities. For days, as he had sensed Renno's approach, Hodano had fasted and supplicated his spirits. Now, using the voodoo powers he had learned in Haiti and Jamaica, he conjured up horrors never before seen on the North American continent.

Gibbering, shrieking, monstrous freaks launched themselves at the brothers from all directions. Part man, part animal, and part creature, these miscreations had never existed on earth. Renno met them with his two blades, but the steel passed harmlessly through them. El-i-chi, however, called upon the spirits of the Master of Life, and the horrors became hollow, harmless, and impotent.

The brothers heard Hodano's wail of fury at the latest failure of his evil spirits. The men turned to see the malevolent shaman atop a mound, arms uplifted. Renno unstrapped the carrying pouch, placed Ta-na-wun-da on the ground, and ran toward his wife's murderer.

The sky darkened unnaturally until the light was an unearthly dimness. The roar of a great wind filled Renno's ears, and for a moment he was thrown back, unable to move against its force.

El-i-chi threw back his head, raised his arms, and chanted, and although Renno could still hear the wind, the violence had gone out of it, and he was able to climb the steep mound, his glittering blue eyes fixed on Hodano's frightful face.

Hodano raised his voice and summoned the aid of all

his dark spirits. The ground shifted under Renno's feet, and he was unable to ascend the mound until El-i-chi, repeating an incantation unfamiliar to Renno, joined his brother, hands stretched outward toward Hodano.

Hodano's hoarse cry of frustration sounded in Renno's ears as he climbed the unstable ground toward the one who had mutilated his An-da, pulling himself along by grasping bushes and small trees.

"Hodano!" he heard El-i-chi call out. "You have nothing left. Your magic is of no use to you."

But Hodano would never surrender, and Renno would not want him to do so.

The sachem closed the distance to the top of the mound and faced his enemy, a deliverer of death with a short sword in one hand, tomahawk in the other. Hodano screamed again in pure fear and made the move to soar. But his feet lifted only a few inches off the ground before he felt a great force pushing him down.

"No!" El-i-chi shouted, his hands still upraised. "There will be no escape, Hodano. You must face your victim's husband."

"So it is to be," Hodano hissed, jerking a giant, steel-bladed war ax from his belt. The blood of victims was encrusted where the handle joined the blade. He crouched, the ax grasped tightly in both hands, awaiting Renno's advance.

Renno moved swiftly, but Hodano was ready, a striking snake that brought the huge war ax whistling toward Renno's midsection. Renno, surprised by Hodano's quickness, barely had time to parry the blow with the blade of his own tomahawk. Steel rang on steel.

Three more times the white Indian met Hodano's attack, adjusting himself to his enemy's style and surprising agility, and startling strength. And then Renno bore in, ducking under the swing of the ax. He could have plunged his sword home into Hodano's body, but that was not his intention.

Instead he swung downward, and Hodano howled as the well-honed short sword bit into the toe of his moccasin, severing his great toe at its base, lopping off lesser portions of the four other toes.

Hodano brought the heavy ax toward Renno's back, but the sachem rolled away, banged into a tree, and sprang to his feet to face Hodano's limping rush. As the sachem sidestepped, the great ax buried itself in the tree trunk, and Hodano strained to loosen it.

Renno stood back and waited for the shaman to free his weapon.

Hodano, breathing hard, looked down to see his left foot oozing blood. Roaring a battle cry given volume by pain and anger, he advanced, slashing horizontally with the ax, aiming for Renno's knees. Renno skipped over the blow and, landing lightly, aimed his own weapon precisely. The sword passed through the toes of Hodano's right foot and thudded into the mulch on the ground.

The pain was great, but Hodano controlled it, deadening his feet. He hobbled to a clear area and waited for Renno to free his sword and come to him.

"This time your left hand," Renno announced, moving in, feinting with his sword.

Hodano held his weapon ready until Renno ran toward him. Hodano swung the ax, but Renno was already inside the blow and bent from the waist. He slashed upward with his sword.

With a scream Hodano saw that his left hand was still clasping the handle of his ax but was not attached to his forearm. The blow had cleanly cut through the bone, muscle, and tendon. Blood spouted from the stump of his wrist. Hodano stood motionless, weeping with anger and fear as his lifeblood poured out.

"I do not have the evil in me to make your death as lingering as that which you gave my An-da," Renno grated, "for which we can both thank the manitous."

He slashed his blade horizontally about two feet above the ground into Hodano's left leg. The blade bounced off bone, so the leg was not completely severed. But Hodano went down, his leg useless.

Moaning in abject horror, he tried to escape the avenging force that stalked him. He screamed again when

Renno smashed down with his tomahawk and broke Hodano's right kneecap and bone, leaving that leg dangling only by tendons.

Hodano pulled himself into a sitting position and clasped his war ax with his right hand. He had had to brush aside his severed left hand to do so. He was crying like an infant, for he knew that he was to die. He uttered curses against the spirits who had promised him so much.

"Now the right hand," Renno said in a deadly voice.

Hodano put all his remaining strength into his final swing, and the ax was a blur in motion. Renno, thinking that his enemy was fatally weakened, was taken by surprise with the force and quickness of the blow. The sharp blade of the ax sliced into his upper thigh. But he didn't look at the injury. Instead, putting all his power behind the sword, he severed Hodano's right arm at the elbow.

Bleeding from all his appendages, Hodano sank back against a tree. "I will be avenged," he hissed. "You will not know how or when it will come, but it will come, for the spirits have not allowed me to live for nothing."

El-i-chi, who had been negating Hodano's magic, climbed up the mound and looked down on the dying man. "I feel the force of the shaman's power fading," he said. "Finish him."

"First he must suffer, as An-da suffered," Renno said.

"You do not have the skill to make me suffer as she suffered," Hodano hissed, his twisted mouth sneering. "And remember this, Renno of the Seneca, before she died I took my pleasure with her again and again."

"That is a lie," El-i-chi told his brother. "He is telling you that to make you suffer."

Renno dropped his tomahawk to the ground and swung his sword. The blade caught Hodano under the throat, whipping his head back against the tree trunk. The sword thudded into the solidity of the tree, and the blade broke just above the handle. Hodano's head, the forked tongue flicking, fell and bounced and rolled down the steep embankment.

The whispering voices that had been with Renno since his arrival at the serpent mound rushed into his ears, and strange words were suddenly more distinct. He felt reassured by them, and praised. He stood, chest heaving, and watched the last feeble twitching of Hodano's corpse.

And then a new sound, a sound that was of reality, came to his ears and sent him crashing and tumbling down the mound. Ta-na-wun-da was calling out for his mother.

El-i-chi gave Renno a few moments alone with his son. When he approached, he found that the sachem's leg was bleeding. Renno was clutching the boy close and crooning to him.

"Mama? Mama?" Ta-na-wun-da kept asking.

El-i-chi insisted on examining Renno's wound. Hodano's ax had grazed the thigh, making a cut a quarter inch deep. El-i-chi stanched the bleeding and treated it with medicinal leaves he found nearby.

Renno, carrying his son, and El-i-chi walked to a small stream a good distance away from the spirit-haunted mounds of the serpent and made camp. Here El-i-chi prepared a poultice of ground herbs and tree bark for the cut.

Ta-na-wun-da slept peacefully in his father's arms. A campfire made a cheery light in a small clearing beside the stream.

"He seems to remember nothing, thank the manitous," El-i-chi said, reaching over to smooth Ta-na-wun-da's dark hair.

"That," Renno said, bereft, "is a gift from the manitous that I would earnestly desire for myself."

General Anthony Wayne's report on his victory at Fallen Timbers arrived in Philadelphia on 23 September 1794. Washington was alone when he read it, and he allowed himself a full smile, as no one was present to see his badly made false teeth. "Thank God," he whispered. "The old war-horse has done his assigned task well."

For all practical purposes, the war against the Indians of the Northwest Territory was finished. Other urgent matters weighed on Washington's mind: In western Pennsylvania residents of a sovereign state were resorting to violence against tax collectors, marshals, and process servers. The victims of the residents' attacks were merely following the central government's instructions to impose one of Alexander Hamilton's tax measures. An impost of seven cents a gallon had been levied on strong spirits. This tax was but one-eighth of the value of a gallon of spirits in the east, but a full quarter of the value west of the mountains. The southwestern Pennsylvanians cried "Taxation without representation," and punished the emissaries of the central government with whippings and with tar and feathers. General John Neville, a hero of the War for Independence, had accepted the post of chief collector. The rebels attacked Neville's home, wounded its defenders, and burned the house to the ground.

Washington felt he had been patient long enough. Although the Supreme Court had declared the western counties of Pennsylvania to be in a state of insurrection, Washington had sought a peaceful settlement by sending commissioners to reason with the rebels. At one time the open rebellion had cut off Washington's communications with Wayne, but still Washington had tried to use reason. Now, as the uprising continued, the President sent American against American for the first time since the Revolution, raising troops to march into the Whiskey Rebellion country to bring the revolt to a swift halt.

Hodano was dead, but something nagged at Renno, gnawing away during his waking hours and disturbing his sleep. He stood in the gloomy clearing in the deep forest and looked at Hodano's longhouse. The stale odor of death assaulted his nostrils when that restless sense of incompleteness came over him.

"I will await you here," he told El-i-chi, "while you go to Fort Deposit for Ah-wa-o and Gao. I will keep my son with me. Tell Roy that we're going home and that I said it might be time for him to think about joining us."

After his brother had departed, Renno built a temporary shelter for the boy and fed him, chewing food to a consistency that the baby could swallow. The sachem spent the night in meditation, sitting with his legs crossed in front of the fire, which he fed just enough fuel to keep a flickering light over his campsite. Across the clearing Hodano's longhouse loomed darkly, and more than once the night wind made sounds that caused the hair on Renno's neck to bristle. At last he understood what it was that the manitous wanted of him.

No manitou came to him overtly, but he felt the close presence of all those who had gone to the Place across the River before him. The white Indian told his ancestors that he had another son, a boy with the blood of a pure Seneca maiden in his veins.

Now and then during the night and throughout the next day he talked to Ta-na-wun-da as if the child could understand every word. He told the little warrior about An-da, with whom they would be reunited someday, and about the boy's ancestors, who would, in the future, join him in his battles, hovering at his side, unseen but powerful. As he told Ta-na-wun-da about Little Hawk and Renna, the longing for his children was evident in the sachem's voice.

Then, finally, it was time. For a night, a day, and most of the next night he had searched for orenda and had talked to his ancestors. After feeding Ta-na-wun-da, he secured the child in a carrying pouch suspended from a stout tree limb, where the boy would be safe from prowling forest animals; then the white Indian entered Hodano's longhouse.

An acrid scent mixed with the foul, rank stench of rotting flesh once again assailed Renno's nostrils. Lining the walls of the evil place were victims, the latest ones attracting ants and other insects to devour the threads of decaying flesh clinging to the white bones. When Renno felt dark spirits fluttering against him, he chanted to the manitous and piled wooden benches, hides, and anything else that would burn atop Hodano's bed. Renno lighted the combustibles with a brand from his campfire. The pine straw and dried moss of the bed blazed up eagerly.

The sachem retreated to stand in the doorway until the flames produced a heat that was unbearable. Then he stood at a distance from the longhouse and held his son as he watched the fire eat its way through the bark roof.

Fingers of flames shot up through the smoke hole, then the entire longhouse exploded. The heat drove Renno backward. The blaze reached for the overhanging limbs of the tall conifers, and small branches burst into flame, then fizzled.

A screech of torment sounded from the conflagration as dark and sinister shadows danced in the flames, wailing and shrieking with sheer hatred and undiluted evil.

Renno, seeking protection, called upon all the spirits of good. His summonses were answered. He felt a warmth unrelated to the fire and experienced a feeling of peace. It seemed to soak into his consciousness from the outside, and then pervade his entire body. The feeling of well-being and relaxation flowed upward until he could stand confidently and watch the spirits do battle in the hungry fire.

Flashing bolts of white heat lanced down from above to shrivel dark shadows, which danced and howled in the flames. The smoky blaze was red, then violet, and finally all the colors of the rainbow as it erupted upward into the late-night sky. With a crash the longhouse collapsed into itself, to become only a crackling bed of embers that glowed and gave off warmth until the sunrise.

A rectangle of ash marked the location of the house of malevolence. As Renno fed his son, pine needles filtered into the ash from the limbs above. Some struck hot embers and flamed briefly. Others began to cover the last evidence of Hodano's presence.

Now the sachem had time to mourn An-da properly with the songs of death. As the days passed, he saw to it that his son had plenty to eat. Slowly, as they stayed in the temporary shelter, Ta-na-wun-da began to regain his chubby health.

Soon El-i-chi and Ah-wa-o joined them again, and in gradually colder weather, they commenced the long trek home. Several times a day Ah-wa-o took both boys to her breasts to suckle.

"They will be as brothers," she foretold.

"A boy needs a mother," El-i-chi agreed. "He will be as our own."

Under El-i-chi's ministrations Renno's leg had healed well, and they were able to put miles behind them. The snows had not come, although the cold mornings were bracing, and at times there was rime ice on the beaver ponds. They crossed through Kentucky to find scenes of devastation made familiar by their stay with Wayne's army. Kentucky and Tennessee volunteers, not distinguishing between the few warlike Cherokee and the peaceful majority, had decimated several Cherokee towns. "Thus we are rewarded," El-i-chi said bitterly as they walked around a burned and ruined Cherokee village.

Roy Johnson had scouted for the legion all the way to Detroit and had traveled with Wayne across Lake Erie to Presque Isle. Roy knew that the power of the Ohio tribes was broken forever. The northern winter was near, so Roy made his good-byes to Anthony Wayne, leaving the general his good wishes and a handshake, accepted his pay in gold, and found a boat to ride to the headwaters of the Maumee. Before leaving Wayne, Roy had received word that Renno and El-i-chi were already on their way home. From there he had a long trek ahead of him, for he had a yearning to see his grandchildren.

Roy rested at Cincinnati and talked with many people. He cursed under his breath to see many representatives of the land companies here, each searching diligently for veterans of the War for Independence who were willing to sell their continental chits, which entitled them to land. The going price was still ten cents on the dollar, which gave the land companies rich, virgin land—Miami land, Shawnee land, and Wyandot land—for ten cents an acre. One agent tried to persuade Roy to invest his pay as a scout in shares of the land company.

"I tell you, sir," the agent boasted, "in three years you will quadruple your money, for this land will be selling at four dollars an acre—maybe more."

"I think I'll spend my money in my own way," Roy said. "I'll buy myself a bottle of hard liquor, and a horse because my feet are beginning to feel sore. Besides, that's

Indian land out there, my friend, and it's been soaked in not a little blood."

Soon Renno's group was away from the Kentucky border area, and they found life going on normally, although some fear existed among the Cherokee that the white man would not be content with burning only a few towns.

In increasingly familiar country, Renno, confident that El-i-chi, Ah-wa-o, and the two boys were safe, told El-i-chi that he would join them in the village soon.

He left the camp and disappeared into the forest, walking and running through the night. He put more miles behind him until, with a start, he recognized a spot where he had consulted with his manitou once before. A great scarp of flint was exposed; a small stream babbled below. With some difficulty he located the very place where he had camped and looked up to see, in the flint of the cliff, the outlines of the spirit knife that had been given to him by the manitou long ago.

Here he stayed for four days, fasting, mourning both An-da and the Cherokee who had been killed and made homeless by the raids from the Kentucky-Tennessee volunteers.

At first, however, the manitou seemed to be ignoring him. His chants and pleas went unheard. He was light-headed from fasting and sick at heart.

Finally the manitou came to him in the hours for dying, midway between midnight and morning. He did not immediately see the shape, for his eyes were blinded by visions of An-da as she was when he first met her—a girl only, bright, shy, dazzled by her infatuation for him, a Sweet Day.

When he became aware that he was no longer alone, his head jerked up to see the original Renno, his great-grandfather, and he let out a moan of anguish, for his ancestor wore the clothing of the white man and had his blond hair tucked under a powdered wig.

"This, then, is the only answer?" he asked. "To be as a white man?"

The manitou was silent.

"Take me then, spirit of my great-grandfather. Let me join you and my father in the Place Across the River, for I am burdened beyond my strength."

The spirit of the great Renno shook his head sadly.

"What more must I do?" the sachem beseeched him. "I fight for the peace of the United States, and their men come against my brothers the Cherokee. I love, and that love is stolen from me in the most unimaginable way. I beg for peace of mind, Great-Grandfather." He extended his arms, and tears ran freely. "Please! Take me to your breast and let me accompany you!"

"Look you," the spirit said, waving one hand. Renno saw a vision of Little Hawk and Renna in the village. Little Hawk was holding Renna's hand, leading her toward Toshabe's longhouse.

"They are the future," the spirit intoned.

Renno nodded, pride and joy in his children welling up to assuage his sorrow.

"And your work is not done," the spirit said, and then was gone.

After breaking his fast, Renno ran, ran hard to purge himself, to expunge the stench of evil that had adhered to him since killing Hodano. He overtook El-i-chi and the others not ten miles from home and entered the village side by side with his brother.

In the doorway of their mother's and Ha-ace's longhouse, Little Hawk, a sturdy and fine-looking young boy, examined his father gravely before extending his arm in the warrior's clasp of friendship. Renno took the arm, but in an instant he pulled the boy to him in a tight and loving embrace. Then it was Renna who hurled herself into his arms, helping to fill the void in his heart.

"Father," Renna said, "don't ever, ever leave us again."

"Little one," Renno said, his voice husky with emotion, "if it were within my power, I would gladly make that promise."

The Men Who Fought

Among the men who joined the fictional characters in this book are several whose lives after the Battle of Fallen Timbers are well-known to even the most casual reader of history.

Thomas Jefferson resigned from Washington's cabinet on 31 December 1793, realizing that he could no longer agree with the President's policies, and built his own political base.

The fate of Alexander Hamilton is equally well-known. Hamilton left Washington's cabinet on 31 January 1795, but continued as a friend and adviser, writing much of Washington's farewell address. He died in a duel with Aaron Burr on 11 July 1804.

GENERAL HENRY KNOX, the first secretary of war under the Constitution, resigned from public service in 1795, after helping to negotiate treaties with the Ohio tribes. He retired to a large estate in Maine and died at the age of fifty-six on 25 October 1806.

GENERAL JAMES WILKINSON received a substantial pension from the Spanish authorities in America until 1800 and was never officially punished for his oath of allegiance to Spain. Ironically, it was Wilkinson who was in command of the American troops that occupied Natchez upon its evacuation by Spain, an event that foretold the Louisiana Purchase and a greater American empire built on the ashes of Spanish hopes.

In 1803 Wilkinson was one of the commissioners appointed to receive the vast Louisiana territories after their purchase from France, and two years later he was appointed governor of the area north of the thirty-third parallel.

From his headquarters in St. Louis, he once again had dreams of personal empire and entered into a conspiracy with Aaron Burr to conquer Spain's provinces in Mexico. For these actions he was tried in Richmond but freed for lack of evidence. In 1812 he was in command of New Orleans. A year later he was promoted to major general and occupied Mobile. In that same year, however, he made a fiasco of a campaign to take Montréal, and his checkered military career ended in disgrace. He died in Mexico City on 28 December 1825, during an effort to secure a land grant in Texas.

WILLIAM HENRY HARRISON, aide to General Anthony Wayne at Fallen Timbers, was promoted to captain but resigned his commission in 1798 to become secretary of the Northwest Territory and, in 1800, governor of the newly created Indiana Territory. In 1812 he was appointed major general in the Kentucky militia and only weeks later brigadier general in the United States Army. He served with distinction during the War of 1812, went into politics to serve in Congress, the Ohio Senate, and as

United States minister to Colombia. In 1840 he became the ninth president of the United States, only to become the first man to die in that office on 4 April 1841, exactly one month after his inauguration.

MERIWETHER LEWIS and WILLIAM CLARK, who formed a friendship during their service with Anthony Wayne, entered the history books with their epic journey to the Pacific in exploration of the newly purchased Louisiana Territory. Clark later served in the territory as superintendent of Indian Affairs. He died of natural causes on 1 September 1838.

Lewis was named governor of the Louisiana Territory by Thomas Jefferson in 1808. When his personal financial situation was ruined by the refusal of bureaucrats in the new capital of the United States to honor his official drafts, he left St. Louis for Washington to clear up the problem. His death, in Nashville on 11 October 1809, remains a mystery, with the question of whether he was murdered or died by suicide.

TECUMSEH refused to attend the negotiations that led to the Treaty of Greenville. He broke with his fellow Shawnee chiefs to fight against Governor William Henry Harrison's seizure of thirty-three million acres of Indian land north of the Ohio. With his brother Tenskwatawa, the Prophet, he traveled from the Great Lakes to the Gulf of Mexico to organize a new intertribal alliance. Tecumseh's army, under the Prophet, attacked an expeditionary force led by William Henry Harrison at Tippecanoe. (Harrison's victory gave him a campaign slogan years later, for the election of 1840: "Tippecanoe and Tyler Too.")

In the War of 1812 Tecumseh and his followers joined the British in Canada and participated in several successful campaigns. When Captain Oliver Hazard Perry defeated British naval forces at Put-in-Bay, cutting supply lines, the British and Indian allies began a retreat across Ontario. Cornered at the Thames River by his old nemesis Harrison, Tecumseh was killed in battle in 1813. With him died the last hope of a grand Indian alliance.

THAYENDANEGEA, JOSEPH BRANT, terror of the northern frontier during the War of the Revolution, devoted his later life to missionary work and translations of the Prayer Book and St. Mark's Gospel into Mohawk. After Fallen Timbers he worked with the commissioners of the United States in securing treaties with the Ohio tribes. He settled in upper Canada, raised funds to build the first Episcopal church in that territory, and died on an estate given him by the British on 24 November 1807.

LITTLE TURTLE, warrior and orator of the Miami, signed the Treaty of Greenville and became an advocate of peace. He was the primary influence in preventing the Miami tribe from joining Tecumseh's alliance.

"MAD" ANTHONY WAYNE, commander in chief of the United States Army, led his American legion northward following the Battle of Fallen Timbers and his devastation of the Maumee valley, to Detroit and Presque Isle on Lake Erie. Estranged from his family and in constant pain, he presided at the negotiations that resulted in the Treaty of Greenville, which opened the Northwest Territory to settlement. He lived to see the British yield their illegal positions on the United States side of the Great Lakes and died of his wounds and his recurrent fever at Presque Isle, now Erie, Pennsylvania, on 15 December 1796, while on active duty.

Author's Note
White Indian 19:
Fallen Timbers

Renno, the white Indian, bravest of all Seneca warriors, was born as a fictional character in 1979, a child of the fertile imagination of the late Lyle Kenyon Engel. For a decade now Renno and his descendants—son, grandson, and a great-grandson—have been gaining friends through multiple printings totaling over ten million books.

Prior to my association with the WHITE INDIAN series, I had carefully avoided writing or reading about the American colonial era. I had been programmed by uninteresting history teachers, as many of us were—and still are, I imagine—to think of the early Americans as boring people who spawned boring children. There was a fellow named John Smith who wouldn't speak for himself when courting a maid, and a few witches lived in Salem at one time, but aside from them and an obscure war that started when Patrick Henry said, "Give me liberty or give me death," not much happened in American history until the Civil War and the era of the western Indian wars.

So it is that I will be forever grateful to Renno and his offspring for opening my eyes to an eventful era filled with fascinating stories, peopled by real heroes and shockingly evil and equally real villains. As the original Renno lived, loved, fought, and influenced the lives of famous historical characters, all of us who were connected with the series found, often to our amazement, that we were mining a richness of material seldom touched on in fiction and often neglected in history books.

The original aim of the series, to depict early America through the time of the French and Indian wars, was expanded as a result of the loyalty of Renno's readers. The first Renno went to the Place across the River to join his ancestors. His son, Ja-gonh, carried us to further adventures. Ghonkaba, son of Ja-gonh, introduced us to the Indians of the South.

Renno, great-grandson of the original white Indian, has seen more of the amazing eighteenth-century world than any man of his time. He prides himself in being Seneca and is fated to be at the heart of those events that determined the future shape and character of the United States.

It is my fervent wish that you will enjoy the newest story and that you might even be a bit surprised, as I was, to find that had not Mad Anthony Wayne—with Renno's help and advice, of course—won the Battle of Fallen Timbers, this nation of ours would today be geographically and philosophically very different.

I thank you for your letters and your continued loyalty to what many have called "my Indian friends." I thank Renno for introducing me to the exciting history that I had previously missed, even if, after the Battle of Fallen Timbers, he did laugh at me for continuing to speak of the western police actions against the Sioux, Apache, Nez Percé, and other small, isolated tribes as "Indian wars." He knew, you see, that the only clashes between the white Americans and Indians worthy to be called wars happened east of the Mississippi and that all the scattered encounters that followed in the west, although dramatic and made exciting by the mobility of the mounted western tribes, were on a much smaller scale. For example, the entire war force of the Apache Geronimo would have made a scarcely noticeable eddy in the great storm of battle at Fallen Timbers.

Thanks to you and millions like you, the amazing Renno will undertake more travels in future books and will fight against evil, greed, and treachery wherever he finds it. He will love again and will see his sons and daughter mature and prepare themselves to play their parts in still another era of immense change for the American Indian.

My great-grandmother, Jane Ogden of Arkansas, was Cherokee, and I spent my childhood in what was once the Choctaw nation in Oklahoma. So I can truthfully say that two men with white and Indian blood in their veins, one fictional and one real, invite you to share with us this Northwest Territory adventure and to join us in future books as we answer a call to duty from Thomas Jefferson, fight with Andy Jackson, and, perhaps, detour along the way for another excursion into adventure in the broader world outside the confines of the early-nineteenth-century United States.

DONALD CLAYTON PORTER
23 March 1989

Here is an exciting preview of Volume XX in the
WHITE INDIAN series:

SACHEM'S
SON

Coming in December 1990, wherever Bantam Books
are sold.

Prologue

~~~~~~

For three days he had purified himself by fasting; with each dawn the attack of the enemy seemed imminent. After one day of mental and physical preparation he had been honed to a peak of readiness, every sense alert, every muscle humming with health and youthful power. Three days of communing with the spirits, however, while cleansing his body and soul through self-denial, had left him tense, uneasy, light-headed. He could not understand the delay. The Chief-Who-Never-Sleeps, the American general Anthony Wayne, had been seeking battle for months, for years. The Ohio tribes were massed before Wayne's position in a labyrinth of fallen trees, three thousand of them, and still the army of the white man did nothing but demonstrate.

When the grandly uniformed American Legion finally marched with great precision and discipline into the smokes and deadly fire from the well-concealed Indians, cold steel gleamed at the tip of their muskets. To the Indian the long knives were unmanly and terrible weapons, but in order to use his bayonet, the legion soldier had to close with men hidden within the twisted, entangled labyrinth of the storm-felled trees.

The young Shawnee warrior Tecumseh had chosen his position carefully. Tangled brush and jagged, broken limbs made it impossible for the bayonets of the American legion to reach him. He killed. He selected his targets carefully, for his supply of musket balls was limited. Beside him his brother, Tenskwatawa the Prophet, who spoke with the

Master of Life, also made his mark with the strength of his arm and the accuracy of his bow.

A storm of sound numbed Tecumseh's ears: the thunder of musketry, the shrill screams of dying men, the shouts of the well-drilled legionnaires as they surged forward, herding the full strength of the Ohio tribes before the awful steel of their bayonets.

Surrounded, Tecumseh and the Prophet concealed themselves and took the opportunity to shoot from ambush into the confusion of swirling gun smoke. The two Shawnee brothers were among the few who continued to fight after the American Legion penetrated the natural abatis. Most of the warriors of the Ohio tribes fled in panic and, emerging from the fallen timbers, ran directly into the field of fire of General Wayne's cavalry. Those who survived sought the promised protection of a nearby British fort, only to be locked out and forced to face the merciless offensive of the victorious American Legion.

Tecumseh watched the rout from the timbers, creeping from his place of concealment to see the shame and hopelessness of it. Tears ran down his face. His brother closed his eyes to avoid witnessing the disgrace.

Never had the Indian fought under a more capable leader, for the Miami war chief Little Turtle had been a wise general who had chosen his ground well. The catastrophic defeat could not be blamed on Little Turtle, Tecumseh thought as he watched the slaughter of those who ran blindly to escape the steel of the legion. Nor could the fault be placed on the individual Indian warrior. Under circumstances of his own choosing, the Indian was as brave as any soldier who had ever taken the field.

The shouts and screams of battle moved away from the fallen timbers. Tecumseh opened his mouth to explain the defeat to the Prophet, then decided that it was unnecessary to speak, for they had discussed the basic difference between the Indian and the white hordes before. The Indian warrior, as courageous as he was, did not have the iron discipline of the white soldier. No Indian warrior could ever be convinced to march stupidly into the muzzles of three thousand rifles. For a while the warriors hidden among the fallen trees had fought well, but when they had faced the cold steel of a bayonet charge, their ingrained dread of the long knives and their lack of mass discipline resulted in a rout.

Thus it was that the dream of an Indian nation north of the Ohio died on that warm day, August 20, 1794, in a storm-tangled woodland near the Maumee River. The vision of Little Turtle and the hopes of thousands died on the long knives of the American Legion.

On a narrow stretch of open ground bounded by the river, the Indian dead lay strewn. No human scavengers prowled among the dead; the Legion, holding its discipline, was still in pursuit of the survivors. Only a small group of mounted soldiers remained on the field near the river, surveying the forms of the fallen in silence. One of the soldiers was not dressed in the uniform of the Americans but wore the war regalia of a sachem of the Seneca nation. Tecumseh recognized the Seneca as much from the proud set of his shoulders as from his bronzed face and blazing blue eyes.

"Renno of the Seneca," he said, half in salute, half in explanation to Tenskwatawa the Prophet. "Again he fights with the Americans."

Tenskwatawa muttered a Shawnee curse.

"And again the Seneca sachem is on the winning side," Tecumseh retorted. "Will it be ever so?"

"The spirits tell me—" Tenskwatawa began.

"The spirits have told you many things," Tecumseh said sharply. "The spirits told you that we would win a great victory here. And now—"

"The Master of Life told me," Tenskwatawa said, his voice low and firm, "that victory will come when all tribes fight side by side as brothers. Here that was not true, for only a few tribes faced the white man's steel."

Tecumseh laughed. "And who is to be the man who, like Hiawatha of the Iroquois, carries the message? Long ago, the Iroquois were only five tribes. Is the new Hiawatha to travel the length and breadth of this great land to speak to hundreds of chiefs and their tribes?"

"Only thus can victory come," the Prophet insisted.

"The Seneca Renno tells all that the path of the future follows the white man's road. Perhaps he is right."

"This is Tecumseh who speaks?"

"The words come from my mouth, but not from my

heart." Tecumseh sighed. "There will come a time when we will meet, the Seneca and I, and then perhaps it will be this that will decide." He put his hand on his tomahawk. "Words have but a short life and are easily brought into being. In the end the spirits decide what is true."

"If words could convince the Seneca and others like him that they are wrong," Tenskwatawa said, "we would be many. In the south the Creeks are strong, and to the west along the Father of Waters there are many tribes. It is you who was given the gift of the golden tongue, my brother. You will be the new Hiawatha. It will be you who will use your wise words to convince all the tribes and all those like the Seneca Renno that we must stand together. You will tell all those who have the blood that we must fight side by side as brothers or be hunted into oblivion by these teeming whites."

Tecumseh did not want to admit that his brother's words wakened pride tinged with righteous anger in his breast, then combined those emotions into a sense of purpose that threatened to consume him. "Come," he said, "we must leave this place of disaster and shame. But let us not forget what happened here. It will be a lesson burned into our minds like a brand. We must convince all the tribes that it is death to face the white hordes in disunion."

They had to make their way through scattered Kentucky mounted militia, but that was not difficult because the Kentuckians had become separated in dense woodlands west of the battlefield. When the brothers were safely into the dense forests to the west, they rested. Tenskwatawa treated the slight wound on Tecumseh's upper arm caused by a musket ball. The tall trees sighed with a night wind around the brothers' fireless camp, and the vastness of the forest seemed to belie the constant threat of white expansionism. As Tecumseh tried to sleep, however, his ears rang with the remembered thunder of the Legion's guns, and his dreams were troubled.

He was twenty-six years old. He had been fighting against white encroachment into the lands of his people all his life, and he had lost a father and brothers to the struggle. His remaining brother, slightly younger, conversed with the Master of Life and received orders and revelations. The Prophet was certain that the Master of Life had given Tecumseh a sacred mission. The way would be long, and it would take years of his life to accomplish the mission. There was left only the need to make a beginning.

Chapter I

^^

"When Renno and I were young men," said El-i-chi, senior warrior and shaman of the southern Seneca, "we traveled far away to a land of the blowing sands and waterless wastes."

Toshabe, mother of two warriors and the warrior woman Ena, laughed. Her strong son looked at her in question.

"It is only because you still seem quite young to me, my son," Toshabe explained.

"My mother herself is young," El-i-chi said.

"Ah. When one counts over fifty winters—"

"One is still young as long as one can laugh," Renno said. He sat between his eleven-year-old son, Little Hawk, and nine-year-old Renna, his pale-haired daughter, who with every passing day looked more like her late mother, Emily.

"Tell how my father killed the mountain cat in the waterless lands," Renna said.

"We must consider the request of our guest," El-i-chi said, nodding at a tall, gangling white man who wore dusty black clothing and whose lank black hair hung to his shoulders.

"You are most considerate," said Reverend Waith Pennywhistle. "I would be interested, of course, in hearing of any feat of daring performed by my gracious host." He made a little bow toward Renno, sachem of the Seneca. "At another time, perhaps, I can hear the stories of the wild Apache of the far West."

Pennywhistle had come to the Seneca village riding a moth-eaten mule. A black hat was pulled low over his burning eyes, and a Bible was in his hand. He had been invited to stay because he told a thundering good tale based on the heroes and kings of the Old Covenant and because of a promise that Renno had made to his dead wife, Emily. The son that Emily had borne him and the daughter who had been given life only days before the death of her mother would, he had promised, know the words of the white man's Bible, would hear the preachings about the God-with-Three-Heads.

"The Apache storytellers speak of the coyote," El-i-chi said, "as a cunning animal who was envious of the owl in the beginning because the owl was the one who had arrows."

"Yes," said Little Hawk, leaning forward in anticipation of the retelling of a story he had come to love.

"And not only did the owl have arrows, he had a magic club with which he killed men."

"Oooooo," said Renna.

El-i-chi made a scary face at Renna and said in a low, growling voice, "And then he ate them."

"Ugh," Renna said.

"He sang *wu hwu wu*," El-i-chi hooted. "*Wu hwu wu.* And when the coyote came to listen, the owl said that he was hungry and looking for men in the low pass of the mountains below. Coyote said that he, too, was hungry and asked Owl to allow him to eat men. Owl sang *wu hwu wu* and thought about it and said that only one could eat man and that it would be decided by the spirits. The one who could vomit human flesh—"

"Ugh," Renna said.

"Be quiet, Renna," Little Hawk whispered. "You've heard all this before."

"—would kill and eat men. Owl said that both of them must close their eyes. Owl closed his eyes but Coyote did not. He watched Owl, and when Owl began to vomit human flesh he caught it in his hands and substituted his own vomit in front of Owl so that when Owl opened his eyes he saw only the grasshoppers that had been vomited up by Coyote. 'Where did I drink in grasshoppers?,' Owl wondered aloud. Coyote showed the human flesh he had stolen from Owl. In his triumph Coyote ran all around Owl and bragged about his speed. He said that because he could run fast, he was to be the one who would kill and eat people. But Owl ran faster and outran Coyote. Coyote said, 'Those legs of yours, Owl, are too long. If they were shorter, you could run much faster. Close your eyes, and I will fix your legs for you.'"

"Owl was sort of dumb in the beginning," Renna explained to everyone.

"So Coyote broke Owl's legs and cut them off, leaving them very short so that Owl could only waddle along. Then, running circles around Owl, he stole Owl's arrows, leaving Owl the magic club. Owl threw the club and hit Coyote, and the club returned to Owl's hand. But Coyote, by cutting off Owl's legs, had stolen some of Owl's magic. When Owl threw the club again, Coyote said, 'Where your club falls, there it will lie.' And the club would not go back to Owl's hand. Owl, without his arrows and without his magic club, slunk away and hid. Coyote used Owl's arrows to kill men, and that is how Coyote became an eater of meat."

"Charming story," said Reverend Pennywhistle. "But, I fear, the product of a primitive mind. We know, don't we, that God made the animals and gave them their characteristics, and then He gave dominion over the animals to His masterpiece of creation, man."

Little Hawk was quite respectful of his mother's God, but he was not at all convinced that the white man had captured God and enclosed Him between the black covers of the Bible. He was reaching an age at which he could read the book himself, and he found it to be a puzzling mixture of meaningless lists of names and accounts of burned animal scarifices, which, in the mind of a Seneca, represented a waste of good food. There were some rousing stories hidden away, especially in the chronicles of the kings, but all in all Little Hawk found that the presentation of God in the Bible was confusing. He could understand Jesus a bit better than the God of the Old Bible, for Jesus, like Little Hawk's father and uncle El-i-chi, could speak with the spirits and cast out devils. A boy of eleven didn't spend too much time thinking about such things, but at night when his father, obedient to the wishes of the long-dead mother, reminded him to say his prayers, he alternated between talking to Jesus, the son of God, and talking to the Master of Life, the supreme being of his father and the Seneca. It was not beyond possibility, he thought, that his mother's God and his father's God shared one face and were, in fact, one and the same.

He had voiced his views to the black-clad preacher. The white man's face had turned almost purple, and the man had emitted a great burst of indignation. Little Hawk had listened carefully, thinking that the preacher's thundering words lacked something, for they did not explain how—if indeed the traditional gods of the Seneca were false gods—they had given gifts to his father such as the magic ax, with which Renno had killed many Chickasaw, and the spirit knife, which had been carved by lightning from a ledge of flint.

"When you shout," he had told Pennywhistle, "my ears ache."

Waith Pennywhistle was vaguely Lutheran and somewhat Baptist. He held no seminary degree. He said that his ordination had come direct from God while he was plowing a rocky field on the eastern side of the Great Smoky Mountains. God had appeared to him, saying, "Go, my son, and carry my dread words of warning to the heathen beyond the blue hills."

Since God's word was not to be denied, he had left the hardscrabble farm the next morning, accompanied by one woeful hound dog that did not live to cross the passes that led to the Tennessee Territory and the first of the Cherokee villages southeast of Knoxville. When the old dog, Pennywhistle's last link to his past life, was killed by a bear, Pennywhistle took it as a sign from the Lord that he was meant to be alone, like John the Baptist, the voice of one crying in the wilderness.

The self-appointed evangelist had marched into the land of the Cherokee at a time when the white man's relentless drive to swallow up Indian lands was momentarily slowed by the conquest of the Northwest Territory. In the year 1795 an uneasy peace existed in that vast area west of the mountains and east of the Mississippi—a peace broken with unpredictable irregularity by encroaching white men and young warriors who scorned the teachings of peace by such sachems and chiefs as Renno of the Seneca and Rusog of the Cherokee.

Pennywhistle's presence in the Seneca village had not been welcomed by all. El-i-chi's wife, Ah-wa-o, the Rose, and Ena, the onetime warrior maiden who was now the mother of the active twins Ho-ya and Wa-yo, were open in their contempt for the teachings of the white missionaries.

"Why is it," Ena demanded of Reverend Pennywhistle on the first night of his stay in the village, "that the first thing a white missionary wants to do is change that which is traditional with our people?"

Pennywhistle had been preaching that a wife should be subservient to her husband, using quotes from the Bible to emphasize the superiority of men. Such so-called teachings did not sit well with a woman of the Seneca and were especially irksome to a Seneca woman married to a Cherokee chief.

In all tribes of the League of the Ho-de-no-sau-nee there existed a semimatriarchy where women exercised the power to name sachems. Among the Cherokee a woman had many rights as well. For example, if a husband displeased a woman, she had only to pack her husband's things in a sack and set them outside the door of the lodge to be rid of him, legally divorced. Remarriages were common, and there was a certain amount of sexual freedom for all Indian women. Most tribes, including the Cherokee, had laws regarding adultery, but were lax in enforcing them unless the offending woman became too blatant in her excesses. In such cases she could be awarded a surplus of plenty by being serially taken by up to thirty men on the theory that if she were given what she craved in such excess she would be satisfied once and for all and would behave rationally in future sexual matters.

Oddly enough, Pennywhistle was to be a witness to an example of the power of women in the Seneca tribe during his stay.

**FROM THE PRODUCER OF WAGONS WEST
AND THE KENT FAMILY CHRONICLES—
A SWEEPING SAGA OF WAR AND HEROISM
AT THE BIRTH OF A NATION**

THE WHITE INDIAN SERIES

This thrilling series tells the compelling story of America's birth against the equally exciting adventures of an English child raised as a Seneca.

☐	24650	White Indian #1	$3.95
☐	25020	The Renegade #2	$3.95
☐	24751	War Chief #3	$3.95
☐	24476	The Sachem #4	$3.95
☐	25154	Renno #5	$3.95
☐	25039	Tomahawk #6	$3.95
☐	25589	War Cry #7	$3.95
☐	25202	Ambush #8	$3.95
☐	23986	Seneca #9	$3.95
☐	24492	Cherokee #10	$3.95
☐	24950	Choctaw #11	$3.95
☐	25353	Seminole #12	$3.95
☐	25868	War Drums #13	$3.95
☐	26206	Apache #14	$3.95
☐	27161	Spirit Knife #15	$3.95
☐	27264	Manitou #16	$3.95
☐	27814	Seneca Warrior #17	$3.95
☐	28285	Father of Waters #18	$3.95

★ WAGONS WEST ★

This continuing, magnificent saga recounts the adventures of a brave band of settlers, all of different backgrounds, all sharing one dream—to find a new and better life.

☐	26822	**INDEPENDENCE! #1**	$4.50
☐	26162	**NEBRASKA! #2**	$4.50
☐	26242	**WYOMING! #3**	$4.50
☐	26072	**OREGON! #4**	$4.50
☐	26070	**TEXAS! #5**	$4.50
☐	26377	**CALIFORNIA! #6**	$4.50
☐	26546	**COLORADO! #7**	$4.50
☐	26069	**NEVADA! #8**	$4.50
☐	26163	**WASHINGTON! #9**	$4.50
☐	26073	**MONTANA! #10**	$4.50
☐	26184	**DAKOTA! #11**	$4.50
☐	26521	**UTAH! #12**	$4.50
☐	26071	**IDAHO! #13**	$4.50
☐	26367	**MISSOURI! #14**	$4.50
☐	27141	**MISSISSIPPI! #15**	$4.50
☐	25247	**LOUISIANA! #16**	$4.50
☐	25622	**TENNESSEE! #17**	$4.50
☐	26022	**ILLINOIS! #18**	$4.50
☐	26533	**WISCONSIN! #19**	$4.50
☐	26849	**KENTUCKY! #20**	$4.50
☐	27065	**ARIZONA! #21**	$4.50
☐	27458	**NEW MEXICO! #22**	$4.50
☐	27703	**OKLAHOMA! #23**	$4.50
☐	28180	**CELEBRATION! #24**	$4.50